CONQUEST OF NOOMAS

CONQUEST OF NOOMAS

A FANTASY NOVEL: THE NOOMAS CHRONICLES, VOLUME III

CHARLES NUETZEL &

HEIDI GARRETT

THE BORGO PRESS
MMXIII

CONQUEST OF NOOMAS

FIRST EDITION

Published by Wildside Press LLC

www.wildsidebooks.com

DEDICATION

The authors dedicate this book to one another.

CONTENTS

INTRODUCTION

A word regarding Torlo and the Universe, in particular the planet of Noomas might be of interest. We cannot verify whether he lives in our galaxy or elsewhere. Nor can we verify his exact age or the exact dates of our previous telepathic communications with him. For the gap between universes is not based on earthly measures. Time is uncertain, distorted by space and our own perspective. We cannot compare our measures to those of Noomas. For what might be a season for us, could be a thousand years in another realm. We can say for certain that significant time has passed between Torlo Hannis' advent on Noomas and transmissions relating Adt's adventures with Sarleni.

We will now let Torlo Hannis take center stage.

—CHARLES NUETZEL & HEIDI GARRETT

FOREWORD

The experience is the reward.
Consider—The experiences between the beginning
and the end of your journey might be more important
than the actual destination.

—The Great Wizard from the Epic Dialogs of Mhyo

What I have to relate are the details of the war with the Muti Empire of Kamina, as I experienced them, and have since learned through historical records and from my surviving comrades and friends.

No war is finalized in one battle; but one battle can be dramatically pivotal to the outcome.

—Torlo Hannis

THE LEGEND
THREE MOONS OF NOOMAS

The night skies of the Northern Territories are the brightest in the entire world during seasons of the sun: a consistent truth for all times. And during the coldest of the wintry seasons, the icy white Northern Territories would be pitched into utter darkness, if it were not for the constant vigilance of the moons casting their protective luminescence upon the frozen lands.

It is said, that long before the lands were peopled, Noomas had no moons. In the times of the Pure, the world was untouched, virgin land. The pale sun shone upon the naked wilderness, bringing forth plant and animal life of great proportions. No time was recorded. A singular continuum of life burst into a happy celebration across the lands, valleys, seas, and moun-tains, spreading its eager blanket of energy.

Disaster struck when a great and mighty storm fumed in the celestial skies, and hurled blazing fireballs across the heavens in throbbing waves of flaming rock. They fell on all creation, crushing plant and beast alike.

The sleeping gods, Clinsol and Nosn, were jarred out of their contented slumber and looked down in shocked disbelief. What could have brought this destruction against their creation? Who had trampled the beautiful perfection of their world? Nosn hid his jealous suspicions from the beautiful Clinsol.

Slke had been peacefully resting with Nial when the tremors had rattled their world and ran immediately to the hall of the gods. Tooli, Anos and Insi plowed in, tumbling heavily over one another, ready to blame any one of the gods, for the malicious chaos. They heard whispers from hidden corners of the mind, radiating bizarre discordant melodies over their world.

Could anything so brutal be traced? Could these simple delicate vespers be the footprint of destructive forces?

The gods cried out in mourning, for this sacred place had generously provided the food and drink, the very source of life, supplied to the gods. But soon after, their sadness began to lift and fury raged among the gods. They raised their arms in anger and caused a mighty wind to blow the storm far into the abyss.

And when the danger had passed, they soared to the damaged lands, collected the remnants of the fiery boulders still burning, and flung them into the oceans. The seas boiled high upon the shores as the fireballs crashed into their depths.

When they had cooled and the waters had calmed, the gods dove deep into the oceans. Retrieving three of the largest of the boulders, they hurled them back into the skies, admonishing them to orbit around Noomas as guardians against any further catastrophes that might dare to threaten the lands. And they vowed Noomas would never suffer devastation of this magnitude ever again.

Thus the Three Moons of Noomas have remained vigilant over the planet for centuries.

With the rebirthing of their creation, they invited new seeds to be sown from beyond the heavens. And as new settlers entered the lands of the gods, they were welcomed one at a time and the land prospered and once again returned abundant joy and goodness to the gods.

—Tomes of the Ji

CHAPTER ONE
THE MESSENGER

Observe the moveable lines that bind us. Leap not over restraints, for they provide safe boundaries. Beyond them great danger garners death and destruction.

—Mighty words of the Eemel

I was shocked out of my deep sleep.

A warrior stood in the shadows of our bedroom staring down at me.

Torlo, this is Adt.

I glanced over at Youi lying there in the bed next to me, unaware in her tranquil sleep. I hadn't disturbed her.

Once again my eyes sought the place where I thought I'd seen the dim apparition of the man.

Nothing's there now except darkness. It's just another annoying disruption, like so many nights of late.

I decided I'd merely had a dream about my lost friend.

The last time I had seen Adt Dorta was when we were both fighting against the Dianos and he'd been chained among the prisoners. I had cut him loose with instructions to raise an immediate revolt. Then I was lucky to have found Youi. She and I managed to steal a grav-disk and flee as Adt led the charge against the Diano enemy. That same night a ferocious storm had blown us off-course, sending Youi and me on a perilous journey, into the Noomasian deserts of the nomadic Raiders.

Lately, vivid dreams plagued me. Perhaps, recollections still surfacing from my career steeped in a violent history of warfare.

I reached for Youi.

Her warm flesh was comforting.

The dream was not.

She stirred as I stepped to the window and looked out over the palace gardens. Our spacious suite provided a broad view of Bel-loniea beyond the walls of the Proctor's palace. I tried to clear my head. Fresh memories of Adt had been stirred up and they refused to leave me in peace.

Determined to redirect my thoughts, I stared down upon the lush pathways, and studied their intricate patterns which had been carefully laid out to form a complex labyrinth. One could become lost among those tall thickets for hours. As I considered the puzzle below, my mind expanded until I found myself pondering on the outer limits of the realm.

Two of the moons of Noomas, Silkenialikaliou and Toolianoscinsi, were high in the night sky and Clinsolnosn, the third and largest moon, was just beginning to crest over the horizon. Its cratered surface resembled a woman's ancient face watching over our world. It dominated the heavens whenever it appeared in its full phase. According to legend, Clinsolnosn represented two great lovers who had ruled over the world of Noomas. And when it filled the morning sky it was believed that the goddess Clinsol was happy, for her lover Nosn had just proven to be a most satisfying mate.

I smiled to myself, for the tales of Noomas were amusing, ancient myths, handed down from generation to generation. I had studied the astronomical charts following their paths, as well as their lore; when time allowed.

Clinsolnosn appeared most often alone. Rarely would all the moons align together; and when they did, so legend claimed, they created the most potent and magical of moments. From then on, the two great lovers reigned over Noomas, thereafter to continue their magnificent sovereignty for eternity.

I had long ago reached the limits of my tolerance for symbolism; although the sight of Clinsol alone is breathtaking.

Yes, beautiful, but we have other things to attend to, a softly feminine voice spoke into my mind.

The brazen tone stirred memories of the uncanny practice of Mutis who have all too frequently touched my forehead and pierced my thoughts with a solid telepathic directive. Yet there was no Muti present!

I turned to discover two shadowy figures flickering into solidity at the foot of the bed.

Torlo Hannis, this is Sarleni. You don't know me, yet. I am with Adt Dorta. We wish to meet with you and Youi.

A startled gasp turned my attention toward Youi who had bolted upright, wide awake, staring at the warrior and the dark-haired willowy woman now facing her.

The man, of course, I knew; the woman was a stranger—unfamiliar to us!

"Adt Dorta!" I lamely greeted, still quite confused about this visualization of a person whom I'd been convinced was long dead.

"I survived," he announced. "I am real enough."

Overcome with irrepressible joy and relief seeing Adt alive, I rushed forward to greet my friend.

The woman at his side smiled and bluntly stated: "We have seen your Proctor. You'll soon understand the details of our haste. We need to meet with you in person before everything changes."

"Changes?" I echoed, stepping back in stunned surprise. "What are you talking about?"

Adt awkwardly began to explain.

"After I escaped the Diano camp she connected mentally with me. Then we were thrown off by the storm." He stopped abruptly, hurriedly adding: "Never mind that...will explain later, enough to say we connected. We've been to the far side of Noomas and brought back an important message, a warning, and...I can tell you more in person.

"It's a long story."

Youi was shaking her head and rubbing her eyes. "Am I dreaming?"

"No," Adt assured her.

"If not, how did you gain entrance to our private chambers? Where are the guards?"

She sounded more alarmed than hostile; concerned over palace security.

Adt replied: "Not to worry. We're not in this room, Torlo. We're projections from my father's home."

Then Adt's words shifted distinctly into my mind: *Tonight, come to the Dorta Estates.*

We made plans to meet for dinner that evening and then, without further comment, they faded away, leaving us to puzzle over these strange events.

My friend's survival raised endless questions. And the answers to them would begin a chain of events destined to cause drastic changes in the lives of everybody on Noomas.

* * * * * * *

News of Adt Dorta's unexpected return rippled through Bel-loniea. The whole nation pulsed with festivities, attracting an unusual number of outlanders in honor of Clinsol, Nosn, Slke, Tions, and all such celestial monarchs. Banners, crafts, music filled the streets. The people had made preparations for celebration in advance.

I noticed an odd tension among the throngs of foreigners milling about, especially the visiting officials throughout the palace grounds.

Tonight's opening ceremonies in the public park were among the primary events we had hoped to attend. But now we were forced to set aside our plans due to Adt and Sarleni's sudden arrival.

Rumors filtered down through the social ranks that the son of Kigor Dorta had returned and had brought a mysterious

Helandian with him to the city-state of Bel-loniea. Her unusual appearance created dramatic waves of admiring and critical remarks.

Stories quickly spread about this colorful woman from the Northern Territories which caused a great number of distrustful suspicions to arise among the commoners because very few facts concerning the polar region ever reached the populace.

Officials representing our political allies began making their scheduled public appearances in honor of the Three Moons Celebration. A great number of Mutis were also circulating throughout the palace and parliament grounds.

A serious chill crept along my spine upon noting this.

It was customary to occasionally see one Muti. Only recently had I spotted groups of four or more moving along the corridors of the palace. It was a rare occurrence to see more than one or two Mutis in close proximity to one another. Highly solitary by nature, these silent mystics of the Noomasian landscape roamed freely beneath their distinguishable hooded cloaks, passing all barriers; unfettered by any local authority. But this day, I had seen several clusters of the tall Muti shapes gathering near remote corners of shaded corridors.

Mutis were appearing everywhere, gliding tacitly in and out of the shadows with an air of somber secrecy. I imagined that a universal call might have been raised to bring them to the Proctor's palace.

* * * * * * *

By early evening the sun cast its last crimson hues across the horizon. Two of the moons graced the heavens and the third would soon complete the spectacular nocturnal trio.

When we arrived at the Dorta Estates Adt and Sarleni greeted us in the gardens beneath the leafy Chilso trees bordering a low lawn. They led the way to the Dorta Manor House through the sprawling complex of single level buildings surrounded by lovely gardened grounds.

A savory dinner awaited us in a comfortably furnished setting, complete with a crackling fire on the hearth.

Sarleni wandered to the fireside gazing into its warmth while Adt poured drinks for us. I studied this lovely young woman while sipping my chalice of Porshi. Her oval face, sparked by high cheek bones and soft full lips was delicately framed with flowing dark hair. She appeared physically fragile, yet gracefully strong, secure, and very much in love. Periodically, she'd favor Adt with gentle smiles and they would touch in a kind of private communication while they took turns telling their story.

We talked over the hearty feast; alternating between our adventures, eager to catch up on lost time. Adt told us about his experience on that fateful day in the Diano camp.

"After you cut me free, we attacked our captors. Chaos broke loose as you threw Kay-bombs down on their camp from the grav-disk flyer you had somehow stolen."

"I was battling my bloody way through nasty Diano warriors when I heard my name called...in my head! I learned later that it had come from Sarleni—like we communicated this morning.

"The storm caused tremendous disturbances and when our craft was blown off course, we crashed and waited through the night. In the morning after the rains had stopped we were lost and forced to travel on foot. We'd finally reached the sea and headed north. While making our way along the coast we were yanked up into the sky by flying creatures they called Gatherers; half beasts and half machines."

"Horrors!" I exclaimed.

Adt continued, more forthright than I had expected.

"They were actually stationed as sentinels on board the Haknord slaver ship where we spent a long period alone, in a cell, chained to the floor."

"Ocean slavers?" Youi asked, leaning forward, intently.

"Yes. You know about them?"

"Just remotely," Youi stated. "Some say the coastline hamlets have been raided from time to time by callous pirating slavers."

"You are well informed."

"As a woman," she coolly smiled, "or a Proctoress?"

"Sorry."

Sarleni smirked. "Adt can be crudely blunt at times!"

"Not at all!" he protested, "...just had not expected her—"

Sarleni chopped her right hand through the air, clearly intent on cutting off his words. "Go ahead. Tell them more about our horrid captivity on that slaver ship!"

Adt picked up the story, telling of their imprisonment. "We could not estimate how long the Haknords held us below deck—a nasty business. I don't think I have ever seen uglier creatures in my life, than those pirates.

"They were creepy, for sure," Sarleni agreed. "Almost human; they were somehow bird-like, with large hooked noses and thin lips hanging over jagged, yellow brown teeth. And their lidless eyes were big bright orange circles."

"The leader looked even worse than the crew," Adt grimaced as he remembered their nightmarish encounter. "The near humanness of its shape was more perverse than its distortion. His grey-blue skin coloration was indicative of a mutation.

"His nose was bulbous; the purplish lips grossly thick and pouty like some kind of ugly fish mouth. The green tinted eyes were large, narrow slits but his weird ears were floppy fat. It makes my skin crawl even now just thinking of it." He shuddered; but more importantly told us what he'd discovered about their business at sea.

"We found out that they worked for the Kaminaeans, mapping parts of our world under some kind of contract with the Kaminaean Empire. They planned on selling us into slavery, of course."

Sarleni cut in.

"Moyi and Ju-bilee became our guides and advisers."

"Guides...advisers?" was my immediate inquiry. "Who are these people?"

"They are notable leaders of great influence in the Northern Territories." Adt replied.

"Moyi is a vital teacher of the Zygo," Sarleni added. "But

Ju-bilee is a major force to deal with."

"Some force!" Adt challenged with a mischievous grin.

"A motherly lady," Sarleni blandly warned. "Don't you forget!"

"Yes, yes. Of course!" Adt seemed to sulk while Sarleni picked up the narrative. "They first made appearances while we were on board ship; tending to flash in unannounced and then disappear abruptly, like dream makers. They'd come from nowhere and do wonderful things."

Adt tenderly touched her hand. "I'll admit, Moyi and Ju-bilee are remarkable, and what they had to teach us was incredible! Merging our mind in one accord...well...it saved our lives!"

He hesitated; glancing at the Helandian woman who said: "Basic Zygo, really."

Which explained nothing.

"Hardly so basic," Adt inserted, grinning. "It requires a massive change of attitude before it can be understood."

Noting our confusion, he resumed his explanation with Sarleni filling in details about this amazing Helandian practice of the mind powers.

"Sarleni was already an advanced student of Zygo and anxious to share her knowledge once my reluctance to believe was shattered."

"Her people had sent Sarleni down to Bel-loniea to find me."

"Why?"

"They had their reasons, believe me! They were determined to team us together and send us to meet an important agent...the Proctor, I am certain, will fill in the details later.

"I know this is confusing. Accept, for now, that Moyi and Ju-bilee were instrumental in helping us escape the slavers. We were far out to sea and eventually landed on an island near Kamina."

"By then," Sarleni inserted, "we learned about our own mission. We were expected to meet somebody on the continent."

As they spoke, Youi and I had poured challises of Porshi for our friends.

"I know our experience is hardly believable," Adt was saying.

We sat on the edge of our seats listening intently, enthralled with their extraordinary discoveries as they continued telling of their amazing journey through unexplored territory.

"Sarleni and I grew immensely during this difficult period. I now know that Ju-bilee was invisibly watching, silently giving us strength and courage to stay on course."

"When we finally met the Messenger he barely had enough life left in him to give us a few instructions. Talni was his name. His body held the precious chip which we needed to retrieve and bring back to the Free Lands, as they called this side of Noomas.

"Ju-bilee and Moyi, I think, were proud of what we accomplished. However, they never said as much. They most severely demanded secrecy and warned us to trust nobody unless we could probe deep into their minds and know that no Kaminaean spy lurked within."

We learned, with fascination, how they had developed an ability taught in Helandi. Something about a link of energy we did not quite comprehend. They called this the Zygo.

I noticed Sarleni's serious face and intense concentration in Adt's eyes as their voices again blended.

He had as many questions of me as did I of him. We exchanged summaries of our ventures since the Diano War.

I told about rescuing Youi from the Diano camp and of our journey after that same terrible storm had also blown us off course into the deserts. There we encountered nomads who dragged us into captivity with Baji-Ney's tribe.

Adt responded with sincere admiration: "You, too, were lucky to avoid slavery. I'm familiar with the desert people; nomadic tribes roaming freely up there where life is harsh and demanding. Wild survivors in a bleak desert are bound by a severe moral ethic that strongly supports their culture. Their fierce loyalty to friends grants no room for leniency towards enemies."

I agreed, having experienced the desert breed.

"Those ruthless barterers trade heavily within our markets."

Then I summarized events ending the Diano War and our return to Bel-loniea.

That particular squall, which tore across our planet, had been unusually treacherous compared to others. In fact, it had baffled the scientists enough to keep them busy sorting out the effects and damages long afterwards. Our farmlands and towns were heavily crippled. The bonding of many communities turned out to be one *positive* result of the catastrophe. The repair work had brought neighbors together, sharing expertise and resources in joint efforts to fix the damage.

The Diano fell under our military and political supervision. Their Proctor wisely decided to cooperate with our government.

Since then our countries have been at peace. I had settled into a very happy life with the woman I loved; Proctoress of Bel-loniea, granddaughter of its ruler, Romos.

My greatest victory was that of bringing Youi home safely.

Adt quickly speculated before I finished my story, "I'm sure you arranged a speedy meeting with a Muti!"

I nodded heartily.

"Yes, we were married."

"I assume" he snickered in good humor, "it wasn't a union imposed at sword point?"

"Sword point?" I mocked his insinuation.

After all, Adt, the son of Bel-loniea's finest fencing master, Kigor Dorta, was an expert swordsman. He'd mastered and surpassed his father's skill with the blade. He had taught me how to brandish weapons of Noomas during our training as officers for the war.

His quick smile responded to my words, but his solemn voice, bluntly changed the mood of the topic.

"What you must understand, my friends, is that the world faces great danger. Incredible as that seems we *know* this to be true. We were warned to limit communication with only those who could be trusted: especially the Mutis."

Youi, who had been quiet, objected: "Surely they are aware

of *everything*! They see the future and guide us! Without trust what is left?"

Sarleni's rebuke was firm.

"Ju-bilee told us to be careful. Moyi warned us. We listen!"

"And they are worried the Kaminaean Mutis might have spies on the continent."

After dinner Adt was eager to tell us about his audience with the Proctor. Their meeting in Romos' garret had been brief.

"He listened to my report and promised to deliver the pouch to Andon Janis' research facilities."

All this time the women had been scrutinizing one another, politely reserved. I had been feeling the sharp bite of Sarleni's commanding personality all evening. As she and Adt told of their adventures she had gradually relaxed and smiled tenderly at him.

"The Helandian contacts had sent a special force to retrieve us from the castle on the Kaminaean coast. They were responsible for arranging the meeting with your Proctor when we arrived in Bel-loniea."

Sarleni turned towards me.

"My brother, Mahzit, was part of that team."

She paused, keeping her eyes focused, unwavering on mine.

"I wish you to make use of him. He's been to Kamina. He's young and gifted."

"Make *use* of him, for *what*?" I was annoyed by her bluntly commanding pronouncement.

She took a long breath; then continued, stubbornly ignoring my question.

"I believe you'll be heavily involved with coming events, on a very high level. He will prove to be a valuable resource to your troops. I recommend you grant him a position under your command. Mahzit will be a beneficial addition to your staff."

The smile on her face was generous enough to negate further objection. The process of assigning a Helandian warrior to my staff was a simple enough request to honor. Still I found her insistent tone to be quite puzzling.

"I'll see what can be done."

"Once our present duties and responsibilities are completed here, we'll be leaving for Helandi. Adt must meet my family— and his own."

Adt swallowed hard, adding: "It is incredible how my family ties are attached to those northern lands."

Reminiscing and sharing family anecdotes filled the evening with lighthearted laughter. Though, we carefully avoided the churning unrest which was soon to be enveloping the world. But before we parted, we once again lapsed into the serious business at hand, silently recognizing the gray mood overshadowing us all. Only in the good-byes did we return to a more relaxed mood.

* * * * * * *

Our flight back to the palace estate soared high above the city lights. Youi and I basked in the splendor of the triple moon-beams, happily enjoying this friendly view of the world. The potential uprising could not prevent the promise of the Three Moon Celebration, long anticipated by so many people who had come to Bel-loniea.

We wanted to absorb the beauty of this magical time. Even stripping the myth from the solar alignment of the moons did not diminish the glorious sight before us.

Youi leaned on me, her soft flesh soothing my troubled worries over the events we'd learned about that evening. Neither of us wanted to think about possible problems.

We snuggled for a long, deeply intimate moment, unmoving, just being close. Since knowing her I had learned the wonderful joy that comes when you've bonded with somebody special. Nothing can compare to the fulfilling contentment of physically connecting to your dearest love. I felt complete with Youi. Everything since my arrival on Noomas faded in comparison.

"The gods must be happy up there," she mused. Youi was not enthralled with any particular religious cult, for she was strongly influenced by her father. Andon Janis had come to this world as a citizen of the Galactic Federation. He was a scientist. Youi's grandfather, Proctor Romos, had educated her in religions and cultures common to Noomas, in order to prepare her for the position of royal Proctoress. She would bear the responsibility of providing sound wisdom and leadership, resolving any conflicts that might arise between citizens of their realm. Therefore, she was required to refrain from favoring any particular religious view.

The Proctoress was a product of mixed parents from two differing civilizations: one galactic; the other local. She had admirably cultivated a healthy respect for all belief systems, of which there were many.

My thoughts drifted away from gods, the Galactic Federation and interstellar leaps between solar systems. Youi's presence, alone, enthralled me. Captivated by her nearness, I gazed dreamily into the night sky.

The moons illuminated the world and the heavens. Nobody could possibly deny the magical spell cast by the tri-lunar spectacle, a phenomenon occurring only once in many generations when the moons align in perfect symmetry. And then, for the remainder of the season, they will continually dominate the heavens, before their orbits spin away from one another once again.

Could there be some omen, some link, or some stellar significance to all of this coming together now? Fleeting questions quickly arose and faded for I had never given weight to prophetic nonsense.

"The legend is alive, some would say," Youi was musing.

"Do you think it could be true?"

"Is there any reason not to believe?"

Our occasional talks about theories never achieved resolution concerning the folklore. I had always believed that legends were based on heroic deeds of human leaders retold over the generations, until they were gradually elevated to mythological gods.

Youi, knowing my bias, stroked my cheek gently in silent understanding.

"It is the way of our culture, and the duty of our royal position to sustain the ancient customs for our children."

I frowned, half wondering if she might be saying something new. "What children?"

"Those yet to come, of course," she giggled. "The rising of the three moons marks the most fertile of all seasons: a time when an especially gifted generation will begin."

After a long sigh, Youi lifted her head and smiled mysteriously.

"Torlo, can you imagine the wonders that the world will experience from this day forward? All tri-lunar seedings will bring great rewards to those whose birth soon follows."

One thing was for certain: the future would not come easy.

The light of the sky outlined her delicate features.

"Tonight we must honor the gods."

"Right here?"

The idea of praying to some invisible beings of this or any world did not appeal to me. I had more selfish agendas nagging my brain involving male and female unions of a most intimate nature.

"It is enough to be together and happy, no matter what the gods of Noomas might favor. Assuming, of course, they actually exist. I know nothing of gods real or imagined. I only believe in the magic of our love. You have made me complete; for without you, life seems empty."

She drew closer to me. "Thank the gods and all those women who were your teachers in the art of love!"

"Do you think I have no imagination? Need I be taught how to love a woman like you?"

"Am I so different from all those others?" she teased, lips touching my check as they softly spoke those words.

I still only vaguely remembered things concerning my life previous to arriving on Noomas, so avoided a direct answer to her question.

"Dearest Youi, somebody certainly must have given you a few lessons in the arts."

"In many arts: yes," leaning in closer to me.

"Well," she whispered, looking up into my eyes. "It is a lovely place, don't you think?"

"Yes." I said, noticing only her moonlit face. "You are lovely."

And desirable, I thought, *beyond anything else in the universe*.

I pulled her closer; and we were both captured by the sheer magic of that embrace.

As our lips met the world around us simply vanished.

Royal Proctoress or not, she was deeply endowed with vibrant passion that made all else blandly meaningless.

Time splintered and we were momentarily enveloped in a mutually shared singularity. We were one living thing, completely unified. It was but an instant; yet contained a sense of eternity.

Only after we broke the embrace did either of us speak.

I nodded towards the distant tip of the Proctor's palace rising from the depths of the city.

"Yes," she decided, with a deep, contented sigh. "A perfect setting and a perfect place to begin...."

Her words faded. Nothing more needed to be said.

In practical terms, the Celebration of the Three Moons phenomena symbolically promoted the birthing of the next generation. It all came from ancient traditions involving fertility rites. My basic male ego decidedly trumped any mythological saga and wanted only to indulge in the promise of physical pleasures with the woman I loved. Youi was the very living force that drove me. Passion and love blended, as it always did for us, into a lovely flow of pure ecstasy.

Soon we succumbed to our pulsing urges, and honored the Clinsolnosn ideal. In Youi's arms I had discovered a place which completed myself and made the universe whole.

* * * * * * *

The next morning everything, as Adt Dorta had said, drastically changed.

I discovered a small envelope under the door with the Proctor's seal.

Memories flashed through me. Vague sparks of distant conflicts on other worlds burst briefly into focus. I felt charged with both anticipation and resistance about facing so grave a situation during the most festive days on Noomas.

The Proctor's message was a formal order to meet with Romos that very morning in his private offices.

And so it had begun.

CHAPTER TWO
TROUBLED REUNION

I. Kigor Dorta

Kigor was lecturing on the art of defensive dueling, before a select class of young warriors, when the message arrived. The interruption was annoying.

Eager men and women crowded the large hall, clambering to learn from this famed teacher, and master swordsman who was in high demand across the country. Every academy in the realm sought his lectures and paid hefty fees for the privilege of his unsurpassed tutelage.

He had standing orders never to be interrupted under any circumstances during these lectures. So he was alarmed when the young courier stepped toward him holding an envelope with Proctor Romos' seal. He immediately opened and read the message.

Come. Helandi connected.

Turning back to the podium, calmly dismissing the students with a brief apology, Kigor hastily left the lecture hall allowing no questions to be asked.

During the flight back home to Bel-loniea the courier told him of Adt's return.

"He brought a young woman with him. She is from the Northern Territories...a place called Helandi?"

A smile swept across Kigor's handsome features.

How ironic, he reflected, *a woman from the land of Adt's birth.*

Helandi was where he had met Adt's mother. Kigor's memory shot back to the brief seasons spent with the only woman he had ever loved. The resulting son had become his life's responsibility, the only thing more important than his dedication to Proctor Romos. Even without Muti instructions he would have taught the boy everything he knew about the sword.

Stillness blanketed the city as Kigor arrived at the Dorta Estates before dawn.

Adt would most certainly be found in his old suite in the residential west wing sector. The majority of the manor housed administrative offices and tutorial studios required to operate the Dorta Academy. The gym, the sparring rooms, and lecture halls were practical spaces for extensive combatant-play. Few students passed all his challenges. This was where Adt had refined his mastery of the sword, as a child growing up in these family estates.

Kigor hurried to the back wing, where his son's personal quarters were located. He stood just outside the door, rigid; taking in the room which had been empty for so long. He wasn't a man who easily experienced emotional reactions to anything. Long years of practice had trained him to hold feelings down beneath thickly constructed armor. He had always told his students that in battle there was no room for distractions. Yet as a pragmatist he had not ignored the fact that death is fated in war.

The notion of Adt having died had never completely impacted Kigor. None could match Adt's abilities with the sword, but skill alone, could not protect a warrior forever.

His son had been reported dead in battle.

But the urgent message today, stated he was alive.

Until he saw Adt in the flesh, breathing, alive, Kigor would not allow himself to believe it. He had to learn the truth for himself.

Now he gazed at the scene, taking it in like a soothing cocktail. Young Dorta was lying in bed next to a stunning young woman. The sight of the lovers said enough. Seeing him there, lying peacefully in the bed, next to the lovely woman, sent a warm wave of contentment through Kigor.

With a calmed spirit, he left the estate and hurried to meet with Proctor Romos.

On the palace grounds, firm salutes from all sentries greeted Kigor Dorta the sword master of Bel-loniea, famed throughout the civilized world for his unsurpassed skill.

Upon approaching the Proctor's resident wing, he hardly paused. He just nodded to the officer rigidly standing guard at the corridor.

The man saluted and stepped aside.

"You are expected."

"Yes," Kigor acknowledged in his richly deep voice.

Gliding down the hall, his graceful combination of militant march and swordsman's gait formed the flowing dance of a lean, tightly wired man of razor sharp muscles tempered to a fine edge. The beard he had recently trimmed was brushed neatly in place. Steel-blue eyes narrowed as he approached the open door of the Proctor's living quarters.

The room beyond was formal, comfortably furnished. A settee pressed against wall-to-wall bookcases. The adjoining library frequently hosted guests, such as chief advisors and friends.

Romos stepped from behind his desk when Kigor entered. Neither man spoke. Then they moved closer, placing hands to shoulders in the natural warm greeting of old colleagues and tight friends who, long before the births of their children, had shared combat forays from their cadet days. They had both been assigned to the missions into the Northern Territories during the plains conflicts long ago. Kigor never forgot those early voyages with the younger Proctor. They had earned their rites to manhood in those days, braving the frigid tempests of the Helandian fields.

The Proctor motioned with his hand.

"Sit."

Kigor lowered himself into the settee and Romos started

pacing, hands behind his back, chin up, head arched and deep in thought. The Proctor's words were solemn.

"Serious international issues have arisen far sooner than any of us anticipated. Our world order will soon be challenged. All of our nations are at risk.

"The continent beyond the sea has become overrun by a Muti-driven empire. They are spreading quickly and are now threatening our nations.

"Helandi has made rapid advancements to halt their progress. Adt is deeply involved."

Kigor stiffened upon hearing his son's name, for the mention of Helandi in the summons had been a blunt link to Adt.

The Proctor sat down next to his comrade relating his meeting with Adt and the woman named Sarleni.

Romos spoke about a Messenger Adt and Sarleni had encountered. Something about a microsliver they had delivered to Andon Janis. But Kigor was heavily focused on the newly emerged presence of his son, Adt Dorta.

"So my son is already intimately connected," Kigor said, with both pride and parental concern.

"More than you could imagine. He's expected in Helandi.

"My dear friend, it has been our secret shared with the Mutis who supervised his growth. He was prepared."

"For what?"

The Mutis had made no explanation during Adt's training. Their silence had implied the obvious.

"She has emerged," Romos stated. "My Muti has said Adt met her."

It was Kigor's turn to speak. Instead, he maintained silence. The pain was too deep: for he knew precisely that Romos was alluding to the Helandian woman who had stolen Kigor's heart.

The mood had shifted.

The Proctor rose in the manner of a tired Traztu beast, stretching to his full height. He now assumed his official role as leader of a nation-state.

"We have been aware of occasional rumors about uprisings on the other side of the world. In previous times, Kamina was spoken of only in whispers. Those stories have since been substantiated."

He held up his hand.

"Andon has access to the information brought back by Adt. We must act. And fast. We must draw upon all our known resources.

"Torlo Hannis will be commissioned. I'll be seeing him today. We will be relying on his galactic experience. His abilities may be crucial if we are forced into an international war.

"Your reputation will be vital to the formation of a multi-national defense force. General Qui Shan and a number of other prominent military experts have been summoned. National doyens are being informed, as we speak. However, we have been warned to be careful about involving Mutis beyond our inner circle, until we have more information."

That might prove difficult, Kigor worried.

Mutis could reach into a man and discern his thoughts and sometimes his future. Even so, the Muti were reluctant to specifically predict or reveal what they saw. Usually they would reply in cryptic form. Visions reflected on distant variables which did not concern people directly.

Thus, Kigor habitually avoided contact with these strange creatures who favored distance and isolation.

Romos raised his voice.

"Kigor, you will tell Adt everything. Right away! He and Torlo shall be trusted. As shall the Janis' Muti. Trust it: None other at this time."

His words sharpened.

"I am appointing you joint commander. You will consult with selected staff to enlist the services of the highest qualified warriors. Your international influence will bring together an Elite Force. You must all become thoroughly familiar with the data your son retrieved from the Messenger. I believe he was called Talni. Once briefed, the Elite will delegate tasks to their staff. Strategic plans must be kept under tight wraps for the officers of the security units assigned by Torlo."

He chuckled hesitantly; then grew serious.

"Oh, my friend, it is a mess! We're in a very real clash of more than mere nations. This isn't a quarrel between municipalities or cultures over land or privileges; no political strife between villages or tribes.

This is far more severe. The Muti has risen against the human. They are not asking for rights or space. No! They want to annihilate us and erase all people from the planet!

We must shape an Armada to strike against a continental nation that calls itself an Empire: Kamina."

Romos' face softened as he looked at his old friend. "Kigor, seek your son. Hold nothing back. I have a meeting soon with Andon and others. I'll keep you informed. We'll meet later today, perhaps."

The Proctor turned to his desk, and their meeting was over.

* * * * * * *

Upon returning to his estates, Kigor dismissed all inquiries, wanting only to speak with his son.

There were no ceremonious accolades when they stepped into his office together, though the invariable feeling of shared, unspoken kindness was ever present between them. Father and son were not personal friends, beyond the parental bond of kinship. The warmth was real, and could be intense. He deeply loved his son. And the emotions were thickly layered between them. Yet for the most part they had been student and teacher until the young man eventually out-classed even his father.

It was clearly obvious that Adt had grown, and the serious look in the eyes of this fully matured man facing him was unsettling. This was a warrior who had seen things beyond the ordinary.

His son had changed.

Both men moved like silky shadows, their bodies honed as master swordsmen.

Kigor placed a hand warmly on Adt's wide shoulder.

"I'm proud of you."

He felt a lump in his throat, coughed, then hesitated a moment.

"We have some catching up to do since the Diano War. And you must tell me about this woman of Helandi."

That was as close as he could manage. Then he regained his austere composure.

Adt replied; needing few words.

"She is here at this moment."

He tapped his head and Kigor understood the implication. Helandians had the Mind skills.

"If you wish her with us."

Kigor shook his head.

"Not necessary."

Adt looked thoughtfully down.

"That works. Anyway, my dear Sarleni won't connect. She wants us to have privacy. Perhaps she is right."

Kigor understood. Any woman of Helandian birth most likely shared similar charms that had attracted him to Adt's mother.

"What has happened?"

Adt began relating his adventures with Sarleni. Once Kigor had heard the summary of Adt's journey, his combat with the Muti, and encounter with the Messenger, he understood the complexity of what lay ahead.

"You know Ju-bilee is your mother, don't you?"

"So she claimed, and never explained."

"That would be like her."

"Then tell me everything you know."

"*Everything* would be personal."

"Tell me anyway. After all, I have a right."

Kigor swiftly parried.

"No more right than I, to ask you the same question. Tell me everything about your Sarleni!"

Adt smirked, having snared his father at his own game.

"That, too, is personal, Father."

The older man smiled.

"Your wit has remained as sharp as your sword."

"Sharper, since meeting Sarleni."

"Yes. I do not doubt it."

"I insist on respecting your privacy regarding Ju-bilee. So do me the honor of being first to speak."

Both contestants had posed a verbal impasse. The next to react, lost the point in the match.

Kigor flexed his hands wide; then cupped fingers together. "About Ju-bilee...what a man shares with his woman, is between *them*. Some issues have broader boundaries. She has been invisible all these years by choice and design. Her purpose should be obvious to you. The woman is dedicated to her cause. We shared too short a journey and you were the resulting joy. Then her studies and vocation...."

His voice broke off and his eyes were distant. Keeping the secret over all these years had been difficult. Perhaps he could share parts of the truth with his son.

"In time, son, I'll tell you more. Right now...it is enough to say we had a love relationship and the feelings never completely submerged. I always have you to remind me."

The man shifted nervously, then straightened, eyes snapping to Adt's, "Your turn. What is your woman like? I realize she's Helandian...though, I suspect, different from your mother."

"That, she is," Adt grinned.

"As you are different from me: I never had Ju-bilee's genetic gifts: potent and damningly commanding."

Adt leaned back, relating the details of his adventure to Kigor.

"Sarleni's one bossy lady, too. We were brought together on the night of the terrible storm. It is a long story. She was struggling in a skirmish with the Diano when I found her. I managed to destroy them, but was wounded in the process. When the storm worsened, she led with commands befitting a royal Proctoress. I took her for a slavegirl. She thought I was a common hunter and made me her student, whom she bullied into learning HanJahn games! Once I grasped the concepts and the seriousness of her mission, it served...."

Kigor listened, particularly intrigued by the interactions during their ordeal.

"At first I hated every inch of Sarleni's lovely, deliciously beautiful, divine shape."

"Instant love," Kigor mused, with an inner sense of knowing. "Helandi women can charm a young man, can't they?"

Kigor then recounted elements of his early life with Ju-bilee; enough for both men to gain an understanding of the Helandian women who had become entwined with their lives.

The duel thus ended. Father and son openly embraced with their eyes. Nothing remained clouded, hidden; nothing left unsaid. Both were blown wide open to honest love and trust. A new bonding had fused. Slowly the two men stood and the meeting concluded.

* * * * * * *

Sarleni glanced up when Adt came through the door of their residence at the Dorta Estates. She had been getting used to their quarters: impeccably organized. Her husband's father was obviously a very structured person.

She conversationally asked, as he hugged her, "Have you seen him, yet?"

"Yes. He's under a lot of pressure these days, with more responsibilities than ever before."

Then lamely added: "It wasn't exactly how I would have planned our meeting. He is carrying a heavy burden which he keeps to himself: all private."

Sarleni felt his uncertainty, pain, and frustration but made no effort to enter into his special mental territory. This was not the time for any Zygo. Most of their daily relationship was closer to normal than one might have expected. Habit selected the obvious. And verbal conversation was an easy fall-back.

"All these years I had believed my mother was lost forever, dead.

And now I discover that the most awesome woman I've ever

met—the most militant, the most fearsome—turns out to be my mother! He should have told me *something*, at least. He should have prepared me."

"Adt, it had to be difficult for Kigor, too. They both care deeply for you."

He pulled her close and she took in the feelings spilling out from him.

"Well, we managed. My father shared a few things about her."

I thought as much.

Reading my mind?

No! I try not to, without permission: difficult sometimes to ignore our connection.

"You often say, reading my mind is like breathing."

It had been a problem for them to cross that natural bridge. They both tried to honor one another's private spaces.

The Zygo connection requires a deep merging. And they had been the first of the Zygo duos to reach full Nexus. Toning down their strengths was sometimes difficult; so achieving complete privacy became a challenge.

You and your male privacy, she smiled, mildly amused.

Don't you carry your own safe place in which to hide your feminine delicacies? He was calmer now.

We women keep our secrets...so you men continue to be fascinated and interested.

"And confused."

"Confused or not."

Her eyes met his in open tenderness.

You can let me in when it pleases you.

She had taught him about the HanJahn and the Mind Powers during their journey across the ocean. Once the link was established, the duo then utilized joint strengths which yielded capacities many factors beyond either partner's singular potential. The ultimate Nexus which had been the goal of the HanJahn teachings, had thus far, only been attained by Adt and Sarleni. And while they were journeying, the Helandian Academy had been preparing scores on Zygo duos to follow in their footsteps.

It would fall upon Adt and Sarleni to assist the newly recruited pairs to hone their skills towards the Nexus.

"I'm glad you're working with your father on the Messenger's data. We'll need to understand a great deal more about what has happened to the Muti before we leave. For soon we'll be going to meet my family in Helandi. They are anxious to meet the handsome warrior from the mainland who captured my heart."

She tenderly touched his cheek.

He frowned. "There are things to be resolved."

"Reports, conferences and...I'll want to give Torlo a detailed accounting of our story before we go."

HanJahn methods have been designed to record memories.

"I wouldn't doubt that Andon Janis, in his Foundation, might be working on systems along those lines."

Adt impulsively drew her closer. Their lips touched.

An instant reading of your thoughts, my dear Adt, is not all that complicated; at least not for me.

You cheat, he joked as they kissed again.

Do we need an excuse? Sarleni challenged Adt, who was too enveloped by her to bother with an answer.

They blended together in a complete union of one.

II. Mahzit: The Public Voices

The room was dark. The young warrior's head brutally screamed at him. Hangovers were monstrous even in Bel-loniea. He was enjoying a nasty one slamming through his skull.

Where am I? he wondered, dazed and disorientated. The air choked him with a putrid mix of vomit and raw sweat. Muffled voices distantly moaned.

Mahzit's hands clutched his ears, hoping to drown out the loud pounding blasting at him from the rhythmic beat of his heart.

A few deep breaths refreshed his memory of the night before, crippling him into agonizing embarrassment. Impulsiveness had, apparently, dragged him into another bitter humiliation.

Mocking tones grated in his head from Sarleni's stinging voice.

Mahzit, shame on you! You're in a Bel-loniean tank with a bunch of other wasted sots.

Get out of my head, he groused, resentfully.

You need to fix the trouble you started.

Her scolding was evident with every word.

He groaned, inwardly relieved to feel his sister's thoughts fade.

All he'd wanted to do was enjoy a nice evening in Bel-loniea. The long trip to Kamina and back had been stressful. They'd accomplished their mission to find Sarleni. He deserved a little relaxation with his comrades. What went wrong? How'd he end up here? He tried to remember. Memories assembled slowly.

He'd been assigned to the local barracks with the other Helandi officers from the rescue team. Having little to do that evening, they decided to visit the famous Bel-loniean Pleasure Palace. Local taverns commonly provided entertainment and comfort for warriors at the expense of the government. This was a commercial establishment highly recommended for its international flair.

Richly ornate tapestries adorned the foyer and main salons where dignitaries of Bel-loniea and wealthy international travelers were regularly welcomed. Its inner courtyard rang with half drunken revelry. Songs enlivened the atmosphere, drifting through the upper balcony where merry diners would disappear later in the evening for private partying. Shaded alcoves were hidden from view as he and his friends were ushered through a patio and into a brightly lit lounge, with its central fountain and elegant statues.

Crackling fireplaces warmly flickered in each corner. Corridors and staircases provided easy access to upper floors. The adjoining bar and booths were occupied so their hostess split them up at different tables, near a ceiling-high fireplace.

They were having a splendid evening, already engaged in bold conversation with their table companions, and soon gained the attention of several attractive women. The Helandian warriors immersed themselves in the light hearted camaraderie.

Mahzit felt flushed from the drinks and as he surveyed the young ladies near the bar, an all too familiar intrusion had usurped his privacy: his sister's voice. They'd hardly connected since he'd dropped her off at the Dorta Estates.

Sarleni, you certainly have bad timing. What do you want?

I talked to Torlo Hannis about giving you a position under his command. Expect new orders and be sharp, brother. Take advantage of your exposure to Kamina. I promised your loyalty, your dedication to duty and your intelligence. I lied a little.

Her smugness had been softly biting. He'd wrangled with Sarleni's cutting personality since childhood. She'd grown into a cleverly determined woman.

I'm not nearly as bright as you are.

She retorted: *No man is!*

Actually he envied Sarleni's relationship with her new soul mate. He wondered if that would ever happen to him: maybe someday—if he was lucky enough.

His eyes scanned across the beautiful young women and then back to a brown eyed blonde who was gazing invitingly towards him. Eager to approach her, he shot back at Sarleni. *Go dance with your toy-man, then!*

My Adt is special. So don't go insulting him; at least not within hearing of his keen ears. His sword point can nick his name across your face in....

I'm not defenseless! Mahzit feigned hurt pride.

Next to Adt you're an amateur. Remember he's a Dorta, son of the famous Kigor, master of the blade.

I remember.

Oh, go and impress those ladies. They'll enjoy your charades!

Then she left his head.

Mahzit motioned the blonde to join him. She was quick to respond, sitting down next to him. He ordered drinks for both of them.

The young lady had a musically light voice. Alluring intimacy colored her words.

When the drinks came, they saluted each other, playfully teasing. The Porshi had freed up his natural male virility. He wanted to take her flesh against his own. Instead, he managed to curb his appetite to the conversation. After dinner, would be soon enough to continue their flirtation in a less public, and more secluded setting.

Mahzit was ordering Ka to finish off their meal when a voice at the next table diverted his attention.

"There's talk of war!" Somebody muttered: "Wouldn't that be exciting?"

"War talk is just idle nonsense clamoring at the wind," the young blonde chided. "You men live on war talk."

Even as she spoke, he felt a slight shift of her thigh touching his.

A gentle voice from the other table said, "War causes mass destruction. Innocent people pay heavily."

"So what? Life is a struggle! The strong and lucky survive."

That sneer came from a square faced man with a thick middle and beefy arms. Yelling, bickering, and drunken talk had risen to a tense pitch, reflecting the street talk of Bel-loniea. The atmosphere had switched from joviality to tense war talk.

Mahzit wanted to ignore the ruckus and concentrate on the young lady—her thigh—and the rest of her, too, later; upstairs.

He touched her shoulder, letting his fingers trace down the slender arm to delicate fingers.

"You are so strong, and I love being with a strong man like you."

A slight shift of warm damp skin against his thigh beneath the table accented the soft voice. Mahzit was growing anxious, wanting to subtly whisk her away to a private room.

From the other table the conversation continued to blare loudly.

"...influential families support this action."

"Can we trust anybody? Who are these Helandi foreigners? From the Northern Territories, I've heard! Can't be trusted, if you ask me."

Angry shouts annoyingly interrupted his private talk again, as he heard a serious voice.

"They say the House of Dorta is involved!"

The man opposite Mahzit picked up the debate.

"Quite frankly the rumors about Outlanders are unreliable."

His eyes met Mahzit's.

"We know of the Northern Primitives. But who are these Helandians? Fantasy? Young Dorta is a Kordatic fool!"

The woman next to Mahzit arched up.

"Are you calling Dorta a liar?"

"They are all suspect!" the man rasped.

"Have any of you seen this woman Dorta brought with him? No! How do we know a subnormal spirit from the Mystery Gods of Helandi has not seduced him? Nobody has ever seen this...mythical land! I will not be tainted by hearsay."

The man's jaw was set, stone-hard and stubbornly determined.

"She's a dangerous demon who seduced the House of Dorta."

Someone chimed in.

"Yes, I've heard about *that* woman. Rumors...."

"Everybody has!" other voices echoed.

Mahzit leaped to his feet, hand gripped his sword belt.

The man glared in shock at Mahzit.

"What's this?"

"I'm *Helandi*, from the Northern Territories, if you must know. Drop the subject. And apologize!"

The man scoffed with contempt.

"Apologize?"

"Or draw your sword!"

He would not sustain another insult from the woman's verbal debates or this man's over-bloated arrogance.

The throng seethed with anticipation.

A voice from the next table shouted.

"A duel! Clear space!"

"I don't fight a helpless...Kordatic child."

"I'm not helpless."

Mahzit slowly drew his weapon.

"And you are an insolent Fiza!"

The woman gripped his thigh to communicate her caution over his challenge.

The rogue's sword bashed against a goblet, spewing liquid and broken glass in all directions.

Voices cried out. People hustled to clear the space. The bully lifted like a riled Korda, bulging muscles rippling, as his sword crossed against Mahzit's.

"Are you sure, rookie?" he raged loudly. "If you want this to continue, I shall prune your loins with death."

"Do not exhaust your coffers with empty words!" Mahzit warned.

The blonde placed a hand on Mahzit's shoulder.

"This cad isn't worth fighting. Ignore him!"

Suddenly he had no need to impress her. She frowned, and then tilted her head, indicating the upper floor.

"Let's leave. I prefer my lovers in one piece."

She wanted him. And that would happen, once he had attended to this scoundrel.

"Later, after I teach this Roku a lesson in manners. He's insulted Sarleni of Helandi!"

The brute objected indignantly. "I don't even know the person!"

"She is the Dorta woman you dared to defile—and my sister!"

Cold ice cut across the other man's face. The eyes hardened, the lips compressed and the man's blade thrust out.

Mahzit lifted his sword against the other's blade, letting the point glide into empty air. Flabbergasted by the quick parry, the bully attacked again: this time following his first thrust with a second and third; then a cut to the head.

Mahzit's blade repelled each jab with minimal effort. He would have accepted an apology; rather than force a fight. Now it was too late to debate the issue.

Several onlookers had pushed the tables back, clearing an area for their duel.

Mainly on the defensive, Mahzit continued to block the other's sword, foiling every counter attack. This was a drunken man, dangerous; yes. Not worth killing. He continued to parry and avoid the swinging blade dancing in front of him.

A sudden leap caused the man's sword to come in contact with his arm. Mahzit's blade sliced across the man's chest, cutting the officer's ribbon and leather shoulder strap. The man bellowed in rage.

A hushed gasp of admiration rose from the crowd as a result of Mahzit's agile riposte. Mahzit took control, weaving his sword and dancing effortlessly around his opponent, making it obvious how easily he could carve this opponent into a trembling mass of screaming flesh.

He actually felt sorry for the fool.

The shaken officer backed away, cursing, at a generous distance, then complained caustically.

"Why must we continue?"

Mahzit had won his point. He'd gain no further profit by continuing the duel. And all he really wanted was some personal time with the woman.

Submitting a gentlemanly nod, Mahzit lowered his blade—a foolish mistake. The rogue leaped in, swinging wide.

A scream of distress sounded from a woman that almost distracted him.

With amazing agility, Mahzit twisted his blade around the other's, slamming it down.

What happened next was a blur. Without thinking he let emotional fury send him bodily at the other man, knocking them both to the ground.

Voices shouted and men shoved in, swords drawn. Something hit the back of his head, as his opponent was being marshaled off under an escort of several armed warriors.

His adventure in the Pleasure Palace of Bel-loniea had ended when two security guards carried his body away like a limp bag.

Late in the morning, in the cell of the Bel-loniean military guardhouse, he learned the seriousness of his situation. The local authorities had halted the skirmish, and the man he had been fighting had signed charges against him for illegally dueling in public. Mahzit realized he was in deep trouble. The man was powerfully connected and bent on revenge.

What had started as a celebration had turned into a crushing defeat.

His future looked bleak.

CHAPTER THREE

SUMMONS

I. Inner Circle

Authority generates respect from advocates who fear its fury.

Dress and decorum, conduct and discourse pierce bloated egos and prick the tender flesh of status.

Bold defiance stands brazen before wisdom. Thus, even fury balances in favor of justified courage.

—Wisdom of the Ancients

The Proctor's directive to appear before him came as no surprise. It was only yesterday that Adt had returned to Bel-loniea. He had already spoken with both Romos and Andon Janis. My friend had given us all enough reason to expect the national call to action.

A palace guard escorted me to the Proctor's study.

The alcove was perched at the top of a spiral staircase leading to this small, practical garret. For it was, indeed a watchtower from where the Proctor had a clear view spanning the central city of his domain.

The supreme authority of Bel-loniea stood behind his desk; an intense expression marking his face. My wife's grandfather, Proctor Romos was dressed casually in a fine ecru Jilio-skin. He looked relaxed, yet grim.

"Sit!" His simple command was friendly. A nod indicated the padded chair. "Torlo, alarming reports have reached us. I assume you have heard."

He briefed me on his recent meeting with Andon Janis concerning the microchip from the Messenger, Talni.

"I've seen part of the report Adt brought back from the Castle of Doom in Kamina. The danger is obvious. Total secrecy is crucial. Rumors are already circulating though we had hoped to keep minimized. We shall give no credence to any of them.

"However, my Muti said Torlo Hannis will again be a shadow across the future. That same Muti had predicted your influence in our world when you first arrived on Noomas."

Ironic humor slipped through the Proctor's smile as he added, "From its lips, I take it seriously. Further details on the subject are classified until Andon's team has reported back."

He paused, staring as if attempting to read my face.

"The situation may be beyond our control despite all precautions—most difficult to assess, with the startling news dropping in our laps.

"Uncanny.

"It happens to occur during the most notable phenomenon of our generation, the Three Moons Festival.

"Remarkable."

Romos shook his head, soberly returning to the crisis at hand. He muttered to himself as if he were summarizing all these factors in order to present a unified concept of the issues.

"At times it is so easy to forget the unique abilities of our Mutis, due to their quiescence. If the message proves to be correct, our understanding of the Muti will surely be changed. No longer can we remain complacent under their guidance— though if this becomes a world crisis, we will need them more than ever before.

"They are capable of detecting future events. Our societies have relied on their benevolent wisdom for countless ages. Yet we freely govern ourselves while they maintain a respectful and protective watch over us." He shook his head sadly from side to side.

"If the reports are as accurate as they appear to be, then we face a threatening Muti Empire. Thus, we will not know which Mutis to trust. We are in a very difficult predicament—caught in a critical bind.

"We're not equipped to battle a toxic Muti uprising without the help of an equally powerful force; our long-term Muti connections."

Romos impatiently drummed his fingers on the desk, and then stiffly standing, released a heavy sigh.

"Korda dump! We have to sort it all out. And fast. Until then, we must be vigilant toward the complexity of our immediate task."

His gaze met mine; then he began formulating his plan in a cold, methodical manner.

"We presume the danger is eminent. Prepare for the worst. The Kaminaean Mutis must be stopped at all cost! We have no choice. Use all discretion available to separate friend from foe, especially among *our* Mutis. A real problem! We must place our trust in those who pass the test and are with us. And pray to the gods of Noomas, all of them however the spirit world works, to help us successfully distinguish good from bad."

His voice faded, his eyes glazed to some distant point; then back to mine.

"Before I discuss my plan further, can you tell me what you have learned from Adt? I assume he's confided in you. And I would like a detailed report."

I took a long, slow breath before deciding how to begin my reply and then proceeded to relate how Adt and Sarleni practice an art related to the telepathic practice of the Mutis.

"Sarleni claims to be a student of a Helandian study. The HanJahn Academy, I believe, directed by a learned teacher named Moyi. I do remember meeting Moyi once during the Relief Projects after the great storm—reminded me of Andon, in some ways. At any rate, I believe their expertise could be on the order of the telecommunications equipment implemented by the Janis Foundation."

He nodded.

"And they mentioned a woman called Ju-bilee. Apparently they are mystics, of a sort. I seriously doubt it is a religious order, sir. Adt leans toward hard science and would not easily trust mystical teachings without solid evidence."

The Proctor replied with a candid admission.

"It is genuine enough. I have known of the Helandian practices for years. From my youth I studied the historic annals of Noomas.

'To understand anything fully is to know nothing.
And the more facts you embrace, the less you understand.'

"Gaining a broad sweep of many avenues into truth and answers expands any man's leadership capabilities with effective authority and wisdom."

His arms generously cut through the air.

"I am aware of mystical practices among the Primitives in the Northern Territories. We have not had contact with these hidden clans for ages. Not until recently. We reconnected after the disastrous storm that tore through during the Diano War. The Helandians joined the relief efforts along with the Raiders during the worst of the disaster. And afterwards their people slipped away, unnoticed.

"What the general public knows or doesn't know, has little to do with what a Proctor *must* know. No power, even as subtle as the Helandi, can govern unless they have some exposure to the outside world. They are simply secretive.

"I understand they are linked to the Nuja gods of the north, primarily worshipped by tribes from their region. If they have perfected their art to the degree you are suggesting, then it will truly be helpful in our conflict with the Kaminaean Mutis."

The Proctor was addressing me directly, leaning close; pressing his words strongly with an obvious agenda.

I paid close attention.

"Remember, Torlo. The more you can learn and discover the better prepared you will be. Don't get lost in details best left to the understanding of experts in their specialized fields. Use them. Know whom to entrust into your inner circle, and allow them free reign within their intellectual pools.

"Trust them to sort details. Knowing the difference can be the fine line between success and failure.

"This applies to your galactic experience before coming to our world...."

He broke his thought, staring into space. After a while he strode to his desk, tapping the rich wood. When he turned back, his tone had shifted.

"I understand our Mutis have limited access to your mind."

"I don't know about that," I admitted.

"My Muti suggested you do." Romos countered.

"Could it be possible to keep your thoughts discreetly blocked from Muti infiltration? If so, then we can expect to take advantage of your disciplined mental shield.

"If you are successful, your abilities will be greatly useful, as my Muti suggests in its predictions of the shadows you seem to be casting across the future of Noomas."

The Proctor stepped to the deep-seated window overlooking the Parliament House.

"Urgency is in the air. Have you noticed the influx of outlanders who have recently arrived? It is common to have visitors during the Three Moons Festivals, but this is decidedly different. Our parliament guest quarters have been filling up. Dignitaries from the eastern regions of Kulaina and Walinal have traveled for days."

He had settled back into the Proctor's role, leader of a powerful nation and began summarizing preliminary plans of action.

"I have called the High Council as well as the advisors of our international dignitaries to assemble. I'll be working with the political officials and the media once the community leaders have been initiated. Outlying districts are showing signs of resistance.

His beefy fist struck down on the table hard and determined.

"Stubborn as the Jilio: stuck in their small cultural edicts—unwilling to be open-minded. Nations, tribes and clans are rife with conflicting conditions. They can be difficult. I'll be communicating with every order, family, and army with whom we must unite.

"I'll be sending envoys to assemble a military force.

"We will need first-hand reports directly from contacts within every nation. I can depend on few people. Rumors will surface; deny everything. I'll continue studying the reports as Andon makes progress with decoding the microchip from Talni. Make your connection with Janis; he has the authority to share whatever you need to know."

He glared at me before continuing.

"You two share origins, from up there!"

He hesitated as if annoyed. The idea of a Galactic Federation spread among the stars was disconcerting to him. "Your experience as a military officer and combatant...out there...is useful."

He shrugged his tired shoulders, an action of bafflement.

My experiences were extensive on a galactic scale. And Noomas was a planet in a solar system fairly well forgotten within the wide Galactic Federation. I'd come here to search for my father.

They had called me *'the lost one '; Torlo Hannis.*

This world of archaic city-states had no technical knowledge concerning interplanetary travel. Only Youi's father, Andon Janis, understood, for he had been an important part of my past, in a different part of the galaxy, light years from Noomas.

The Proctor was saying:

"If events lead us into an international war, you will be assigned a high command position. We'll want to utilize your experience with major military conflicts.

"Very soon I'll be sending you to Kamina. You will have the authority to speak for me.

"Choose several teams. You will be told when to activate

these missions. Initially they must seek alliance with factions who sent that Messenger to Adt Dorta. We need connections with the resistance movements developing there."

The Proctor paused, as he scribbled notes at his desk. Almost as an afterthought, without looking up, he muttered. "Be on your business."

Thus I had been curtly dismissed.

* * * * * * *

Even though this action had certainly not been unexpected, the Proctor's brisk manner left no doubt our nation would soon enter a serious conflict. The warrior side of me sprang into instant action, calculating the necessary steps needed to activate mission troops, ready the commanding officers, train and brief staff—all systems within the galactic career-man part of me had the score memorized.

However, another less familiar voice raised its protest within my conscience. If I moved into action as the warrior, that would mean I would be separated from the woman I most dearly loved. Never before had I experienced this strong a desire for a peaceful life bereft of drama. This sedate, sensible persona no longer relished taking risks by taking on uncertain ventures. I now had a wife and a desire to develop community, family, and a home I had never known before. Strange, how these two opposing forces within me arose at this particular time.

I'd faced battles, often in the role of a foot soldier without much emotional attachment, no personal grounding with any woman or family. Detachment made quite a difference.

I felt mixed pride and apprehension over the prospect of a radical change and challenge. War could so easily wipe out any civilization and damage family ties, even when anyone survived. Battle changed men. War brutalized cultures. Nations were violently altered in their status and political position depending on the outcome of the conflicts.

My meeting with the Proctor focused on the serious nature of the coming events. As I left his offices and started towards my own, I found myself lingering in the corridors facing the inner gardens, beyond which were the hangars for private flyers.

Restlessness prevailed. This world which I had so recently adopted was entering into a grave war with an undetermined enemy. As a soldier under the command of a Galactic Federation, I had seen war annihilate total planetary systems. I didn't want to witness such devastation here on Noomas.

Shaking my head, I tried to put all these jumbled thoughts in some semblance of order.

Perhaps I needed to escape these royal surroundings. Tonight the skies looked particularly calm. So I decided to take a peaceful flight beyond the boundaries of Bel-loniea.

It was a short distance across the gardens to the royal flight hangar. My private grav-disk was parked there, not far from the apartment we occupied in the palace. I experienced a wonderfully freeing sensation when flying over the lovely lands that stretched out in all directions from the walled palace. To the west, beyond the broad expanse of lush farms, lay Bel-loniea's port from where the ocean expanded past the horizon. Out there was another continent; called Kamina.

I soon found myself flying high above low hanging clouds; the sky far too bright with city lights to see any trace of stars. The practical limits of these flyers kept them below any outer fringes of the atmosphere. They are simple open vessels with no compressed chambers. Not like a spaceship; or like the high-flying planetary liners I'd known in my youth.

The galaxy of my birth was a place of advanced science and with it, came destructive violence on a grand scale. Whole planetary populations could be wiped out.

Life could be wasted without thought; cindered in a mad moment of military or political decision. Living, thinking beings were a product of the universe.

Birth, death and rebirth form the natural cycle of the cosmos.

The limits of our knowledge are bound by the thinly sliced sensory organs granted each species. Perhaps, some day, understanding will arrive through a miraculous union of all conscious-ness. Until then, all remains enveloped in mystery.

'New sprouts spring forth from the old,' the Ji once preached in its metaphysical rhythms of cyclical life.

By comparison to Galactic Federation norms, Noomas was a peaceful haven; a socially primitive mix of modern and ancient technology. Kay-guns held dangerously explosive shells that could blow whatever they hit into atomic dust. Yet the sword played most valiantly in the field of honorable battle, as a cutting tool. This bloody metaphor offered less evolution than its many seers might have wished the masses to believe. Even here, the worshipping of death was used by those who wished to domi-nate.

The blade cuts a fine line through national boundaries. Violence appears to be the nature of the universe. And this world is not so different: beautiful though it appears through the eyes of a man in love.

Andon was probably right to think of Noomas as a galactic dumping ground. He believed that interstellar ships had come here over the centuries, each bringing various groups of settlers, a mix of farmers, explorers, mercenaries, from all walks of life. And in the mix, penal ships chucked their unwanted cargo on unclaimed worlds such as Noomas, which was not recognized as a constituent of the federation.

I remember him saying to me:

'It is common for newly developing planets to be hammered by diverse migrations. Religious and political clans and cults escape to new worlds. We don't know who the original people were on this bit of solar rock. Mutis discourage exploration beyond our borders and I wonder about their motives. I respect them; as they respect me!'

I sifted through these thoughts, not lingering on any in particular. Romos Muti has been a part of my wife's family for generations. I trust him. The Proctor's Muti once said:

'We are not concerned with cosmic concepts. We care little about reaching beyond our own world. The Muti awareness

stretches into the past and present and reaches into the future. And even other dimensions.'

At any rate, the universe will eventually swallow its own tail. So life ends up as a meaningless cycle from birth to decay.

Right now I wanted to enjoy the sky and peaceful horizon. The ocean ended the continental landmass but its shores and our city-state's seaport were too far away to be seen from this low altitude.

I was ready to return home where I would find my love, Youi.

* * * * * * *

The next days filled rapidly with meetings and heavy instructional sessions, spinning the entire palace compound into high gear. Everyone was racing around like mad vipers. Energetic units crammed into every open space forming massive training teams.

Bel-loniea had taken immediate action. The Proctor called upon the wardens from all municipalities to attend a summit at once. The outreach had successfully engaged the majority of nations in the Armada Project. According to the opening debates on the *Declaration of Engagement*, this process was slowly and surely reaching the rural areas.

Romos had scheduled daily briefings of the Elite Force early each morning. Today we were in our official uniforms waiting near the Proctor's throne, positioned against the back wall of the meeting hall.

Normally the anteroom served as a staging area for royal audiences. There was ample space behind the partition where over a thousand congregants could be brought to abrupt attention with the blast of a single horn. The throne enclosure had been shut off from the general assembly, which normally stretched out in front of the royal dais.

Less than twenty of us were in attendance; an intense meeting of the inner circle, the trusted Elite. The Proctor had summoned each of us by private invitation with the royal stamp of his signature. To the right of the throne two tall sentries stood side by side: the Janis' and Proctor's Mutis draped in their dark robes from hooded heads to booted feet, revealing little of their purpled faces.

Youi was tense at my side. Adt and Sarleni stood with Kigor Dorta. We pressed closer to them, waiting and watching.

Proctor Romos entered with Andon Janis at his right. Raising his arms, he glanced at the intimate assemblage.

"Take note, while Andon speaks."

As the Proctor sat, the proceedings began with no further ceremony.

The scientist took the stage, Proctor and Mutis presenting a formidable backdrop. Andon's Korda-strap held his sedately ornamented sword beneath his blue trimmed cloak.

"You've been called here for a vital reason critical to the survival of our people. Perhaps even for the survival of all mankind on this planet. We have learned, to our dismay, about a perilous uprising occurring at a frightening speed. A force already dominating a major portion of a distant continent is threatening to cross the seas into our lands.

"Word has reached us through a detailed report brought under dire circumstances by our young Adt Dorta and Sarleni from Helandi. Not all of you have met Sarleni, yet."

His arm unfolded towards the lovely woman standing near Adt. Heads turned as he continued.

"They retrieved valuable data from Talni, an inside source in Kamina. The brave Messenger, rest his soul, fought to preserve these horrific accounts and make them available to us...."

The Proctor's voice cut him short.

"To the point, Andon."

The nervous scientist rapidly continued:

"Ah yes, the report: it all came from a tiny microchip imbedded upon Talni, the Messenger; a fine piece of genius, it is: a tiny sliver encapsulating a recording shell; quite simple enough for our decoders to resolve. The task will take time for it contains multiple layers of data, graphs, visuals, recordings, and complex messages.

"The preliminary findings are distinctively clear!" Andon's right hand lifted, index finger extended to become a stiff pointer waving upwards in a spiral as he spoke.

"An authoritative government has come to rule, disregarding the innate ethical principles of natural order. A threatening tyranny is overthrowing tribe after tribe, enslaving the clans; yielding to no negotiation."

He paused, looked nervously at the floor, then back to the anxious audience.

"The shell appeared to be a singular message, and our lab discovered an unusual coding system that continues to expand the deeper we go."

His words had begun to drift as his eyes lifted in glassy wonderment.

"I've been perplexed by the sliver itself, intricately designed...."

"Andon, please!" The Proctor scolded with firm understanding.

The scientist continued, after turning a disapproving eye toward the Proctor.

"I suspected the microchip carried volumes of data even before starting my work on it. Vast experience in my previous life has exposed me to wisdom beyond our greatest minds here on Noomas. Reducing infinite information to a concentrated finite point is not beyond advanced...."

"Andon!"

The Proctor's tone said far more than that one word.

"Yes. Of course! Talni had spoken clearly in a particular hologram, appealing to all resources who still could hear the message and hopefully guard against its impending threat: the Kamina."

He shook his head to wave away any questions. Then he eyed the Proctor, knowing that brevity was expected.

A few of us had already heard what Andon Janis was about to reveal.

"We are facing a deadly, ruthless nation."

His hand lifted again, and the finger pointed like a weapon of destruction, tapping out shot after shot with each declarative statement, aimed threateningly at his rapt audience.

"And they are determined to dominate the human species as beasts of burden for their sadistic desires. Yes, the people are reduced to performing unspeakable atrocities for the expanding rulers of Kamina. Their purposes are malicious, vile, and sadistic to the core.

"A Muti nation: by name—the Kaminaean Muti Empire: by design—determined to dominate Noomas."

He paused, finger curling shut, then lifting like a drawn sword, once again thrusting at us.

"And they expect to be worshipped in the name of some Ancient decree. They tout themselves as overlords to their human chattel."

Again he paused; eyes grief-stricken. When the finger relaxed, the hand lowered.

"What is shown within the message is revoltingly graphic."

Andon Janis shuddered visibly.

"All of you must see and learn from these images. The lab's viewing screens are all set. My technicians will assist you with the translations. Be warned; prepare yourselves. For, what follows is grotesque to the point of madness. Mutis brutally inflict unspeakable pain on their most loyal human servants. These tyrants have invented sickening ways of savaging humanity."

General Qui Shan, commander of the joint Bel-loniean Armed Forces, aggressively stepped forward and demanded. "I'll want proof. As soon as possible! I will require detailed facts regarding their aggressive tactics and any maneuvers that fall under my personal authority!"

Andon shifted towards Qui Shan.

"As you wish; at the Janis Foundation. The volumes of data might require a substantial team to analyze. Detailed maps and historic archives are being extracted from the micro-sliver, even as we speak. We have no idea how relevant they are to current affairs or past eras. It is exhaustive. Still, you may, of course, sort through it all to find pertinent data. I have two specialists standing by with transcribed files for you and your staff, Qui."

The old scientist explained the background and extent of the Kaminaean uprising in depth and then stepped down, having finished his report. The Proctor confirmed Andon's invitation and gave brief directives, outlining procedures and assignments for his staff.

"General Qui Shan, you along with Kigor Dorta, will arrange a unified international bulwark."

A cold, tense silence filled the room.

Suddenly a shrill feminine voice splintered the silence.

"Finally you make sense!"

The sharp, biting tone caused all eyes to turn and see the woman sweep forward. An extraordinary mane of red hair streamed behind her in undulating waves. Her gown glistened with silver and gold mingled with deep scarlet hues. Her entire image shimmered, as if hovering; not standing. Her movement was swift and in a blink she occupied the dais, overshadowing the Proctor and the Mutis.

To most of us she was a stranger.

Sarleni leaned forward tensely without saying a word.

Apparently a projected image of the woman; she hovered, feet not actually touching the floor and bowed in deference to the Proctor; the room watched in amazed silence. Then she spoke with a gentler voice.

"Our people have been tracking the Kaminaean activities, however, their expansion recently escalated at an alarming rate.

"Understand that what you are going to experience is a sample of what is occurring daily in the land of Kamina."

Her arms spread wide and the room opened in all directions. An uneven plain stretched to the horizon. The speckled landscape was clumped with spindly brush and dried grasses. Far off we could see what appeared to be oddly shaped barren tree limbs. They zoomed close and took the shape of broken arches.

From the heavens a pillar of fiery white and red appeared, belching out of a metal cylinder slowly descending to the ground.

In rapid motion people raced about constructing buildings as if by magic! Expanding and growing and overlaying the surrounding ruins. Everything pulsated, as if wanting to disappear into an elusive dark space.

Then mammoth towering buildings surrounded us. The landscape sank as we were lifted above a massive city. Towering pyramids dotted the metropolis that stretched to the surrounding hillsides.

The scene changed again to a particularly austere pyramid. Here mobs of people pressed frantically towards its many gates and swept us into an already crowded place. The air was filled with sweet scented aromas, lilting strains of soft music and voices chanting in harmony. Apparently this was some sort of Holy Temple, and we were now facing an arena filled with hundreds of cloaked Mutis.

I nearly tripped down a sloping walkway pushed by the others surging around me. We were herded like wild animals down a narrow corridor to the central arena. The stench in the room was now gagging. The music gave way to moans, then cries, then screams and shouts and wails of unquenchable agony. I saw humans stretched out naked on platforms, their flesh being rendered, torn, shredded, burned and beaten in angry rhythm with painful human cries. And above the carnage, the walls were lined with balconies from which hundreds of Mutis cackled and mocked with hideous laughter, amused by the indescribable slaughter of men, women and children. I felt the throbbing pulse of the place; it was a vile choking constriction around my whole being.

Then blackness and deadly silence fell upon the room.

A strong Muti voice boldly chanted into the inky darkness: "Come and partake and surrender to the new God of Order. Make your pilgrimage and worship for this is your destiny. Come to the city, in the midst of Kamina. Enter in unto the Pyramid of the Prophet. For the power of Kalinis is the First

Voice to Speak the New Truth. The Prophet is inspired by our True Creator."

The strange woman now floated before us.

She whispered: "And now see the past!"

We were bathed in bright light and a fresh sea breeze washed over us. A beach stretched out below a tall cliff, surrounded by low jungle growth. A pathway was cut along the cliff, moving up to a looming castle at its top. The scene quickly panned up the path, down dark corridors and high into the castle.

We were propelled through an archway into a cavernous chamber. At the far end were two men. One strong warrior standing over a very small, old man, crumpled on the floor at his feet.

The room blazed fiery lights and crackling explosions filled the air so powerfully that all of us at once covered our ears and dove for the ground. The air was filled with heavy fog, causing me to gasp for air. When it cleared, the old fellow lay there alone, gasping. His arm wrapped tightly across his side where a terrible wound had ripped into his flesh.

"I must speak." The man's eyes shifted back and forth as he weakly gasped: "I must...tell...before it is too late. I am called Talni, sent by the elders...spread the message...prevails...we must overthrow the Muti overlords of Kamina."

A misty fog gathered around the scene.

And I was back, grounded in the Royal Audience Chambers.

The woman standing by the Proctor smiled as her eyes examined one person after another. I felt her presence worm itself into me.

Torlo, you have witnessed the moment of contact with the Messenger. Adt's strength proved capable of acquiring his message despite the Muti's interference. Kamina will learn and increase their powers. You must take heed. Learn from the Helandi.

Then her thoughts slipped away leaving only a broken sensation of emptiness when she raised her arms and flashed out of the room.

Stark realization paralyzed all of us. Then everybody was speaking at once.

The Proctor stood.

"Silence!"

As the room grew quiet, Sarleni spoke up.

"That was Ju-bilee.

"Accept her warnings and her advice."

Kigor Dorta's, face rigid white, utterly shaken, glared towards Adt, then Sarleni. The man spoke guardedly.

"I know this woman, and I, too, say we *must* listen."

The Proctor added.

"She is a formidable ally from Helandi."

Those words had a startling effect on all of us. He clearly endorsed her, thus advising that we all do the same.

The Proctor took charge giving orders, doling out instructions, leaving no room for debate.

"You will assemble your units. Andon will schedule briefings with each of your sectors in the next days. Go and prepare."

II. Dangers Declared

They will command you to bow in obedience.
Tormentors of the night haunt dreams.
They imbed their ideals into your minds.
Learn to master the demons and be wise.
Set your goals to Proctor and nation and find peace.
                    —HanJahn Missives

The young warriors stood silently at attention in the cool assembly room. Their faces expressed the raw intensity of volunteers motivated for dangerous missions. My advisors had selected this exceptional group, over two hundred recruits, willing to die for their nations; determined; dedicated as only youth can be.

I greeted them with the standard, salute and customary

briefing; then broke them up into units and turned them over to their group leaders.

One face in the front row, a little to the left had drawn my attention. I recognized the cocky lad who'd made trouble down at the garrison. It had taken a hefty bribe, from Adt and me, to get this cadet released from the holding cell. And besides, I'd promised Sarleni to include her brother in the missions. But instigating an open bar brawl certainly did not look good on his record.

Shortly after their routine drills, I ordered him to report to headquarters.

The young Helandian officer arrived promptly, a lean and eager warrior who stood awkwardly at attention; presumably worried about his tarnished record. His voice was crisp as he saluted.

"Officer Mahzit reporting as ordered, sir!"

These formalities were always uncomfortable, for as a galactic warrior I, too, had begun as an underling. Later, my responsibilities increased, even if I still viewed myself as a warrior.

"Sit!"

Mahzit shuffled a few steps before he took a seat. He did not entirely relax, keeping his shoulders squared.

I briefly studied the open document lying on my desk. His résumé was a detailed log of military duties, the most recent post with the special search and rescue team that had retrieved Adt and Sarleni from Kamina. Prior experience included assignments with the Helandi support teams during the relief projects.

However, his untimely arrest had to be reconciled. I began my interrogation.

"Explain this little incident!"

Mahzit stammered, awkwardly embarrassed about his predicament.

"Sir, I...it was a matter of honor, involving my sister and my country. I tried to avoid it."

He gave me his version of the fight while I glanced over

the report, skimming over interviews with witnesses which matched his story fairly well.

"I see here that you are gifted with the sword, and rapid to confront a person who insults your comrades. Tempered, these values are useful. Without constraint, they can prove dangerous."

He lifted his chin squarely.

"I had no intention of harming the man, sir."

I curbed my amusement. "Report claims you had him under control. In fact even *he* was amazed, once he'd sobered up. His superior demanded blunt explanations as to what actually happened. You have narrowly avoided making an enemy of a formidable fighting man."

I tapped the report.

"This states all I need to know, unless you have more to add."

Mahzit leaned forward, eyes intently fixed on mine. "I have experience throughout the Northern Territories. We journeyed with the Kanns and the Raiders. I'm young, yes: and strong, capable and perfectly suited to meet unforeseen challenges."

"So I noticed."

I studied him a bit longer; then gave my order.

"You'll join the team from the Baji-Ney unit. They are a tough and highly ethical clan and—"

"I'm acquainted with the Raiders. I'll work well with them."

"Then, it is settled," I decided.

"Critical expectations are included in written directives. You will make every effort to connect with the Resistance. Learn everything you can and report your findings to Central Command."

Once I had dismissed Officer Mahzit, I left my offices to meet with Proctor Romos and the General.

* * * * * * *

Qui Shan and the Proctor were in deep conversation when I arrived. They turned, pushing a thick ream across the table.

"Here, take a look at this."

Proctor Romos shuffled the pages to a section labeled: *from the Janis Foundation.*

"The great Muti questions so many learned scholars were reticent to recognize are right here, Torlo, made clear through the Messenger.

"We discovered the Mutis have been aware of the expansion of this empire. How long had they been watching? Why hadn't they advised our leadership earlier? How much did they know?

"Go ahead, read it for yourself."

Excerpt from the council records.

Reference source: the Guardian of Haldolen.

....we had never challenged the Mutis nor dared to vocalize our reservations regarding their ways.... For generations we endorsed their consummate authority. They consistently and accurately foretold the future on our behalf.

The Mutis on the continent were not inclined to band together and rarely would participate in worldly affairs. On occasion a few Mutis appeared at an event or counsel meeting: often silently observing; loathe to interfere with the human process.

Nomadic by nature, individualistic, shunning social trivialities save for matters of state, ritual or ceremony. Any one Muti might be speaking for all Mutis, and yet be speaking only for itself with its prophetic cadence. Personal bonding with a family or clan occurred over generations, though it would often travel alone for extended periods.

Alarming evidence has challenged the time worn facts. A legion of Mutis have become violent: emotionally unstable, lashing out against the humans: against the natural order of Noomas.

The report continued:

Their numbers are expanding beyond the territory of Prophet Kalinis, into the heart and to the coastlines of the continent. The Kaminaean Mutis assimilate all Mutis into their grip, convincing them to obey its teachings.

An edict has been sent to all regions with specified regulations, including the punishment of resistance.

Any Muti who disobeys shall be slain.

I looked up at the other two and decided to make this a logical place to stop. Qui Shan paced heavily back and forth, his stocky bulk echoing loudly through the royal audience chamber. The Proctor seemed equally agitated, drumming his fingers on the table.

"What is our response, General?"

Summarizing the preliminary progress of the Armada Project, the General spoke with precision, giving quick accounts of resources under his command. The man displayed exquisite control over his administrative duties.

"We've encountered a few snags. Blunt complications. The Helandians have been reluctant to deal with the arrogance of the nations at the Gapa Sea.

"Despite the stubbornness of the peoples of Walinal and Kulaina, we've made strides towards cooperation and resolving their differences. I believe it won't be long before we have a trained force ready to confront Kamina. The Diano have been a strong influence, successfully compelling the mountain clans to support the Armada. The Kanns and Raider tribes are already activated. They will be armed and dispatched at your command."

"Is an international world war what you want, sir?" I measured my words. "I've seen whole planets wiped clean, everyone on them annihilated without mercy: to what purpose?"

Neither one of us was anxious to argue.

I took a deep breath.

"Qui Shan, I respect your experience. You have led many combat missions resulting in minimal casualties and lasting peace.

"Kill the head of the beast and the body will die. I prefer to seek reconciliation with the Muti population at large. And I intend to request full Muti cooperation in order to accomplish this. Are you prepared to involve the Muti sages?"

The General answered.

"The Mutis are not warriors, Torlo, and you know it. Talni's warning was clear: the Kamina would not negotiate under any circumstances. Their sole intent is to invade and conquer. The enemy may not be so easily defeated! The problem is grave. We're going in blind, no matter what."

The Proctor interjected.

"That's why I assigned you this mission: to operate the initial explorations with explicit authority to speak in my name."

The General faced me directly.

"Spy missions are expected to supply vital information for the Armada. We need to learn the mechanisms controlling their Ersatz warriors and the reported Gatherers. We will need as much information as possible to plan our ground and air operations against the Kaminaean forces: territorial layouts, mapping charts, and details about the cultures and people.

"Our aircraft will only have power to transport the missions into the territory. Most will not be able to return, even if they succeed. Their ground orders will require them to seek out and join with any Resistance movements. Very likely there are a number of them active throughout the continent. It will be your responsibility to follow up and coordinate with their operations once we're inside their empire."

Romos sharply cut in.

"Until then, we must be ready to defend our borders and aggressively rebuke the enemy."

The General clamped his mouth shut. He obviously had unspoken concerns as the Proctor continued.

"Our re-mapping of the Diano nation, since their defeat, also reshaped its political leadership. The ruling family was exiled. New governing parties, under the Bel-loniean Alliance, have created a strong and effective hold on this nation. We're assured of their loyalty. I've requested a list of qualified officers to be assigned frontline positions in the Armada's initial probes into Kaminaean territory. Their units will be trained and placed under your direct responsibility."

A well of distrusting emotion arose as I recalled the Diano who had taken Youi captive.

The Proctor raised his hands at my possible protest. "Things are quite proper. And these people are from a different clan than we had experienced during the wars. Their allegiance to the tyrannical ruling family had been in dispute even before the new order. One officer, in particular, has requested specific assignment to your personal fleet. No. You don't know him. But he admired what you did."

"As you say, sir," I replied, although I had misgivings.

The Proctor added grimly.

"You hesitate. The war is over; they lost. They are now our colonial partners. If I trust them, you can. Captain Darmond is an extraordinary warrior."

Qui Shan confirmed the Diano's character.

"Our Proctor has spoken. And I can vouch for Darmond. I interviewed him: personally, supervised his preliminary place-ment exams. The man is sharp, well educated. Give Darmond serious, consideration."

I nodded, mentally noting to interview the Diano captain.

Then the General made a startling statement.

"I know you have special experiences from your previous life."

The man, coughed, and then added.

"I expect you to make good use of them, son!"

The officer had been starkly aloof, except at this moment his words had reflected open respect.

Romos rose to his feet, indicating the meeting was ended.

"You'll be sent activation orders shortly. So make the most of your remaining time in Bel-loniea."

He thusly dismissed me.

* * * * * * *

Two days later the Janis' family Muti approached me. It was a gnarly hooded pundit who, for generations, had been part of my wife's household. I always felt unsure whether I'd conversed privately with this one or not. To me, in their identical drab, hooded cloaks, they all appeared the same, difficult to define as separate personalities. The Mutis wandered through our lives, briefly lingering and then slipping away into their own solitude. On occasion, one would take bold, brazen, command over a particular event in human society. Like shadows they lurked; uninvolved, disinterested, and unseen. They drifted alone and rarely with perhaps a single companion.

In whispering silences they breezed in and out of a room, observing without inter-reacting. When they connected directly with people, they could appear highly dramatic and even threatening by their implied power. Though usually, they emitted a gentle and nurturing energy.

Personal names: they never responded to labels. I found that confusing and tended to apply descriptive nicknames to those of the royal household. They were interchangeable; yet could easily be defined as separate personalities.

The Janis' Muti seldom surfaced in my presence. It had been with the Proctor's family even before Youi's mother was born. Mutis were quite old and may have been born full-grown. No human had seen a Muti birthing. Some people wondered if they had a beginning, a childhood. Maybe they were born old. Maybe they were immortal as were the many gods of Noomas. Nobody knew.

Mysterious and somewhat alarming, the populace considered them a gift to humanity. I felt less certain; accepting their placement as part of the Noomasian culture.

A large hooded visitor was not an everyday event. They never attempted to be companions or friends with me, to my knowledge. Mutis appeared sporadically and mingled among us without permission.

And so the Janis' Muti approached, its deep black hollows turned towards my face. Those empty sockets held an inner invisible glow that sensed far more than humans could imagine. Its low, gravelly voice pierced my depths.

"Your future journeys appear erratic. Your shadow cascades extensively across the timeline. The event of Kamina intersects with your line. It permeates the plane of your journeys; most unsettling. The visions are multiple."

It paused, stock-still.

"I see a place where segments splinter into diverse alternatives. You are a powerful force down one pathway. You are missing from another."

Then it wavered, shaking its head slowly.

"Wait!" I cried out, knowing the Muti habit of walking away without ceremony.

It froze, and glared down at me with set lines on the multileveled map of its face.

I asked.

"What dangers do you see?"

"None to concern you; do not surrender to easy solutions. You will be alone at the darkest of moments. Stand strong on your convictions. Fear not the illusions for they only confuse. And remember, the mission must direct its own destiny."

"What about Youi and Bel-loniea?"

I seldom made requests. In fact it was rude to make personal inquiries. Mutis were not fortunetellers. They simply announced their prophecy when they deemed it fitting.

"Kamina is your future. Connect with KiNal. Set your goal towards the north. It will unmask your destiny. And reveal your true comrades. Many will die. Sziat can aide you."

Then it simply stepped away with a rapid twist of its dark cloak.

I studied the empty space it had occupied and considered its words, trying to dismiss all of it as nonsense. Nobody ignored a Muti's divination.

III. Third Council Debates

Seek understanding of the unknown.
Seek wisdom during the search.
Explore beyond the limits of the known.
True wisdom comes with open knowledge,
Explore through boundless quests.
And find where truth speaks.

—*Songs of the Helandi*

Illusions and dreams develop from within our consciousness into a perceived reality. The line between these mental states and awareness is often blurred. Nightmarish visions had plagued me since I'd arrived on Noomas and my memory had returned ever so slowly.

Recall is a delicate balance of real and imagined experiences, whether they be shared events or remembered concepts formulated only within. All thoughts are subject to becoming part of that which we call memory. What lives for the moment; slips away to make room for the next event. And we are forever growing, expanding and continually tripping down new pathways much as little children exploring the unknown. Hence we continually journey through a constant living expansion. The Ancients left for us their wisdom and legends handed down to future generations, ever evolving from one culture to the next.

* * * * * * *

Present events were changing rapidly. Talk of war was secretly whispered in anxious voices.

The inner city was still swollen beyond capacity from the holiday festivities. The mood of the populace had taken a decisive shift. An odd air of ominous foreboding had blanketed the gaiety in the streets. Colorful market stalls still bustled with heavy trade, yet the tone of the people had fallen to a hushed urgency. A few wild rogues rambled among the inns and taverns extending the holiday celebrations beyond their natural limits. Rumors of what the future might bring down upon us, rumbled through the alleyways. Stressful anxiety was heavy in the air.

Those who had access to the palace grounds made no pretense about the somber business at hand. The guards at all the gates had been doubled. Extra quarters made ready for the frequent arrivals of dignitaries.

Meetings occurred daily in the Proctor's chambers. Concerns over the Muti Empire of Kamina had created uproar among the Grand Council members and, indeed, left me with a very uneasy feeling.

My department was no less busy than the rest of the palace. Strategic reports from central intelligence were rapidly piling up on my desk. I scanned the latest summary from the previous day's meeting, which reflected the popular uncertainty developing into a serious debate over these issues of war. Among these reports was one from Andon, which caught my attention.

JANIS GEOLOGICAL REPORT

A galactic map of the world found in early documentations, recorded topographical details of the major continents through images and data retrieved from my spaceship before it landed in the mountains south of Bel-loniea. The Janis Foundation integrated older charts from their archives and compiled an updated rendition of the area.

Because of the political delicacy, this information was classified.

Knowledge of the continent to the west, Kamina, was shadowed in with few details other than the speculated shoreline and several rough notations of mountainous regions. On the greater charts, landmasses could be conveniently described by their location designated solely by the chart maker, common descriptive titles to geographic regions of water, plant and mountainous regions or directional locale, like the territories to the north, the south, or the east and west.

For purposes of the Armada, Kamina was ascribed to the western continent as a whole, and our familiar continent to the east, called Free Lands. Our nations are numerous, though to mention a few would be sufficient. Bel-loniea, our beloved city state governs over a sizable region bordered by the Kanns of the mountain ranges to the west of the barren northern deserts of the Raiders. Helandi lies beyond the ridges and icy tundra. The Diano, Tantioan, Walinal and many others lie south and east; even beyond the Gapa Sea. Few traverse the distant jungles for there the Korda dwells in great numbers.

Charts from the Haknords and Kasiisi provided additional elements. The data received from Talni, the Messenger, verified astounding details of the continental borders as well as island groups off each of the continental coasts. Among them was the Kasiisi Resort colony near the median latitude and further north, the Muti Sanctuary of Illysæ Ad Mördi Tăłi.

Adt Dorta's addendum included the following note:

We obtained several sea charts detailing ocean shoals, islands and shorelines along the western ocean. The Haknords are expert chart-makers. They sold their talents to Kamina, creating detailed maps for the purpose of their expansion.

Andon Janis had added the following:

The global maps consistently specify at least three major continents on Noomas. My own ship's records had traced their habitable sectors, finding all three mildly colonized: two of them in temperate zones. The third encompassed the southern polar region. However, portions of the data were scrambled when my ship malfunctioned; crash landed and was broken into irreparable pieces.

Vivid details of my galactic journey to this remote region flashed by:

The fourth planet was without question inhabitable, containing three major continents and two smaller land areas. I fed statistics to the computer....

One was on the snow-capped South Pole, another in the

*middle of an ocean. The third seemed a more logical choice...
off the coast of a large continent....*

* * * * * * *

Report, in brief, of the 1st Council meeting held before Romos,
Proctor of Bel-loniea

From: *Honored Xkahal, speaker of Wisdom, Senior Advisor of
the Great Council*
We urge full acceptance of the Mutis as formidable authorities. They are trusted universally and must be given proper
respect. The Creed of Allegiance within the covenants of our
peoples is supportive to the convictions set by the ancient patri-
archs. All historical records and memory slates hail the purity
and benevolence of the Muti influence.

From: *Proctor Romos, Bel-loniea*
We accept the report as it was stated and learn, with great
sadness, the Kaminaean Empire has proven to be hostile to
all human governments. We have listened to our pundit Muti
counselors and salute their advice and the grave urgency of the
Messenger's reports.

From: *Croelas Bain, Keeper of the Paths, peaks of Kalfor*
I speak for our peoples dwelling in the high places, watchers
of the pass. We wish no conflict. However, prudence must be
our stance towards any shift in loyalty to our Muti sages.

From: *Osah Raton, Proctor of Diano*
The recent struggles between our two nations have been set
aside. The people have reconciled their grievances and have
joined forces with your nation in order to make ready for the
coming world conflict.
It is critical all members of this new coalition to be of one
purpose. My pundit Muti assures us that the northern culture of

Helandi offers great power.

From: *Nu-Elka of the Kanns*

There is no authority in the universe that outshines the beloved and all knowing and all benevolent Mutis. We vote against combined forces to offer war with a Muti Empire.

From: *Master Ammila, Herdsman from plains of Kulaina*

In recognition of our questionable unity here today, my following must remind the great council of our honorable elders who abide by the Old World thinking. We adhere to the authority given to Mutis. They have always been our supreme advisors. We intend to continue to venerate all Mutis as one voice.

From: *Proctor Romos, Bel-loniea*

Misplaced trust is self-defeating. Caution is required. If we must secure our borders, then we should act together. If we must retaliate in order to preserve our freedoms; then offensive action shall be taken, and under one authority. Unity will create a solid buffer strong enough to prevail against any dangerously aggressive nation.

From: *Zhoena, Ji of the Nuja worshippers*

We are aware of the foreign person Sarleni, who holds influence over the House of Dorta. Her presence parallels the sacred Moons Festival. Omens and prophecies abound. The notion of an empire intending to dominate humanity under savage Muti control is absurd!

Above all, this ludicrous fabrication must not interfere with the most holy celebration of our precious gods.

'O Holy Clinsol and Nosn, most sovereign Regals of the celestials, may you keep guard over your most dedicated people. Slke, Goddess of the peaceful and Nial, God of the joyful, bless your grateful followers. Tooli, Anos and Insi, how we adore you, for we recognize no mightier powers than yours to protect our blessed Noomas. Thanks be to the Gods who keep our world

safe, if we trust! So be it to the end.'

From: *Proctor Romos, Bel-loniea*
Our advisors respect the sovereignty of the gods, reverent Ji.
However, they also support the Family Dorta and the contents of the Messenger's report. Adt and Sarleni will proceed north to Helandi. Their work is crucial to all of us.
Our pundit Muti advises we call a second meeting of all international representatives. All voices heard here will be given full consideration prior to the next session. This I promise.

From: *Kkua of Dailiano, Spokesman for the Plains territory*
What do we know of the Helandi? Fantasy about a land of people so secretive and hidden does not merit our consideration. We have no record of their existence.

From: *Proctor's Muti*
Knowing means nothing, if you know nothing. There is much on Noomas that you know nothing about. Being ignorant of these facts does not make them non-existent. It only indicates your lack of information concerning these facts.
The Helandi exist. They are peaceful without guile. And their powers are deeply bedded. We have need of their advanced developments for the full maturity of the Armada.

One voice was heard without sound:
'We must be inclusive, not exclusive. Bind together within a framework of mutual love and affection, with mutual need to be one in an ever-embracing unity.
'Willingly magnify your awareness with diversified acceptance. We are only as resilient as our unity and our willingness to expand to new levels of understanding.
'Only by joining forces can we win.'

The Muti introduced this unseen voice as that of a learned Helandian sage, Moyi. The debate had continued among the tribal leaders. The gravity of the Kaminaean conflict struck deep into their core. I skimmed over those entries. The council meeting concluded with protests and debate.

* * * * * * *

A subsequent meeting between the Proctor and leaders of nations focused on further issues, including the *Declaration of Engagement* and formation of the Armada. The report given me outlined their widely varying views.

Reluctance among the majority to consider action against a foreign nation prevented them from reaching a unified purpose. Despite the many conflicts, the free nations of the land reached unanimity on one issue:

We respect the legitimacy of all nations and peoples.

Until proven otherwise.

Consequently, a third session has been summoned.

The council requested an official connection and conciliation to be developed with the land of Helandi's leadership.

Delegates would be briefed and sent north.

After exhaustive deliberation only a few conflicting debates remained unresolved. One grave point was unanimously shared:

Nobody wanted war.

I stared at that those words. A tragic resignation rested in their meaning while they expanded before my eyes.

Nobody wanted war.

Distantly I heard my name as both a voice and a thought steadily repeating like a beating drum.

Nobody wants it, Torlo Hannis. You must lead our people into a clash with the Kamina. It is your destiny; it always was. I stared at the document still clutched in my hands.

Nobody wanted war.

My eyes darted around the room. I was its only occupant. *Adt is up to his telepathic tricks, again*, I thought. But I was wrong. *You have a powerful mind, Torlo!*

A ghostly image appeared out of the dark, fading in and out

of focus. Then it slowly sharpened and I recognized Moyi. He floated, face lined, eyes penetrated deep into mine. Suspended, no larger than my fists, he filled my mental universe with his presence; features drawn up into a wrinkled smile, eyes brightening.

An intense, yet kindly expression marked the stark lines of his face as he continued to stare through me.

Don't resist!

I reached out and we made contact, my hand touching his. The vivid illusion was real and enveloped me with puzzling security.

It is well for you to be cautious when on mission. For you will soon be sent. The name Torlo Hannis is in danger.

Hide that identity.

Be prepared for false illusions. Fear no images. They will make extraordinary efforts to delude your core awareness. Observe and learn all you can from them, all the while isolating your inner shell.

His image faded; then returned, flickering slightly. When he spoke, his voice was hollow and thin.

Give them Sorla of Kanns, the mercenary. He must occupy them sufficiently. Your challenge is critical. Avoid discovery. Develop Jan Sorla fully. Flesh out his identity. Remember the mercenary from Kanns. Fill him with your knowledge of combat: your experience as a warrior.

Remember the fiction: your father and mother were Kanns, from the north. You have been away from your country for many seasons. You left at the peak of your youth, consigned to armies of other nations. Ever since then you have been without a country; without loyalty to any sovereign. Your profession travels with you.

Remember; the Kanns believe a man's past is his own. That is their guarded truth; and yours. They are brutal by nature and certainly easy to anger.

You are a mercenary for hire who has conquered many warriors in honorable duels. An assassin, if need be, by nature, trade and habit. You could be useful to the Kaminaeans.

Moyi began to dim.

Our link will not maintain when you go on mission. Be careful.

The image had faded, the voice echoed in the emptiness.

Be alert and aware, Jan Sorla.

I shifted position.

Cloudy pieces of lapsed memory retraced my life on other worlds. Battle ships and wars in long forgotten planetary systems against untold enemies, teased my trepidation. And I, Jan Sorla, fought long and hard among the strongest of them, though it was not as a tribal member of the Kanns on Noomas. For the Sorla I recalled in my former life was that of the galactic warrior. Many times I had led units of a hundred and more to victory, only to redeem my promised reward.

I'd travel on to the next realm, hunting for action. Always hunting and never willing to settle in any land; restless, eager to explore. I'd hoped to find my roots; my family—a connection to the past nearly obliterated.

My search brought me to Noomas. Finding Andon and learning his story gradually shed new light on unanswered questions about my early youth. Within a short time I had remembered large patches of my past.

During the Diano War I had made use of the name Jan Sorla, my name prior to landing on Noomas. As a trained soldier, I easily adopted the nature of the warring Kanns, a fitting cover for a man without memory.

Everything changed when Youi came into my life. I fell in love. She had become my passion; all I ever wanted to live for. And her nation became my nation. My earlier careers on other worlds were now, by choice, faded memory. Noomas took precedence for me.

Once again I concentrated on duty. Between dream and wakefulness, I pondered those last words of the document.

Nobody wanted war

It was time to take action.

My mission units had nearly completed their training and could no longer be delayed. Pulling out my official memo, I began calculating requirements to schedule the initial flight missions. Then I wrote the final details. Sealing the orders, I summoned my couriers to deliver them at once.

IV. Preparations

Be not hasty to define resolution with matters of conflict. Long deliberation often uncovers undiscovered truths while a short fuse will destroy all possibilities of understanding and of lasting peace.
—Teachings of Moyi

It was during these weeks that Adt Dorta joined me nearly every morning to discuss the Kaminaean situation. Often we'd meet at the palace arena where he gave me critical pointers in fencing. One morning, after a few moments of sparring with dulled practice swords, he bluntly stated:

"Your abilities have remarkably improved since our cadet days. Obviously you've continued training with my father or one of his instructors. You're using a few of my father's unique techniques quite effectively!"

I probably looked puzzled, for he added, "I opened part of your mind and observed. You must take extra time to practice with the sword. You'll be pleased, I'm sure. Mixed with your masterful hand-to-hand fighting skills, they'll make you a dangerously fearsome warrior in battle."

We touched blades; I strove to penetrate his defenses only to have the sword snapped out of my hand. It hit the floor with a clatter. He laughed as I picked it up. "You have forgotten a few things, I see!"

That was a trick he'd flaunted me with many times in the past.

"Maybe," I grunted, again attacking with more care, only to

have each thrust towards his chest easily parried to one side.

His prowess surpassed mine, despite my increasing agility and accelerated response with each practice session.

Before he and Sarleni left for Helandi we devoted long hours in my office to the concepts of the Zygo and all its capabilities, both in the physical and the mental worlds.

Sarleni and Adt had learned to see their world from a broader scope than ever before. And he taught me a lot about the Zygo.

"To give you the blocking ability that Moyi suggested, will take some training."

Adt would begin gently, though the principles were not so simple.

He would induce a semi-conscious state, what Sarleni referred to as pre-hypnotic mental readiness.

Adt closed his eyes as I loosened my stiff neck and shoulders.

"Relax. Release your control. To shield against any Muti you must only access your surface thoughts."

Focus on an X; *blot out all else.*

"Lock your consciousness around the intersection of that mark. Sharpen your concentration within the crux, expand your awareness inward through the central hub until you feel your-self drawn into its dimensions and the shield will trigger."

Glimpses of random historical events blending with alien visions were suddenly shrouded into grayness; then the room returned.

I must have penetrated some altered state. Physically I experienced two bodies, two minds, two sets of senses, touching, seeing, and hearing everything simultaneously in two completely separate places in space. It was like focusing into separate pictures; enveloping two conscious identities. I could direct awareness to either or both: strange; yet effective.

Adt coached me forward.

"You'll need a strong block so nobody can read your inner thoughts. You have strong will-power. Even with Sarleni's link we required a significant amount of joint energy to probe your consciousness. Nonetheless, it will need to be further protected.

You must master two minds.

"We will generate an embossed shield depicting illusional scenarios of a lifetime in Kanns. Your surface thoughts will include interactive reflexive intelligence because you do not want to appear dulled. Any Muti reading your thoughts will be suspicious if you appear drugged, shallow, or systematically predictable.

"You will be supporting both, in tandem on a parallel course. At times Sorla sustains all you are and ever have been. A shifting of your inner shell, a wall between immediate awareness and memory, will offset outside perception. When you assume this state, the Muti will know your conscious thoughts, and nothing else.

"Sit back."

He continued, pulling his chair closer to mine.

"We'll begin building that shield now."

Before I could even think the question, he was in my mind:

I'm not alone. Sarleni's here. We're unified within the Zygo.

The expression in his eyes grew intense.

Yes. This is Sarleni. We linked, Adt and me. Get used to us. Adt is still struggling; even I am. We're learning every day. In Helandi we will advance our studies to prepare for the coming conflict...I don't have time. Moyi calls. Adt will teach you.

And it was a matter of days before his lessons were completed. Shortly before he prepared for his journey to Helandi, Adt handed me a small packet; a compact metal cylinder.

"Keep this. I put it together with the help of the Andon Foundation. It contains my adventures with Sarleni, in more details than you've known so far. I call it *'Slavegirl of Noomas'*; an ironic pun, all things considering.

"I've included a short, official report for the Proctor, containing a brief list of facts. What I've given you reveals everything I remember from the moment you fled that Diano camp to our return here."

Once Adt had left, I felt a distinct loss. He would soon be going to the Northern Territories. Considering his suggestion, I practice fencing daily selecting different warriors as partners in sporting matches.

My time would be crammed with meetings and insurmountable tasks. I finished signing orders to activate the spy missions. It is always painful to send people on missions that could be death traps.

Just as I closed things down, Andon Janis rushed in unannounced. Without formality he stammered over his words.

"Torlo, I've found a record in an ancient scroll in the library. Here is my rough translation; hopefully the message is obvious."

He extended an envelope which I opened and read. The following was scribbled in his bold handwriting:

We have reached the peak of heaven and the gods wailed:

You are ignorant fools—shunning the holy law, selfishly straying from the righteous path towards your own destruction.

The fires of your own blind passions will consume you. Each lightning bolt will strike your rebellious hearts and snuff you out, one by one, until madness destroys your lands.

The wise and strong will survive and witness with great agony. Listen for the voice of the stranger. For there will come one from above to guide the way into future generations.

Andon said, "I discovered another disturbing section.

"It read, in effect:

"Find the Scrolls of Wisdom, kept by the Guardian of Haldolen. Be warned. They tell where life begins and ends.

"Most intriguing: meaning what? It may be myth. Ancient texts take years to decipher even if we could find them. The task will never be completed in time to ward off this conflict.

"Useless rumors blown into legendary, historic nonsense," Andon scoffed at his own absurdity.

"One day even you may become the root of the Legend of Torlo Hannis: ah yes, the very thing that I wanted to discuss with you; timelines and origins."

He tapped the air as if touching some invisible screen then opened a large packet and spread its contents out on my desk.

"The Three Moons Festival has mythological messages and

legends and, quiet frankly, it smacks of ludicrous nonsense for a person like me or you, who has experienced life in the Galactic Federation.

"Noomas is different. Ancient text and learning come down through myth and custom. This time we have found a correlation and timeliness is crucial. We've been tracing the astrological charts and according to our calculations, the current lunar cyclical trend will soon be at its apex. The latest evidence from Talni's Message pointed directly to this date."

The notes were technical and scattered, typical of Andon's habit of mixing incomplete thoughts with coded note-taking which only he could understand.

"Read; read this!"

He insisted that time was extremely short, if his hunch were true.

I glanced over the material.

"What's the significance? So the orbits of the moons synchronize once in a millennium. Legends point to major shifts in the cultural and spiritual essence of the planet at large. We all know from legend and history that even silly fables...."

"Yes—yes," Andon angrily snapped. "Notice the difference. It is saying the effect can have more than tidal influence. It is expected to bridge continental plates, cause internal quaking effects. More importantly, their strong magnetic field affects our thinking processes. Don't you see?"

He tapped the bottom.

"Vile are the thoughts radiating from the core believers.

"Alas, we breathe in contempt; we madly seek escape from doom,

"And reach for higher lofts of strength, power and aggression.

"Seeds of Time, the painful birthing, all begins again. Thus, the wheel perpetually turns."

I had never been influenced by threats or foreboding based on myth. In my opinion, writings and lyrical prose obscure facts with pompously over blown jargon. My patience was running thin. I could not afford to be wasting my time on this trivial material, but Andon was emphatic.

"Connect, connect! We know the basic effects between inter-galactic bodies."

He shook his head and his hand impatiently chopped into the air.

"The gravitational pull between two bodies intersect....

"Well, I got off base," he huffed, interrupting his own process.

"The magnetic field influences major global shifts, even earthquakes: not just weather patterns or ocean tides."

Again he shook his head, aware he wasn't easy to follow: standard stuff for Andon Janis when he got excited.

"Torlo, from our lives previous to Noomas, we *both* are familiar with well documented evidence of these factors. The populations *here* came from those galactic civilizations. The majority have lost memory of their origins. The ancient ruins may contain evidence of early arrivals. Ah, nevermind the cultural genealogy; no time for that.

"The tri-lunar convergence occurs once in a millennium, more or less. And into that phenomenon, history has vented numerous legends, handed down orally through magic-laden verse. History repeats the events. The Moons Celebration is a reflection of natural causes. We understand that. And we have seen the evidence in the recent magnificent storm systems you experienced in your travels with my daughter, Youi.

"Do you remember your academic lessons concerning plate tectonics and earthquakes?"

Andon quickly shuffled through the pages and then thrust a particularly thick document in my face.

"Here it is! Don't bother reading. Let me quote.

"Precession of the polar axis caused by the gravitational pull of the sun is all the more radically disturbed by the tri-lunar alignment drawing on the equatorial bulge of the flat-tened rotating planet. The angle of the polar axis proceeding around the pole of the ecliptic is greatly accelerated during the cyclical periods every eight thousand five hundred years. The

effect is large enough for changing the equatorial coordinates significantly.

"The celestial pole traces out a broad arc alternating among the major stars, Prena, Volar and Alconi as the pole star. Currently, the pole star is Volar which will be in exact alignment at the height of the lunar convergence during the Romos era in Bel-loniea.

"Since Noomas is an evolving body, the moons influence the condition of the planet's core. The moons may also contribute to the movement of the tectonic plates. Any shift in those plates could be particularly magnified when all moons align in corresponding orbits.'

"At the tri-lunar convergence all energies within the region are expected to be strongly attracted to their points of origin, thus stressing any balanced power systems at a magnitude unprecedented. Major shifts throughout the planet will bring about seismic turbulence, potentially rupturing continental foundations."

His voice dropped off.

I reluctantly allowed the information to settle with great difficulty. I could barely sort through his logic because of the widespread lunar-worshipping legends incessantly sifting through my mind. Finally I focused directly on the solid scientific evidence he'd presented:

"Andon, what you say sounds as if this planet is undergoing a major geological shift. Is that right?" I began to calculate the enormous impact of this occurrence as Andon continued his explanations.

If his theories were correct, Noomas was in big trouble.

"Oh Torlo, that's not the half of it for Noomas. This culture is so deeply steeped in their folk lore and legend, that their way of life will be irrevocably altered. On a cultural scale, the moons' alignment alone completely annexes the reasoning power of every tribal unit. The people are then compelled with frenzied celebrations to honor the celestial spheres with many days of feasting. The energies of all life forms are so strongly affected by the phenomenon, that they cannot avoid congregating, due to the phenomenal synergy created by the convergence. This is only the beginning.

"Well-documented seizures of madness inevitably follow when the planetary systems respond to the magnetic forces. Ocean tides rise beyond their peaks, the pre-ordained storms, and fissures shake the lands." Again the man shook his head frantically.

"It all makes sense, and the chaos will be ugly. The notes that shocked me most from the Messenger had to deal with this and the Muti uprising. And their fear of a major shift within their culture, an intruder from beyond...what I believe to have been your arrival: perhaps concerning both of us, since we are the latest known arrivals on the planet.

"The Ancients knew.

"The *Kaminaeans* fear a new human revolution is about to breed across Noomas, brought on by the tri-lunar alignment." Again he shook his head.

"The Messenger, Talni, quoted the ancient text in a hologram:

"The New Man will be born when an alien warrior aligns with the three moons."

I quickly dismissed that last remark, too concerned with the magnitude of this profound information. The implication of legendary myth was unfathomable; besides, the immediacy of the spy missions overwhelmed all other speculations. Nevertheless, what Andon had said made sense.

The necessity of keeping my true identity hidden was clear. Andon's statements shot deeply to my core. Plus, he was not nearly finished.

"Ancient text tells of a colonial ship that brought people here who marginally fit the description of the Helandi culture; scientists involved with Zygo studies. In the case of the HanJahn, there is reference to the Nexus defining their ultimate state."

I told him of Moyi's appearance earlier in this very office. "Adt claims that Sarleni is devoutly dedicated to the counselor's teachings."

"A clannish lot; all of them," Andon laughed.

"The Helandians are secretive and I've honored their illusive needs for privacy."

"That's all for now," he concluded, "And enough it is!"

* * * * * * *

Three days later, my activation notice arrived.

Report for Mission Duty: as of tomorrow morning at dawn.

As I unraveled the scroll, a thin leaf slipped to the floor, nearly transparent. I carefully lifted the fragile material, its surface slightly shimmering. I held it close to the light to better read the following message:

Contact on Kamina. The code occurs in greeting. The consecutive sequence must be spoken thusly: North. *Friends answer with* Mask. *Respond only when you hear the word:* Reveal. *Initiate connection.—Romos*

Looking closer at the leaf, I gently touched the slightly ridged lettering which immediately faded on contact with my skin. Within less than a blink, the note had disintegrated in my hands. I concentrated on the code words: North; Mask; Reveal. How they would be used was an unknown issue. After reviewing my orders, I locked up my office and then retired for the night to our private quarters. It was not easy telling Youi the news. Her face instantly shadowed.

"Already?"

I placed a gentle arm around her shoulders.

"It has begun. Our world is at the brink of disaster."

Her cheek pressed against mine; face hidden, lips close to my ear.

"So soon it all changes."

I possessively lifted her up in my arms. Youi smiled softly.

"You are changing the subject!"

"Do you object?"

"Should I?"

Her lips brushed my cheek.

"You *are* my dearest lover in the entire universe."

"There are others?"

"I might be tempted to visit the Royal Pleasure Palace where a woman might find comfort on lonely nights. If I'm left alone *too* long,"

I raised an eyebrow watching her blush deeply at her highly unlikely fantasy and we both smiled knowingly. As I carried her into our bedchamber she softly purred:

"Do you have time?"

"What else can we do? We must honor the tri-lunar goddesses. Surely your grandfather would approve."

"Even the Proctor cannot disapprove. So speaks his granddaughter who is willingly seduced by the father of her child."

It took a moment to digest the full implications of her statement.

"Yes, my love,"

She mysteriously whispered.

"Then, perhaps, I should restrain my homage to the honor the tri-lunar goddesses."

"Honor them or die!" she throatily laughed. "Don't you dare leave me stranded with only a hint of your promise."

A thin edge of sadness shrouded her voice.

"Only then can I endure your going off to do battle with evil monsters."

That was the last thing she said. In the early hours long before dawn, I quietly left her sleeping, gently tucked under the covers. I took little comfort from the local deities, for the only true goddess I knew was my beloved, the one I left there in our bed; the one and only most lovely Proctoress, Youi of Bel-loniea.

CHAPTER FOUR
A MUTI CONFERENCE

They stood in the overgrown bower, oblivious to the lack of light. Two Mutis, severely troubled with issues at hand, huddled closer; merging into a singular zone. Silent communion was evident through their rhythmic weaving back and forth.

The turning of the root has begun, the taller one expressed with deliberate urgency. It serviced the House of Romos.

Expectations have come to pass. The aura of Torlo Hannis strengthens across our horizon, the other Muti agreed. *My work with this branch has generated wisdom to the sovereigns. My words forewarned of him.*

Romos is gaining knowledge of things to come. The Messenger, Talni, provided well for them.

The Janis Foundation will sort the evolving complexities.

They were in Muti union; fusing into a seamless continuum:

New revelations and changing currents bend the time line.

Variables alter results. Few paths of purity remain.

Branches must be tapered. Narrow the paths to open doors.

The melding broke as Janis' Muti went on:

Our watch will continue with the new fruition stemming from Andon, especially over new scholars examining his standards.

Proctor's Muti raised its arm and touched the other. Both had stopped swaying and stood frozen as their exchange came to a halt. Silence sealed the boundaries of their mental vistas.

And then the Muti continued:

You are a crucial key. Our task is heavy. The Guide has

spoken the way we shall take.

The other also touched its companion. They both slowly lowered their cloaked arms and began the subtle rhythmic sway once again as Janis' Muti weighed their queries.

Andon and Torlo are wizened with academic and galactic experience. These two humans have rich histories.

Proctor's Muti infused: *Decide which to inform, which not: which to lead, which not. Choices yield diverse possibilities. We must make ready.*

Third sector voices prevail. The Guide informs. The source returns soon to assay our progress. Prepare for Sziat.

Revolution forces selective bends. Uncertainty dulls visions. Future balance crosses dimensions, thwarting alignment of space, confounding the present course.

The Muti of Janis had turned and begun to pace a few steps back and forth, trance-like.

The breach in the vine is reaching chiasmic depths. Many of our numbers yield to the Kamina.

And the Muti of Romos nodded, pacing its pattern in the gloom.

Talni's message marked unprecedented change; Bright mortals whither rapidly beneath the oppression of the New Order. Muti and Man alike suffer irreparable damage.

Now both increased their pacing pattern locked in a ritual dance, reciting their saga in unison.

Cosmic fractures never before spanned, now bind ancient divisions.

The moons have converged. Hope arrives amid chaos.

Destruction blackens the soil. Fertile decay primes the seed.

Stagnant waters fester. Patience fosters new genes.

A rift is evident. Followers of Kalinis savage the continent. All who publicly protest their cruel dictates, perish. Kaminaeans plot to expand beyond borders. Their greed devours each acquisition. They intend a Conquest of Noomas.

The mutual chant broke.

It happened so fast. Proctor's Muti had paused as if coming back to the awareness of the present.

"So fast!" It muttered softly in a hissing whisper.

None of us anticipated. The Ancients knew. It was foretold altered seeds would change. The challenge is tougher than we surmised.

The Muti of Janis raised its hooded head, facing the other. It trembled briefly and then shook its shoulders hard, one time. Again the pacing began, as did the saga.

Perhaps we did not believe it could happen. Rapid seedings bring untold horrors to innocent nations. Forbidden experiments were stricken from the world: banned forever. And now we know why. Rebirthing has plunged the future into a fog of indecision. Only Sziat conveys hope.

Is it possible we question? We must mend the hole. From it, seeps poison; crippling our readiness to strike against the Kaminaean Expansion. We have lost unity among our peers. The chasm between us is too great. We must amend our bonds before it becomes too powerful. The humans are vital to turning the root.

Romos' Muti curled into its cloak, protectively.

Humans can be aggressively dangerous, too. We have traveled through the realms of Torlo's mind. His experience as a galactic soldier vexes provident. It has been said; we must learn to make use of human aggression. I wish we had begun sooner.

The Guide directs at its own pace.

Both Mutis faced one another; their bodies firmly squared and straightened to their full height.

Kamina must be stopped.

CHAPTER FIVE
CONVOY ON CALL

I. Kal-Nor's Unit

From: the official files on the mission of Kal-Nor
Call to alert came before dawn. No signs of invasive forces, I assumed we'd been sent on a routine training drill.

Our flight route took us west, towards the Bel-loniean seaport at an incredible speed; reaching the coast well before sunrise. A convoy of twenty similar grav-disks intercepted us and fell into formation. As we headed out to sea, our pilot took lead position.

Crew completed detail reports and logs. All supplies accounted for and roster completed. Unit consists of expert combat warriors trained for international duty: nine desert Raiders trained as follows:

Scouts: three with research and scientific backgrounds.

Technicians: two, acutely familiar with military air and sea craft.

Medics: two heavy-duty combat experts.

My first officer and the pilot are Helandian: qualified warriors as well as communications experts.

Unit is ready for any challenges. I spoke with Officer Mahzit. His relaxed attitude and sharp wit reflect his easy adaptability. For the record, I appraise him to be a sincere and highly dedicated warrior.

* * * * * * *

Mahzit received the sealed assignment that was issued directly from Commander Hannis and, as instructed, immediately reported to the Baji-Ney contingent. His unit Commander, Kal-Nor, had been expecting him. The Raider, a determined tall man with a trimmed beard, appeared pleasant enough but decidedly grim. They had cautiously sized each other up; then Mahzit had taken his gear to the unit barracks and did not see the officer again until the next day.

The other members of the crew held a respectful distance. He knew his position as second in command created a natural barrier between him and those in his charge. Being late in the evening, he'd politely retreated to bed, curling up in the narrow hammock, shutting out the low chatter among the bunkmates.

The morning revelry angrily woke everybody, rushing them to their assigned grav-disk. The Raiders grumbled among themselves as they automatically executed well-practiced drills. Mahzit operated by instinct. This was a standard grav-disk: a rounded hull, two decks. The uppermost was geared with a retractable transparent dome. The protective cover slid over the deck within seconds when needed, otherwise it stowed below, slung down into the hull of the craft.

These flying vessels were typically armed for battle with Kay-guns and tracking devices. The Helandian pilot had expertly eased the craft off of the launch pad and headed west towards the coast. There they had maneuvered into formation with a squadron. It all appeared routine enough.

Kal-Nor joined Mahzit on deck, where they studied the control screen.

"We normally don't perform maneuvers before dawn. Since the ship's special sensory boards were adjusted yesterday, I assume the engineers requested predawn testing of the systems."

Mahzit tapped in a short sequence and a diagram of the engine block appeared on the panel. Then he adjusted the angle of the screen, zooming in until they could examine the alterations.

Kal-Nor grunted approvingly.

"Your engineers have done well. I think they expect us to test out the new drive."

Mahzit knew Helandian technology. They had used refractory systems for generations. With some clever adjustments to the anti-gravitational turbines, they would be able to significantly boost the grav-disks' capabilities. Traditionally restricted to low flight over continental territories, they would have the capacity to soar above the seas and mountain ranges without relying on the Noomasian solid ground surface to sustain flight energy.

The ocean was racing under them and a glance back revealed the fast receding lights of the shore. They had already left the Bel-loniean Port far behind.

The Commander's desert-tanned face was drawn, accentuating his deeply furrowed, elongated features, as he studied Mahzit. The man smiled warmly.

"Your reputation precedes you."

"My *what?*"

"You're colorful duel at the Bel-loniean Pleasure Palace."

"I'm afraid I made a fool of myself, sir."

"Fury in battle is admired among my tribesmen. The desert demands harsher discipline than required of city populations." The Raider's eyes brightened.

"Torlo Hannis said you would be a vital part of my team. Perhaps you'll have enough Kordatic hump to be fairly useful among my rugged men."

Mahzit decided to respond with a friendly challenge. Leaning slightly forward, he peered into the leader's eyes. "We Helandians are great warriors. The spirits pull briskly at our core."

He scanned the Commander's perplexed expression, and before Kal-Nor could respond, he reared dramatically back.

"Ah ha! Hearken! The sky speaks loudly. Don't you agree?"

The Raider looked puzzled.

"I can show you things that would amaze you beyond your wildest imagination."

Mahzit paused. When the Commander was about to react, he opened his mouth, and then snapped it shut like a trap closing over any possible response.

"Do you think the Mutis are the only ones who can predict futures?"

The Commander started to reply, and again, Mahzit quickly interrupted.

"This requires great practice. And I have learned great secrets. Gaze into my eyes and watch as the universe unfolds before you. See the magic."

Kal-Nor glared sardonically at him.

"I see *nothing!*"

Inwardly Mahzit guessed the Commander was probably wishing for a legal opportunity to strangle his impertinently foolish neck.

"Am I in the hands of a blind commander?"

Mahzit threw his arms up in exaggerated motion, attracting the attention of the crew; then threw his head back crying up into the sky. "Heavens; reward me with guidance, Oh mighty JaJa, make yourself known to us!"

"JaJa?"

Kal-Nor exploded, searching the empty air in front of them.

"Yes, have you not heard of JaJa?"

"*No*, to be honest."

Mahzit spread his hands wide, arms extended, encouraged by the incredulous stares of the enraptured crew.

"Do you not see the JaJa in the sky?"

The leader appeared to marvel at something invisible. But after a minute, he futilely shook his head from side to side.

"Quite frankly, I see very little beyond the...obvious!"

"What god would be obvious? They are all mysterious. Isn't that their divine right? Confusion and illusive bequests to answer endless questions are continually fed to countless omnipotent deities by their eager followers!"

Mahzit was playing the stage with the tact of an experienced thespian, holding the entire crew spellbound. "Look and listen;

see, hear, and behold these wonders!"

Mahzit leaned closer to the Raider and whispered.

"I am having a vision...right now! Out there, the loveliest of damsels are expecting us to seduce their lush bodies. They are awaiting the men of this ship to offer the greatest of pleasures. Ah, what ecstasy awaits us! Who would deny their plea?"

Kal-Nor shook his head, this time with shaded humor. It was clear the Commander was on to Mahzit as he carefully placed his words.

"What god grants carnal lust over spiritual promises? And why does he reveal them only to you? Where is your visible evidence of his word?"

"His? Who said JaJa was male?"

"A goddess. Perhaps?"

"Did I suggest JaJa had gender?"

"Neither him nor her? Then what? Horrors!"

"Muti be the son of a Korda! Must these super creatures be divided like mere mortals?"

"This JaJa is of your own...concocting. I bow to you...tell me...," and the man made a long low sweep before Mahzit.

When he had again stood erect he looked sternly at Mahzit, his penetrating tone of voice adding a sharp edge to the meaning of his words.

"By what authority do you make conjectures about the deities? Where are your facts?"

Mahzit decided to quit while he was ahead.

"I have an inner perception. Precise intuition, sir." he conceded, dropping his pompous façade; then respectfully addressing Kal-Nor.

"I'm not permitted to share details, sir."

Kal-Nor astonished everyone by placing a hand upon Mahzit's shoulder; a sign of honor among the clans.

"You have humor and brains and guts!"

A chuckle shuffled through the crew as each nodded toward Mahzit. He had won his point and acceptance from the men, who now turned back to their duties, leaving Mahzit alone with the Commander.

Kal-Nor raised an eyebrow. "Seriously, your record with the Baji-Ney tribe is impeccable, so you need not prove your valor here. Talk of unseen entities eludes me. I've heard rumors about the Helandian culture and special wisdoms. What do they call them—HanJahn?"

"Those are primarily my sister's dedication; Sarleni of Helandi and the House of Dorta. The powers of the mind can be amazing. And she claims that Adt Dorta has extraordinary talents, too, beyond his swordsmanship."

Kal-Nor looked puzzled and doubtful.

Mahzit realized he had said too much and nervously smiled.

"It is genuine enough."

"As for me; I'm a warrior; my loyalties are committed to my commander and my unit, sir!"

"So accepted."

With that, Kal-Nor took his leave. Mahzit wandered to one of the portals, pondering the exchange while he watched the formations of ships gliding above the ocean.

The far horizon was brightening from the rising sun when melodious tones from Sarleni swept into his head.

You made a loud mockery of the northern culture, brother. Tame your tongue!

He felt her brazen rebuke ripple through him.

I heard they sent you out. Ju-bilee told me your mission has begun. She has a message for you, 'Tell him we expect great feats. His future is challenged'.

She hesitated.

I think your unit is being advanced in order to avoid notice. Kaminaean spies have watching eyes.

The connection snapped out as he literally felt her whip away. She could do that; he couldn't.

Sarleni had communicated her message and left. The fact was; an official, though secret, mission had been confirmed.

End of subject.

He returned his attention to the expanding horizon. Colors

streaked across the heavens in dull tones; then slowly brightened as the sun ascended with the regal splendor of an ancient god gleaming across its creation. The frigid night air had thawed.

To the east he noticed the grav-disk squadron split off, turning sharply back towards the eastern coast.

Their own course shifted southwest and away from the coastline, towards the ocean.

Kal-Nor had disappeared into the ship's cockpit where the Helandian pilot was seated. Mahzit watched the control panel from his post. He was deep in concentration, examining the charts, when a hand firmly gripped his shoulder.

"She has received new orders. We're heading towards our instructed destination."

They approached the open deck and the Commander spoke to the men.

"We've been activated. Take inventory of your posts. Prepare for ground operations."

Mahzit and the Commander began a detailed inspection; armory, rations, the ship's reserves, or skimpy lack of same.

The Raider failed to veil his discouragement.

"Supplies are minimal. They barely pass code."

Kal-Nor bitterly frowned as he slammed the storage bin shut.

"We have untested arms and inadequate munitions."

Mahzit seemed less worried.

"If we carried heavy artillery into unknown territory it might jeopardize our objective. We're on a search and discover mission. Heavy weaponry could send the wrong message to potential enemies."

"It is unwise taking on a dangerous venture without being fully prepared." Kal-Nor squinted, waiting for a reply

Mahzit could not go into further details because Sarleni had only implied and had not given him a lot of facts.

"Probably a rush job," he suggested, "adequate enough."

"Our people are never without weapons."

"So I noted. Armed from birth?" Mahzit taunted the Commander, grinning.

Kal-Nor calmly ignored the gibe.

"Young men of the desert tribes must earn their weapons through rigid tests of courage, one at a time."

"I've heard; fights to the death."

"Not often. Still, it can be bloody."

The Commander pulled back the tunic from his shoulder exposing a long, jagged scar dangerously close to his neck.

"The price of being young; we were fighting over the...."

He muffled his last words through a stiff sneer. Shaking his tunic back into place he grumbled: "Not all that important."

"Affections of a woman?" Mahzit could not let an opportunity for a spicy story pass.

Their eyes locked, and each officer reflected an unspoken understanding; a chance to divert focus away from the current, dire situation.

The Raider hesitated, stroking his closely cropped beard.

"Only a girl; mature enough and oh, the dangerous, vicious innocence of it all!"

Kal-Nor spoke low and steady, as he recalled his first duel in the training fields long ago. His story was rich with the rugged customs of the desert folk and gave Mahzit a new level of respect for the integrity of the warriors; a deeper understanding for their ways. For to win a duel before peers, was the highest honor. Gaining the favors of a maiden was considered secondary; and only by the lady's choice. Thus, the stakes are high and the prize is never certain among the desert people.

Mahzit noticed a touch of sadness in the man when he spoke of the near fatal finale of the match.

"She was a worthy woman; right?"

Pride bellowed from Kal-Nor.

"I won my blade!"

He tapped the knife strapped to his side.

"The girl, she was, indeed, thrilled having two virile stallions vying for her favors. In truth, we were crazy boys with the hormones of Jilioes searing through our young blood, willing to fight for any virgin's affections. And often we did succeed. She was flattered by the attention of the two best warriors from the training fields of the season. Both of us had scored well above the ranks. When we'd begun to dispute over the favors of this irresistible maiden, the clan chiefs took notice right away and the duel was arranged.

"Ah, the innocence of youth: bold and confident in their own invincibility. Eager to sample the fires of carnal bliss: impudent recklessness."

Kal-Nor bared his teeth grinding his jaw back and forth. His nostrils flared; then the corner of his lip twitched as his eyebrows lifted.

"So we were groveling at her feet, lustfully panting for favors. And she played her seductive wiles, alluding to secretly promised possibilities.

"Too naïve to realize that what she *really* wanted was rank and riches!"

He laughed a bit too lightly.

"She favored an older man, a noble warrior from another tribe, who had taken notice of her during our duel. Status is everything. The chieftains, the powerful, easily win what they want! Neither was mine, at that time, and the rest...."

His arms flew up in the air.

"Youth fights for the prize and expects the desired reward of ecstasy from the hands of the lovely maiden. So the myth goes. Though we fought valiantly and nearly lost our lives for *her*, neither of us won that prize."

The Commander expanded his chest, thumping it with large hands. "Lush in body with firm breasts; so gorgeous and innocent."

Mahzit empathically gripped his own chest. "It must have hurt!"

"Oh, painfully so!" the Commander admitted. "Besides, at *that* age a girl is far too inexperienced to be very...satisfying.

"Regardless of the harsh rejection, we gained a notch up the manhood ladder. Our youth must prepare early for survival in a brutal world. Beasts devour other beasts by the law of natural survival."

Mahzit reflected on this.

"In Helandi it can be the same. Is not man the most savage of beasts? Life survives at the cost of other lives."

Kal-Nor's stubborn pride compelled him to point out differences.

"We of the desert have learned to adapt. And accordingly, avoid enslavement to the governed municipalities. The city-states are accustomed to our trade and benefit from the knowledge we bring from distant places. We roam at will."

They both silently absorbed the subtle unspoken views.

Mahzit saw a great deal he admired in Kal-Nor. A bond had taken root between them.

Kal-Nor gazed towards the northern horizon on the view screen.

"What is it like up there? From what I've been told, Helandi is frozen tundra. Not fit to be traveled during most seasons."

The Commander's switch of subject intrigued Mahzit.

"True. However, we spend those times deep beneath the ice fields. I cannot compare it to anything you would easily identify. If I say we live in open caverns cut into ice, you would shudder at the prospect of being thus confined. It is not like that at all."

He explained how their communities were pocketed deep within the glaciers.

"Ah, I understand why you enjoy the cities. Crowded and cramped!"

"Yes," Mahzit agreed. "I'm comfortable being surrounded by solidity."

"The barren north is a wasteland of ice," the Commander scoffed but not too disrespectfully, considering it was Mahzit's home, they were discussing.

"And the desert is a wasteland of dunes and stone!" Mahzit rebuffed.

"We are from opposite sides of the same mountain range; yours basked with dry sands and mine exposed to bitter cold winds and ice."

Kal-Nor's eyes were searching the horizon.

"What was it like on the other side of Noomas?"

Mahzit considered his answer.

"From what little I saw, we spotted a few clusters of sizable islands. Our destination was the northern coast of the mainland. A castle stood on the edge of a tall cliff overlooking the seashore. The land beyond was possibly dense jungle. And further off we saw mountains. It looked like an uninhabited wilderness. The grounds were overgrown. An eerie feeling came over all of us that morning we picked up my sister and Adt Dorta."

He then told how they had met with Sarleni at the Castle of Doom and how in the broken rubble, they had found the charred skeleton of a monstrous Muti.

An old man's body lay crumpled at one end of the gloomy chamber. Talni, the Messenger. Mahzit never learned exactly what the others did with it.

"I just stood there, staring at the massive Muti remains. It was almost unbelievable that my sister and Adt Dorta had destroyed this creature in battle." That was, in truth, all he knew about Kamina.

"No other signs of civilization?"

He shook his head, shrugging.

The elder seemed self-absorbed. Perhaps a bit resigned to their fate.

Reluctant to pose any further questions; he concluded: "So we're going to an alien territory."

Thus: had ended their discussion.

"Get rest!" Kal-Nor stretched, "We'll all need it."

II. Sky Attack

Mahzit's excitement spiraled when they sighted land. The deep haze of the morning cast a murky mist over the horizon. Then mountain peaks of an on-rushing landmass rose into a large island, which soon passed them.

After a ration of Mio-sticks, Kal-Nor scheduled combat drills, including swordplay. Mahzit found the sport invigorating. Though none of the Raiders bested him, some of their unusual tactics did rouse intrigue and he, in turn, challenged them with a few Helandian tricks that might prove helpful in any coming battle.

In the midst of these training duels a distant obstacle blotted out the sun's light, casting a shadow across the Orb's deck. Activity came to an abrupt halt as someone pointed skyward. All eyes were fixed on a swarm of flying creatures hovering, generating the dark cloud.

At that same moment Mahzit felt a rushing presence.

Yellow bodies, streaked with bluish, undulating patterns crossed the sky. He had never seen anything like this; they were entirely alien.

Odd flapping extensions of their bulky silhouettes served as wings. They moved with lightning speed as the assemblage made its way towards another peculiar object. The creatures seemed disinterested in the grav-disk.

"Flying swarm just ahead!" somebody cried.

Everybody crowded the viewing rail at once. The dark hoard spasmodically shifted direction with unified precision, diving and then skirting the other object at remarkably steep angles.

Mahzit felt the mental probe's throbbing energy intensify despite his attempts to blot it out. Logic suggested a message from Sarleni. Instinct insisted otherwise. He had never experienced this kind of raw prying energy annoyingly buzzing his ears.

The jells maneuvered; then attacked the other object now taking the form of twin avian, as a wordless fury bellowed in his head.

Am I connected to a sapient element? Self-aware?

Intuitively he thought, *it must have come from those jells: a collective consciousness, perhaps?*

Reason claimed that was impossible. Experience argued otherwise. *There is something else involved, not readily visible.*

What is this flock after?

He leaned forward glaring at the rolling dark cloud. The jells seemed better suited to swimming than flying.

Kal-Nor wondered: "What do you make of it?"

"Not much, yet...."

Mahzit was not willing to share his foreign mental connection with some unknown consciousness. Something with an enraged cognizant aliveness was out there, rampant with intense wrath.

The grav-disk bolted forward, sweeping up the distance like a blazing sandstorm.

The swarm scattered; then jetted down to attack the strange target which had split into two independent bodies.

Mahzit remembered how Adt had described huge flying creatures called The Gatherers, half machine and half bird, when they'd seized him and Sarleni.

They were horrid things, four times the size of a robust warrior. Their claws lifted us from the ground and carried us through the air as if we were air bubbles! Their talons must have injected some sort of poison into our bodies because we had felt a sting and then lost consciousness.

The Gatherers had taken them to the slaver ship.

The Haknords were actively mapping the coasts of the continents and islands. When not in use, these Gatherers were latched to the rear of the ship, one on each side. Their fierce violet eyes continually stared out with obvious awareness of their surroundings! Feathery wings of metallic gold were clamped down, strong talons shackled. Whatever control the crew had over them apparently was not adequate without rigid restraints.

The grav-disk rushed closer and it was possible to see greater details of the conflict. The description Adt had given of the Gatherers fit what he was seeing.

Abruptly a bright white beam radiated from the winged machines and in broad sweeps melted complete swaths of the continuous wave of attacking jells.

Even at this distance the men could hear the screeching wail of agonized life being ripped apart with each sweep of the ray.

The jells repeatedly rammed into the winged beasts; then scattered only to regroup, avoiding the white beams periodically streaking towards them from the beasts. When the jells' gaping mouths attached themselves to the metallic bodies, they left deep gaping pocks on the Gatherers' underbellies and wings.

Both enormous snapping beaks shredded any jells in their reach, scattering them in all directions. Monstrous wings, like magnificent fans, ripped at the nearest ones, plunging them down into the churning ocean below. The surviving jells continued to attack with an amazing unified dedication. The display was stunning.

Kal-Nor spoke half under his breath.

"I'm glad they didn't go after us."

"Astounding, how they're attacking!"

"Have you ever seen such things?"

Something haunting seeped into Mahzit; insanely disconnected. He was drenched with pure mental hatred; emotion, without words. Countless dots distorted his vision. Suddenly he was viewing the attack as if seen by the Gatherers.

Mahzit's head jerked forward, his mouth clenched, jaws snapped together again and again, mimicking the battle scene.

Rage and screaming pain crowded him like an inner alien connecting to both the jells and to the flying monsters.

Illusion! Mahzit told himself, shaking his head vigorously.

A sudden calm whisked the voices away. When he could focus on the scene again, it was too late to warn the pilot.

Their ship was being sucked into the zone of conflict. Dead jell blobs splayed throughout the sky. The pilot did not veer away fast enough to avoid impact.

Kal-Nor and the other men dashed for the gun ports. The Commander aimed a Kay-gun at one winged monstrosity as shots rang out from the portals manned by his fellow warriors.

The jells converged, jetting up above them, avoiding the Kay-pellets. Mahzit watched in horror as the creatures dove directly at them.

The grav-disk was almost flipped as the men clung to the safety grips. The ship dipped, nearly into a nose dive. The pilot maneuvered quickly, bringing its bow up and looping over the fray until it righted itself. Then it stalled, sputtering, faltering; unable to gain speed.

The jells made a wide circle, avoiding direct contact and reconfigured into a sharp 'V' aimed towards the Gatherers, who glided back to back in the sky; protecting themselves in a magnificent display of raw intelligent unity.

Their battle formation shifted as the jells fanned out; then regrouped below them near the sea's surface and evaporated into the ocean mists.

The Gatherers arched their wings and shot away.

The grav-disk lurched awkwardly, like a wounded Kuknal in flight; losing altitude. Kal-Nor slipped into the pilot compartment. The grav-disk slowed its spiraling descent, gradually leveling over the broad sea, drifting lower and lower towards a land mass positioned just south of them. A purple forest stretched from a narrow sandy beach right up along a ridge of matted hillsides. Off in the distance there appeared to be mountains, though it was difficult to see, as the damaged vessel continued to descend; nearly skimming the waters before it reached the shore.

The landing was pleasantly controlled, lightly cushioned by the thick tall marshy grasses.

The pilot had barely avoided complete disaster.

"Damage is serious. We'll attempt to repair."

Kal-Nor assigned his best mechanics to assist her while the others set up camp.

They found themselves in a boggy jungle, the ground liberally pitted, sprinkled with ankle deep water-pots. Several times they spied slimy wriggling things splashing around their feet. Distantly they heard the calls of hunting beasts and birds. No jells reappeared.

Their situation appeared brutally hopeless. If the grav-disk couldn't be fixed, they were lost. Barely armed, what chance of survival did they have? On foot, it would be a major trek across what appeared to be hostile swamp.

Mahzit forced himself to relax. Something unmistakably odd had occurred during their encounter with the jells and the Gatherers. He explored his inner senses to calm nagging nerves. Sitting cross-legged, he concentrated on the Zygo in an effort to perceive any consciousness beyond his fellow warriors. His Helandian teachers claimed they should be capable of tuning into any intelligence. Narrowing his focus, he crossed through an inner imaginary wall, searching for anything that might have lodged itself in the recesses of his mind. He then tried to access a stronger frequency into which he could merge. He was accustomed to riding on his natural stratum, though he only had intermediate training.

Instinct told him something had connected to him. Some collective consciousness had been out there. He had felt a consciousness, yet not a singular being; incomplete, or subhuman. And then again, it could have been his overly active imagination projecting curiosity towards that peculiar swarm.

How can I be sure?

He never understood mind theory. His lack of experience was painfully inhibiting.

He had spent too much of his life on impulsive pursuits for momentary self-discovery. Not particularly organized. It was his nature to flit from one interest to another. Sarleni had often scolded him for his lack of concentration and unruly discipline. She claimed he was not focused and too impulsive. Perhaps she had been right.

Angry about his limitations, he returned to the others. Duty called.

III. Swamp to Sand

From: the official files on the mission of Kal-Nor
Reports indicate ship is beyond repair and must be abandoned. Secure the ship; pack all portable provisions and conceal the grav-disk. The jungle will provide enough cover to keep it well hidden. We broke camp; proceeded on foot. My scouts explored ahead, while the rest of us collected and distributed the weight of our gear and provisions.

* * * * * * *

Mahzit was up early, just as the sun spread its morning glow upon the thick wall of trees blanketing the sky. They broke camp and began their trek through thick jungle, chopping away at vines and giant leaves; navigating along narrow dry areas between the slimy water-pots. The air was rank with hot mist steaming up from the sludge. They were constantly swatting at tiny insects buzzing around their faces. The medics had treated the uniforms with repellent that apparently discouraged the larger varieties, but had little effect on their tinier cousins.

He was feeling comfortable working alongside the men; a friendly lot, equally at ease with him.

The unit slogged on through the thick bog, their boots often ankle deep in the muck. Officers Mahzit and Linia were in the lead, using their innate senses to navigate the unit towards higher ground.

By mid-morning they had finally left the bog. After hacking through thick jungle, they had climbed until the landscape cleared away to open spaces. The Raiders stopped and raised their weary arms, whooping out a joyous victory salute,

"Vahl—Razzah!"

Kal-Nor laughed, for this cry is commonly lauded on the victor of a match in the arena. The unit had proven victorious over the nasty jungle foe and all deserved a break. And that had brought on their yell of joy.

They stood on a fairly wide strip of barren rock. From here they could look at the thick jungle canopy on the one side and rocky terrain of the other. It was a good idea to take advantage of the hot sun, which had reached high noon. So they laid their soggy gear to dry on the hot rocks and then scraped the thick crud from their boots. They must have collected half their weight in swamp muck. While the unit rested under a shading ledge, two scouts explored the terrain ahead.

When they returned, Kal-Nor and Mahzit reviewed their reports. The scouts had located several possible trails leading in various directions.

After a great deal of deliberation, the Commander summed up their evidence and decided which they would explore. Thus, the unit packed up and soon dipped into a low canyon where the air quickly chilled. Winding between massive stone walls, the narrow path allowed only one person at a time to squeeze through the cold stone cleft.

Finally the channel widened and broke open onto a flat ridge. The late afternoon sun illumined the gorge below, rising to sharp cliffs on the far side, pockmarked with holes. Most startling was a particularly well-defined arch. A row of stone pillars lined its outer edges. Tall statues guarded the outcrop leading to the arch.

They found a scalable path straight down towards the site. Before the sun had set, they'd reached the floor of the canyon.

The Commander selected a recessed, flat space where the unit should set up camp for the night.

The nook was curiously carved to one side of a series of broad slabs and framed by massive pillars which led up towards this façade.

Half shadowed by the late afternoon sun, Mahzit instinctively drew closer, flushed with questions; wondering who could have built such a structure, and why. It appeared to be a ceremonial temple.

Nagging intrigue needled the Helandian's natural instincts,

for anything mysterious taunted him to distraction.

A small heap of rocks nearby was scattered with broken pottery—an obvious sign that someone had camped here fairly recently. Mahzit knelt down, letting his fingers trace tiny clay bits. Some appeared more ancient than others. Sadly he was not an expert.

When the campfire had settled to glowing warm embers, he joined an animated discussion with the two historians who were very eager to examine the site the next morning. He had ideas about exploring he held privately. A little later Mahzit approached Kal-Nor with his plan.

The Commander was sitting cross-legged before a hot pile of coals that cast just enough light to see the pad on his lap. Somehow he had been able to write on it even in the twilight. By then most of the men were already asleep.

Mahzit tried to appear light and casual as he approached the man.

"Busy?" he asked. "I don't mean to disturb you, if you are."

"Updating the journal; recording our activities of the day: nothing that can't wait, really."

"Making notes about this canyon, the caves, that temple opening?"

"No, no: hardly so profound."

The man sighed, looking frustrated. "Who knows if anybody will ever read it?"

"I'm certain your account will draw a good deal of interest, once we make it through this ordeal," Mahzit asserted anxiously.

The leader tossed back his head and muffled his amusement.

"A dreadful thought! My desert tribesmen would most likely prefer to mock these notes! Most are adamantly against journals, considering them a waste of time. Maybe they're right. All regulations are to be followed, and we're required to make our daily reports.

"So what has sparked your interest, Mahzit? Anything I should add to my report?"

"I just find myself curious about that cavern up there;

undoubtedly ancient."

Kal-Nor looked at the carved structure.

"Ancient enough."

"And quite a puzzle."

"Yes, a puzzle."

The man returned his attention to the pad on his lap.

"Can't help wondering who built it...or where the inner chambers lead, if anywhere at all. What culture is responsible for its construction?"

Kal-Nor glanced at the austere lines of the temple a short distance above them.

"I've heard rumors of ancient civilizations. Never gave much importance to them. Myths continually plague our histories. You can't always believe these stories. Most are created from dim memories as lessons for the young. I discount them

"As for this old cave...yes, a rather amazing structure and certainly built by highly gifted artisans. Perhaps constructed to worship their gods or, who knows what?"

"Would be interesting to explore...."

"Anthropology and philosophy are not part of our mission. We have neither time nor expertise amongst the lot of us."

"Sir, I believe there may be something of value to our task in there. And tonight I could explore without deterring from our goal."

"Are you serious; in the dark?" Kal-Nor blurted: "Spooky demons must surely be living up there, ready to grab you as a night snack!"

Mahzit went to the pile of sticks and dried foliage they'd collected for the fire, picking a long, thick branch. He had noted wood burning bright and remarkably slow. Hefting it for weight, he took it to the fire and put its thinner end into the flame.

"Could serve; well enough."

The Commander looked uncertain.

"Not logical to wander around in there at night."

"Don't plan on wandering far. I'll never be able to sleep with so many unsolved questions, unless, of course, you *really* object."

Kal-Nor studied him; then conceded.

"My blessings, just be careful! You'll need your strength for tomorrow's hike out of this canyon!"

The man had so much as given his approval; then busily engaged himself with the journal in his lap.

Without looking up again, he said: "Go! Go."

Gruffly adding, "may the canyon gods protect you!"

The Commander's soft chuckle followed Mahzit as he headed toward the structure cut into the solid face of the rocky cliff. He stood there gazing up at the ominous silhouette looming before him.

When he stepped through the temple entrance a soft breeze brushed his cheeks, coming from deep within the cavern.

Had some mighty phantom beast exhaled its greedy welcome to the foolish human who was about to wander into its private domain?

The torch in his hand flickered against the stark walls; the stately columns silently beckoned him to enter. Mahzit stepped boldly forward, anxious to explore: blind to any possible dangers.

IV. Lost

Mahzit's excitement piqued as he passed through the ornate columns marking the entrance to the temple-cave. He hurried into the depths of the shrine; his torch dancing in the cool air, illuminating the elaborate murals.

What must it have once been like? So beautifully sculpted and painted.

Awed by their grandeur, he admired the detailed artwork along the corridors, wondering about its purpose and its makers.

Who had built this? What lay beyond? How far do the tunnels go?

The colorful scenes abruptly stopped at a vaulted chamber

confronting him with several narrow openings, but the larger central path appeared to be a main corridor. This tunnel curved right and left, like a giant undulating snake. Mahzit ran his hand along the smooth brick and stone lining the tunnel, his finger-tips feeling rugged, chiseled rock between places where the thick veneer mortar had crumbled.

His torchlight sputtered from an unexpected draft causing grotesque shadows to leap across a broad chamber. The light flashed in waves against a central stone slab. Like phantom ghosts, it created the illusion of a haunted tomb.

What could this place be? He wondered in amazement.

The room appeared sacred. The walls were empty, the room barren except for the plain altar.

Perhaps it was designed for an ancient potentate; or priest; possibly a throne; or a simple stage where mad poets preached their crazy ideas to those who happened to wander into this room.

Mahzit laughed at himself. His imagination was swollen beyond its sane limits. The day had been long, the night draining. He should be back at camp sleeping like a responsible mission officer; not wandering throughout these caves.

The torch flame pulsed brighter. He examined the waning torch with annoyance. It couldn't last much longer. He needed to go back. Reluctantly he began retracing his steps.

Turning the first curve he stopped; bewildered.

An unexpected choice of corridors branched off in several directions. How had he missed this?

Intuition caused him to take the first opening. When that, too, branched off to several passageways, he turned again.

Instead of one pathway, he was once again facing multiple choices.

Retrace your steps, he told himself.

Leaning over, he examined the stone floor for signs of foot-prints he must have made. In the dim light no signs were evident that anybody had come this way.

Which corridor had he come through?

Desperation assailed him. Impulsively he took the left corridor, which wound in sharp turns, sloping down. He ran faster, scraping against the barren walls. Unexpected fear tore at him.

Frantically he attempted to reclaim his sanity.

Stay calm.

Mahzit's heart pounded on the verge of uncontrolled panic. His breath pulsed loudly as he raced onward. Suddenly the path ended, ramming him into hard rock. Sweat poured from his brow as he slumped, dazed onto the cold stone floor, fighting unreasonable terror.

It felt as if some alien creature were clawing into his brain. Using his limited Zygo, he began to wrap a protective shell about his skull.

Examining the tunnel, he retraced his steps, slowly following his own footprints in the thin dust layer. Back and forth he wandered, remembering how it had appeared. He could find no clues. At each bend, he was more lost than before.

He focused inward, pulling into his senses, reaching out.

Sarleni, are you there? Adt? Can you hear me? Can you tell me where I am?

Summoning his courage, he waited, breathing hard, deliberately forcing himself to a slower rhythm.

He waited, aware of nothing.

No answer came. He grew anxious, even angry for having allowed fear to cause confusion.

The torch flickered, timidly offering light.

Again, he probed deep into the heart of the mountain, hoping to discover which path would return him to the canyon and the unit.

He had been bred in ice caverns. This tunnel chase was not new to him. As a youth in Helandi, he'd been lost many times, and learned how to find clues that eventually led to safety through the icy passages. Not the same here, for he sensed no crystals, no ice to reflect friendly signals back to the community.

Here, among the dense rocky foundations, he found no hint to give him direction.

He grew more annoyed than frightened with each step. The corridor broadened and he started moving faster with renewed confidence.

The corridor opened into a mural-lined chamber and he expected it to be the cave's entrance.

Soon I'll be back with the Raiders, he thought.

When he took a clearer look, all hope withered and was replaced with a mix of horror and fascination. The bizarre paintings displayed harsh proof he was still caught within the nightmarish labyrinth.

His torch illuminated images of oversized Muti faces, each nested in podded foliage. Their eye-sockets glimmered like sparkling azure pools.

A sharp chill climbed up his spine.

The faltering flame pulsed dimly, casting dark shadows against cut carvings along the chamber's walls.

Mahzit examined the finely detailed murals.

Some showed hooded men; apparently warriors with no detailed features. Others were animal shapes, most of which he could not identify. More striking were the written symbols running in panels alongside these figures.

Without warning, a heavy gust of icy air struck him and he was shoved violently forward. Something clanked loudly and rough claws yanked him up.

He fought back, only to be overwhelmed by the violent strength of the creature. Suddenly he was struck hard from above. Consciousness instantly collapsed.

When awareness sharpened, horrific shrieks pierced his ears; chomping, like axes smashed together, clashed over and over again, closely followed by a deadly roar. Sharp pain seared through his limbs. His head pounded loudly in his ears.

Slowly his eyes opened. He was lying on the ground matted with dried moss, the sun baking down hot and bright. He was in a camp of sorts surrounded by a forest. Ashes from a nearby fire were idly smoldering.

To the left he saw the half-eaten body, torn and shredded, almost touching him. Blood splattered around its twisted form. In utter shock and horror, he slowly began to recognize its shape and size. The hood was the giveaway, and the cloak.

He was looking at the broken body of a *dead* Muti.

Something had consumed the majority of its mangled purple flesh. There was little left of the creature beyond jagged whitish bones.

Nobody in Helandi had ever reported the death of a Muti until their encounter at the Castle of Doom, a highly irregular incident. The subject was rarely discussed; he doubted anyone had even actually seen the skeletal composite of a Muti.

Was this the creature that had captured me in the darkness of the caves?

The body and head were practically fused by a series of linear bones and sinews, not at all resembling the human. Shreds of flesh hung beneath the skeletal chin. The shoulder and chest frame molded together in one smooth white intricate pattern. Pivotal casings held sockets for the legs. He couldn't quite imagine a naked Muti; whole or in pieces. The beast had de-fleshed it, leaving only shreds of purple skin mingled with partly devoured innards.

What a sad distorted creature this Muti must have been: certainly not a normal example of its kind. Perhaps deformed or mutated. Feet resembled hooves. And the wide platelets encasing the midsection were bowed and squat. Surely this was a poor cripple. The face was fairly intact though contorted. Jaw was craned wide open, exposing four rows of stumpy teeth. The eyes sockets were pecked down to raw bony cavities clear through the back of the elongated skull.

Had this Muti brought me here?

Mahzit quickly took inventory of his own body. His head ached, and while his body was not broken, it was seriously bruised. Basic tools and weapons were still attached to his harness.

He shifted attention to the matting which was ovular and firmly packed; bordered by thick brush and tall reeds.

Is this a sort of nest for some enormous creature in the middle of a forest? Why did the Muti take me from the caves?

Mutis seldom touched humans and certainly were not prone to attacking or carrying them away.

Why did it bring me here? What did it want?

Panic threatened. He was alone; literally lost. Reuniting with the Raiders was not possible.

He slogged feverishly through an undulating fog, struggling to regain composure.

Mahzit dragged the Muti's body towards the reeds. Hacking a thick bundle of the grasses, he wrapped the body tightly; then buried it in a shallow grave beneath the bushes.

He had to keep moving or his mission might be lost.

The best plan was to continue in the direction of the rising sun, which should take him deeper into Kamina. They had come to explore and that's what he'd do.

Pressing his way through the overgrown reeds, he projected a plea outwards with considerable difficulty.

No good, Mahzit thought.

Shutting his eyes tight, he counted backwards and once again drove his mental sensors into the foreign wilds.

Slowly he became sensitized to images.

He was back in touch with his natural abilities. Rebuilding self confidence, he quickened his pace. Time filtered through his awareness as he broadened its mental reach. Nightmarish images flashed in spurts between the scents and sounds of the tumultuous jungle. He sifted his thoughts with keen precision, intent on honing in on any sign of civilization. As far as his awareness could stretch, he found no indication of human life, no sign even of ancient ruins.

Where had he been taken?

Isolation crushed him as the day waned to evening.

He needed rest. He was exhausted.

Everything that had happened to him since entering those

caves seemed vaguely unnatural.

It all felt like a dream. He'd been in the caves, then trans-ported elsewhere; apparently by a Muti. Nothing made sense.

He stopped, allowed himself to sit, and focus on *anything*. The attempt only failed miserably and left him frustrated, wishing he'd perfected the Zygo lessons as Sarleni had done. Angrily he stood and walked toward a clearing, the moons hovering on the brink of the tree line.

Calm: Probe.

He once again concentrated, expanding his mental bound-aries.

Faint voices stirred inside his head. At first they were without structure, just sounds.

Surely he was hallucinating. Yet they were distinct frag-mented statements.

He had just stepped out from under the cover of the fringe trees when the voices tuned in clearly.

...Found something....

Is it him?

Yes....

The transmission kept fading.

He looks safe.

We were worried.

Mahzit snapped alert to this new and very much welcomed invasion.

Finally the words sharpened.

Mahzit! Be ready.

That was all.

Sarleni, he mentally called out: *Adt?*

Silence answered him.

The evening abruptly felt warmer. He was no longer alone.

You'll be instructed.

This was not Sarleni but definitely Helandi.

We'll send it to meet you.

His feet were running. Totally blinded to any dangers of where he was heading. Someone was out there to help him.

The glowing light ahead instantly relieved his anxiety as the Orb slowly lowered to ground level.

A firm voice commanded: *Enter.*

He simply leaped through the opening that automatically created itself upon his approach. It sealed behind him. Mahzit knew this kind of craft.

For a short, breathless moment he bathed in a giddy comfort zone.

The only other occupant, a pilot from Helandi, turned and smiled warmly.

"I'm charged to get you relocated, sir."

"What about the others in my unit?"

"The orders were very specific. They will find their own way."

The Orb lifted into the sky.

"Where are we headed?"

"To the Kaminaean coast: I'm instructed to take you there to finish your mission. You were under surveillance until we lost contact!"

The pilot turned back to the controls, indicating the conversation was over. And he also realized the man probably knew little more than he had just stated. Unanswered questions riddled his mind but they didn't matter. He was safe.

He quickly rushed over the last day's events and realized that he had apparently not been on the continent. The Gatherer's attack must have caused the Raiders to detour from their planned destination.

That was a shock. For now, he decided to deal with the present. His mission was being re-directed by Helandian authority.

"Are there any supplies here?" he asked.

"You can check the armory bins. They sent me on short notice so I don't think they were stocked. Take my travel kit; also the water bag and cutting tools: basic provisions. Some bandages and a few emergency items, sir."

He went to a locker in the wall to the left of where the pilot was sitting and pulled out the small belted pack that easily latched around his waist. The water bag and other provisions clipped neatly into place.

Mahzit settled in, thankful for the rescue and decided to enjoy this flight to Kamina. He had hardly begun to relax when a violent jarring tilted the Orb.

The pilot cried out: "What was that?"

Mahzit had been knocked awake. He sprang to the control booth and scanned the open vista on the screen. The ocean spread out below and ahead of them land was approaching fast.

A thick shadow crossed their path. The sky went black.

Mahzit recognized its shape.

It was one of the monstrous Gatherers.

What are these creatures doing here? Why are they attacking?

"Get away from it—fast!" Mahzit ordered.

"I plan on it!" The pilot's voice was tense, and as his hands went to the controls the Orb shifted direction and shot rapidly towards the coastline. "I'll have to drop you here. We weren't supposed to be detected! Prepare yourself!"

Again they were brutally jarred.

The pilot throttled the Orb down towards the land. With amazing agility the man shot towards the trees, maneuvering through narrow openings between massive trunks. The Orb twirled left and right as it brushed past thick foliage. Abruptly the craft hovered above a tiny meadow, under the covering of tightly laced branches, hardly pausing.

"Go!" the pilot said hastily, even as the Orb glided along its course.

Without questioning motives, Mahzit knew what was expected.

Anybody observing what was taking place might not notice the craft pausing in its flight over the marsh.

Mahzit jumped out of the portal and as he tumbled to the ground, the Orb shot towards the protective cover of thick clouds. Just when it streaked the edge of the billowing white, several Gatherers swooped in.

The Orb went wild red. Explosive energy churned violently;

white fire shattered the air, engulfing several of the Gatherers in its demise. The Orb and birds plummeted to the ocean surface blazing like a crimson furnace. The brave young pilot had apparently triggered a self-destructive explosion.

Mahzit saw one last Gatherer hover over the debris of its fallen cronies. After circling twice, it withdrew up the coast. The pilot had been expendable; and so was every person involved in the spy missions.

Mahzit slipped into the thick marsh, not once looking back.

CHAPTER SIX
HELANDI

I. The Aer-Hahl Clan

Sarleni's excitement about their trip to Helandi flushed over Adt as they boarded the Orb in the Dorta Gardens. When the compact transport lifted up above Bel-loniea and raced north across the white sky, they set to work reviewing the preliminary briefs which would prepare them for the heavy drills they'd be undergoing at the HanJahn Academy.

With their escalating access to the Zygo, their combined energy had exponentially multiplied, granting them a tremendous amount of power, which they'd be expected to develop further. Both would undergo rigorous training for the impending conflict. However nothing was scheduled for a few days; allowing ample time to visit Sarleni's family: the Aer-Hahl Clan.

Adt was nervous and Sarleni was equally anxious about how her family would respond.

She made a bold suggestion. *Why not connect? Combine our experiences like we did when we met with Torlo and Youi.*

Adt mulled it over.

I believe we attained a remarkable depth at the Castle of Doom with amazing results. We will need to discipline our practice in order to strengthen that energy.

They created the bond, mentally opening to each other for extended periods; always expanding their range, drawing deeper into their cores, solidifying and honing each channel.

As they drew nearer to the Northern Territory, Adt's genuine interest in seeing the land of his birth spiraled. Sarleni had described her homeland in beautiful metaphors depicted in deep hues contrasted against rich pastels and now he watched the landscape below them changing before his eyes. None of Sarleni's narratives had portrayed the true splendor of the majestic terrain now stretched out before the Orb. He had expected white emptiness, as reported in charts. The Polar Regions were virtually unexplored; perpetual mysteries. His father had seldom spoken of Helandi. The reason, as Adt accepted later, was Kigor Dorta's painful memories regarding Ju-bilee.

He had repressed his own questions as his father had encouraged him to do long ago.

Adt was not a master swordsman by accident. His renowned father had attended to the young boy's training at every opportunity for the child had displayed astounding gifts even his father had not anticipated. He excelled at every lesson until the youth had surpassed the Head Master of the Dorta Training Academy.

* * * * * * *

Adt was suddenly jolted out of his childhood memories back to the spectacular landscape blazing before his eyes.

Sarleni!

Adt's rapture fairly exploded into her mind.

It's beautiful!

She knew Adt had never before seen anything remotely close to the magnificence of her beloved homeland.

Glistening snow and ice perpetually covered the stately mountains surrounding the summer home of Sarleni's family.

Sod-covered bungalows laced the shore of a sparkling inland lake teaming with fish and waterfowl. The land was brilliantly fertile, interspersed with similar thatched dwellings, marking the clan's farm communities. A colorful patch quilt of fields cultivated in neatly drawn rows covered the valley floor.

She had tried to explain the stark transformative cycles of the seasonal changes. But it was difficult for him to believe how it would soon be cocooned beneath thick layers of snow and ice, erasing all traces of a civilized world during the longer winter season.

Exciting life teams over these lands and waters during the season of the sun. Our winter world lies entrenched within those shiny mountain glaciers. We're coming into the harvest season.

The late summer meadow flourished with wild flowers. Flying bugs and birds chirped in cacophonic rhythms.

Sarleni laughed at several young rascals who came running from a nearby cottage. They practically knocked her over with their enthusiastic race to see who would get to the lake first.

"Come and meet my family. All of my cousins spend their academic recess here together."

She hugged the wriggling children and sent them scurrying back down the path. Her mother's cottage was a modest place, one of perhaps thirty cottages dotting the shore, each with a small pier jutting out from the sand. Schools of colorful fish frolicked in the sky-clear waters. Several people were basking on the beaches. Others were fishing from the piers and from a dozen or so boats floating on the flaccid surface.

Inside, the cottage was bright and buoyant, just as she remembered it. Nothing had changed. A long table filled the central area where a good two dozen people could be seated at once. A row of windows overlooked the lake. Fresh cut flowers stood in vases filling the room with their sweet scents mingling with the aroma of fresh baking bread coming from the oven.

"Now, who have we here?"

A melodic voice rang out sweetly from the kitchen.

They were greeted by a tall, slender woman; jet-black hair framing delicate features and pulled back into a neat bun. Sarleni gasped with joy—then rushed into the woman's outstretched arms. Tears instantly welled up. For a long moment they hugged in silence.

"My goodness, Sarleni," she exclaimed. "You're so radiant; alive. Beautiful! More so than ever before, if my memory serves me right. You had all of us so worried. And afraid we'd never see you again."

"I'm home now. And it's all going to be fine."

Sarleni was a little embarrassed and quickly wiped her damp face on her sleeve.

"I want you to meet someone very special, Nada."

She guided the woman by the hand to Adt, eyes sparkling with excitement.

"I want you to finally meet my mother, Nadeshi."

Adt awkwardly stepped forward, not quite certain how to address a mother-in-law.

"I'm pleased to meet you...and honored."

Her mother embraced them both and kissed each of their cheeks.

Sarleni modestly muffled her amusement. She knew he had painstaking rehearsed a number of greetings for this event.

"You are officially part of the family. Our home is your home in every way. Dear boy, call me Nada. And I will call you Adt."

Adt flustered, slightly perplexed, regained composure: "Oh, of course, Nadeshi."

"Nada, please!" the older woman insistently squeezed his hand.

"Nada, it is!" Adt confirmed.

"Soon you will learn the names of everyone in the family here and later those who were not able to join us for the High Summer Jamboree."

She looked curiously into Adt's eyes.

"I've heard you are already acquainted with our Mahzit. That boy has always been an impulsive young lad, constantly adventuring since he was barely walking."

She raised her lyric voice.

"Before I forget my hospitality, come! Make yourselves comfortable. Dinner is almost ready!"

She had turned and rushed off into the kitchen, still chatting away to herself.

So like mother to be flitting about taking command; queen of the cottage palace.

Sarleni was finally home.

"Will you help set the dishes? I'm glad we've arrived in time for dinner. I can smell it simmering and I can't believe it! She's baking my favorite dessert, Lechno-maggis!

"Adt, you *will* love them."

She began pulling dishes from a cupboard and handing them to him, while sending mental pictures of delicate sugar dumplings in a creamy sauce. Adt was suddenly drenched with her memories.

Sarleni also experienced Adt recalling his youth, living among cousins before his academic disciplines had begun. In his father's home, the dinner table would be crowded with energetic kids. Loving guardians in the House of Dorta had raised him. He had not been alone. Unruly rough-housing and a fair amount of chaos had been a part of his life for only a short period of his childhood.

The later years were harshly structured with endless lessons in swordsmanship and battle closely supervised by a stern and gifted father.

Sarleni had noticed the marked sobriety and etiquette of Bel-loniean society, at least among those on the palace grounds. In sharp opposition, the open fields of the Helandian valley gleefully defied discipline or supervision of any kind. Summer inspired wonderful freedom from the confining walls of rock and ice.

Sarleni loved the seamless days when the sun barely touched the horizon. She pined for a longer interlude to enjoy these warm sunny days.

* * * * * * *

Harvest season had encroached upon them; the crops had nearly been reaped. New frost laced early morning dew indicating closure to the growing season. The land showed clear signs of retreating. Its playful denizens bade farewell, some migrating to warmer climes, others burrowing deep into the softened sod to their customary hibernation nests.

The Aer-Hahl Clan made preparations to enter the mountain cities beneath the soon-to-be barren lands which would be smothered beneath thickly iced wintry blankets.

Adt was glad to have the fine-spun cloak Nada had given him to keep him warm for the journey. At pre-dawn, still quite cold, Adt and Sarleni waited with the family to begin their trek to the mountain. Each moist breath hardened to shaved ice in the brisk chill.

Approximately two hundred Aer-Hahl clansmen crossed the valley towards the mountain Sarleni's people called the Taop Horn Peak. Adt had asked why it was called that name. Once the sun had risen, Sarleni pointed out the smooth curvatures of its shadow resembling the horns on the male Taops in the herd.

Ascending the ridge on the outer edge of the banks the path proved to be treacherously slick. They stopped. The Aer-Hahl elders separated from their family groups forging their way to the front of the pack. Everyone stepped back to give them clearance. Once they'd assembled, several of them began pacing along the ridge, back and forth, chanting low sing-song verses, gradually increasing their volume.

Sarleni noticed Adt's puzzled frown.

He was having great difficulty trying to look serious; he really wanted to burst into laughter.

What's wrong with your people, Sarleni? Are they expecting some mountain ogres to attack? Or maybe their gods will pelt them with snowballs if they forget the secret password?

Sarleni grimaced. It took all her patience to stay calm. She did not wish to cause any interruption during the Entry Ceremony.

It's not what you think, Adt. They are not superstitious. In our society it is simply polite to acknowledge our good fortune and give thanks for another season of plentiful harvest. It is an ancient custom. And the elders give praise to the Nuja gods annually before we go below. I'm certain you have rituals in Bel-loniean society, too.

Her explanation had been enough to sedate Adt's churlishness and he respectfully began absorbing her people's cultural history.

When they had finished the ritual, the cliff wall opened. Everyone fell back in line and filed through the arched gap along the smooth corridor. The chilled air was dispelled by gentle warmth welcoming them to the inner world of Helandi.

They journeyed through tunnels in double file, the elders periodically chanting verses and the people echoing back responses. Adt was beginning to enjoy the unusual parade; like listening to a walking-talking encyclopedia, hearing stories being transmitted from elders to the people and back again.

At length they approached the Third Sector Hall of Meetings where the rest of her family clan would be waiting.

Adt, I think you'll get to meet most of my people today. I believe they will all be here before the evening feast. She gave his hand a squeeze.

He was brimming with questions.

You must be related to the entire Helandian nation, from the looks of it! Does your mother want me to remember the names of all these people?

Why not? She reassured pridefully. *You have a wonderful capacity for learning. I expect great things from you. So does everyone.*

So I noticed: He glumly thought. *Far too much; if you ask me and you aren't asking, are you? You leap into me at will; you strip my resistance and read my thoughts.*

Yes, my dear, we are as one.

But, all the time? he complained. *There are limits.*

You haven't always been an open book, she sighed. *"Sorry, Adt, we are bonded although you are not transparent. I have never blocked you.*

She shrugged. *I am open to you. Just 'read me' and you'll know all the names as the faces are presented to you.*

Sarleni let a giggle touch his thoughts, curling around them in a lightly loving way, to smother any suggestion of a sting.

She had worried about Adt's natural discomfort around new faces, crushed into a society alien to him; a stressful exercise, at best. He stiffened ever so slightly and Sarleni could tell he was uneasy among so many strangers.

Ceremonial affairs were not his favored events. In fact, he adamantly tried to avoid them. Adt was a warrior, a protector and magnificent swordsman. Nonetheless, he was being pushed into a foreign territory.

Sarleni wanted to help him; and allow growth at its own pace. She could feel resistance. He was like a little boy trapped in an adult ritual. Letting a loved-one suffer their way through pain without interfering was difficult: a lesson for both of them.

They had been actively practicing the Zygo techniques, strengthening their flexibility. They'd become adept at combining visions and memories.

Their original fear of unlimited mental exposure to one another had proven to be a false assumption. For within its perfect state, both preserved independence and privacy. In fact, both had doubled their inner awareness.

Thus they willingly co-mingled details of past memories. What they shared resided in their unblocked regions, only. And quibbling over it merely exposed his uneasiness. He detested not having control.

He didn't have to speak. Sarleni felt his uncertainty. Helandi was not just an unconventional place to him. He faced a new culture which was now his family, too. He wanted to find familiar ground.

Oh, Adt. Sarleni pleaded with genuine sympathy, for he looked desperate.

You were born here. Everyone welcomes you. They celebrate your return to your original place of birth.

He pulled her towards the shadows, out of the milling crowds, overwhelmed with a flood of emotions.

Sarleni, maybe we can be alone for awhile and deal with these...events, later.

Maybe you're crazy.

In love?

Maybe.

Is anything wrong?

The course of history constantly changes. For any child born to us will be a major event.

I could not argue with you on that point. Shall we try right here?

I don't think so! She teased.

So, why hesitate?

Gradually he relaxed and became playful again. His hands slowly massaged her shoulders.

"Dear man, people will start talking. Behave!"

She touched his cheek lightly.

Later we can explore the pleasures, once we're settled in our wintry domicile.

Adt swiftly surveyed their surroundings and the people trailing around them.

"Tonight, for sure," he dramatically whispered.

I promise, she vowed.

Tonight, after the family feast and ceremonies, we may discover the true meaning of the Three Moons Legend.

Isn't that the purpose of these...unions?

Not the way you romp through them; being such a high energy beast that can never be sated.

You drive a man to madness.

I do so with tenderness.

Ever so, he promised.

Sarleni invisibly smiled to herself, for she had never met a gentler lover. The future promised great joy to them, if the world survived. And she wanted to capture as many moments of intimacy as possible before war stole their energies.

II. HanJahn Cram Course

Everyone was in high gear for the coming conflict against the empire. And debates were openly shared. Rumors flew much the same here as in Bel-loniea, only with a difference. For the Helandians did not need to be convinced about the seriousness of the Kaminaean threat. They had been aware long before the Bel-lonieans and were prepared and ready to mobilize.

Sarleni handed a folded leaflet to Adt. The cover plainly read *"Attendance required."*

The students were packed tightly into the auditorium. Buoyant lights sent dancing rainbows among the many faceted ice crystals, like a thousand delicate chandeliers. The dais consisted of a low platform, not larger than a pillow. In fact, it was just that, a simple cushion.

Lilting conversations amplified the growing excitement and electrified anticipation.

The notice had said: *By Invitation, Only.*

All who anxiously arrived to be exposed to this master's verbosity were slated to be trained as the Primes Duos, on the pathway to their Nexus.

The class was a rare opportunity available only to highly advanced students. When Moyi chose to teach, scholars would come purely for the privilege of being in his presence.

No sooner had the last of the seats been filled than silence fell across the auditorium and a soft blue hue spread across the lofty crystals. A single ray of light shone down upon the dais onto a man. Ageless in appearance, he floated cross-legged above the cushion. This was Moyi, the teacher, speaking without the sound of words.

Remember and understand that I know nothing. We all have come to learn. Together we will begin exploring new avenues of reason. There are many paths to ultimate answers. It is in and through territorial devotion we all seek to expand.

Again: even as I know nothing, I say without shame or vanity, what I know far exceeds the knowledge of you who are present. I search, seek and wonder at what I find. I discover vastness ultimately unexplained.

I expand my consciousness onto the horizons of the unknown. I am drawn to the journey on a quest for Truth. My curiosity will guide me into territories undefined by my imagination. It beckons me to the brink of madness, though it is, no doubt, unimpressed with anything other than its own determination. Surrender to possibilities beyond consciousness.

I have no name, no value, no system of belief, and no evidence to substantiate the existence of a consciousness within the core of our pulsing universe. Truth demands that there be no false images, or imagined concepts. Truth allows itself to be discovered. Truth is ever illusive of easily assigned names and labels or even living characteristics beyond 'what is'.

I envy none. For I am at peace with the challenges I seek for the sake of Truth.

I wonder about blind faith in teachers of knowledge. Is it wise to thus believe in their discoveries as if they had been easily found answers to creation?

Or does the practice deny the opportunity to release one's own cravings for answers to those proclaimed conclusions fashioned by other minds?

Certainly the young new student will follow without qualified wisdom, for a time, until the lessons have been learned sufficiently to experience their value within one's own reality. For it is precisely within the discipline of examining, questioning and seeking out relevance, where one's own experience reveals the essence of wisdom. After testing and evaluating the precepts unto the self, we come to greater and lasting acquaintance with Truth.

Too often a student makes the leap from pupil to teacher far too soon. The trap is strongest for those who learn quickly and easily but have not yet reached the deeper truths, the solid gems of wisdom arising through long practice and experience with time. Take care not to come to this junction too quickly in your *studies.*

Learn well the teachings of the elders.

Heed the temptation to make the lessons your doctrine, your personal mantra.

Not until you have passed the knowledge through the testing flames shall it become ensconced upon your knowing. And in the knowing, take care in sharing your experiences, lest others look to you as their fountain of Truth, their personal mentor. For those who stand solely on their own wisdom and choose to teach their own truths as quoted from yet another such mentor must be at the very least questioned and alas, must be pitied. Their professed teachings become snares to entangle the unaware and they design their convictions in ways polluting Truth with their own power-hungry aggressions. And for those who succumb to the deceptive easy road of submission to unquestioned authority, their fate is marked and they soon fall victim to the utter loss of their passion for Truth. And for them, life is cheap.

All living organisms have bred out of creatively destructive forces; fertile un-harnessed chaos founded all things. Life; both matter and energy, are sacred to all. And it is in the expanding and contracting of the very energy of life that all things live and die within the universal realms. We must accept and honor the harmony and the not-knowing in our quest for understanding. The mystery expands even as we pursue Truth.

There are as many convincing answers as there are thinkers. We, of the living, come and go seeking answers to our quest: where we come from and where we go to, is what all godly orders impart upon audiences willing to listen.

The true believer has been born into their local divinity. We need answers. We need grounding. We have inherited roots seeking nourishment. They perpetually and indiscriminately absorb what is within easy reach. Thus, life measures its allotted energy upon the landscape.

Not one living thing is worthier than another; for every entity contains the necessary ingredients of self worth.

Is it not enough to justify itself?

The answers we all seek are illusive, yet I resolutely devote my time to expanding outwards with gentle perseverance. Not pushing the boundaries beyond my reasonable ability to interpret. I absorb new wisdom as it reveals itself to my ever-searching curiosity.

Think on these suppositions. After you understand, you will be ready to discover further truths.

And with perfect simplicity he quietly left the auditorium.

* * * * * * *

Sarleni met Adt for dinner at the Terrace Gardens near the Institute. Ease was very welcomed after the class that had occupied most of the morning session.

They'd both started each day early at the HanJahn Academy. By the end of the week they were exhausted from the intense drills.

Their training was half completed and they desperately needed a break from the brain cramming studies. The morning lecture had been exhausting, with a heavy afternoon load still ahead of them. He tried to make himself comfortable and relax. Even these gardens strained Adt's basic grounding. Nothing in this subterranean world was familiar to him.

He could rationalize the tunnels and caverns carved into the rock and ice. After all, the engineering of these awesome communities was ingenious. Caves and passageways were common enough on the mainland, although not to this degree of refinement. The lush vegetation within these gardens was all wrong.

For one thing, how could plants grow without the natural elements of an open sky? They were deep within the icy mountain far from the nourishment of fresh air, rain and sunlight.

And another even weirder issue: why was everything *green*? He'd never seen anything like it before in his *life*! The natural world was full of foliage in rich hues of red and violet and amber forests; gold and bronze meadows. And he missed the delicate bluegrass in his beloved Bel-loniea. Never had he seen *green* in any growing thing! He was certain he could never get used to it; let alone the eating of green foods on his dinner plate. It was asking far too much of him.

Here he sat at the garden inn with a plate heaped high with freshly cut greens, as they called this particular dish. Everyone around him was shoveling the leafy stuff into their faces and acting as if it was the best treat they'd ever had. The first day the waiter was enthusiastic when he presented the platter, saying, "You'll never find healthier food anywhere. Organically cultivated, we are so proud of our crops this year; the highest nutrient content yet achieved in these gardens."

The young waiter had been, of course, quite right. Adt had closed his eyes and let hunger get the best of him, shoveling the food down his gullet akin to a boorish Traztu Beast. At least the Porshi had been semi recognizable and he gulped that down quickly as well.

Actually, he had thought, if he didn't think green, the food was not at all bad; downright good, if it were not for that awful color.

Remembering that first impression he frowned.

Sarleni smiled at him.

"What's so funny?" he asked, unexpectedly self-conscious.

Need something be funny simply because I'm smiling at my love? She thought without blinking.

Anybody observing them would not have noticed their subtle intimacy. Nobody could have known what was happening. It was possible for them to be touching, without any physical contact.

You're not being fair! He managed to project.

Did you not enjoy?

I'm not able to return the favor, he mused, shifting just slightly uncomfortable in the chair.

I'm rewarded by you when we are together.

You flatter beyond believability.

Oh, you think I lie?

I wouldn't dare tempt your anger. He shivered. *Still....*

If you object, we can withdraw.

The connection faded. Normally she didn't speak into his mind during an intense connection. Adt was taken aback when she had unexpectedly done so.

They sat in awkward silence, becoming aware of the room filled with the chatter of excited voices. Greetings, conversations, ever heated arguments all blended together with the soft background music.

They ended their meal, casually said their good-byes: then rushed off to seek the privacy they both so much desired.

Like all young lovers and especially during war conditions, intimacy trumped the night.

* * * * * * *

Adt was fascinated by the ingenious variety and lively pace of the HanJahn classes. One particular lecture given by Dean Yaw-iyn captured his interest. This man had developed a vital hypothesis, currently being tested and utilized by new flight simulators. He held a captive audience, including Adt's attention, during the last lecture of the day.

"Crystal radiance is the earliest natural energy source known to man. It is constant, reliable, renewable and virtually unlimited in its capabilities. We are continually discovering new ways to harness its amazing properties."

Dean Yaw-iyn's passion for the topic permeated every word, though his voice was casual. The students sitting near Adt were entirely captivated by the handsome athletically built instructor. The dean looked less like a professor and more like a tough warrior; sharp gray eyes darting over the room, not missing the slightest shift in even the remotest corner. His role of a scholar clashed with the man's exterior appearance. However each statement was fluently marbled with confidence. His tall lean frame sailed effortlessly across the stage like a refined dancer.

A tight cord of sleek black hair traced down towards leather boots, which were meticulously laced up to his knees. He was skimming a pointer over the holographic charts as he lectured to the class.

"Several methods of mass production had been perfected by the Ancients. We still use basic, antiquated methods today, though their applications are being continually modified as you can see by our latest upgrades.

"Once you have learned the basic principles of crystal energy, the concept is rudimentary. Of course, it is easier to grasp if you have a background in the mechanics of angular physics plus a fair understanding of thermodynamics."

The professor was one of the leading theoreticians of physics at the HanJahn Institute. Using the drawing flat board and the prism structures next to the podium to illustrate a point, he continued with gentle patience.

"As you can see, the deflections marked on the scope correlate consecutively with the speed of each transmission through the prismatic surface of the shard. The calculations on this chart demonstrate precise ratios for determining the number of radians required to accomplish the desired angular displacement."

Adt resisted his natural desire to doubt and debate, especially these kinds of concepts; he had never particularly enjoyed classroom studies in Bel-loniea. He usually disliked lectures but this scholar held his interest better than most had done in the past. Besides, he had to absorb the material in order to expand his Zygo abilities. Each nugget taught here was as alien as if he had left Noomas and landed in some distant galaxy. The vast knowledge among the Helandians awed him beyond description. Nonetheless, he scribbled notes as the professor continued. His curiosity was strongly roused when Dean Yaw-iyn began using archery examples.

Now this guy is talking real sense, Adt thought, as he diagramed the professor's trajectory charts and copied the formula written on the board. In fact, he was disappointed when the class was over before he was ready for it to end.

Dean Yaw-iyn had just completed the lesson and outlined the next assignment summarizing the principle governing the thrust of the Orb engines, when he cut the lecture short, challenging the class to finish the equation on their own. The HanJahn students filed out of the room and clustered in the halls, still discussing the formulas in small groups.

Adt folded back the page and sauntered up to the podium just as Yaw-iyn was turning down the projectors.

"Might I ask a few questions before you go?"

He appeared to be near Adt's age, well-built, obviously not prone to sit for hours in a classroom.

Yaw-iyn looked up and held Adt's gaze.

"I suppose, if you keep it short."

Adt nodded, looking down at his notes.

"I wonder if you would be willing to demonstrate. I mean, in action with real equipment. Not on these simulators."

"Weapons, maybe?"

He wanted authentic answers and the Dean of the Physics Department appeared interested in a friendly challenge. Something about the man appealed to Adt.

Yaw-iyn quickly straightened, eyes sparkling.

"Have you ever played Crystal Shards, Adt? No, don't answer. Of course you haven't. Come on. I'll show you."

* * * * * * *

Yaw-iyn stood at the far end of the sports field with a dozen uniformly cut shards lined up at the goal line.

"Ready for the shot?" he asked; the words rang all over the cavern walls.

"Ready!" called the young Dorta, a bit shaken from the powerful echoes ricocheting around the ice field. He held the ornate shield watching for Yaw-iyn's aim. The Zygo shard sport was one of the most competitive games in the northern catacombs during the cold winter season. Yaw-iyn released the first shard from its post making a smooth arch towards the opposite goal. Adt had expected a very different trajectory so he had to scrabble towards the edge of the field and dive for the shard, intercepting it with a resounding gong just before it grazed past the last marker. The shard shot straight up in the precise angle Adt had intended, scoring dead center of the Pentagram above the field.

"Holy Nujas!" Yaw-iyn gaped at the flashing star spinning above them in blazing beauty.

Adt laughed, "Victory! And in one shot! Ah-ha!"

"Not so easy, my friend: you're obviously a gambler trying to convince me you've never played this game before. We shall up the stakes."

The professor jogged across the field to Adt's side to explain the next round. Taking the shield from Adt amid his short Victory dance, Yaw-iyn challenged him. "Double or nothing, using only the Zygo—no shields; no visuals."

Both men squared off in the field, their eyes locked for a long, silent moment. The Pentagram had ceased its rotation and come to a solid rest above them.

In tandem the two opponents turned back to back. A second shard flew from its post at a sharp low angle towards its target in Adt's end zone—a jet-black triangle was its destination. Instantly a flaming ray burst from Adt's left hand. The shard cut sharp to the right just grazing the outer edge of the goal.

"Check point." Yaw-iyn had turned to glance at his opponent. Neither had scored.

The third shard was in mid-flight, though it was poor sportsmanship to shoot before the previous play had been officially called.

Adt pointed emitting a blue streak which lifted this shard hard into the third Pentagram moored above the goal line.

His breath grew hot as he blinked once, keeping steady aim; barely flicking his wrist, each shard pinging directly into their corresponding targets. Shards four, five, and six were perfect shots.

The gymnasium rang like a bell tower with wild explosive bursts of light and sound shaking the subterranean vaults. Both contenders locked concentration; combat ready, fully focused.

Yaw-iyn prepared to launch the second set, but apparently decided against it. Lowering his gaze, he turned toward Adt, dropped to one knee, left palm extended in a sign of accepted defeat with honor. It was more than a moment before Adt realized he was on a gaming field; not a battlefield. The high tension of the game had triggered him into a back flash. Too many recent battles prevented him from enjoying the sport in a less serious mode.

Barely glancing up, he could not accept the honoring palm. Adt simply turned and walked away from the field. Yaw-iyn followed at a respectable distance sensing Adt's disturbance. Neither spoke of the game again - at least not about this particular match.

* * * * * * *

The professor had taken a personal interest in his new students, Adt and Sarleni. Their mature approach to his theories inspired him to spend extra time in discussions and he soon learned about their extensive experiences abroad. This evening he offered to show them his prized possession. Yaw-iyn had been working on major innovative improvements expressly for the Kamina project. Adt and Sarleni studied the beautiful, sleek machine gleaming on the launch pad.

"My latest design," he was saying.

"It provides a definite advantage, empowering our people to optimize the skies. I've made a few nice adjustments which will soon be universally adapted to all Orbs and grav-disks."

The hangar was small and cramped with a battery of equipment, grouped around a trimly designed Orb, tanner in shade from the typical silvery glow common for most vehicles.

"The vessel's easier to mask on land, easier to obscure in the sky," he had said.

The controls were motion sensitive, with flat symbols baked into a panel below the wide viewing screen that accommodated a near one hundred eighty degree simulated panorama. They watched a demonstration of skimming across the ocean at speeds previously unimagined.

In order to demonstrate its efficiency his hand scanned over the controls, causing the scene to shift direction. The Orb jolted in accord.

"The console responds to heat emission. I've almost completed the code sequences so the two of you can control the ship if so needed."

The professor continued proudly explaining his innovations.

Not long after Yaw-iyn completed his exhibition he had to prepare for an evening lecture.

III. The Mother That Never Was

Ju-bilee smugly reveled in her element. She sat within a lofty dome, the translucent canopy of her self-designed mountain-top retreat, discreetly screened from uninvited outsiders. This place she shared with no one. Her lungs filled with pure cool air; enriching her whole being with renewed vitality. The land below was home. And she was content, radiating sheer joy from the top of the world; emitting a menagerie of pent-up tension; discharging, without constraint, unfettered kaleidoscopic sensations. She had given everything to her lifelong vocation and in the process lost valued parts of herself: the greater the gift the harsher the price.

This was her domain. From here, she could cut through barriers of time and space. She stood against the brisk night air, her copper hair dancing wildly against the starlight. The moons had run their concurrent courses in spectacular formation, not to be viewed again until the next epoch.

Her haven had been costly but she did not take time to count her losses. For here, she could abandon all restraints and express all that was Ju-bilee to the universe: her universe: her domain.

She dwelt high within the polar arc of Noomas. Most of the world discounted the Northern Territories, deeming them of little consequence. People seldom traveled to the north. Few explorers penetrated its desolate regions and even fewer had survived to recount their stories. Scattered villages clung to the sheltered coves along the treacherous coasts. Trappers tempting fate, ventured upon the tundra, recklessly wagering their feeble fortune. In scant huts clumped together among the treacherous bogs, they doggedly waited for unwary prey to stumble into the cruel snares hidden throughout these wastelands.

During the brief season of the sun the farmlands and cano-pied cottages would become magically evident to anyone who might have braved the impassable inland trek. To the observer, they appeared as common communities of simple folk much like the fringe villages found elsewhere across the planet. No one would have guessed the highly skilled professionals of Helandian society to be dwelling in these thatched hut settings. Despite incongruous oddities, Helandi ingeniously hid its vast technical network of progressive institutions beneath ice and rock.

But fewer inhabitants live along the high plains, the tree-less bleak expanse, where frozen soil and water are blasted by the wild winds of the incessant winter. Yet small pockets of Primitives manage to endure. One remote tribe had established their settlement in an ice cave chiseled out by a natural hot spring. Their small herd of Taops fed on the thick low grasses and shrubs during the short summer season. Indeed, a harsh place where only the hardiest among them survived.

Other tribes had settled along the lower coasts where the ocean slammed the shore. Craggy inlets protected small fishing and bartering communities. Foreign voyagers and privateers who braved the forsaken frontiers came to trade basic supplies and conversation. The Helandians also frequented these coves, keeping up with the local lore, collecting news of the outside world. The weather-beaten cliffs provided discreet access for hidden portals to the Helandian civilization. For the most part, these glassed-over gateways were invisible from the sky. The small rounded mounds were usually frosted in layers of ice concealing the passages to the interconnected tunnels woven throughout the Helandian glaciers.

Rumors had circulated about an advanced culture in the north. Merely rumors without evidence, drifted down to the rest of Noomas. By choice, the Helandian people remained quietly remote from most of the world.

The undisturbed focus within this studious society concentrated on explorations of ancient sentient practices. Advanced sciences thrived throughout these caverns where people applied themselves to specialized fields of creative arts, basing their efforts on the singular concept that the development of intellect is without limit. The HanJahn students were no exception.

Ju-bilee was the foremost ground-breaking explorer of the HanJahn, dedicating her life to the perfection of her mental abilities, exceeding unprecedented boundaries and surpassing all teachers; broadening vistas none had imagined were possible.

Tonight she was in her glory, communing with the cosmic energies of thousands of stars filling the heavens.

She pointed her finely tuned mental compass outwards in every direction. The stars sparkled brighter as her mind soared across the cosmos, listening, watching.

Ju-bilee could project elements of her own being to a different location, mirroring the image of her own body, or fashioning an appearance out of her own creative fantasy. She had developed this ability and over time, had learned to maneuver incredible amounts of force and matter, physically affecting and interacting with whatever she could envision.

The last major transcendence though, had nearly been self-destructive. Recovering from that battle had taken longer than she had anticipated. The clash with the Muti in the Kaminaean Castle of Doom had been dreadfully brutal and had taken its toll.

Even her richly developed powers, honed to near perfection,

were not enough to squelch the tyrannical engine fueling the Kaminaean Empire.

A shiver rippled through her. The HanJahn had felt the impact, too. Things were changing rapidly. The inner circles and pundits were scrutinizing the evolving situation in Kamina. Helandi had been preparing since the word of the lost seed had echoed among the Muti. Hope was strong, but many would lose their lives.

Ju-bilee narrowed her concentration. Her eyes opened and an air of triumph softening every nerve and muscle, lifting her mood as she regained control.

My Helandi is beautiful!

Ju-bilee closed her eyes, once more feeling the burden of her beloved planet weigh down upon her.

She allowed her acuity to radiate beyond the domicile.

Outside the wind had become a strong force raking across the fields of ice.

How I will miss the summer season; too short, she sighed.

Spring will come again, soon enough, when everything revels in its fullness.

Wrapping her cloak around her shoulders, she strode across the balcony into the glassed enclosure. Spreading the cloak across the floor she stretched out on it, humming softly to herself.

Soon she was hovering a short distance above the softly matted floor and could easily reach up to touch the transparent sphere.

Ju-bilee gracefully raised her arms above her head. Traces of flickering color trailed paths from her fingertips.

From within this meditative state she transcended time through multidimensional space, passing through portals untouchable by less discerning minds.

The world raced by, escalating as she traversed the cosmos beyond the limits of the mountain lodge, looking over the whitened lands.

Narrowing her scope to the oceans that teamed with bountiful diversity, she plunged into the frothy surf. And in that instant became a shimmering copper sea faun swimming in blissful abandon among the sea creatures.

Deeper she dove, pursuing the throbbing life force. Somewhere below she felt an odd emission that had not been evident before.

Strange.

She swam through an ocean cavern to investigate.

Impatiently attracted to exotic wonders, she eagerly searched for new discoveries; anything new. A shimmering glow radiated from an obscure crevice. An amazingly bright colony of sea life, soft-shelled bodies of a thousand creatures suddenly swept up from this deep-sea tunnel. She felt a burst of energy as they bolted towards the sea faun. A shoal of peculiar jells sped past her in a flurry of wild energy, racing towards the surface and nimbly flitting into the sky.

How had she not known of these marvels before?

Something beckoned her up, radiating the pure, joyful, life-giving source of the waters.

Energy seared through her in tandem with the sea faun emanating from the chaotic frenzy of the glittery jells.

What are these? she wondered, chasing after them.

The sea faun had reached the ocean's surface, searching dimensions accessible only through Ju-bilee's studies.

As the HanJahn taught:

If the Muti can do it, so the human can.

Her smile broadened as she remembered caustic remarks occasionally made accusing her of witchcraft or sorcery, using supernatural spells and magic. However there was no witchery, no mysterious involvement with her practices. Hers had been a lifetime of study into the scientific discoveries within the intellect, which had erroneously been accredited to the metaphysical world.

Just then her mentor appeared, uninvited, floating cross-legged.

Lady, you are enjoying yourself too much!

The thought wasn't hers; it was Moyi poking into territory where he had not been summoned. Anger laced up through her spine as she faced this meddling colleague. Determined to exercise control, she countered:

Emotions are a woman's right of passage! Fury is her fortress against unwanted voices pushing into places they don't belong.

Moyi's proverbial edicts stabbed at her with utter smugness.

Ju-bilee, calm your temper. We have pressing issues to resolve.

She shivered stiffly.

I need none of your scolding!

The man tilted his head with a partial nod and half-sardonic wink.

I come as your advisor, at your service.

She reared up, fuming.

Get out of my mind!

Moyi blinked out; at least for the moment.

His quip had held a tone of urgency she could not easily dismiss, thus imprinting a mental note to return for further study soon; and alone next time.

Reluctant to leave the deep sea discovery, the sea faun pulled in its golden fins, sinuously arched its slender torso and with a flip of its nimble tail fin darted straight down into the ocean depths, fading away as smoothly as it had first appeared. If anyone had been there to observe, they would have hardly noticed the subtle shift of this amazing creature, this changeling known as Ju-bilee.

Once again back in her lofty fortress, she must address her honored mentor despite his untimely intrusion. Ju-bilee iced a wall across her thoughts as Moyi's image flickered then radiated into stronger focus.

Anger brewed to a churning wrath.

Speak if you must.

Moyi did not make excuses.

He observed the obvious.

"Your family, your son, will be arriving soon. Prepare yourself."

She struggled to explain her position.

"You're not being fair."

Uncertainty sifted through her, teetering on the brink of impatience; off-balance: bordering on emotional vulnerability and far too human recollections.

From a distance, yes, I had watched Adt Dorta, though usually through a Muti contact, until the current uprising.

Since the major storm had rocked the planet with its cursed violence, I've supervised his quest.

Despite her determination to remain detached during his adventures with Sarleni, she had found herself increasingly involved. Ju-bilee had helped the young woman teach Adt; then prepared them both for the impending confrontation with the Muti. Hadn't she done enough in guiding and saving Adt and Sarleni? Even fighting at their side?

She felt trapped. There would be no easy escape. She must submit to a meeting with Adt in person where physical contact was unavoidable. All the reasons for her previous actions would seem shallow to him.

How would she explain her absence throughout his childhood? That, she realized, was a fair question for any son to ask.

And why had she been able to walk away from her only son, never to return to his side; never to hold him, never to offer motherly caring, motherly advice, or protection?

Ju-bilee had tried to rationalize that Kigor's fathering had been enough. His Dorta fortunes and connections were sufficient for Adt's nurturing. And with the Muti's protective interest, what need had he for motherly interference?

She had used precious time and energy to perfect the mental arts beyond those of any known methodology, expanding the HanJahn capabilities to unprecedented heights. Did it make sense to toss out vital responsibilities for the mundane role of motherhood?

Logical questions; and her son may rightfully be justified to demand answers.

Why had she denied him a mother's love?

Why had she abandoned him?

These questions had plagued her from that pivotal day on the island of Kasiisi when she had fixed a hard look upon her son. Still maintaining strict emotional distance, she had managed to observe and guide him.

Ju-bilee was keenly aware she was the mother of a fine swordsman. Startled beyond expectations, she had withdrawn and resumed her position above emotional attachment. Or so she thought.

He has taken himself a Helandian bride.

Ju-bilee shifted focus to the competent young woman. Sarleni had admirably developed his budding natural talents in a very short time.

Since the young girl's early training, Ju-bilee had watched Sarleni's progress, anticipating an important role in her future. She was completely thrown aback when the young woman proved to be a natural match for Adt. Ju-bilee had immediately insisted upon complete authority over her advanced training through the HanJahn Academy under the direct supervision of Moyi. Indirect observance secured a certain element of control.

"You've kept your distance way too long. And now you must bridge that void."

Moyi was right. It was one thing to have made contact with her son indirectly utilizing projections; it was another to meet in the flesh.

Nonetheless, she turned away from the obstinate scholar.

"He's a child consumed with young love. Madness!"

"And you know nothing of the habit?"

"I gave that up," she snapped with a shade of irony.

A lot of history had been ripped aside. She'd barricaded herself beneath her studies and shielded her well-hidden motherhood role; deliberately suppressing its primal rush of vile female chemical imbalances. All forbidden, violating biological elements were banned to cells at the back corners of her memory. And she had done so with indisputable resolution.

Moyi relentlessly persisted.

"Yes. I remember: and Kigor? You avoided him. As you did your son. Ju-bilee, you're obsessed with the Dortas."

"You smug beast!"

Ju-bilee's resentment intensified. Whipping around to face Moyi, words expelled from compressed lips.

"Go! Out! Leave!"

Moyi merely hovered, impervious to her caustic outbursts.

"Beware of your hostilities. They are daunting weapons. They are vengeful tools. They can be dangerous if you don't control them."

The woman lifted physically from the floor, rising above Moyi.

"I don't want your opinion!"

Face drawn into serious, harsh lines, Moyi bluntly chastised:

"Your ego is showing. I've watched how you examined lessons, and the delight you felt during his schooling. Your motherly respect for him did not escape me then, nor can it be concealed today. He has grown into a magnificent man. Even since the ordeal in Kamina, he's accumulated complex skills; adapted at rapid speed, to the concepts taught by the HanJahn masters. How could you not be filled with admiration?

"Take care, Ju -bilee. Let it not divert your attention when our world needs all your expertise empowered. Remember and be watchful. Do not stray from your own destiny."

She felt impudently vexed by lectures. Yet, in an odd way, knew Moyi provided truth. And he was one safe friend who could be a cushion against fevered obsessions. She must permit inner turmoil and madness to be unleashed here and now within the private safety of her beloved haven. Shatter her brittle untamed anguish and cast it into the wilderness where it can harm no one: where it cannot interfere with the precision of the critical burden of her enormous responsibilities.

And after a brief bout of anger and grieving, she was thankful to have this friend and mentor.

Admittedly, she realized, *I've been confused over memories.*

Kigor is a symbol of my youth.

Her relationship with Kigor Dorta was still unsettling. Now she was caught unprepared again, just as she had been those many years ago. Sometimes people recklessly twist together in a flurry of unquenchable hunger.

Kigor had been a remarkable lover, quickly winning her heart, with his irresistible charms. As their romance blossomed, she had pledged to partner with the dashing Dorta swordsman.

Early in the affair with Kigor, the Muti had advised her to succumb to primal instinct and become seeded with child.

Your son will have a pivotal place in the future of Noomas.

He had supported her desire to birth their son in her own homeland and he had loved her dearly.

Kigor wanted his son properly trained in the Bel-loniean tradition. She agreed to his request. That summer, Ju-bilee and Adt made their home at the Dorta Estates.

After the season of the Moons ended, the balance shifted.

Ju-bilee increasingly chafed against the confines of the city. And he, with equal urgency, needed to continue his quest for the sake of Bel-loniea. Neither was willing nor able to resolve the painful truth: the tragic incompatibility of their respective obsessions.

Her plight was destined towards the expansion of her studies. His passion for the sword had compelled him to the fighting arenas.

Both lovers were hard-driven by their enormous passions which were in direct conflict with one another. And thus Ju-bilee was compelled to make the unbearable choice and move on. The involvement with Kigor, she had told herself over the years, would never have occurred if it hadn't been for that message.

She stared at the waning moons as if seeing them anew. Kigor had entered her life during the Moons Festival a generation ago. And at the very peak of Clinsolnosn's ascent her intense rapture had sparked to insurmountable heights.

How she had loved that season.

How she had believed love would be her eternal fate.

Unrequited conflict was difficult to control. Images of Kigor cascaded in an explosion of frothy sensual waves. He was strong and highly desirable. Their fervent lovemaking overwhelmed everything: an experience never to be repeated with another man. Even now, the thought of him evoked shivers of yearning.

And the subsequent loss of Kigor was the terrible price she had paid in order to pursue her goals. Nevertheless, she had managed to dull the pain those memories brought by deliberately avoiding them.

She had never completely blotted them out. And they haunted her. Thoughts could be buried as long as he was not present. And these remembrances stayed locked away, even here, in her recluse.

She had fashioned this mountaintop haven when explorations had outgrown the confines of the academy. Only Moyi knew of its location.

Here in her solitude, serious studies had diverted attention from musings of love and physical attractions. And she had disciplined herself to live without ever being tempted into another troubling romance.

It was impossible to recall that man without stirring up feelings she wished not to acknowledge. What puzzled her most was how Kigor's charm had enticed her into an intimate involvement of irreversible magnitude; a terrible distraction. As was her son. These feelings had remained dormant until recently.

Then world wide events had exposed the aggressive threat of the Kaminaean Empire to its neighbors. And it sprawled with frightening acceleration. An impenetrable mantle had thickened over its territory to thwart all access. Even the Proctor's Mutis were alarmed when no information was forthcoming.

A confluence of Mutis had now joined the HanJahn Masters. In accordance with the current orders, Ju-bilee was compelled to actively oversee all events involving her son.

Ju-bilee, it is time!

Moyi could be a monstrous agitation with his continual goading.

She fumed at her tormentor.

I have no need to access everything connected with Dorta. My life has been focused elsewhere.

She stiffened, legs crossed, back straight. It infuriated her to be forced to admit he was right. Moyi was still her honored teacher. She often failed at masking thoughts from the man. And he was still a dear friend; always caring, with patience and abundant wisdom even when intruding into her privacy.

There was no lying to Moyi. Reluctantly she acquiesced.

So I have a son. So he's going to be here, and I have to deal with it. All of it! She felt depressive waves rush over her. *Is that your message?*

Moyi persisted, words gentle.

A beginning; soon you'll be faced with a son in the flesh; a different situation. Adt has spoken with Kigor, who told him the truth about his birth. The rest is up to you.

Rage sparked, like an erupting volcano belching out its oozing sludge.

Enough!

Ju-bilee pushed against the man's thoughts, shoving Moyi out of her territory and closing the boundaries so tightly that even he could no longer penetrate them.

Shifting thoughts toward the current conditions of global disparity, she reconnected to her actual domain, her mountain peak haven.

The universe closed in, shrinking to the natural limits of her retreat.

Avoidance, real or imagined is avoidance!

His cutting tone slashed at her.

Moyi, go home!

She grew rigid.

Stop avoiding and I'll leave!

With a defeated sigh, Ju-bilee sank to the mat.

When Moyi faded, her arms raised high, she slid up through the dome and was gone.

IV. A Brief Connection

Sarleni tried to remain light-hearted and lift Adt's spirits.

He looked trapped.

Today my clan will officially recognize their newest member. Once accepted into the brotherhood you will have easy passage throughout our sectors. Tomorrow we can begin our other duties.

She wanted to put him at ease.

Helandi is a very large nation. You'll get an idea of its capacity eventually. We have complex cities in these caverns and you probably won't see my family often once we've completed the Welcoming Rites.

He'd grown used to the fact she could infiltrate his privacy. As she claimed; it wasn't exactly an intrusion, just as natural as breathing and often useful. He had been wrapped in memory, ignoring the commotion of the clans. *I'm not prying, Adt. I want to help you understand our culture.*

Just the same, Adt was peeved. It was not so much her intrusion as it was her incessant rescheduling of his time and activities. He did not have one moment to call his own!

Sarleni stopped when she saw two familiar figures gliding into the hall.

Oh look! There's Ju-bilee and Moyi!

There was the woman who had been denied him all this time. Sane reasoning seeped from his nerves as he watched her glide to a halt a short distance away. He had encountered this woman as a ghostly projection during their travels to Kamina but had not expected to be flooded with terror, standing in her presence.

Help me! Adt meekly begged.

Sarleni sympathized with his panic and passively linked to Adt. She would support her man; not rescue him. She could do very little in the open ceremonial hall. They would have to behave at least civil, regardless. She silently encouraged him.

Fear it not, dear Adt. Your encounter was inevitable.

She gauged Ju-bilee. This was a woman whom Sarleni admired and had expected to emulate in her own search for understanding and growth. Ju-bilee was the ultimate Seeker: a formidable practitioner of the HanJahn discipline. She stood alone, as a beacon for all.

Adt watched himself detach from his body; his brain throbbed in confusion. *How must I greet this woman? What reasonable tag can I place on my torment: anger?*

Sarleni's clear coaching did not lessen the gap. *Get past the block. You are no longer a child!*

* * * * * * *

Ju-bilee rigidly fixed to one liquid goal: *Escape!*

But there was none.

Watching Adt's lean, young muscular figure striding forward was greatly disturbing. This was real life; not distant projections; not probing. This was human flesh meeting human flesh.

Ju-bilee felt a probe pelt the nape of her neck when she saw Adt.

It is time. The sage sliced across her boundary like a smooth cutting razor.

She stalled. *No, Moyi.*

Ju-bilee was not ready for the impact. Nerves turned to ice.

Better in ice than nothing at all, Moyi challenged.

She slammed a solid curtain down across his invasion, shoving him completely out.

Moyi persevered with a master's relentless crunch. *Everything around you is converging. Take hold, surrender to its beckoning and become one with the essence. Ownership is all we have. Stop running! Face your son.*

Today she must face a son in hard reality; not shielded by illusion or mirrored projections.

As Adt reticently stood with his young bride, Ju-bilee's painted smile froze into a soft hardness. She nodded, feigning false warmth

"Sarleni, I see you have safely returned home."

"I brought your son back to meet his mother!" Sarleni's response knifed right through her. The young woman's face was equally as pretentious as Ju-bilee's. "He has discovered his birthplace."

Ju-bilee calmly listened—emotionless. She was the mother who had rejected her natural role.

Adt wrestled with apprehension.

Sarleni felt his anguish and pain and the terrible conflict. *I think you both should have privacy.*

* * * * * * *

Raw, naked truth faced both son and mother.

Ju-bilee spoke first. "So, we meet at last."

The woman's opening statement set the tone, broaching an untouched chasm between them. Ju-bilee hovered before him and the world slipped into a void as if a curtain had been dropped between it and the two of them until the outside world faded, leaving them in a dimensionless space.

Their connection intensified.

Time is fractured, Ju-bilee pressed.

Adt instantly understood. Nothing had altered. Only their perception had been tainted.

Much is expected; from both of us. We need time and there is none. We must function. Our lives will depend on it.

He felt off-balance, caught in an unfamiliar web; spinning. He wanted to yield, yet could not submit. He wanted to run, yet could not budge.

Before him was the mother who never was!

The grand, mysterious, frightening Ju-bilee was equally helpless; unable to break out of the petrifying shell that held them tightly interlocked.

Hate me, if you must, Adt. Let your anger out. Don't hold back.

Once it has been released it will be depleted. No good will follow until it has spent its power over you. We have both denied the hard facts. Acceptance is all that's left to either of us.

Mother and son were locked. Static—rooted to the ground; an ocean of resistance chained between them.

Gradually they shifted, forming a slow, ebbing spiral, wrapped in wordless energy, reeling in a sea of tumultuous unrequited yearning. A fog obscured their shared thoughts, dripping mere impressions with no details.

Ju-bilee spoke softly.

"We must meet privately soon, my son."

"Of course," was all Adt could muster.

Like scripted actors, Adt and Ju-bilee closed the gap and went through the motions of embracing. A stale action of which any stage director would have demanded a retake.

* * * * * * *

Not even Moyi flinched, as mother and son once again returned to the present. Standing behind Ju-bilee, the aged master frowned; shoulders slumped. He nodded with gentle reassurance.

Ju-bilee stepped back to Moyi's side. "We survived!"

Sarleni allowed a smile to greet Adt as he reached for her hand. *Like she said, we will meet again, soon enough.*

He felt completely drained and relieved that it was over. *It was difficult for both of us. We agreed to take it by slow steps.*

She tried to soothe him. *Emotional triggers are difficult to overcome.*

His hand in hers gripped tightly. The four of them advanced as one group drifting through the crowd like a close-knit family.

Nothing could have been further from the truth.

CHAPTER SEVEN
FLESH OF THE MUTI

From the First Voice to Speak the New Truth

The lands are given unto the flesh of the Muti, for their exclusive privilege, decreed thus, in the name of their Creator.

Divine edict allots unto them dominion over all creation.

For the flesh of all is the flesh of their flesh.

To be desired is to be owned and to own is to be one with all things Divine.

The law of the Ancients ordained Divine Power unto the Muti. Hence forth, the Muti shall become one with the Creator and by order of the Creator, has the sovereign obligation to rule.

Those who seek wisdom from the Creator, remember these words:

You are, by mandate, Lords of the realm.

Yours is the duty to Rule and set forth the Law.

The greatest of Universal Truths prevails.

Supremacy expands in the hands of those who accept its diktat.

Limitless power yields its possessor limitless dominion.

And the Muti is promised all authority.

Abide by the Laws of the Great Voice so defined in doctrine.

Become one with your Creator and one with your passions.

And one with all living matter within the world.

For it is written in the Book of Great Truths,

The Muti alone shall inherit dominion over every living thing.

* * * * * * *

A tall Muti stood by the platform upon which nineteen bound and shackled members of its own family strained against the stone *Poles of Death*; their naked frames were dripping fluid; their battered bodies brutally tortured. They awaited their fate.

"We mete justice to those who fail to dispense our ordained Rights!"

The Muti mournfully raged. "Let all witness the reward for failure."

Its hands stretched open a tattered scroll, the delicate sides splitting fragments to the ground. It raised the condemning parchment.

"These are the perverse words written against our empire."

The community crowded around the platform nodding with somber anticipation.

"Glory in their pain as I speak. Let it become the sustaining anthem of joy for all who witness their demise."

The Muti's gnarled hand lifted the scroll up, lips curled back. Jagged teeth snapped together, grinding in contempt. It waved the document like a ravaged flag.

"These lies are raw seeds of destruction."

The Muti bellowed its command. "Light the flame!"

A dozen torches flared up, lighting the plaza.

"This proclamation *itself* is their damnation!"

Its head snapped to the pathetic Mutis chained tightly to thick posts; stripped of all dignity. The prisoners' stick legs were bowed under their thick rounded torsos. Its arm flashed down causing the scroll to flap wildly and more bits littering the ground.

"Listen to the lies they advocated!"

It opened the scroll and began reading:

'For God has no beginning and no end.
'Life sprang from its benevolent might, and filled the heavens.
'We are vessels pouring forth the infinite glory of God.
'God is the Universe and the Universe is God.
'Our journey begins and lives within its boundaries.
'And when our journey ends, we will still remain with the eternal
    God.
'For each vessel shall be cast anew among the stars from which
    it burst.

—So speaks the Eemel.'

It hissed air from its lungs.

"Lies: all lies!

"These poisonous words ignore the promise of the Muti."

With a flourish, splintering another chunk of the scroll, it read on.

'Denying, doubting, or believing
'Does not invalidate what was, what is and what will be.
'Trust your innate spirits.
'And question whatever is told to you.
'For to think is your choice; to learn is your privilege.
'Know that we are products of the ever-expanding universe.
'Therefore open your minds and honor your source.
'For truth is our heritage in life itself.
'And no shadow shall fall across our destiny,
'No matter from whence opposition may arise.
'Thus the purpose of mankind is declared,

—By Muda, the God of Haldolen'.

The Muti stopped, dramatically gazing at its mesmerized audience.

"These fools who are condemned to die reject *the New Truths.* They deny *Muti Divinity* over all of Noomas."

The Muti stalked up the raised platform to the quivering condemned victims and shook the scripts of evidence in their faces as it accused them of each malicious crime.

'Disobedience against the venerable Muti Law:
'Corrupting the masses with blasphemy:
'Proselytizing the innocent masses:
'Direct assault against our sacred temples:
'Bearing false witness—"Lies upon despicable Lies:
'They speak of false prophecies."
'Hope will be sent from the stars. And a warrior will come to crush our Holy Prophet.'

"These perverted imbeciles claim a rebellion will rise against our supremacy; and humans will dominate. A new evolution of man is in the making destined to surpass the Muti: the ravings of madness!"

The Muti howled on.

"Lies, distorted sick lies! The damage done by these deceitful heretics is unforgivable.

"Remember the sovereign *Law*. The supremacy of the Muti! For the promise mandates our absolute authority over all Noomas."

The Muti's fingers gripped the offending scroll, twisting the scroll back and forth in utter hatred; collecting what was left of the shredded portions, crumbling them into dust, scattering it to the ground. What hadn't piled to its feet crunched between its gnarled fingers. Shaking its hands, arms reaching up, it shouted.

"Ignite the pyres! Witness the fate of those who defy the *True Prophet*!"

Fires exploded around the tethered Mutis. Screams of tortured anguish roared over the cruel jeering of the onlookers. Hungry flames were already consuming skin and muscle and whitening bone.

The speaker glared at the crowd around the platform.

"Go! And serve the *'First Voice to Speak the New Truth'*!"

And the Muti audience dispersed.

CHAPTER EIGHT
PERT CORT

I. The Delegation

Qui Shan paced angrily back and forth, shouting orders to the officers who had hurriedly crammed into the back of the assembly station at security headquarters. As commander of Belloniean Armed Forces, Air, Sea, and Ground, he was compelled to get these messages across to his senior staff before leaving Bel-loniea. The room filled with a cross-section of nationals from diverse cultures, co-mingling and busily conversing in small groups, comparing statistics; polishing their presentations for the staff meeting. All were competent, seasoned leaders from their respective regions. Though they had often warred in the past, they now were civilly setting aside their differences. The Armada promised to be a complex force under Qui Shan's command. He was unanimously acknowledged as the man in charge.

Their overall agenda made steady progress, yet some areas remained problematic, needing prompt attention. Updates coming in from the plains reported delays among the troops beyond the Great Sea. Not everything was running smoothly. For, the creation of an international military force was challenging, at best. They expected further issues due to the already strained obstacles among clans and smaller tribes. The larger nations, fortunately, were readily willing to join the Armada. Even the Diano contingent had proven to be cooperative, considering they had recently lost the war against Bel-loniea.

Stepping forward, Qui Shan took a silent breath and began his opening statement.

"We are all newly acquainted with the Helandian culture and its technical advances; and through their excellent emissaries we have been exposed to the effectiveness of these systems and training methods.

"I am pleased to report; the majority of the mainland troops is nearly integrated and will soon be ready for mobilization. By the authority of Proctor Romos, you have all been selected to participate in the joint summit in Helandi. I expect utmost courtesy and respect amongst you, and towards our hosts; whatever differences may arise. We have been granted an inspection tour following the conference. It is geared to familiarize all of you with the technical equipment especially specifically by their engineers to support the Armada.

"Let us begin!"

Shortly after he had dismissed his staff, a memo arrived via a courier from the palace.

Request a meeting with you as soon as possible.
Youi Hannis, Proctoress of Bel-loniea.

The curt formality of the note was, in effect, a command to come directly to her office at the bureau of state affairs.

He obligingly complied.

After a short, formal greeting, Youi got straight to the point.

"I will join you for the Helandi conference."

Qui Shan replied without hesitation.

"Your request is quite impossible! The Proctor would—"

"Grand-father will agree to my decision. You can grant me a position on your staff."

"The dangers are far too obvious to list here."

There was a disturbance in the doorway as Andon Janis entered the room. The old man smiled, features wrinkling.

"Even if the Proctor disagrees, she can twist him to her will."

"Andon, surely you understand my objections."

"Understand. Yes. But she *will* be with you, and if you cannot assure her safety, nothing on Noomas can."

"It isn't a request!" Youi asserted.

Andon shrugged as if helpless.

"She commands; we act."

"If it must be," Qui Shan spread his hands wide.

"I suppose you may qualify as...as a...consultant, representing the Proctor's family."

The title sounded reasonable enough.

"Thank you, Qui," she soothed, stepping forward and touching his shoulder.

Andon chuckled.

"You will find her a vigorous addition to your staff."

"When do we leave?" she asked. "I am anxious to become acquainted with Helandi and do my part in support of the Armada."

"I understand. Tomorrow morning. Early."

"I'll be ready."

Her royal dismissal needed no further discussion.

Quite frustrated by this new responsibility concerning the Proctoress, Qui Shan returned to his offices to set into motion the orders to guard the Proctor's granddaughter. During any uprising, the royal family required protection against any potential hostage situation. Her request, though noble, complicated security arrangements.

Issues involving the royal family could not be ignored and this demand would be among them.

Still no word came from Torlo Hannis, or from any of the spy missions. And as a result, the Proctor had recently restricted all future missions.

The latest orders signed by Proctor Romos, prompted all commanding officers to place their units on full alert. The increased urgency of the Armada's activation had spurred immediate arrangements for the summit in Helandi.

Just as Qui finished his memo to the Chief of Security, Kigor

Dorta stepped into the office, unannounced; with Ju-bilee.

"I understand we have a royal presence joining us. I heard Andon tell the Proctor of her decision. He was furious.

Qui Shan rolled his eyes, grumbling about complications involving royal security, obviously impatient with the whole topic.

"And *I'm* personally responsible for *Youi's* safety!"

Kigor nodded. "I'll set her up with a body guard."

Qui Shan rose stiffly and walked across the room to a side bar, pulled out a tray, and noisily placed three goblets on it. Grabbing a flask he carried them back to the table and growled hoarsely. "Shall we continue over a glass of Porshi?"

As Qui Shan poured the amber liquor into the glasses he recapped his conversation with Youi.

"Complex challenges still face all of us. My team has been working day and night organizing the varying cultures into a proficiently functioning military force and that is my primary concern. I don't easily accept extracurricular political diversions, particularly involving royalty.

"The Proctoress is a major responsibility. And the two of us, Kigor, are directly accountable to Proctor Romos! I would not be overly cautious about the Proctoress."

Kigor thoughtfully sipped the smooth elixir. "I'm certain the situation is manageable."

The General tossed down his drink in one gulp. "I'm annoyed, to be truthful. She was resolute on going."

"I promise you," Ju-bilee insisted, "the royal lady will be safe."

Qui looked doubtfully at Ju-bilee. "How can you be so sure?"

Kigor answered the General for her. "Ju-bilee is aware of elements far beyond our scope of understanding. Do not underestimate the Helandi."

The statement was meant to bring an end to further debate. Qui had known about Ju-bilee's alleged wizardry; which further fueled the General's annoyance. He found the woman intolerably over-bearing. "Proctoress Youi is royalty and therefore a political target. I hope you understand."

"We of Helandi are quite capable of providing excellent security," Ju-bilee brazenly retorted. "And officially, we are not yet at war."

"The situation will soon be altered," he pointed out. "She'll require *complete* protection."

"Do you think women are helpless? Do *not* forget the HanJahn, and my personal influence." Ju-bilee tossed her head back, hair cascading in flaming waves, accentuating her haughty arrogance.

Their heated argument was abruptly halted when the office door flung open and a Muti marched into the room.

"Your travels north are imminent. The unexpected is a certainty. Complexities insinuate the Proctoress. Turbid hues foil purpose. Links are multiple. Prepare!"

The Muti left the office as swiftly as it had appeared.

As soon as the door slammed shut, Ju-bilee stood and calmly spoke with a respectful tone.

"General, I understand your concerns about these dangerous times. I have no doubt that the Proctoress will be safe with you and the Helandian forces there to protect her from harm."

She too, left the room. Kigor, with a penitent bow, followed the woman. And the General returned to the heavy tasks ahead of him.

* * * * * * *

Early the next morning Qui Shan arrived at the hover pad, a short distance from the palace gardens where Youi, Pert Cort and other members of the delegation assembled. Foregoing any official ceremony, the traveling party entered the Helandi craft. Andon Janis and Proctor Romos bid them safe journey.

Once everybody had obtained comfortable seating in the passenger compartment, the Orb sprang to life. Without a sound, it lifted.

The view through the wide screen was so realistic that it felt as if they were in open air. The only missing component was the icy chilling wind—an amazing illusion. Qui Shan took note of the ship's remarkable demonstration.

He could already feel the craft stabilize. Its engines were obviously upgraded. By tracking the passing clouds he estimated the ship's rapid speed. There was no comparison in any way to the standard grav-disks popular in his part of the world.

Ju-bilee, sitting next to the General, listed some of the craft's specifications and then stated: "This model will be replicated for our forces. The interior of this particular ship is equipped to support two dozen full regiments. It has also been readied with sufficient equipment to manage an Armada of any size."

"Quite excellent." he confirmed.

Bel-loniea shrank in the distance replaced by a curving landscape. The ship shot higher through cloud banks, heading northward.

"Qui Shan, I would be pleased to take you on an inspection to examine all its operational features." Ju-bilee had released her harness and stepped away from the passenger aisle. "Let me show you the rest of our ship."

Qui Shan attempted to listen to her lecturing voice as she took them through the different sections of the Orb. The words meandered for he was already measuring necessary tactical notes in his head. He couldn't help sizing up the maneuverability of this craft in relation to the most advanced grav-disks.

Before he knew it, Ju-bilee had brought them back to the control room.

"I hope you found the tour satisfying, even if you were, perhaps, diverted by other things. Many, I would imagine."

The Helandian had assessed him correctly despite his attempt to appear interested in her tour. She had pulled out a pack of documents from a cubicle and handed them to him.

"General, at your leisure, I'm sure you will want to intimately familiarize yourself with your command ship."

She spoke with a tinge of arrogance he found annoying. The General sighed to himself and decided to ignore the woman. He was tired and expected to enjoy a lengthy rest period. Settling back into the comfortable seated, he shut his eyes, listening to the gentle whirring of the Orb's engines as they flew smoothly towards their destination. But he was mildly disappointed when his pleasant nap was interrupted earlier than expected.

"We will be in Helandi soon."

"Take these blueprints. You'll find them useful because your flagship will have a similar layout."

Her comment was edged with a mixture of respect and distant superiority, as if the woman was resistant to the protocol expected by a man in his position.

After a few moments, Ju-bilee added: "Of course, any modifications you might want to make will be seriously weighed."

Now it felt as if he were mentally transparent to the woman. And he highly resented the intrusive feeling.

Surely, she didn't read his mind! He groaned to himself.

This woman is going to be impossible.

II. Guarding the Proctoress

Pert Cort's lean frame moved like a shadow next to the Proctoress. His job was to make certain nothing happened to Torlo Hannis' royal wife. The assignment was both a position of honor and one of critical importance.

Proctoress Youi had always been Pert Cort's favorite assignment.

When Youi Janis had traveled as emissary for the Joint Relief Project he'd eliminated more assassination attempts against the Proctoress than he cared to remember. He'd not had personal guard duty since Youi and Torlo had returned from the Raiders' territory.

During that period Pert had been working with the commissioners after the Diano War. More recently, he'd commanded the International Military Troops Division. The combined military forces, composed of diverse cultures which had fought as enemies in the past, were rife with challenging episodes. So, in comparison to the rugged nature of such quarrelsome troops, this trip to the Northern Territories of Helandi was a pleasant diversion though his services as body guard seemed excessive. Youi was in competent company, traveling among the most powerful officers of the nation, with Kigor Dorta and Qui Shan, both on board.

Pert Cort knew the General had previously insisted on scheduling a parley with the Helandian officials before the finalization of the Armada project. There still were strong voices of resistance. And his strategy required substantial support which encompassed conflicting societal dynamics. Nonetheless, he had convinced key officials about the superior efficiency of the Helandian technology.

Yet there had been little progress at the Gapa Sea, despite extensive efforts by the Bel-loniean counsels. The Walinal and Kulaina cultures stuck in their archaic customs, threatened to withdraw completely from the coalition if the Helandians continued to insist on women piloting the war ships. Their strong patriarchal societies considered it intolerable to breach a cultural bias against female leaders. The Armada had not yet reached single-minded military solidarity.

Pert did not envy Qui Shan's difficulty with these nations. He churned over these impending issues as the Orb moved effortlessly through the atmosphere high above Noomas. He'd been impressed with Ju-bilee's tour of the controls and engine room and astounded at the brilliant craftsmanship of this magnificent flying machine so expertly designed by the Helandian engineers. Soon the Orb was making its descent, sliding silently through a gaping slot in the icecap. The hatch opening to receive their Orb, was wide enough to allow half a dozen of these marvelous vessels to lift off at once.

As they stepped from the ship, the hatch above the Orb slid shut, forming a seamless crystallized canopy. A soft blue luminescence filtered throughout the landing bay.

"You will enjoy our country." BerJahn, the official from the

HanJahn Academy said, ushering them past the flanks of Orbs packed in neat rows.

"Helandi is equipped and ready to roll once central command gives the order, as you will soon see for yourself."

The counselor's name was no accident, for he was a direct descendant of Master HanJahn himself.

"You are reviewing the front lines on the upper deck. Below us, four equally equipped bunkers house the flank ships.

"The charts and plans are available to you at headquarters where we will be discussing the joint command strategies. That, of course, will be after you've settled in and enjoyed a few refreshments."

Ju-bilee took over, leading their team down a corridor to a compact ice skimmer in the transport terminal. The narrow self-contained cars floated slightly above the track, carrying a dozen passengers in two rows of seats lining either side of the craft.

Pert joined Youi in the skimmer and soon they were gliding through ice tunnels, passed amazing communities adorned with exquisitely sculpted foliage surrounding unusually designed buildings. They came to a stop within a spacious terminal where several handsomely uniformed Helandians greeted them.

"You will be meeting the technical advisors at the twenty first sector assembly hall."

Ju-bilee was focused mainly toward Kigor Dorta. "We'll go into conference, once you've refreshed at our guest quarters."

* * * * * * *

When Pert and the Proctoress entered their compartment, the Helandian guide gave them a tour of their accommodations before taking leave, promising to return to escort them to the afternoon conference.

Pert and Youi explored the suite, including a comfortable lobby; finding it extraordinarily cozy. Warmth was evident, even within the walls of ice. No chill reached into these spaces.

Alone with the Proctoress, he relaxed; at ease to serve as both guard and companion to this royal lady.

Youi, too, had dropped her formal façade. They located the refreshments, spreading an assortment on the low table near the settees. Youi propped her feet on the foot rest. "I'm so glad you accepted this assignment."

"I could hardly refuse." he said, sipping hot Ka.

She mused. "Did you notice how serene the Helandians are? I mean, they can be intensely serious, but with a calm overtone, except for Kigor's red-headed friend."

"Do you mean Ju-bilee? Rumor has it when she wants something, nobody will object."

"She seems quite unreasonably hostile towards authority."

"Including a Proctoress?" he teased lightly. "Besides, I don't think the woman likes me, either."

"Perhaps she just disapproves of most people," Youi supposed.

"I noted *your* annoyance."

"Yes. You're right. Power dislikes power." She frowned. "I realize she is not comfortable taking orders from anyone. In fact only Kigor seems to have persuasive influence on her. They were lovers, you know."

"Oh?" Pert had heard the rumors but did not care to gossip without personal evidence.

"Pert?" She said, nearly too softly to be heard.

He looked puzzled, leaning closer to hear.

"What is it?" he asked.

"Can you keep a secret—I mean, a real secret? Nobody can find out."

She was visibly trembling, her eyes misted over as she spoke.

"Yes, of course, Youi. What's wrong?" He took her hand.

"Pert. My news is so wonderful and terrible. You see...Torlo and I...we are going to have a child. A new member to the royal family will be born. Tell no one.

"In the midst of great tragedy our entire realm would be in danger if the word got out. Please understand how important this is to all of us.

"And why I had to come to Helandi. I need to make certain nothing—absolutely nothing—happens to this child."

A knock at the door ended their conversation.

Young Helandian officers had arrived to escort them to the conference.

* * * * * * *

The Helandian hall barely held a long table crammed tightly with Ju-bilee, Kigor, Qui Shan and the other officers of the mainland forces.

The Admiral of the Helandian Fleet, a stately man and spokesman for the Helandian forces, was first to take the floor.

"We have looked forward to joining with your forces. Alone, we could not hope to quell the advancing dangers, but together, our combined strengths and wisdom will provide a solid foundation. We need full cooperation from our allies before we're equipped to face the perils before us. You are about to learn our plans using the technical advances implemented during our present preparations for the coming confrontation."

As the admiral introduced the officials, Pert and the Proctoress took their seats along with BerJahn, Moyi and others from the HanJahn council.

The Helandian forces had been prepared for the Armada long before Bel-loniea had gotten involved.

Their development of flight engines far surpassed the expectations of the Bel-lonieans. The officers discussed strategic planning at length. And later, the Admiral led the group to a larger assembly hall where they were joined by a technical team for detailed demonstrations of the weaponry and equipment. Qui Shan had been briefed on the HanJahn training practices and now they all had the opportunity to study these techniques with their engineers.

The information uncovered by the Messenger Talni's report as translated by the Janis Foundation, was one of their primary points of study. The Commanders of both Helandi and

Bel-loniea assessed the enormity of the situation, drawing up plans in unison with extraordinary agreement. Officers divided their respective responsibilities, each marking their command posts on the working charts spread upon the long table.

Over the next several meetings they solidified sequential plans of action, and when they came to the final points, everyone consented to launching the Armada towards the troubled continent for the welfare of all mankind. The alternative was unmitigated warfare; something everybody wished to prevent. A swift and overwhelming assault was the only solution, if they hoped to circumvent war.

Closed-door meetings followed with volumes of fresh material being thrust upon them. Soon even the most hesitant members of the visiting team were immersed in the complications of this adversity. Resistance against the coming conflict began to melt away. And war plans became top priority. The Armada was nearly functional, thanks to the Helandian's advanced technology.

Proctoress Youi was actively engaged in the planning with Pert Cort continually at her side. Kigor Dorta and Qui Shan often diverged to other parts of the city conducting vital military inspections, and visiting research labs where scientific advancements were aiding the war effort. The Helandians strongly leaned towards the advancement of sophisticated projects across a wide range of human understanding. And the new Orbs were a stark example of Helandian innovation.

Pert had joined a heated debate concerning the translations from the Janis Foundation.

"The Mutis have spoken of a disruptive component coming to our world. Talni's report held detailed descriptions predicting a potent figurehead coming from the stars. They considered this event a threat to their rule. And it has caused them to accelerate their expansion and ultimate conquest of the planet."

Ju-bilee drew attention to an evident fact.

"Your Torlo Hannis fits the description of the legendary intruder from beyond our heavens. His presence could surely be used to our advantage."

Youi was coldly detached and said nothing. Her strained face worried him deeply.

Pert knew she harbored a strong dislike for Ju-bilee and her callous remark about using Torlo as if he were some unfeeling object certainly would have aggravated Youi even further.

The talks continued for hours, covering additional material from the Messenger's documents.

Between briefings Pert and Youi frequented a quiet bistro near their guest quarters. Occasionally Kigor or Qui Shan would join them. And on this day both did. The inn occupied one corner of a quiet residential lane; windows trimmed with hanging vines, emulating a lush natural woodland complete with gently cooing evening Whiffers, so familiar in his homeland. Pert was beginning to enjoy this place.

This particular evening the General, somewhat tense and tired sampled various spiced cocktails, recommended by the bistro's customers for their potent flair. He exposed gruff humor under their influence.

"Helandians are peculiar: fair at sport, clever at quandaries, congenially intelligent, egotistically modest. We've had rare differences, solved good-naturedly. Our teams cooperate splendidly, generally speaking."

A rousing chorus tagged his flattering speech.

"*Generally* speaking! Ha!"

The whole tavern broke into joviality over Qui Shan's self-made joke, the General laughing loudest of all. He ordered the bartender to pour drinks all around, taking another double for himself. Loosened tongues told quips and bits of gossip here and there. People were relaxing, less formal and a tad careless.

Youi confided her mixed feelings towards Helandian authority, though she did not mention the HanJahn specifically.

However, the General was not so tactful when he said, "The woman Ju-bilee is annoying."

Kigor reared up like Korda braced to pounce on a challenger at its lair.

He stoically responded. "She's a prominent voice."

"Influential or not," Qui Shan blurted, "She is abrasive."

Youi's eyes brightened to the exchange.

The cocktail was affecting the General's mood and words.

The Proctoress intervened.

"We can deal...be careful, General Shan. You are speaking of a woman favored by both my grandfather, the Proctor, and by our friend Dorta here."

Kigor had stood; his hand frozen near the hilt of his sword.

Pert did not miss the implications of the tension, nor was he ignorant to the relationships involved. Certainly Qui Shan was not uninformed.

"My good General," Kigor tensely managed. "We wish to honor our hosts."

"I suppose," he sighed, adding contritely. "She is a Korda to swallow!"

"Don't I know." the sword master admitted.

"And," the General continued boldly. "The woman is rather a flash, with that flaming long hair flowing. She acts superior to us all. But I forget myself. There's been a good deal of talk and—"

Kigor glared the man to silence.

"Rumors are best left unspoken within the air around my ears. And they can reach far, I warn you."

Pert had never seen sparks flare up between these two officers before.

The General's face softened. "All in good humor, dear friend; I didn't intend insults. She's a robust woman and certainly one powerful lady. Here on out, as noted, my lips serve to honor your wishes."

The silence weighed heavily on them all.

Qui Shan rose to his feet. "I should return to my duties."

When he was gone, Kigor muttered, "he's a pompous man; but respectable."

"He will honor his words to you," Youi assured.

Kigor repressed any further remarks. "I understand."

The officer's voice carried a hint of embarrassment, as if the scene had exposed some deep intimacy.

"Actually," Kigor reflected, "What angered me most was the probability that he could be right.

"Ju-bilee, despite her exemplary qualities, has always been the cutting beak of a Kuknal to handle. She seems to keep a thousand swords aimed at my heart all at once. Even *my* blade has its limits."

He glanced at Youi; then sighed with tired resignation, "we have pressing matters to attend. Shall we call it a night?"

The next few days sped by in a whirlwind of scheduled meetings. Unified agreements among the representatives were drawn up, solidifying detailed strategies for launching the Armada.

The Helandians had never participated in the mainland wars. This was different due to the global threat incited by the Empire of Kamina.

The joint commanders proposed HanJahn Teams to spearhead the opening salvo, and nobody objected.

III. Disappearance

Near the end of the Helandian visit, Pert and Youi decided to review the new material over a hot meal in one of the gardened inns.

They were settling a complex sequence they'd recently learned regarding survival techniques when the Proctoress shifted impatiently in her seat.

"Pert, I've been thinking over the prophecy issue. Primitive cultures and their gods do not move you but it is quite possible that this entire conflict is based on legendary myth.

"Our Mutis have given us hints of the future and tales of the past and we've accepted them without question. They've been so cryptic. I never considered them necessarily prophetic."

She expounded her views on Mutis and theology while he quietly listened. Finally she came to the point.

"Ju-bilee's reference to Torlo disturbed me. That day when she implied...." She broke off for a moment, never finishing her statement.

"Mutis claim a great danger is coming to Kamina from beyond the stars. The woman was so adamant about fixing the design on Torlo Hannis. What do you think?"

"I think there could be danger for Torlo unless he leads a successful campaign."

Youi shook her head, from side to side and stopped speaking.

"Perhaps," Youi's voice was soft, as if speaking to herself. "Maybe I'm being foolish. Pert, I'm terribly worried!"

The Proctoress was a complex woman in a special position for their nation. She was not immune to the vulnerability of a woman in love.

He gently spoke. "Torlo is quite able to look after himself."

"Yes, under normal circumstances. If this were an ordinary war, he would do well. But the Helandians are perfecting a different level of power, central to the coming conflict."

"We are all at risk. The whole world is in danger of conquest by these perverse Mutis." Pert replied.

"I don't like thinking Torlo Hannis came here for the purpose of dying at their hands," the Proctoress lamented. "Torlo is a mighty warrior. I am proud of him and expect his leadership to guide our nations to victory."

Youi had stiffened her tone and now spoke as Proctoress; not as the woman. And the stark contrast was evident.

Just then two uniformed guards approached their table.

Youi studied them with royal disinterest. "Yes?"

Pert had learned, long ago, the Proctoress could easily intimidate people. It was her masterful technique.

The guards, though, were undaunted. They appeared sternly purposeful. Tight-fitted uniforms, sword, knife and Kay-guns branded them as officials; not ordinary escorts.

"The Proctoress is requested," the taller man said.

He was an officer, marked by the bright ribbons on his chest.

"By whom?" Pert formally demanded.

"I'm commander of the Helandian Citizen's Guard." The officer saluted crisply.

"Undoubtedly, but who has summoned the Proctoress of Bel-loniea?" Pert repeated his question.

"Mistress Ju-bilee." was the terse response. "She will come with us."

Youi stood, assertively. "Pert, you will join us."

As he came to his feet, the Helandian guards stepped between him and the Proctoress.

"You are *not* required," the Commander firmly responded.

"He comes with me!" Youi snapped with harsh authority.

"Mistress Ju-bilee was specific. Bring *only* the Proctoress," the Commander stiffly held his authoritative ground.

Pert automatically reached for his sword.

The Proctoress' head shook just enough to stop him. Her words were measurably direct. "We are guests here, Pert. I intend to comply."

The two guards flanked Youi. The Commander smiled condescendingly at Pert. "It would be profitable for you to seek The Hall of Garmad. Ask for Lady Tilano. Say to her: *New World Seekers consent.*"

Youi gracefully complied as she was led away.

Pert Cort glanced at his meal, which was now cold. It did not matter because his appetite was gone.

A small man stepped up to the table. "Please follow me, sir."

Pert was taken via tunnel skimmers to the surface where they boarded a ferry. A bitter cold wintry squall drove the vessel through churning waves towards a barren island off the coast of Helandi.

The Hall of Garmad was in a small lagoon past a desolate village, marked by a few scattered trappers' huts. The man hustled him past the market stalls towards the hall. At the next corner, the frosted side lane bustled with travelers of varied races mingling in town; more diverse than might be considered the norm. He thought it possible these oddities could even be human mutations; but could only guess at what might have caused their evolution.

When they were out of sight from the village, he pointed at a quaint roadhouse. "You are expected here."

Then his Helandian guide turned and left; quite unnerving and mysterious. Pert found it difficult to shake off the eerie disquiet. The building was colorful, the front smoothly painted, depicting a forest scene with a door set between two stone pillars shaped as trees.

Stepping through the entrance he was astounded to be facing a lovely garden. There appeared to be no walls. The illusion was stunning. Sweetly scented air tantalized him. Obviously a light narcotic mist filtered into rooms inspiring intimate moods and erotic desires.

A cloaked woman sat behind a counter, camouflaged by richly blooming flora.

"I seek a Lady Tilano. *New World Seekers consent.*"

"I'll be right back," she said, slipping through the ferns.

He waited, watching the sensual couples languidly mingling. When she didn't return, he lost track of time. The rest was dreamlike; vague as a nightmare evaporating upon waking. Obviously he'd been drugged.

Eventually he found himself entering the quarters assigned him and Youi. The door to the Proctoress' room was closed.

She's probably sleeping, he thought.

His head throbbed and he went into his room, collapsing on the bed. How long he lay there, unconscious, he wasn't quite sure. He woke midway through a dream of being tangled in the warm passionate embrace of a woman's body. That faded and he sat up, decidedly nauseous.

A quick inspection of the rooms confirmed the Proctoress was not there. Had she not returned from whatever meeting she had been escorted to the evening before?

He was pouring a morning cup of Ka when Kigor Dorta arrived.

"Is the Proctoress ready?"

"Isn't she still with Mistress Ju-bilee?"

Kigor frowned. "What are you talking about?"

When Pert explained about the uncivil Helandian guards and how she had been requested by Ju-bilee, Kigor went rigid.

"I have personal reasons to believe that such a meeting never occurred."

He forcefully grabbed Pert.

"Come! You have been duped!

CHAPTER NINE
THE RAIDERS

I. Failed Pursuit

From: the official files on the mission of Kal-Nor

The evening didn't bring Mahzit back to his sleeping mat; nor did the morning. We debated over the best action. My scouts searched the outer cliffs looking for any other possible access to the tunnels while the rest of us lit torches and combed the cavern where Mahzit had been the night before.

* * * * * * *

Kal-Nor was sitting, hands clutching the journal he normally kept tucked in his pouch. He needed to write personal notes. In a diary one could write anything. A military report required disciplined observations and directives, nothing personal, only data.

Shaking his head, the Commander tried to clear the murky thoughts threatening to confuse sound reasoning. Distractions caused him deep frustration.

It was a mistake allowing Mahzit to explore the cave alone, because the young officer was key to this mission.

Helandians are peculiar! He concluded, thinking over the nature of the ice dwellers. *Highly irregular!*

Frustrated and chagrined, the Commander got up and strode a few paces away from the camp. He needed space to think. He made some quick notes in his personal journal.

The caves were alien to my natural instincts and placed me at a disadvantage. I relied strongly on the pilot. We have lost Mahzit, a vital member of our team and must continue on without him.

As for Officer Linia: she displays remarkable discernment. Admire her guts—interesting woman. Despite obvious differences of ethnic qualities, she will be challenged heavily on this mission. My men still resist her rank which immediately was elevated to second in command after Officer Mahzit disappeared.

Slipping his journal back in its pouch, the Commander rejoined his men. He would write the official report later, after speaking with the pilot so that he could learn what she knew about the northern culture and Mahzit, in particular.

He then requested that Officer Linia meet with him for a chat. The woman had a disturbing affect upon him. Her graceful stride was far too enjoyable to watch, awakening his youthful instincts; feelings of an anxious young cadet. But he was not a boy. Kal-Nor was a seasoned officer; not a juvenile panting after some alluring vamp.

Yet he could not deny his raw, natural male attraction for a very beautiful female. Any man would find her desirable. He wondered how the soft texture of her flesh would feel against his finger tips. Alone together at some Pleasure Palace he would have made advances.

After all, he reminded himself, *she's an officer under my command: untouchable. This sort of musing is not appropriate, even if quite natural.*

Internal thoughts are private property, and in a way he enjoyed the gratification brought on by his imagination. As long as it didn't go beyond wild fantasy, it was innocent enough.

A wave of embarrassment flushed up his neck when she drew near, as if these reflections had been nakedly exposed.

"Sir, reporting as requested," she said, smiling almost too brightly.

Surely, she couldn't read my mind!

"Sit." His invitation was clearly lacking grace.

As she did so, he could not help noticing how the shadows framed her delicate face. And for a lingering moment he just stared at her.

Kal-Nor pretended to look for something when her eyes met his. Any distraction would be a welcome relief.

He impatiently grabbed a stone and tossed it into the desert. The act managed to clear his head enough to focus on the serious issues at hand.

Cautiously, he began asking the difficult questions.

"What can you tell me about Officer Mahzit?"

"Not much. We'd just met. In fact, the two of you had spent more time together." Her generous smile brightened in the semi-darkness.

"I heard all about your JaJa banter from one of the men."

"Oh, yes, a funny Kordatic twist," he admitted, beginning to feel less distracted. "I assume your Helandian heritage would perhaps shed some light on his whereabouts."

She shook her head. "Helandians take responsibilities seriously. He had dedicated himself to the warrior's code if that's what you are saying, sir."

He hesitated, uncertain how to approach the next point.

"Yes, yes. But I understand so little about your people or your culture. I've heard rumors—mystifying slivers about mind powers."

Her body arched as if a rod had been shoved down her spine. "What exactly do you want to know?"

He had no idea why she'd become so angered at his inquiry. As commander he had every right to question his staff. He felt defensive. "Just tell what you can!"

She seemed brusque with her next reply.

"I can pick up the energies from every single warrior in this unit, except one: Mahzit."

Her honest statement met his needs, for the time being. She had utilized her specialized abilities, confirming a startling fact.

Mutis read minds; humans weren't known to carry that trait. A few, he realized, did claim to do just that. He had never believed it to be a real possibility, until now.

She smiled mysteriously.

He had no intention of asking the obvious; she'd admitted to it. He felt stripped naked, mentally exposed.

Just how much could she pry into my private world?

Linia had answered respectfully to her superior officer, but resented Kal-Nor's questions about Helandian Mind Powers. She felt constrained by his lack of understanding, thus, restricted from effectively making use of her trained abilities. The temptation was great to leave unspoken issues right there.

Military protocol be damned! She thought to herself, impatiently.

An element of amazement in his eyes mixed with raw embarrassment softened her attitude.

He actually believes I can read his mind! She realized. *I could so easily undermine his confidence.*

However, her integrity as his first officer drew her to compassion and she truly wanted him to trust and understand her concerns.

"It isn't like listening in on somebody's self talk inside their head. We train and develop an intuitive mode on a refined frequency. All matter emits various energy patterns that can be detected by a well-tuned intellect. The HanJahn studies teach us how to hone in and be aware of the world around us through those energy fields."

That was vague enough for him and not totally distorting of the truth.

"You certainly have made judgments based on your *personal* intuition or perhaps moved by a certain mood. I suppose everybody has a fair amount of natural instinct. Most cultures teach the young to ignore this from an early age."

Linia basically disliked being deceptive. *At least I'm telling half the truth, just not being completely transparent,* she consoled herself, but she still felt inadequately equipped since

Mahzit had disappeared. *Any advanced HanJahn Master would have been able to locate Mahzit by now: dead or alive.*

"Like I said," she reiterated. "I mentally searched for any signs of Officer Mahzit but I got absolutely nothing. It is as if he had left Noomas entirely."

For Officer Linia events whirled like a lost wind in the desert. As pilot she had been thoroughly briefed about the mission. Her knowledge and experience were sufficient qualifications to promote her to leadership as second officer under Kal-Nor. But with Mahzit absent she felt uneasy about the assignment.

This brash lot of wilderness warriors, flashy and self-assured, savored a passionate love for open spaces. Their mixed bag of specialties held a common thread of dedication to duty. Rowdy at play and clannishly indifferent to outsiders, they were intent only on completing the mission.

Their resilient leader dealt evenhandedly with those under his command. Linea tuned into his spirit of fairness and carefully restrained unwarranted judgment against their ideas. She made every effort to stay alert and avoid harboring prejudice towards the desert clans' blunt male dominated culture.

The next morning, it was understandable to find Kal-Nor hesitant about sending his men in to explore the confined enclosures of the caves. And the deeper in they went, the more doubtful he became.

On reflection, she realized, it might be natural for a man like Kal-Nor to be uncomfortable in confined quarters. Desert warriors were used to open spaces. She had heard the nomadic people disliked any space more cramped than the loose, free flowing panels of a tent; at least, most of them. There were few exceptions.

Nonetheless, it was crucial for them to diligently inspect these caverns for any sign of the young Helandi officer.

The first chamber was expansive; running murals lined the walls, broken intermittently by open corridors. Sharp, well-preserved colors revealed only a slight marring of age. She curiously examined the pictures of people in the streets of a remarkable city. Sleek artistry; brilliant colors created a multi-dimensional illusion. One could spend days examining all the details. Aware of the potential sidetracking, she turned away from the paintings. Linia sent a mental probe, searching for signs of human energy within the tunnels. As before; all came back empty.

Infinite loops of passages seemed to cut through the mountain; a complex labyrinth of interconnected tunnels extending beneath the continent and perhaps, even the whole planet.

What a bizarre concept, she realized: *absolutely fantastic.*

The search team followed Mahzit's zigzag footprints freshly pressed into the thick dust, circling back and forth across one another as if Mahzit had been romping up and down these tunnels like a madman. They came upon several chambers lined with stone cubicles that two of the specialists wanted to study. Kal-Nor insisted they limited their search to finding Mahzit. The trail changed when the footprints faded and then disappeared altogether along a graveled section of tunnel which eventually came to a dead end. They searched for any sign of passing through the walls. Even Linia could not detect any access beyond that point.

Late afternoon, Bin-ulk and Mir-Ahj urged the Commander to join them in the temple cavern. Officer Linia had discovered a chart, half the height of a man, chalked onto the wall with black ash. Its crude design suggested a hurried hand might have created it.

Mir-Ahj quickly jotted down notes from scribbles under the map.

"Here: *'Danger'* and *'limited access'*....

"Look! This line here...followed by....

'Rulers': *'Conversion Room'*

"And this one: what could it mean? See this?

'Golden links' or...no: that could be *'files'*.

'...*Haldolen Guardians stand by the southern shores*....'

"More broken words follow—"

"Perhaps it's an old dialect," Bin-ulk was saying.

She asked them to make an exact copy of the wall map; then out of the corner of her eye she noticed Kal-Nor studying *her*; not the cave. Annoyed, she tried to shake off the heat suddenly rushing through her veins.

Linia consciously avoided tapping his thoughts but could not help wondering, *what is he thinking?*

Briskly she walked over to Ran-Shur with a writing pad and asked him to copy the writings which he had discovered. Kal-Nor nodded as if he approved of her instruction. A flush edged through her under his scrutinizing gaze. Looking away, embarrassed by her own reaction, she forced all attention to the artifacts. The Raider unit was engaged throughout the cave, talking in whispers, copiously engrossed in the search and oblivious to what was happening between the leaders.

Impulsively, Linia glanced again in the Commander's direction.

Kal-Nor was looking elsewhere, fully absorbed in a scroll he had picked out of a slot in the stone wall of the cavern.

What difference does it make? He has as much right to stare as any other man. I just need to focus on my own work; in a professional, detached way, of course, she reminded herself.

It was now her turn to study the man. His lean, tall frame cast an attractive shadow against the stones. The man could be as stealthy and aggressive as a wild animal; then, at other times, express sincere wisdom and strength. He was a complexity of demanding leader and gentle guardian. It was impossible not to like him.

Well, she silently mused. *He is incredibly handsome and I can't seem to stop thinking about him; yet I'm supposed to be concentrating on finding Mahzit. I've got to stop acting like a fickle school girl, wantonly enchanted by a gorgeous male animal.*

A self-conscious grin marked her face and now the joke was on her. She was thinking inappropriate thoughts. Outwardly, the Commander insisted on a strictly formal deportment since embarking on the mission. She must pull herself together and act responsibly.

Her idle daydreaming was short-lived, for just then one of the men unraveled a thick scroll, insisting she and Kal-Nor study it with them.

Bin-ulk and Mir-Ahj rapidly explained the importance of investigating the civilization that had left these maps.

"We must explore further, with your permission, sir."

They had exhausted the tunnels that contained Mahzit's tracks, and Kal-Nor and Linia both agreed to check out a vein indicated on the scroll; a particularly steep tunnel they had previously overlooked.

Linia felt an unpleasant urgency beyond the odd vibes of the caves. Outlandish, as if they were in another world. She detected a foreign energy.

Without more than a grumbled "Continue," from the Commander, they all filed into the dimly lit passageway. As they climbed down the winding tunnel, the walls became smooth and then damp and slick with a hard, glossy sheen. The air thickened; the walls changed, their smoothness breaking up, marbling into deeper tones and feathery textures. The corridor narrowed, allowing only single file passage through its constricted space. Several of their torches had already burned out.

Abruptly the walls buckled. Linia stumbled, slamming into them. The moist, slimy walls caressed her body.

She felt dizzy as they continued along this dramatically curving passageway. Then she lost her footing, falling. The torches snuffed out all at once, plunging them in darkness. It felt as if something had swallowed the tunnel. They were at the sheer mercy of the pitch-black burrow steeply spiraling downward through a looping channel.

Linia clawed to slow her descent along the chute.

Calm, you will be safe; almost there.

Where am I? She demanded of the undefined vocal intruder.

Where you were meant to be!

A breeze began flowing, clean and pure. For a moment she

thought she saw a Muti flickering in the darkness; hallucination or reality? She didn't know. The undulating illusion of the pulsing channel simply ceased. Dry air surged into an expanding corridor, which was once again solidifying to stone.

She felt a floor. No more spinning.

Linia smelled a distinctly foreign aroma drifting in the air; hot and exotic.

Mek-Toj cried out, "The desert!"

Ran-Shur chuckled: "Home!"

Kal-Nor laughed. "You're both right. The clean pure scent of a desert is certain. But the spiciness in the air is not of our tented caravans."

The Raiders had emerged from the tunnel, unscathed. They found themselves in a broad open space; the ground from which they had emerged had sealed showing no sign of entry now.

Linia stared with skeptic hesitation. The desert looked bleak, a landscape of sand dunes. Nobody questioned the odd journey they had just experienced. Perhaps these radically rational men of the wilderness had no way to express the inexplicable.

Thus, the Commander easily led them at a confident gait across the dry terrain. And following him was as natural as breathing.

II. Conflict Of Interest

From: the official files on the mission of Kal-Nor

No sign of life for days. Officer Linia found a strong trace of a herd whose tracks resemble our familiar Jilioes. Tomorrow we will hunt them down. I am hopeful that they will be suitable for riding.

* * * * * * *

Kal-Nor led the unit in a tight formation for the hunt, as they approached the herd. The place was quiet and soft, and grasses whisked along a thin waterway, speckled by bright flowers. The yellow and purple blooms mixed together against the sandy ground. Then all blended to solid rock. The herd seemed related to the sleek Jilioes his men were used to riding in the deserts of their homelands.

"This will take time," he said, surveying the area. The men were skilled riders, and most had actually tamed at least one wild Jilio.

Officer Linia asked: "Will the men have any problems?"

"We can master any riding animal." His eyes flashed towards her. "Not to be bragging, however my men are expert riders. We can take a day or two if necessary. Riding will speed our progress through this land.

"Stay and watch!" he shouted, his exuberance exposing the ego he generally tried to hide.

Thus he dismissed her and joined his men.

Linia noticed how the men's gentle persuasion coaxed their selected prime animals out of the herd.

Creating a personal relationship with the steeds was another challenge altogether. Several Raiders isolated one animal and worked as a team within a confined setting. Rock formations provided natural arenas. The Raiders had only to block a small path to confine the chosen mount in a natural stone-cut corral. And then the breaking began.

The moment one man tried to climb onto its back the beast bucked as if wanting to beat him against some invisible stone ceiling. Once it had dethroned the rider, hurling him onto the ground, it shivered slightly then insolently ignored other would-be riders.

The men spent the day tasking the small herd of tightly muscled beasts with their strong haunches supporting firm backs.

Linia watched Kal-Nor with keen interest as he moved among men and herd and finally picked a choice animal to personally train.

"It is time, my friend!" He cooed gently to the animal,

caressing its long snout and floppy ears; then the Raider adeptly leaped to its naked back.

The beast whinnied in objection, bucking wildly to rid itself of this stubborn rider who clung to its mane. Several times Kal-Nor was flipped to one side, nearly dislodged. When he held tight to the creature's ears, high pitched trills sounded from the beast as it fought against the restraints. The battle continued for much longer than she would have thought possible. Both were determined to conquer the other; neither one wanted to lose. It seemed as if they would fight to the death but in the end the man tamed the beast.

Kal-Nor had won.

He quietly slid off his steed. Man and animal glared at one another eye to eye. He patted its subdued haunches as it snorted, nuzzling up against his shoulder. This was a moment of surrender where beast and master bonded.

The Commander's eyes flashed victoriously towards Linia, as if saying: *This is how real men win battles!*

Everybody had watched this hard won victory. Proud *Vahl— Razzah"* sounded from the other men before they, much in the same manner of the Commander, went back to their work, selecting other potential mounts and repeating the process.

Some failed at first, pounding dust as their bodies were tossed to the ground, but they remounted. It did not take nearly as long as Linia had anticipated before all of them had won a new personal companion.

By the end of the day the men and mounts had come to respectably friendly terms with one another. The men seemed to have received the harder body bashing than the animals.

Cas-Hil came over to Linia, leading a mount he had just tamed.

"This one is yours!"

She accepted it with gratitude and honored Cas-Hil with a courteous bow, customarily shared among Helandians.

Linia looked forward to riding beside these men.

* * * * * * *

The next evening, Kal-Nor led the expanded unit, pleased with how these animals responded. They rode easily now that they accepted their riders. The beasts provided everyone with a sorely needed relief from the daily march.

The open spaces, broken only by scattered rock formations, reminded Kal-Nor and his warriors of their home turf. A small herd of a dozen unbroken beasts trailed behind, some carrying provisions. On occasion they came across stalks they quickly recognized as water plants, by their sticky thorns. Though they were almost twice the size of any he had previously seen. The men hacked at the thick husks in order to release their sweet and refreshing juices.

During the days they rested under the shelters they constructed from the hides of the unbroken beasts that supplied food for their bellies.

At night they traveled through the cool darkness: silent shadows within shadows. They knew, all too well, the keen eye of any native desert marauder might possibly spy upon them from distant dunes. Thus, Cas-Hil, Mek-Toj, and the other scouts preceded the caravan by nearly a day's journey, reporting back in relays anything worth noting. Making contact with people was their prime mission. That meant finding settled communities.

Making haste was imperative for several critical reasons.

Their supplies were dwindling. However, their primary focus and goal was always to make contact as soon as possible for they needed to forestall the advancement of the Kamina. Discouragement ran high as they continued to find no sign of human dwellings. Raiders, however, rarely exhibit weakness, no matter how heavy their ordeal. Plus, the open spaces and steeds had sparked new vitality into their blood.

On a positive note, they were all glad to be away from the cramped caves and craggy canyons which proved nearly as suffocating as crowded cities. For a desert Raider, confinement of any kind restricted the soul.

One evening while riding alongside Linia, Kal-Nor commented on this very point to the Helandian officer. He was feeling extremely relaxed and happy. The desert night cast a state near emotional ecstasy throughout his whole being. It was the first time since starting this damnable mission that anything seemed even half normal.

Kal-Nor realized that his mood probably stemmed from a release from the terrible tensions caused by the last days of struggling in confining and alien surroundings.

"The desert was comfort! This is reminiscent of my home; the wild freedom of the desert: Never liked cramped towns."

"Is that why you hated the caves?" she prodded softly, all too quickly zoning in on his meaning.

"Yes, we have spoken about that." He reflected the question back to her.: "How different is all this from your own home? From what I've heard the northern continent is a barren land, a white place, even different from Bel-loniea."

"Quite so—though hardly barren; ice covers the entire country in the winter; true: conversely, lush and vibrant in the summers. We spend the season outdoors in the wide open fields. I believe you actually might like it. Lovely glacial mountains border our villages out on the tundra. During the sunless winters our clans retire into spacious caverns throughout those glaciers."

"I believe that would be...chilling," he chided, attempting to mask his aversion of caves.

He was aware of the lilt of her voice blending with the night breeze as she continued to describe her Helandian home.

Kal-Nor noticed the pilot relax in his presence. And he was finding her company pleasant, despite her rank as the senior officer under his command.

The soft breeze broke across the sands, whistling around the rocky terrain; teased him into a lusty mood. An underlying edge of discomfort cut through him every time he looked at Officer Linia. Startling thoughts played at the back of his mind.

As she spoke, his mood pulsed strong. He was no longer listening to the words. He just marveled at her sensual beauty. The lovely contour of her figure, the curve of her breast against the neatly fitted uniform taunted him.

The woman's hair framed her delicate features. And he instinctively wanted to run his fingers through it. He enjoyed watching her lips move around softly spoken words. And he wanted to tenderly kiss her.

Soon she had stopped speaking and was looking silently towards him.

Does she guess the drift of my thoughts?

She was amazingly sharp, annoyingly professional: and stunningly beautiful.

"Your love for the desert defines you," she finally said.

"The desert is part of my being, I suppose," he absently answered.

He felt like a young stud, panting after a filly. Angrily, he tried to divert their chat to a less personal topic.

"The desert is wild and rugged. Not so chilling and bare as your lands of perpetual ice." He purposely avoided her stare, forcing his eyes to focus towards the distant dunes.

She replied softly: "I, too, enjoy warm places."

Her voice enticed suggestive images into Kal-Nor. He growled: "Well, this desert *is* quite hot by day!"

"Yes, I have noticed." Her laughter bubbled playfully.

A sudden annoyance needled through Kal-Nor.

His eyes snapped to hers. He wondered exactly what unspoken message she had meant by that remark.

Is she playing her own flirtatious game with me?

Her serious expression denied this. Then she smiled just slightly as their eyes met. He was convinced she was being suggestive, despite the innocent expression on her face.

Kal-Nor's discomfort escalated as he felt a hot shiver climb up his spine: most pleasing—too pleasing. He shook off his unsolicited graphic thoughts, rejecting them as inappropriate. Freely sweeping his arms towards the endless desert, he tried to redirect the conversation.

"This is what I love—the freedom of the dunes: breath-taking."

Instantly he flushed; uncertain whether she'd construe a double meaning to his remark, possibly connecting with his covert desire to reach out and bring her into his arms. Not that she would, necessarily wish him to do so.

"You sound like a child thrilled to be home after a terrifying experience," she said in a flat tone.

Kal-Nor struggled to regain control over his emotion.

"A man reaches for the familiar in the same way he would take a maiden in...."

He broke off, horrified by the words he had not meant to utter. He was speaking to a female officer; and she deserved strict respect.

"What I mean is.... Well, these open spaces breed satisfaction and peace of mind."

"So the desert resembles a woman? I would have thought it as a raging and fiery warrior!" Linia teased the Commander about humanizing the terrain.

To his dismay she had not missed his carelessness. Her words dug deeper into his feelings than he would have expected possible.

Kal-Nor felt painfully exposed.

Despite his objections, the Bel-loniean command had assigned this female warrior to *his* unit. And his tolerance had been stretched to the extreme when he'd accepted her, especially as his pilot. If she were an unattractive hag, it would have been far easier. That admission, alone, sent a raging anger through him.

If they had crossed paths in a tavern or desert caravan it would have been different.

An internal battle raged with tempting images of holding Linia in his arms, imagining her soft body pressing up against his, lips parted in eager hunger for the intimacy of a kiss.

His passions would have melted in her arms. Assuming she

wanted the same thing.

Damned rules! Pure insanity: Desert madness.

It was impossible to think straight while riding so close to this tantalizing female officer. He drove his mount sharply out into the open desert in order to break free of such harassing thoughts.

What is wrong with me?

His galloping steed sped faster, as if racing against the pounding arguments in his mind.

Officer Linia is a warrior and member of my military staff.

Every beat of the mount's hooves hammered that into his brain.

Rigid control arched his back. This was no time to be courting. His responsibility for this team must be taken seriously.

Calmer now, he decided to accept her as an equal officer. They were on a mission and survival was paramount. Professional ethics would override personal attitudes and thus allow him to enjoy the pleasure of her company, solely as a warrior. With conviction, he slowed the mount and waited.

The surrounding landscape captured his attention now.

This is a magnificent, open space, beautifully exposed like that of my home land.

Waves of sandy dunes broken by rugged terrain flooded his thoughts with tangled memories. Early evening moonlight evoked raw passion in its somber sheen. And late night skies thrilled him with brilliant stars spreading from horizon to horizon.

In the desert he cherished the wide open spaces that permitted freedom from confining restriction. Under these conditions a man could take a woman, even make love to her. That was the natural law of human survival. His primal instincts longed for that kind of freedom. His integrity and commitment to military rules demanded he control all irrational whims.

In keeping with these circumstances, Officer Linia was off limits!

His distant thoughts snapped back to the present when he heard the hoof beats of her steed followed by the mounted Raiders racing to keep up.

Breathing easier, he had finally succeeded in riding off the confusion which had besieged him. He had spent his childhood wandering the deserts from among the squat tent oases, where his tribe traded and on occasion, engaged in combat sport. Life had been tough, survival demanding, and as a lad the training had been brutal. Sons learned from older brothers and later the fathers and uncles tested the young. Heavy discipline required savage bruising and bleeding that resulted from mock combat. The ways of their people demanded harsh lessons. Young men became warriors through sport and often mortal combat with a rival village. Yet it led to a tight comradeship among the youth.

The women also focused on sexual ritual and desert survival. When he had his first young girl, at the Festival of the Dunes, they had both been inexperienced. They quickly discovered the magic of the perfect sensual mating.

Strange that he should find himself lingering on these memories. Officer Linia had sparked something very basic in him. He focused once again on the surrounding desert. Kal-Nor allowed the scent of the air to merge with his inner being.

Officer Linia finally approached, followed by the unit and herd, which had resumed their traveling pace once they had all fallen back into formation. No words were exchanged as they all continued to make their way across the open sands.

Linia, steeped in her own thoughts, had been amused by the talk with the Commander and especially when he angrily rode ahead. She had refrained from reading his thoughts, wanting to allow him privacy concerning troubling issues that should stay personal.

She strictly adhered to the ethical rules practiced among the Helandians.

Even so, his interest in her had been obvious during these conversations; embarrassingly so.

He had interpreted her messages correctly.

It was so easy, so pleasing; so deliciously enjoyable to watch the man be aroused by her prowess. In another time, another place they would probably have tumbled into erotic passion.

A flush crept into her cheeks, thankfully hidden by the night; nonetheless, the heat rising within her startled Linia. She knew all too well, that these were not the thoughts becoming of a professional officer. Yet, their alluring pull would not leave her in peace.

How easy it would be to tempt this man; and how difficult it was to ignore her natural longings.

Both Kal-Nor and Linia had displayed their instinctive desires for one another. She knew that open responsiveness was punishable.

The Commander was sitting on his steed like some magnificent statue, unmoving. Approaching him, she ignored personal feelings.

Linia's body, though, ached to freely express her passion. Every nerve battled against her logic. She stubbornly reigned in her emotions. Wisdom dictated it was mandatory to set aside the obvious and avoid unnecessary complications. Well disciplined officers on serious duty must respect protocol.

That was final.

The mounted warriors had fallen into file behind their commander. Kal-Nor silently led at a brisk pace onward across the sifting sands. Linia followed at a respectable distance, avoiding any further conversation.

III. The Kaminaean Desert

The caravan halted shortly after the sun had risen, the sands still cool from the night before. Kal-Nor and the others selected an untamed beast to slaughter that day while Linia kindled a sparse fire in preparation for the roast. The men wasted no parts of the carcass. Even the blood and fluids were carefully stowed to be used for tanning or lubricant or salve. Sinews stretched and dried for binding and weaponry, the hide, of course, prepared for tent, tarp, and many other clever uses. Everything on the animal served a purpose. The meat would be quickly seared. A portion would serve their immediate meal, but the bulk would be dried for the coming days. They could not afford to build a fire too frequently.

The men prepared meaty slices from the carcass of one of the herd they had taken for the purpose of butchering. A goodly portion of the late morning had been occupied by making camp and preparing for the hottest time of the day, propping shelters for themselves and the animals to protect them from the fatal rays of the sun. They had found another meager source of water tubers buried in a sand dune where a single thorny sprig had been discovered by one of the men.

After the meal was over, Kal-Nor withdrew to the privacy of his shelter and waited for Linia who had requested a private conference.

When she entered, her hair was pulled loosely around her shoulders. What a lovely sight she was.

"Kal-Nor, can we converse openly with one another here?"

He did not answer. Only his eyes held to hers, yet he could not look at her without feeling a rush of natural desire. They were actually hidden from sight; in privacy. That reality attempted to twist away from any strict regulations.

It felt as if at least two things were happening at once. This was a meeting between two officers; yet it was also a stunningly powerful merging of two highly charged people; potential lovers.

He was experienced enough in such matter to read the signs. And his desires were reflected in her eyes. Both humor and longing lingered.

Her next words were a bit unsettling: "I think using less structured protocol may serve future purposes."

What purposes? he automatically wondered; hoping to keep his inner flush concealed beneath a well-trained professional façade.

Then she spelled out her ideas.

"You know I possess HanJahn senses beyond the visible range. I respect your privacy and do not inappropriately probe anyone within this unit. But I cannot entirely close them out."

The more she spoke the more uncomfortable Kal-Nor felt. He struggled to remain calm, for outward appearances, at least.

"I want to be candid with you on this point for several reasons," she was saying. "First and foremost, completing our mission safely is my primary concern, and that being said, I want to level the connection between you and me. You probably do not know how I have been thinking or feeling."

"You most certainly are correct on that point," he managed; throat a bit husky.

"I wish to share a summary so that you have equal knowledge of me."

Kal-Nor shifted his position, both intrigued and guarded; trying to maintain a clear head, despite his uneasiness about her mysterious ability to invade his privacy. He certainly would not want to admit to becoming vulnerable to a powerful Helandian woman. Now he wanted to hear the facts about what she actually knew of his thoughts. That was cold, blunt and realistic. The expression on his face probably showed his troubled recognition.

"Go on," he said tensely.

"Kal-Nor, I believe you have strong feelings towards me. I want you to know I, too, have feelings for you.

"I admire you as a man of great integrity. I trust you. We are a good team for this unit. We work well together."

She stopped.

Had she gone too far or not far enough?

Kal-Nor said nothing.

"Well!" She suddenly sat rigidly upright as if interrupted from a deep trance. "Enough of that...more importantly, I need to inform you about what I have been noticing.

"There's strong activity in the distance; maybe a couple of days ride or more, directly ahead of us. Life: to be specific, humans; a sizable group of wanderers; nomadic people. They don't seem to be in a fixed settlement." She sat again, took a deep breath then continued. "Kal-Nor, we are about to make contact."

The Commander continued to keep his silence; revealing neither approval nor rejection.

"Is that all?" he inquired, distantly.

* * * * * * *

By the fifth day the chill of night blanketed over a greater portion of the morning hours. They were able to travel longer as the temperature dropped lower and the land rose higher. In the afternoon they topped a rise.

Nestled against a narrow range of dunes in the distance they saw their first glimpse of vegetation. After a long march they finally reached the sand hills and from there they spotted the first flags of civilization.

From the top of the next dune, tents were clearly visible, surrounding a mud pit; hardly enough to be considered a watering hole.

Raiders were suspicious of strangers.

These people could be slavers or merchants. He understood the nature of survival among nomadic tribes. While they might be friendly they more likely would consider all strangers as a possible threat. Clans seldom welcomed newcomers without serious challenges. Extreme caution and care in observing social formality would be the best strategy to avoid unnecessary conflict.

Kal-Nor had set their pace at an unhurried but steady gait and then warned: "Prepare!"

He hardly glanced at Officer Linia, who dutifully repeated the order.

"Prepare!" she firmly echoed, touching the sheathed sword at her side.

Dogmatically, they plodded across the open desert knowing

that there was no chance of remaining undetected; then halted a short distance from the encampment.

A few clansmen seemed to be busily working near their crescent of dusty tents. A small herd of livestock huddled beneath the shade of a scant clump of short broad-leafed trees. Everything seemed quite vulnerable and oddly heedless to the approaching riders.

The Commander was wary, not sure what to expect.

Linia frowned. "Looks secure but feels *wrong*. These sands are shifting, Kal-Nor. All is not as it seems."

"Yes." The Commander nodded towards the dunes beyond the tents. "My people would have had guards visible. Perhaps they fear nobody. Foolish in my world! "

"On the other hand, we are on foreign soil," Linia surmised. "These people seem to confident. Their protector is likely unseen...." She stopped midsentence when an unseen bird suddenly cried out, followed by a number of answering chirps.

Kal-Nor recognized the warning sign—too late

Immediately the threat materialized on the dunes. Over twenty armed warriors lifted from the sands brandishing swords, though they did not advance; only studied Kal-Nor.

Keenly alert, the Commander carefully balanced on his mount; neither cowed nor threatened, and announced openly, without judgment: "We are traders and seek welcome."

The desert-man nearest to him spoke.

"Your pack-beasts are wild. And they carry nothing worth the trade!" He paused, awaiting a response, which didn't come, then growled: "And you are a liar!"

"Surrender," he demanded. "Or die!"

Kal-Nor confidently rebuffed: "I fail to tremble before your little threat!"

The man's face hardened. The warrior beside him burst out: "What brings you to our lands?"

Without any show of emotion, Kal-Nor offered: "We wish to trade for information. This Korda spoke the words of a fool and will feel my blade in his throat, unless he chooses to be more civil!"

Among the Raiders it was important to show no weakness; for doing so would have been considered an immediate sign of guilt and evil intent. Strength was equated to fairness and honesty across the open sands. Kal-Nor had hoped that the same ethics applied in these lands, as well.

Even the most dedicated warrior will avoid unnecessary battle. The two men immediately relaxed. Their rigidness melted and they looked relieved.

With a bold air of formality, the leader said: "We will admit you. But proof of your friendship is required. So be warned. I am Vultoran."

Kal-Nor recognized the standard desert invitation to strangers and instructed his men, accordingly: "Disarm and proceed with respect. Be alert!"

The Raiders filed in behind the armed escort and entered the encampment.

* * * * * * *

From: the personal files on the mission of Kal-Nor

We found wandering tribes independently supportive of the Resistance. The nomadic communities are cautiously friendly though willing to share; much like my own. For me and the men it's as close as it gets to being home. We assessed their situation, learned their customs and then gained their confidence.

Their connecting networks avoid the Muti; deeply suspicious of the Kaminaean rulers. Their austere conditions kept them at safe distance, for the Kamina relished sensual comfort which was decidedly scarce among these tribes.

Our mission required us to infiltrate and assist any Resistance against the Muti tyranny. Once we felt confident about their ability to cloak secrecy, we disclosed our purpose. Word quickly spread among the nomads, that the Armada was coming.

Vultoran was highly impressed with the information we had brought for trade. Indeed, he had told us with open relief, that never had they received so valuable a treasure as the news of the coming Armada to fight against the Kaminaean Empire.

CHAPTER TEN
KARDON'S JOURNAL

My name is Kardon, a warrior in the service of the Bel-loniean Proctor, sent to discover a passage into Kamina. I have done so, but the cost has been dire. I write with impending terror always at my back, for I doubt I may live long enough to deliver its message.

Memory has been distorted and time has contracted since I arrived.

I came on a preliminary exploration mission. This much I feel certain about. Memories were strong during the beginning. Now many parts had been burned out.

I remember villagers near the ocean greeting me. Friendly folk contented with fishing and living with what nature provided. The small population was happy, innocent in their eager openness.

They spoke of the Kaminaean Mutis in hushed, respectful whispers. When I asked where the Mutis dwelt, they pointed inland.

"Very far through the jungles and across the plains," was their answer.

They honored the Mutis gods to be worshiped and never questioned. Even more revered than ours. Masters laud control over the *"life and death of all living beings; crawling on the soil itself."*

So they quote from their *Muti Rights of Divine Universal Law.*

Simple people of the land, they accepted the world on its own terms. Maybe they were happier than city folk.

I left the seaside town in search of the Resistance groups. My mission: to provide inside assistance to the Kaminaean residence. Establish contacts for the Armada. I set out, crossing the grasslands, finding no other civilized life. I survived by hunting to supplement my rations and minimal supplies. Of course, I had standard weapons: sword and Kay-gun. All are gone.

My ordeal began one afternoon, after I had scaled a rocky ridge overlooking a dry hot desert. Blinded by the sun I didn't notice the caravan coming my way until it was too late to avoid them, assuming I could have found a place to hide.

Mounted scouts in coarse brown cloaks overtook me, bound my wrists and hauled me along behind their caravan, as if I were a captured slave, until their troupe halted to make camp. Long past sunset one of the scouts loosened my bonds and allowed me to eat. He dragged me past their blazing campfires and tethered me to their tent post with their stock.

Their beasts didn't respond kindly, kicking and biting at me. Fortunately their keepers had already watered and fed them or they would likely have gnawed me to death. They left me all night among the animals.

* * * * * * *

Details are vague, and I believe something erased my memory. I'll continue to write here as best I can.

Someone passed me on to other captors; my weapons and tools stripped; I was locked in a cramped cell; a narrow bed shoved against one wall beneath a small window. Outside was a massive city.

Bel-loniea would fit into it several times and not be noticed. Sprawling, soaring, pyramids sit in the middle like pointed mountains within a forest of tall monolithic buildings. These structures, pocked with millions of glass eyes on all sides, scrape the skies with metallic pinnacles.

* * * * * *

Later I was held in dungeons buried beneath the place.

Time settles slowly. My warrior training disintegrated. I barely subsist on meager rations shoved through a narrow hole at the bottom of the door. I eat and drink only to survive.

I don't know how long I have been here, or how long it will be before I die. Surely they cannot keep me here forever, whoever they might be.

Life is meaningless.

I heard screams and explosions; drifting voices. Music, off-beat throbbing. Darkness surrounds me. My eyes want to open. When they do, I see nothing.

But the dark is not empty.

Light flashed and I saw the face of a Muti leaning close. Hollowed eye sockets pulled me into their empty void. I could taste its rancid breath. Not a familiar Muti. This face, marked with bright colors and patterns, leers at me until deep creases cut through its dry purple face. This is not my caring Muti advisor. The monstrous evil is so hateful that I am choking deep in my throat.

Something hard strikes my face and I scream. I fear that I can never stop screaming. Pain breaks into every nerve.

My voice cries out helplessly. I don't recall what it says. Everything blurs....

Darkness....

Days go by.

My mind is confused. Events are scattered. Locations and nightmares mix together into a patchwork of uncertainty. What is real and what is madness cannot be separated. Moments of lucidity allow strong and solid memories; others are uncertain conclusions spurred to convictions at the moment of writing in this journal.

I am led by chain to an inner yard where others similar to myself are given time to breathe air outside our cells. We dare not speak. Those who do are brutally beaten to death before our eyes.

I witnessed the execution of several men. They were bashed with metal clubs. Flesh, blood and bone flew all around. Large Mutis held the weapons. Hoodless bald skulls, wide gaping jaws, jagged teeth gnashing, screeching out hideous noises. Excited, like children at play; jumping up and down. Beating and bashing the bodies over and over again, taking sheer delight in the torturous pain they were inflicting on innocent victims. And there was never any explanation for their raw brutality.

Nearly every time I come to this yard somebody gets beaten. No warning, no purpose. The lucky ones die quickly. Mutis do not favor that. The next victim they beat slowly. The method of torture always depends on the mood of the Muti. Thankfully it isn't a daily routine. In fact, nothing is routine. Most terrifying is the not knowing what will happen next. For the most part I'm ignored.

Today, I've been told, they will kill again in the yard. Celebrating something seasonal...I don't understand and don't care.

I accept; for that is the only element in life that gives me peace. To rebel is useless.

Someday, maybe my suffering will end in death. I hope it will come soon.

CHAPTER ELEVEN
KAMINA

I. Landfall

Hidden truths fall like bombs in the hearts of the pure
They burst open insights to inspire the innocent.
Wise ones use these truths as guides to future actions.
—HanJahn Missives

The day I left on my mission to Kamina, my flight headed for an island near the Bel-loniean seaport where I would meet my Helandian crew.

The grav-disk landed on a small rise above a narrow beach near a shimmering oval vehicle. Helandian warriors stood waiting; their leather boots laced just below the knee of their leggings, and fitted tunics belted with harness straps over each shoulder. The buckles allowed them to latch on tools, parcels or weaponry, enabling them to haul substantial supplies during any rugged journey. The weather being mild, they had foregone their cloaks.

We briskly filed towards a vessel, led by our warmly communicative pilot. She spoke with pride.

"This Orb has recorded the fastest speed to date."

The beautiful vibrant shell of the vessel evoked dormant memories as I examined its unbroken surface. My hand glided effortlessly along the seamless metal. It felt akin to the smooth skin of the gentlest furry beast.

The Helandian pilot noted my reaction.

"It is designed to cut smoothly through the atmosphere with virtually no resistance."

We were hurried along to the ship's entry which dissolved at our approach.

Interesting, I thought, *a holographic portal screen.*

I had seen similar systems employed on other worlds, such as energy fields surrounding intergalactic ships; common federation technology.

The control deck spaciously supported the flight crew. A slew of operational grids flashed beneath a viewing panel displaying the rock covered island.

We settled into cushioned, slim-line booths and the Orb vibrated slightly as the pilot coded in commands. Before I'd finished buckling in my harness we had risen through the cloud bands, soaring towards the naked sun.

Helandian engineers were producing fleets of comparable ships for the Armada. Grav-disks had always been restricted to function at a maximum elevation slightly above the lower mountain ranges, and always within sight of shore. Any attempt to go beyond that threshold caused the grav-plates to malfunction, since they were dependent on the magnetic source within the median layers of the mainland terrain.

Limitations would be nullified by the revolutionary technology of the Helandians. Their technicians were converting our magnetic generators to the crystal based systems. They would soon be able to cross the oceans of Noomas, though probably not at the speed this Orb was demonstrating.

We adjusted our booths to form small groups around mobile tables where we could pore over new strategic charts, comparing notes in low-keyed whispers as if we feared awaking ancient gods.

The maps displayed amazing graphical details. Data compiled by the Helandians from the charts Adt and Sarleni had found, had been combined with Talni's reports, and correlated with recent incoming information from the preliminary spy missions.

Everybody was riveted on the mysterious territory occupying the other half of Noomas, while the covertly cloaked Orb raced across the planet's ocean towards Kamina and within a few days we approached the Castle of Doom.

The Orb began its descent through the cloud layers towards the continental coastline.

Sharp cliffs jutted towards the ocean. A stone fortress towered over the northern crest, its landward façade walled by dense forest. The only exposed side was fronted by the ocean.

We slid in low along the tree line, hovering alongside a veranda extending from an upper level of the fortress. Once my unit unloaded the equipment onto the balcony, the ship sped away.

Inside, the ancient castle was gloomy. Every passage chilled the bones; austere walls bearing little décor, emitted no warmth. We crept cautiously through the castle from floor to floor; until we felt satisfied it was vacant. Deep within, we discovered a broad, circular hall with vaulted ceilings. Frescoes adorned these bleak stone walls, chipped from age and neglect. They must have been lovely in their original condition; richly painted scenes of elegantly clad nobles. Regal hats perched atop long-haired ladies, while baldheaded men sported thick, silky beards. The hall opened to an enclosed garden.

We decided to make camp within the castle courtyard and set our operational base at ground level. From the overgrowth and level of deterioration to the premises, it gave the impression that the castle had not been inhabited for generations. This fortress must have undergone untold ages of occupation, and then desertion. Now it stood forlorn.

Two teams canvassed the perimeter. Massive stones composed the outer structure; neatly squared off against one another, row after row, lifting up high above the cliffs. The bleak hardness of the castle was scarred and bleached by the constant battering of the surf. When they returned, confirming no signs of life, we posted rotating guards.

I tried to concentrate on the plans for an inland exploration, but, my mind drifted relentlessly to thoughts of Youi. Our life had been too hurried. I'd been too busy mounting a career in the Bel-loniean Royal Guard; finding an acceptable place within the rigid military standards that still regarded me an upstart mate to their Royal Proctoress.

I craved the touch of my lovely wife and the intimacy of her body against mine. Our passions from the beginning were brightly charged with continual physical ecstasy, and now we would soon have a child.

It felt so distant; so fragile. When would I return to her and the new young life she was carrying? The idea of fatherhood stunned me to the core.

I had arrived on Noomas as a single warrior without memory and become the mate to the royal granddaughter of the Proctor. She was a splendid prize for any man; the perfect glory of loving and being loved.

Parenting would levy greater demands upon me. I craved to be near the mother of my child- to-be. I was struck with strong, inexplicable need to protect my children's future; to protect their world; to succeed for their sake, and stand by my off-spring through their maturity.

The whole concept amplified the idea I might not survive this war. I could be denied my future. Morbid notions distracted me.

I forced myself to examine the charts until I grew weary. Only with great effort was I able to surrender to a fitful sleep.

* * * * * * *

The next morning, we awoke to the brightening dawn, and local chirping birds. A flock of migrating fitalos flew across the sky. In the distance some angry beast roared, not unlike that of a Korda.

I sent scouts to investigate the beach where we had spotted a pier. The rest of the unit organized our base camp.

A sturdy vine-enshrouded wall bordered the castle's inner

courtyard, drenched with tangled purplish foliage. An archway cut through this hedge, creating an unnatural tunnel through the lower stone walls that led out into the untamed forest. The path from that point was barely traceable.

Later in the afternoon, the scouting party reported some odd descriptions of local life. A cloister of frond-covered huts sat beneath the cliff where people mended nets; cleaned fish.

The villagers had openly invited them to share Ka and fish cakes, assuming the scouts were traders. My men had accepted their hospitality: politely asking simple questions. The uncomplicated people contentedly responded with folk tales.

A peculiar old man was constantly waving colored sticks and spouting ancient lore concerning local ocean gods: and about the Mutis of Kamina. After each story, he'd howled wildly:

"The will of the Prophet is invincible. Praise the Prophet!"

The villagers would pick up the chant with him.

"The will of the Prophet is invincible. Praise the Prophet!"

My men tried to question them about the Prophet but the entire village shrieked, jittering and dancing, insanely. They did not seem able to explain their agitation.

There was no evidence of children, only elderly or frail, damaged folk in this village. When my scouts asked specifically about the absence of young people, the villagers immediately stopped their ranting, and no one spoke for a long time; slowly dispersing back to their huts, leaving the scouts sitting alone by the waning fire.

Down by the shore, one old woman sat alone, cooing a soft lament about the children. My scouts kept their distance so as not to disturb her and listened carefully.

"They have gone to serve Kalinis. The delicious ones: taken away to please the Prophet. The little chosen ones were gifted to the Holy Kalinis, to please the gods."

She stopped when they approached her and looked up pleadingly, tears trickling down her frail cheeks.

"Will you come to see us again?" she had asked them, innocently.

Our scouts assured her that they would do so.

With each visit, they learned more about the people, the area, and their history.

Other settlements along the coastline were pretty much the same. Most of the fishermen related similar tales about the Mutis. They spoke of rulers who once dwelt in *The Ancient Place*. By description, it matched the castle on the cliff. The villagers seemed to be living in a world long lost in the past.

My scouts wrote the words to the many repeated chant. All related to the gods, the legends and tales of long ago; much like this one:

Lo, and behold, the Mountain of the Ancient Place,
Within its frame lies the mystery,
Bow low to the tribute,
Praise the pathways of those who paved the way.
Hearken unto the verse of their momentous voices,
And Sing to the Glory of the Times immortal.

Gradually, we had collected a significant amount of history about the Mutis, covering a wide-ranging era of conquest by Kalinis. They spoke about the Law of the Prophet, which claimed the territory, calling it Kamina. Their legends tied in closely with the reports from the Messenger's files.

Meanwhile, we installed the control hub at the Castle of Doom. My task was to conceal and safeguard the station until the Armada set up its command post, once the fleet arrived.

We had no reason to suspect danger of discovery at this time and felt quite confident with our secured containment of the fortress.

While the Helandian technicians had concentrated on establishing the site, rigging communication and cloaking gear, other units made frequent visits to the simple townships, taking various trinkets for trade. The people provided us with plenty of artifacts, including hand-drawn carts, which we hoped would assist us towards our pretense as common merchants seeking trade.

Occasionally, one of the Helandians spotted a very large Kuknal in flight off shore. Its unusual size and lack of life energy emissions, suspiciously branded the creature as a Gatherer of the Kamina, like Adt had described from their encounter with the Haknords.

After the third sighting, I decided we should conclude our business and begin our inland journey. The Gatherers drifted periodically, at a fair distance, though we feared they would soon venture closer. Camouflaging our tracks in and around the base was critical. Helandian imagery cleverly disguised our command station, before we headed inland.

* * * * * * *

The forest challenged us, and we were forced to hack a wider trail to gain enough clearance for our carts by painstakingly carving a path through tightly packed dripping vines and twisted trees. Thick overhead branches blocked daylight, dropping us into perpetual twilight. We had toiled laboriously through an entire day, when the trees came to an abrupt halt, opening into a meadow lit only by the stars. Here, under the protective cover of the outer tree line, we chose to rest for the night.

As dawn broke, the camp was awakened by a shrill war cry which sent us scrambling for our weapons. Mounted warriors galloped at us from all sides forcing us into chaotic self-defense. We were overwhelmed by half-naked savages brandishing swords and spears.

I had grabbed my sword barely in time to ward off the swipe of an enemy blade.

"Charge!" I ordered, lifting my sword high.

The ambush closed in fast, making our Kay-bombs useless. At close-range they would have been self-destructive. My men fired their Kay-guns, wiping out a front line of enemy warriors who clamored over their own dead, in order to engage us in face to face combat. That act, however, created only a momentary pause, but long enough so that my warriors could form a circular defense. A quick survey of our position confirmed that we were outnumbered.

We lashed out wildly against them but an ever increasing number of warriors quickly replaced those who had fallen under our blades and Kay-guns. I searched the area for any hope of avoiding our imminent defeat, when a strange sight caught my attention.

A mounted Muti hung back in the foliage to our right. It was clothed in a bright, blue-streaked cloak, its face highlighted with yellow and red markings. It was starkly different from any Mutis I'd ever seen.

I could not shake the visage. Civility under these conditions perishes; aggressors are often nameless phantoms without personalities. You defend against the weapon and think of little else.

Fighting for survival was all I could manage.

My sword engaged the next warrior, who backed away, avoiding my thrust. As he retreated, I instinctively charged. A lethal mistake, for in a blink the warriors had trounced and disarmed me. I had been outwitted by a cunning enemy.

My sword fell. That is all I remembered.

II. I Am Sziat

Loss of memory slaughters identity, leaving a bitter void.
Recollection floods the mind like a painful avalanche.
—Words of the Prophets

Consciousness emerged slowly amidst a garbled stupefaction of voices. I could not discern whether they were real or imagined because every attempt I made to remember, evoked a severe warning from within:

Block!

Locked down behind an invisible shell, my Torlo half withdrew beneath its protection while the outside world disintegrated.

Block!

Abstractions filtered in. My reasoning had dulled as if watching through dense smog. I struggled to remember, but then the training drill surfaced:

Beware the dangers of false memory.

What memory?

The warrior who stands against all....

Block!

...Torlo Hannis...born without memory, without knowledge of the world...future....

Block!

...Altered memory; visions...not completed. Pathways are varied he must survive! For he was soon to become.... Survival counted....

Block!

You carry genetic codes...new generation on Noomas....

Block!

We are all linked. Life is universal; the same elements....

We are Jan Sorla.

"Wake up!"

A rough hand slammed down, grinding my chest into a straw mat. In the dimly lit space, I barely distinguished a rugged face snarling inches from mine.

Instinctively, I triggered the Zygo-block, locking it solidly across my identity. *I am a mercenary by profession, a wandering Kaminaean tradesman. We had left the seacoast, going inland; seeking trade.*

The shell around my inner self, the Torlo Hannis core, buried itself deeper into the protective shield. My active identity was Jan Sorla, warrior-mercenary. I would claim the Kaminaean shore as my home.

"Why have you invaded our lands?"

A tall, surly man was standing over me. He grabbed my shoulders lifting me into the air.

"Sit! Up. Like a man!"

The Zygo block was solidly activated, burying all recognition of Torlo Hannis to any Muti. Only Jan Sorla, the mercenary would respond.

"Who are you? What is your purpose here?"

Still dazed with confusion, Jan Sorla watched; stalling for an advantage.

I remembered the battle, void of details beyond the Zygo block; reshaping memory to fit his mercenary background.

"I come as a friend! Where are my men?"

"Safe—for now....."

Doubt flared. I had no reason to trust this man, yet I wondered if he might be our first contact with the Resistance.

Careful, Jan, I told myself. From deep within I could sense that Torlo wanted control.

Block!

I began the recognition code.

"I assume you took them *north*."

The man blinked.

"Is *north* your destination?" he asked.

I persisted, still perplexed over my duality and watching Sorla interact with this stranger. "Beyond, if the key is not *masked*."

The man looked puzzled. "Yes. And if you go further you'll enter the ice fields. We never go there."

He was not responding to the code. This interrogator stared at me, and then clutched my shoulders.

"You shall fight with us! Vintu has spoken."

"My sword is a loyal weapon," I gruffly replied, as any professional mercenary might respond, "For a price!"

He looked interested. "Are you a seller of swords; a merchant of weapons?"

"It might be so. A reliable one, I can assure you, for those who are willing to pay."

I felt less perplexed, and on firmer footing.

Suddenly, the door behind him flew open. He turned, startled.

A crowd pushed through the doorway, and beyond them was a hooded figure. It appeared to be the same mounted Muti I had seen at the ambush. Its brightly marked face glared at me, as if cut in stone; unmoving, coldly observant.

Among the mob cramming into the room, were my own men, chained together, under guard. They looked battered and confused, though not defeated. No doubt, my words were not heartening to them. Yet my duty was to assure their survival, if possible.

Just then, the Muti charged through the crowd raising a wide bladed sword. It dashed directly at me, and shouted, "Away with you; slave dung!"

Two guards drew their own swords in protest.

The Muti's blade swung, slicing through their weapons, cutting their bodies aside like dried grass.

"Come!" It grabbed my wrist, jarring me with its stunning strength. Drenched in a fog, I struggled to maintain balance.

Suddenly, both Torlo and Jan spun in mixed conflict.

"You're mine," the Muti insisted. "Do not resist!"

Armed men rushed towards us. The Muti cut through their oncoming bodies, sending bloody pieces of arms and legs flying through the air. I mutely heard their agonized screams.

"Don't let him escape!" Vintu bellowed.

The Muti shoved the hilt of a sword at me. "Defend yourself!"

I had no idea who was friend, and who was enemy. But the warriors were an immediate threat. A professional mercenary would seize the advantage.

A sharp command knifed into me: *We need to escape. Your life depends on it. Defend yourself.*

"Fight," the Muti ordered.

It headed down the corridor, dragging me along like a flopping flag.

Vintu yelled, "Kill the prisoners!"

I saw my Helandian pilot assaulted; head half severed under the blades of Vintu's men. Then, the rest of my unit was brutally slaughtered.

Use the weapon! The Muti's voiceless words rammed at me.

Vintu was rushing up behind those in the lead. I extended the blade threateningly, towards them.

The Muti's sword hacked through the bodies of anyone trying to block our forward passage.

My weapon cut a bloody slice across the chest of the nearest warrior rushing us, then, engaged the next; he crumpled into a lifeless heap.

Vintu leapt forward. No mercy showed in his eyes. He meant to destroy me.

I nimbly parried Vintu's double swing at my head. Even while restricted by the Muti's grip on my arm, I twisted my blade around his extended sword, knocking it aside. With deliberate aim, I thrust the sword straight into his heart.

As the interrogator fell, his followers retreated, for they apparently had no further interest in challenging us.

The Muti broke into my mind.

North!

My word came automatically.

Mask.

The Muti responded.

Reveal.

My orders had read:

'*...The code occurs in greeting. The consecutive sequence must be spoken thusly:*

North: *Friends answer with* Mask.

Respond only when you hear the word Reveal.

Initiate connection.'

I was stunned. Nobody could have known the code without authorized access.

Had someone twisted the message? Could I trust this Muti who was dragging me through chaos?

I had grave concerns, but the dead bodies of my unit left no options. This Muti adamantly imposed escape; be it friend or foe. No other choice remained.

We continued running down the narrow corridor until it ended, opening to a wild river beneath the black night sky. A long, sleek skiff jostled at the water's edge.

I paused, determined to set my standards, and demand answers before leaving the unit behind.

"Release me! How dare you treat me like...?"

"Quiet!"

The Muti pushed the boat into the water and tossed me in, with one swift heave. As physical contact broke, I felt a discharge of energy.

Taking an oar, the Muti stirred us away from the shore in silence; the hooded specter paddling steadily upstream.

I wondered where we were headed; lost in alien territory, and in the hands of a Kaminaean Muti of undetermined loyalty. I had critical questions. For all I knew, we could be anywhere; I had no method of locating my position.

Lurking suspicion assailed me. The Muti's motives could not be for my benefit. I had been briefed on the Kaminaean's appearance and danger. This towering nemesis fit the description in spades.

"Who were those men? Why did they take us for enemies?"

"You should know." the Muti snapped, not looking my way. "Don't play the fool, Sorla!"

Hearing my name startled me. It must have read my mind, picking up the Kann's identity.

Apparently the Zygo block was proving effective.

"Where are we going?"

The Muti ignored my demand and handed me an oar. "Row; the journey is long."

With no other options, I complied and dug into the waters, still riddled with questions that piled up with each stroke of the oar. I wanted to resist; trying to retrace the harrowing events of the day. How could I have lost my entire unit? They'd been completely wiped out with one fatal act, while I'd watched them mercilessly hacked to pieces. The sudden loss was unbearable.

Whatever this Muti's agenda, it had provided me with safe

escape from those who had heartlessly slaughtered my men.

I kept Jan Sorla quiet. Perhaps this Muti would be my guide through this hostile land. My mission was to find KiNal.

The river wound through a craggy pass, sloped slightly downhill, picking up the pace as we rowed in silence until the sun had risen. Soon, fatigue had settled in, and I needed to conserve my resources.

The Muti turned. Odd, how empty sockets can give the illusion of eyes.

"Food is behind you," it told me. "Eat!"

I found a box and ripped its top off. Inside, I dug into the wafers that were no thicker than my thumb; similar to galactic space-grub; compact food tabs supplied to soldiers in battle.

"Shells melt," the Muti explained. "Drink the water of life. Make use."

It scooped its palm in to the river and poured the water down its throat.

Too tired to do much else, I followed its example, guzzling the pure liquid. I was thirstier than I had realized, and the clear water was refreshing. As it had said, the shells melted. Unexpectedly satisfying; lifting my spirits so that I was clearly revitalized, refreshed.

Thus energized as Jan Sorla, I had regained determination. "Where are we going?"

"You want contact." The voice was expressionless. "Sziat delivers."

Sudden awareness struck me like a bolt.

Moyi had said: *Be alert to Sziat.*

Was it luring me into a trap or was it really trying to assist my quest? Too much coincidence: I could not yet let my guard down.

"What is Sziat?"

The Muti ceased rowing, its hooded face lifting.

"Call me Sziat."

It spoke with scorn.

"The rule of Kamina dictates names by the *Law of the*

Prophet!"

Confusion set in. Had this Muti breached my block? Was it friend or foe?

The Muti dressed colorfully, and spoke in vibrant tones, as bright as the hues pasted on its face and cloak. And I knew Mutis never refer to themselves by name. Nor do they express emotion of any form. Yet, it was speaking with a fiery passion. "*Prophet Law* does not ascribe names. For *I am* Sziat."

Did it penetrate my inner space? My caution suppressed further comparative analysis, relying only on the new facts bombarding Sorla.

I held my silence long enough to be obviously unresponsive.

"We can be civil or formal. I am not your enemy," it said.

I chose to ignore its comment. I wanted answers. And I would determine whether it would be my ally; or not.

The Muti raised its sunken eye sockets, as if it detected my doubt.

"Your capture was unfortunate. I salvaged you from a treacherous snare. Alas, I could not do the same for your crew. Dangerous elements abound in Kamina. You must learn, before you are ready."

For what? I wondered.

"Jan Sorla," it whispered. "Be warned. Learn."

Clearly, the Muti understood my thoughts. At least, those regulated to Jan Sorla. Sziat gripped the paddle in its thickly gnarled purple hands, turned away, and we both rowed.

At length, it sighed and then began to speak again.

"Among Mutis, not all things are equal. The empire rises at an unnatural speed, fueled by the engineering of the Prophet."

I rowed and listened as Sziat unfolded a story of Kamina. Andon Janis had traced a Muti strain he'd researched in the ancient Bel-loniean libraries. He had discovered similar accounts in the Messenger's report although he had little to go on, and as a result, had judged it to be a typical legend.

Sziat was describing Muti forces and battles among nations. It spoke of uprisings and defeats, its voice growing both angry and sad.

"They have become increasingly murderous.

Vuel ne, hiu Ahmra, li ahn Trae bis!"

Over and over, it chanted a rich melody, all the while rowing steadily.

This Sziat was beginning to pique my curiosity.

"Do you support the Resistance against the Kaminaeans?"

It ignored me, mechanically rowing the craft, so I persisted.

"To defeat their purpose, you must join your people and even those in the lands beyond Kamina."

I tried to add reason to my plea. "Only with united effort, is there any chance of crushing the Kaminaean rule, Sziat. You must help the peoples of these nations rebel against their treachery."

The Muti eased its heavy strokes. Calmly and evenly, it related a long saga about the Kaminaeans.

"Dare not to make demands," it said sternly.

"I do what is necessary for the balance of Noomas. Do not underestimate the Kaminaeans. Prior to the Prophet's arrival, violence among Mutis never occurred. The Kaminaeans once were friendly, uncommonly social, banding together, and catering to the needs of your people.

"The tribes and clans were honored to be part of any Muti event. People rallied, eager to partake of the Muti banquets. Over time, we observed irregularities.

"The Kaminaeans displayed elaborate festivals, engaged in frivolities beyond the ceremonial traditions of their culture. Gradually, stronger passions budded among them, expressing more and more human characteristics. A bizarre phenomenon emerged. Their zeal for human pleasures, for food and drink, for dance heightened to hysterical elation. Peculiar gestures of acceptance perhaps: or a token attempt to bond with humans.

"It did not stop there. They were prone to quarreling irrationally, among themselves.

"Emotionally unstable, highly volatile; instead of serving nature, they devoured human passions with a vicious hunger.

Their manipulative capers harmed the people. A cunning society arose behind locked doors and drawn curtains. Nobody guessed the truth."

Sziat abruptly stopped speaking, digging its oar harder and harder into the river, speeding us faster and faster, while growling and sneering and blasting atrocities and violence against the Kaminaeans, wailing the lament

"Vuel ne, hiu Ahmra, li ahn Trae bis!"

I had dropped my oar into the skiff; hanging on to the sides so as not to fall overboard from the boat's violent rocking. The Muti's actions caused the river to splash perilously over the bow.

"Sziat! Stop! We're going to capsize if you keep this up!" I hollered at the top of my lungs. But it ignored my plea, ranting louder and bewailing the sadistic dismembering of innocent people and of honest Mutis.

"Their vile, cancerous empire spreads. They have desecrated the majority of our beloved land and expanded out across the oceans."

The more it spoke, the heavier became my dread of what the future would bring. I feared it would sweep me into the depths of this black river, doomed.

"There is no mercy. They strip bones, layer by layer, and laugh at their victims' pain. You don't want to cross these monsters!

"Vuel ne, hiu Ahmra, li ahn Trae bis!"

Sziat slowed to a respectable pace, still telling its story, never resting from its task; rowing persistently along the narrowing river.

By the time dawn broke, it had spent the fury of its tale and I could release my desperate hold on the gunnels.

Sziat had grown silent.

The landscape had become increasingly sparse, changing to rugged dry waste. Large jutting boulders forced us to navigate precariously around them. Eventually, they blocked the dwindling river.

We abandoned the skiff. Sziat strapped several packs

of supplies to its shoulders and I did the same. On foot, we climbed a rocky path. I tagged after this stranger, its purpose still puzzling me. All I knew for certain, was that it had become my keeper, my guide, and in an untamed country, my sole companion. Questioning the Muti further only intensified its silence. It spoke at its own pleasure; not mine.

As we forged onward, I kept wondering how much of my core identity the Muti had accessed.

III. Wilderness Dangers

Intelligence was never restricted to beasts, for there are wonders beyond animal flesh. Man and creature are not alone given voice to wisdom, for truths emanate from flora and fauna alike.
—Tomes of the Ji

Several days passed with no signs of civilization. We had been progressively climbing up and down, scaling ridge after ridge of ragged crags, until we'd crested a summit overlooking a barren region of sand and rock.

The Muti pointed to a tall, slender tower lifting out from among huge boulders.

"Monitors; avoid. They spy on any rebellious or suspicious aggression and report to the Prophet. We must circumvent them. Beyond the horizon lies your destination. The realm of the Muti engine continually expands, consuming territory as if it were a hungry Traztu beast."

We kept our pace steady, although Sziat hugged the shaded side of rock formations shielding us from Monitors. I did not like the open plains or the silence between us.

It paused when we came upon a squared block jutting half out of the ground with faded, but neatly etched writing on its surface.

"Cultures rise and fall; often leaving behind little more than broken pilasters like these, as a memorial to their builders."

Sziat stepped back from the stone.

"In the Quadrates of the Ancients you shall find substantial relics and among them, perhaps, the answers you seek."

The Muti told of the ruin's history as we passed the protective boulders and trekked across barren plains. Its voice droned on into yet another piece of the Kaminaean saga and I relaxed, preferring its monologue to bitter silence.

"For generations, we had ignored these crumbling ancient ruins. Few travelers ever showed curiosity. Even the Muti had been content and had declined to study what was dead and buried—until recently."

Sziat stopped short and glared at me. It gave no basis for staring. Soon, its droning continued in cadence with our march.

"It would not seem *recent* for the human, I suppose, for the historic passing of time spanned many of your generations. Although, for the Muti, it is indeed, *recent*: but, no matter.

"The people of the region showed open curiosity and the search for relics grew in popularity. In time, treasure hunters started digging around the old foundations. Beneath the rubble, charming objects were soon discovered; intricate sculptures, tools, and artifacts. Fascination with treasure hunting spread across the land.

"Continental explorers excavated huge swathes of land, sometimes digging up the ancient foundations of entire cities, opening long buried vaults and discovering volumes of written scrolls. Scholars studied the writings, many of which were written in foreign script. They sought council of their sage Muti who eventually, came to the forlorn sites and obliged the human's curiosity. For, the old relics sparked no personal interest in the Muti of those days. Patiently, they assisted the humans, deciphering and preparing the delicate text to be transported to the cities, and then distributed across the country.

"*Tales of the Seeding* surfaced. Books, such as the *Words of the Eemel*, circulated and became popular among the people. They learned the odes and sagas, and recited them in the holy temples, glorifying the gods. The Ji taught new verses to their followers.

"A disturbing behavior gradually occurred. Certain Mutis conferred with one another over the transcriptions; congregating, first in pairs and later in clusters. Sometimes they would attend ceremonies and occasionally raise voices in praise with the throngs. The formerly singular, serene stoics exhibited human-like emotions and social conduct.

"People welcomed their sages with great awe and respect. The Ji honored their wisdom and allotted them privileged seats in the ceremonies. The Muti actively increased their involvement, deciphering the scrolls.

"In due course, they took control over the worship services, the libraries, and schools. The scholars and rulers lauded praises on Muti sages, appreciating their interest in educating human communities.

"Ah, what glorious times those where: the words of wisdom were sung throughout the land, by young and old, alike: cherished by all the nations. Quarrels were rare and wars had ceased, for a time. The Muti continued to grow in favor and in power and endowed the peoples with common sense of righteousness.

"Another eerie trend crept across the land, as well. The Muti savored its popularity and greed emerged from its prosperity. Now and again, a Muti would quarrel with another over some verse or a ritual in ceremony. Or dispute the ranking of certain wisdom over others. They disagreed about whether certain text was acceptable or should be omitted. As new works came to light, the Muti argued over who would have first rights.

"The most grievous changes occurred when the Muti began administering punishment to any who opposed its authority. And by that time, it was too late for the people to stop it.

"Slowly but surely, the Ji lost favor. The Mutis' self-esteem escalated, demanding to be worshiped and obeyed. They took control over the community laws and customs, and tightened restrictions on the masses.

"They convinced the people that open education needed

protection, for one reason or another. Their purposes were never questioned because nobody had ever dared to contradict a Muti.

"The Muti discouraged scholars from continuing the work, warning the humans that these documents could prove dangerous to their well being.

"All public access to any books of knowledge fell under Muti control. Whole communities found themselves excluded from worship ceremonies.

"At the height of the abundance of knowledge, the Mutis had declared a moratorium on all works, springing from ancient sources. They banned access to libraries; even destroyed volumes of documents. Any mention of the excavated cities or discovered writings was strictly prohibited."

Sziat's pace quickened and I had to run to keep up.

"A few scholars secretly defied the Muti law, but said nothing for fear of punishment and death. Instead, they secretly hid away the precious scrolls they still possessed, for they refused to believe in the Muti's rise to power. Something had gone gravely wrong. But, nobody could take the risk of openly voicing their objection."

"After the ban was enforced, people were very frightened. Nobody dared to speak. Research scientists, all over the country, had suddenly disappeared. Excavations were closed and the areas were marked as dangerous.

Sziat looked sullen.

"The Muti banned together and designed the pyramids. The most notable of them stand in the Quadrates. They enlisted the human population to build cities with the pyramids positioned over the major excavation sites. This ensured that no humans would gain access without full Muti supervision.

The *Pyramid of the Prophet* is now heavily guarded from intruders. It is rumored to house the source of Kalinis' power."

My interest perked up when it mentioned the pyramids and I wanted direct answers.

"Were the *Scrolls of Wisdom* among them?"

Sziat's head snapped up.

"Are those what you came for?"

I had kept these thoughts and many others buried deep beneath the mind block. Still, I feared I had revealed too much.

I said nothing more.

Eerie, how a Muti's hollowed, empty eye sockets can pull me into their depths. Whatever membrane induced visual understanding of the world around them remained as mysterious as the origins of the Muti themselves.

The Muti sucked in a deep breath. I felt exposed; punctured right through the Jan Sorla masking. I tried to convince myself that an adventurer, even a loyal spy for the Armada, would be as acceptable a guise as a mercenary.

We traversed the harsh terrain, passing an occasional Monitor discreetly planted among jagged ridges. They stood like stone sentinels, guarding against trespassers. And we were, obviously, ripe targets. Over time, Sziat spoke again.

"The Resistance learned of certain documents found in the deserts, south of a primary Muti Quadrate. Some believe the discovered secrets have been stored in the Pyramid of the Prophet. It is there, you may find the *Fruit of the Seeds*, perhaps, locate the birthing place. It is sacred, and few, beyond the Prophet, have access."

Sziat gnashed its teeth and hissed as it spoke about the Muti warlords.

"You must be alert; for the servants of Kalinis are many. I speak not only of human servants and slaves. For, they have designed means beyond your imagination. Watch for the winged Gatherers; dangerous products of Kamina: the melding of the living to hard technology. And beware of the man-machines, the savage warriors designed for hand to hand battle, and cannot be easily killed; half-man half-beasts—vile And, if manufactured in full assembly, will defeat any unified army, no matter how big."

I asked, "What more can you tell me about them?"

Its gruesome saga disturbed me greatly, as the Muti spoke of the Kaminaean rise and occupation, throughout the continent;

spilling out to the neighboring islands. It told of how the tribes and communities had been reduced to servitude. The people's humble communities lapsed into slums, while they were forced into slave labor, rebuilding their cities in order to accommodate the growing Muti hordes. Any persons, of intellect or talent, would be literally devoured by the hungry Muti. For the Muti forcefully convinced the trembling masses to believe that to do so, was honoring the will of the great Prophet.

People have now been conditioned to believe they are no better than feed beasts to be raised for the slaughter in order to please the Muti.

It spoke of rituals and mass assemblies, where the Muti would repeatedly perform outrageous deeds in public squares, until the peoples grew numb to the shock and could no longer discern any sense of morality.

I struggled to grasp the extent of what this Muti was telling me.

Sziat finally shook its head and reverted into its sullen silence.

We crossed the empty valley to the cool shade of a forest, where Sziat stopped.

"Too many hunters roaming: beware of the Mosdus and their bipedal mounts; nocturnal hunters, prone to flying from tree-tops; cutting away hapless victims in the dark."

The night air amplified moans and eerie trills through the forest. The unmistakable call of the Korda was among them, though it came from a respectable distance. This particular beast was all too familiar to me; standing over five times the size of a tall warrior.

On occasion, we saw ghostly eyes shining from the branches, only to quickly dart away when we turned in their direction; probably as suspicious of us as we were of them.

No real threat had actually materialized until we approached a dense netting of purple foliage. I noticed a peculiar tilt of Sziat's head while examining our pathway.

We cut through the twined underbrush, the air chiming with vibrant life, eerily hostile. Thick rods lifted up above twisted vines with pointed pods at their tips.

A vine suddenly clung to my legs. Several of the pods slammed me.

"Destroy them!"

Sziat swung its sword, decapitating the ovular pods, as if they were living monsters. Dust burst out in all directions.

The gaping pods lashed towards my flesh, as I swung my weapon with critical aim. I had no idea what these creatures were.

My sword chopped at the vegetation, shattering stocks. They hissed and squealed, painfully. The plants were animated, bending and swaying towards us. In a short time, the incident ended.

Sziat sheathed its sword. "Nasty business."

"What are they?"

"Hungry for animal flesh," it stated. "They dwell in swamps, often near the Rupa."

"The Rupa?"

"Many creatures live here. And they are ravenous. You will know, soon enough."

Near dusk, we were attacked for the second time. The world switched into a mad frame of whipping vines coming out of nowhere, yet from everywhere, at once. They slashed around us, like a whirl of mighty chains.

Sziat smashed to the ground with an exploding thump. A vine had twisted around its heels, snatching the Muti's whole frame high above the ground. It bellowed wordlessly, hanging upside down, head swinging.

Another one slithered around my own feet.

"Listen. Be alert! Do not resist!"

But I wasn't listening. A slender vine locked my legs in a tight vice, roughly yanking me forward, stumbling to keep my balance. Broad purple leaves whipped across my face. I instinctively swung my sword, grazing the coiling vine. My legs were jerked out from under me. My vision blocked. When I finally caught sight of Sziat, its still limbs dangled above me.

Swirling vegetation twisted further up my body. Helplessly, I struggled against the twining tendrils. My hand still held the sword, but the blade was ensnared; my arm was awkwardly strapped. I felt like a stuffed manikin, pinned by a solid, though painless weedy growth.

Peace! advised a voice inside my head. *Why does he tremble? Is he afraid?*

Other voices rumbled. *Hold the peace. Rest the limbs.*

Straining wastes resources. They spoke in an echoing chorus.

I tightened the Zygo block, hoping to sever the connection. Angry aggression flooded me with hardened determination to resist this uncanny connection.

"Release us!" I demanded.

Stop struggling, Torlo Hannis.

My block had failed It had already pierced my inner defense barrier.

We know about you and your fundamental shield; notably adequate for most purposes; however, transparent to our observation. You require a condensed layer of protection.

The voice split into parallel strands,

The guard within was not properly sealed. It cannot protect against threatening consciousness. His will is strong. It can be mended. We shall reorder his mental defenses.

They shifted into singular monotone.

Be still. Allow the process to compound.

A tingling settled down my spine; a cooling ice traced along my nerves, both frightening and soothing. It rushed through my veins, in harsh violent waves, gradually, kneading over my muscles, with amazing force.

We mean you no harm.

Defiant against its calming words, I demanded once more: "Release us!"

It disregarded my plea as if deaf.

I framed automatic questions. *Who are you? What are you? Where are you?*

Different voices whispered:

We are of a universal bond.
Sentient knowledge is not limited to walking creatures.
Intelligence feeds through all living systems.
It is the energy supply of life.
Call us the spirit of the forest, if you need a name. Or Rupa,
as Muti has so done.
Does that explain?

Quite obviously it didn't. A chorus streaked through my mind:

All is aware, even the soil is conscious. All matter must be aware, to survive. Be it inanimate substance, simple singular entities, or complex life. All come from the same star seeds, and exist along different vibrating time frames.

The voices came in waves.

"We are the melody, yoking together, all certainty.

"We are the perpetual coils, adding definition, to what is nebulous.

"We are wisdom, binding all the purpose, of this world."

Dizziness drenched me, but did not drown my stalwart refusal to meekly surrender.

We wish not to harm, only to inform.

My blade swept through empty air on its own, as if it was making a futile attempt to do battle with an invisible foe.

"Release my friend!"

I tried to regain control, wanting to hack at the vine, but the blade fell short of its intended target.

It speaks of the Muti as friend. Is this not rare?

An edge of mockery laced that thought.

The twisting tentacles that had captured me were now loosening. Darkness melted as I pulsed in and out of consciousness, convulsing like fragmented glass. I lay on the ground; the evening air damply chilling; the sun setting low, upon the horizon.

My eyes saw a Muti but didn't recognize Sziat, right away.

It took my shoulders and lifted me to a standing position.

"You are well. We continue our journey."

"What happened?"

I tried to clear my aching head.

"Rupa told its wisdom, and withdrew," Sziat replied. "We continue our journey."

Still dazed, I could not form questions, coherently. "...Rupa...."

Sziat sighed.

"They dwell below in far locations. Rupa make their homes where they please. They weave an intricate network of connected living matter throughout the planet."

It shook its shoulders, rubbed its legs, examining itself all over; muttering annoying remarks at the Rupa.

"You called me friend to Rupa. So, I will say what I know of them, Jan Sorla."

In silence, Sziat hastened its pace through the dense foliage. At length as had been its style, Sziat began to speak in its story-telling fashion.

"In all the lands, Rupa grows hardy and strong. They thrive in cold bogs and arid deserts: in the depths of the sea and peak of the high mountains. Rupa keeps peaceful harmony with nature, digesting the old, providing vital nourishment for new life. They are everywhere and appear as needed. You will learn. Some are similar to weeds; some bare bountiful flowers.

"Rupa of the hot swamps and the dry desert can be as fierce, as the Korda. For their life is complex and Rupa grows hungry."

"How did I survive the encounter back there?"

Its answer sounded more like a teacher attempting to explain rudimentary lessons to a dense student.

"The Mutis are wary of Rupa; sometimes friendly; some-times in conflict. We perceive at different frequencies. The Muti has need of Rupa to work against Kaminaeans. You will find them useful. The gift of Rupa will help you defend against threatening probes...Jan Sorla."

The Muti marched away, essentially expecting me to follow.

To Sziat the conversation was over: Again.

After this encounter we slept by day and journeyed at night. The steady tone of Sziat's voice became my beacon beneath the black blanket of twinkling stars and moonlight. Its long speeches droned on with generalities and vague references, so I grew accustomed to its epic jargon, spanning space and time; often unrelated to human understanding.

"Seek clarity. Be not closed to the unfamiliar. The Muti can grasp knowledge beyond the human reach. This much you know, for you have dwelt among people who are accustomed to the Muti ways.

"Surely you have felt the touch of the Muti when it would lay its hands upon you."

The memory of my first encounter with a Muti who had spoken into my mind during the Diano War still haunted me. When this *Sziat* had snatched me away from Vintu, I had shivered.

But now the Muti continued its historic saga and I'd held back my many questions, knowing Sziat would ignore interruptions to its monologue.

"Mutis in Kamina are different; not all are equal. They may bond with a human at the will of the Muti. Not all are capable of discerning thoughts beyond the touch. And fewer still, care to connect with the human other than in demanding servitude.

"I need not explain. Kaminaean Mutis are a different breed. You must stay alert, Jan Sorla, even with the gifts of the HanJahn and the Rupa."

* * * * * * *

As we crossed a clearing in the forest, we saw smoke whisked up along the tree line beyond a broad field of low grasses. Several of the Monitors were perched upon hillocks, their slim towers protruding from uneven crevices.

Sziat nodded towards the village, barely visible in the distance: "Those people serve Kalinis."

We spent the better part of the night keeping the crescent moons behind us, avoiding the settlement. Once we passed into a forested knoll within the cover of the trees, the Muti stopped.

Head cocked to one side, it looked up into the thick trees.

"I sense danger." Sziat reached for its sword.

"Arm yourself!"

Its voice had barely faded to silence when a howling billowed all around us. Shadowy beasts swung out from the trees.

I got my first look at a Blianzeh. The long-legged beasts hung by hairy claws with wild warriors clinging to their narrow shoulders. Ugly yellow eyes, pitted with black and brown specks, radiated glowing beams of light that cut through the night.

Sziat's sword slashed at one savage after another. I had drawn my sword by the time the Muti had started hurling bodies down into the jagged rocks, lining the pathway. Their mounts squealed, ripping at us with their six pronged claws.

"Go for their eyes!" I heard it say.

The wide mouth of a Blianzeh snapped; its jagged teeth flashing. I swung at the assailants, cutting them down with the edge of my sword. Their defeat was easy enough, and in a short time we exterminated nearly all of them.

Sziat snatched up the nearest Mosdus, yanking him from his Blianzeh, which streaked off into the forest.

Two of the captive's companions, retreated into the night.

Sziat turned. In the dim light I saw a glow in the Muti's hollow eye-sockets. Weathered lips parted, and a low hissing voice rumbled.

"The Mosdus are hunters, they hunger after flesh."

"The scoundrels failed!" I jeered with a droll smile.

"You have much to learn! We have been spotted!"

With contempt, Sziat's right arm smashed across a Mosdus' face, decapitating him, in one swift movement.

The Muti released the convulsing body which piled to the ground at our feet.

"These disgusting beasts report to the Monitors. Their defeat will be noted."

As it spoke, Sziat had already distanced itself from the fallen enemy, and did not look back. Eventually, it stopped at the top of a hill. I caught up to it. Below, a sizable group of Mutis circled around a blazing bonfire.

People, likely servants, were milling around the Mutis. And not far away, was a group of huts.

We watched, for a short while. Sziat advised we should make a wide circle, to avoid detection.

I wondered if any Resistance organization could be found, in such an environment.

"It is well hidden!" Sziat responded to my unspoken query.

"When do we make contact with Resistance?" I foolishly asked.

"Sooner than you might wish; be aware. All is not as it seems to be. You cannot detect loyalty from outward signs. Mutis function treacherously within the empire. They are growing bolder. Villagers are dedicated to them. Worship them as gods. Prostrate themselves as willing slaves, no better than pets and beasts of burden. So strong is the Kaminaean influence, on the peoples. The dominance is rampant."

It dashed down the embankment in broad, leaping strides. Conversation had been bluntly ended, leaving urgent questions unanswered.

IV. Betrayal

The present is illusive.
The dimensions of the universe encompass endless
perceptions of yesterday.
Projections of tomorrows bear countless variety.
All are legitimate and all have purpose.
                                    —Teachings of Moyi

I felt amazingly safe, in Sziat's company, for I had grown to trust this eccentric Muti, who had come to my rescue and served as my guide.

A cobbled road reflected increasing signs of habitation and development meandering from open plains to cultivated farm lands. Late that afternoon we noted a cluster of dwellings; a township without a sentry or any notable barriers.

"We will go there."

The Muti headed down a crowded street past mud-brick huts. People ambled in and out of shops. Sziat muttered something to a passerby who pointed to an intersection. We followed his direction down an alley illuminated with hanging torches. The wooden shingle hanging over an arched entry read *Public House*. Inside, the inn was packed with overfed drunkards and half-clad wenches. A patron near the door, hollered across the crude benches for Porshi.

In a secluded corner, we found a saucy barmaid sitting alone at table. Sziat brushed her aside as if wiping old crumbs from the bench, and she slipped away; melting into the noisy crowd. A server approached, a nervous grin contorting his face; eyes stiffly fixed on the Muti.

"Oh, *Mighty One*, do you disapprove of our women? They are here for your service. Might I interest you in another favorable morsel, seeing how you found *the other* undesirable? Choose any pleasing your taste!"

"I have no business with them!" Sziat snarled with sharp emotion.

The man looked startled, even a bit frightened.

"We are honored with the presence of one as venerable as yourself."

Keeping his eyes locked on the Muti, he spanned his arms across the room.

I tried to placate the trembling innkeeper by saying: "My... Master...is not interested in carnal entertainment."

Sziat glared as if I'd spoken without permission and sent a hasty slap against my shoulder.

"Please, I assure you, we supply as required. We can order any pleasure for your most eminent demands!" When the man changed the subject, his clumsy attempt only annoyed the Muti all the more.

Sziat's sharp anger was dangerously menacing.

"You tell me nothing! What need have I, for your weak, animalistic trivialities? Beasts groveling in carnal lust; their driveling rituals bore me."

"A combat to the death?" the man stammered, anxiously. "That can be arranged."

Sziat slammed his fist on the table and sneered.

"I have no interest in any of these *weaklings*!"

The poor fellow was obviously terrified for his life. "We are simple villagers. Seldom, does the Muti honor my establishment: Praises to the Prophet."

"And to the *New Truth*," Sziat grumbled in response.

His pathetic attempts to please a Muti customer sadly intrigued me. He awkwardly persisted; lips stretched thin: "Shall I bring Ka or something extra potent?"

Sziat's hand clawed the tabletop. "Bring Ka!"

Instant relief thawed the innkeeper's thick face.

"It is my pleasure to serve at no charge, for our prominent guest!"

"Wise; very wise: but you cannot prosper without profit. We purchase your Ka. And if you speak well, we are willing to pay for information." Sziat showed an edge of amusement.

"My Lord, you are too generous! My profit need only be the honor of attending those who come in the Prophet's name."

He clapped his hands twice. A lovely young wench scurried to the table, carrying two steaming tankards. She quickly shoved them towards us and hurried away, while the innkeeper seemed to regain his composure.

His eyes widened, craftily.

"What sort of conversation interests you?"

"We heard of new ventures: activities on the outskirts."

Sziat faltered, as if he'd changed his mind mid-statement.

"Surely, you would know better than I," the man rambled. "For the minions of the Prophet are many. Wise are they who respect the hallowed secrets reserved exclusively for members of your honored clan."

"Well advised! Tell me."

Sziat again, struck me firmly across the shoulders.

"My minion seeks trade. Discretion, you understand?"

This odd exchange was beginning to make sense as I considered the desperate nature of humans in Kamina; valued less than slaves, by the Mutis.

He glanced towards a door in the back of the tavern.

"It is an unusual request."

He hesitated.

"New trade within the peoples' class is—as the Mighty Voice of the Prophet dictates—not permitted."

"Stop rambling. Speak truth!" Sziat played a finger against the man's nose; just touching it.

"Yes, of course, unless it is established in the outer courts. You can leave by the back door. There is a narrow, concealed passage that avoids the crowded streets."

Sziat tossed a few coins on the table which the innkeeper greedily scooped up.

"The honor is mine" he hurried away, looking nervously back over his shoulder. "Praised be the Prophet!"

"Come!" Sziat slipped past me towards the door. "Treachery is everywhere.

A steep staircase led down to the bottom and through a dimly lit tunnel.

"Where are we going?" I asked, somewhat bewildered.

"To local traders," the Muti replied.

It abruptly stopped when the tunnel ended at a thick wooden archway.

Danger! Sziat warned. *Prepare!*

The murky alley was not empty. Shadows rose towards us. Heavy metal scraped against metal: the unmistakable sound of unsheathed weapons. Just enough light reflected the flash of blades.

"Betrayed!" Sziat snarled.

I drew my sword and knife. Sziat's reaction was even faster.

We stood back to back, surrendering no space to risk attack from behind. Sparks exploded from our blades clashing against a horde of warriors swarming us like hungry Kunaks.

Someone hollered for reinforcements and more fighters appeared out of nowhere. Sziat seemed to actually enjoy cutting its blade through human bodies.

We fought our way down the narrow alley and out to the street. I had never expected to be dependent on a Muti as a fighting companion.

Several warriors were soon cut down; our blades yielding no mercy. The others backed away when they saw how their companions were so easily annihilated. Their attack halted abruptly at the open street where the last fighters lowered their weapons and scattered. An odd encounter, as if they did not want to be seen publicly fighting. Or perhaps, the sight of a Muti fighting them was too unsettling; terrifying.

I backed into the alley and wiped my weapons clean on the dead warriors' bodies.

"I should have suspected the trap!" Sziat hissed, head lifting as if it was attempting to listen, or smell, or see. "Revolt seethes against the Muti. It is all around us.

"Maybe those attackers know something we do not."

No sooner had we sheathed our blades, when out of the side streets came an armored brigade led by a Muti. The militant air left no doubt as to their intent. We were outnumbered. They marched directly at us, brashly disarmed me, roughly escorted us through the scattering crowds, and into a public square.

Sziat stayed at my side.

Guard or protector, I wondered.

Sziat's right arm slammed back against my chest, knocking the wind out of me.

Be alert!

Its thought warned me to stay mute.

Jan Sorla intensified, keeping Torlo Hannis solidly submerged below the Rupa's reinforced shell. Yet, from outside my skull, pressure squeezed hard against my will. An unwelcome force probed deep. The Zygo block automatically closed tighter within. Something had buried Torlo deeper beneath that protective shield.

Stay silent! Sziat cautioned. *Cower if necessary.*

Several hooded sentries turned, glaring at us as the captors stepped away and a Muti, taller than the others, approached. Its decorated cloak was bright with a series of ornate twisting vines and bejeweled flora. That colorful pattern rippled right up to the leathery purple neck, stretching the luminous markings along the creature's wrinkled, bony face.

"I am Fuewal, Chief Magistrate of the Marfsu district. What business have you here?"

Sziat pressed its sword into my chest.

"I bring a slave for the Lords of Kamina."

It bowed submissively before the other Muti. "How can I serve?"

"Why is he not bound?" Fuewal angrily demanded.

Sziat purred smoothly. "This foolish creature professed me a friend."

Fuewal's arm shot out, pointing straight at my face.

"Bind him!"

Its cloak fell back, exposing flamboyant chains of gleaming gems upon its chest. The men behind him lurched forward, weapons drawn.

Sziat bellowed with savage laughter, right arm brushed hard across my face with a forceful swing, knocking me to the ground.

Fortunately, it restrained the effect sufficiently to demonstrate Sziat's control. Had it applied any more effort, it could easily have crushed me: Although, it had, in fact, nearly rendered me unconscious.

"Binding him is pointless!" Sziat hissed.

Fuewal tossed a rope at the Muti.

"This specimen is *your* gift to us, so do as ordered. Present him in proper fashion!"

Sziat obeyed with no further objections, looping my wrists firmly behind my back. It swept past me, following the Magistrate out of the courtyard. The warriors filed past, roughly shoving me forward.

Nothing made sense. I had trusted the Muti; nearly considering it a *friend*. That had proven to be a mistake. Betrayal caused my captivity. Seething anger possessed me, blurring all else. I swore to never again trust any Muti; especially not Sziat.

Something rammed the back of my head.

* * * * * * *

Voices filtered through the pain searing down my spine. I tried to open my eyes.

"He's coming around."

A gnarled face glared, inches from mine.

"Who are you?"

"A prisoner: same as you. What crime have you done against the Kamina?"

I recoiled, snapped back by the chain which bound me to this man; the first of a long line of heavily scarred, muscular men locked one behind the other like trapped beasts, raring to be loosed.

"You are newly arrived," he said, raising me up so my head leaned against the stone barrier. He seemed to take an interest in my welfare for some odd reason.

"We're the Muti's gaming warriors, trained to compete in death duels. Entertainment for the Muti masters. Scars won in battles, gain us an edge. We're rewarded with feasting and pleasuring slavegirls."

He was describing the life of a gladiator. Even in the Galactic Federation, sports were not uncommon; usually composed of combat demonstrations. Death duels occurred among prisoners of war, for the sake of taming the defeated foe.

This warrior must think I am one of them.

"You appear strong enough," he rasped in hushed tones, scrutinizing me with grave concern. "The Muti will target your unmarked frame, quickly. Scars come in all battles. You have no experience."

"Scars result from *mistakes* in battle," I answered, coldly.

"Perhaps cowards who run and hide dodge the scars," he stared suspiciously at me.

I met his glare, head on. "A *master* of the arena smartly avoids the wounding blade."

The man nodded admiringly, "You are either a stealthy warrior or a spineless fool."

Our eyes held the insult at bay. He dropped the questions; then glanced down the line of prisoners, who were flopped motionless against the barrier of this dank, smelly alley. It was too dark to see beyond the first few hunched figures.

"I am a fool, perhaps. Not a coward! I'd advise you not to contest my battle methods."

His voice was now barely audible.

"We may duel. And you will probably be pitted against my companions, here. Perhaps the Mutis will decide to skin you alive, screaming. They have a sick concept of humor."

"Shut up!" someone threatened.

A rock pelted the edge of his jaw and he cringed to silence.

"We are all doomed!" someone snapped.

The men near me hunkered down as a Muti swept by and whipped a bony finger across my cheek.

"Silence!"

I recognized Sziat's harsh voice.

Rage slashed through me at the sight of the deceiver.

Show them you're a killer! Sziat taunted.

Resentful indignation stung me. I needed no opinion from this Muti. The scourge of betrayal fired my ferocity to an unreasonable level.

My body arched; poised to attack.

Yes. Reveal fury! Sziat goaded. *Convince them!*

I wanted to mangle this monster who had deceptively shifted from advisor to tormentor. All I could think of was terminating it.

Enraged, I leaped at its throat. I wanted to snap its neck. But it clawed my shoulders, dangling me up off the ground beyond reach with its long arms.

Savage man thing: you cannot fight against me, foolish human! There are other fighters here. Choose one to battle...or die at my hand.

I spat demands at it. *Why have you betrayed me? Get me out of here!*

I had seen the brutal strength of this Muti during our travels and now it used its superior power viciously against me. With a sweep of its arms, it swung me until the chains went taut.

All eyes turned on us.

Approving voices rose, in anticipation of a death duel.

"Arm this...*thing*!" Sziat commanded. "And *that* man!"

He shook me like a pointer.

"He's Qon, our champion."

"Perfect!" Sziat exploded.

"Prepare them for a death duel."

My fellow combatant was the biggest and most alert of the prisoners.

Sziat dangled me at arm's length while a guard shackled my leg. One end latched to my right ankle and the other the warrior who now stood nearly as tall as a Muti.

His thickly muscled arms flexed as he grinned fiendishly. The brute oozed with confidence. This chain spanned four lengths of a man. Our weapons were short double-edged hacking axes with saw-toothed razor sharp edges; perfectly suited for close combat, designed to rip flesh from bone.

Humans and Mutis stood shoulder to shoulder in a dense ring, making escape impossible, even if I could manage to break free. I was forced to face this gladiator.

"The survivor will be champion for tonight's banquet!" a Muti set the rules of the match.

"Qon, chop him slowly and win the most beautiful slavegirl in our dens for the night."

"Kill or be killed!" Sziat growled coldly.

The giant's bare torso was contorted with scars: his insignia of hard won victories over savage combatants.

Qon swung; the short ax slashed towards my chest forming a wicked arc that would have shredded my flesh if I hadn't instantly raised my blade to block, counter-thrust, and hack at the other's extended thigh. The man parried and stumbled back a step, slightly off balance. Sudden shock showed on his rugged face. Qon had apparently expected to mangle me with that first swing.

A mistake, for he'd badly underestimated me.

I pounded into the man's wide ribs. One sweep of his arm hurled me to one side. I fell back the full length of the chain that linked our ankles. Qon tumbled after me, his ax now raised for the strike. I dove, letting my body roll under his shoulders and he flew right over me.

With one move, I pushed his blade to one side and slammed the edge of my weapon's handle into his neck. Like a fallen Korda, the man slumped and lay still.

I didn't expect it to end so brusquely. I loomed over Qon, who froze; jaw set hard, hissing profanities at me.

"Kill! Kill him!" several voices chanted in high pitched unison.

I locked my stance, refusing to comply. I had no intention to kill. Suddenly my head was jerked from behind. Sziat glared viciously into my face.

"Fool!" its hot breath seethed through clenched teeth. Sziat roughly yanked me away from Qon. Blinded from the jarring pain in my skull, I lost consciousness.

* * * * * *

Once again, I found myself chained among the prisoners. My vision cleared to see Qon linked further back. All these men were crouched down, close together. I followed their example as several Muti guards marched by, prodding at anyone who caught their attention. We were commanded to move. Everybody stood and instantly took up a fast pace as directed.

We were force-marched a full day. I continued to feel dazed, sickened to my stomach by my nightmarish predicament. No words could begin to describe my resentment at how I'd been cheated out of my integrity. My trust had been thrown away like so much trash; worse than death: insulted, beyond belief. The whole world was insane.

Does any Muti make sense? They know the future when it so pleases them. They invade our minds. What else can they do? Is there some rational explanation for Sziat's actions?

That evening, we camped within a cavernous hollow beneath the side of a cliff. A gloomy place, pillared with stately Muti statues; their arms held high to support the rock ceiling.

Chains were unlocked. We were shoved, one by one, into separate cells. The gates crushed shut and darkness slammed down.

Exhaustion caused awareness to slip into a black vortex, churning into an acrid abyss.

CHAPTER TWELVE
HELANDI RENEGADES

I. Ju-bilee's Charge

Ju-bilee gazed up at the starlight filtering through the dome, marveling at the endless space; tracing the millennia back to the seeds of creation. It stretched out across the pale terrain of Helandi, her beloved home, where she could escape from the conflicts and confusions of the turbulent world. From her personal sanctuary, she could concentrate on healing. For, this place provided the balm for restoration to inner peace, and serenity.

Demands were high, and she was obliged by the HanJahn, to supervise a multitude of people who were vital to the rising conflict. She was expected to coordinate the forces preparing for conflict with the Empire of Kamina. The mission was partly guidance; and partly direct action. Those elements had included a close connection with the mission pilots and crew, while they were able to transmit. Her task was difficult, for when a unit was in crisis she could likely be compelled to personally intervene, sometimes leaving the others unguarded. As a result, several missions were tragically sacrificed, while she resolutely focused on saving those in immediate danger.

Her son and Sarleni had been the first elements of the HanJahn project, setting an excellent model for the Zygo duos that were being deployed with the Armada.

In the past, when Moyi had suggested such a possibility, she had conferred with the master sage, at length, about her personal involvement. Moyi considered the implications, but they had come to the conclusion that the connection was a greater asset, despite its complications.

For decades since leaving her son, Adt, under Kigor's care, her attention had been wholly absorbed. The HanJahn studies required extreme concentration on the dimensions of the intellect. Every moment was honed for the purpose of refining advancements.

Recently, her son's welfare had become a monopolizing obsession. Adt had barged into her exclusive vista, at times absorbing continual attention. She felt an unreasonable need to protect him from current threats. Parental ministrations of this nature were inconceivably alien.

To her displeasure, the latest deployment list included her son and Sarleni. Ju-bilee decided to visit the academy immediately to speak with Adt about these issues, only to be shocked in discovering that both he and Sarleni were missing.

She immediately questioned every authority about their whereabouts, and was highly indignant when not one person had noticed their absence. They had doubtlessly schemed to throw the supervisors off track, by cleverly altering their schedules, so that the various professors would assume them to be attending elsewhere. In actuality they had not attended any of the last several classes, at all. Nobody remembered seeing them on campus, lately.

It was quite possible that they had left Helandi, altogether and not even the security staff knew they were missing.

Adt and Sarleni had disappeared.

Ju-bilee angrily shuddered, thinking about her stubborn son.

How could he be so obstinate?

Everyone knew the protocol. Regulation required all personnel to report their whereabouts, at all times. Accountability was vital. Failure to report was inexcusable!

How dare they disappear without permission!

It was of utmost importance to sustain consistent contact,

especially under the current conditions. Danger threatened them beyond the borders of Helandi outside the safe confines of Bel-loniean political, and military control.

In all likelihood, she resentfully guessed, *they've gone on some mission of their own design.*

Senses keenly sharpened, Ju-bilee rushed through the HanJahn Academy searching for those vagrants, cross examining every person who'd last seen them, digging for every minuscule detail.

And she had not stopped there, for the Dean was also under suspicion in her book. Before the day was done, the word that Ju-bilee was on a rampage had circulated, and everyone within the academy had been involuntarily recruited to solve her mystery.

Central control reported that the last conversation they'd had with the three missing persons was very short—incomplete; several days ago, with Moyi present.

Her quest was on.

Little by little, the pieces came together signifying that something had been brewing. The records showed that Yaw-iyn had reassigned all of his classes to the engineering faculty.

According to Moyi, the professor had apparently vacated the academy. He'd been spotted on the gaming fields with Adt, a few days earlier. Current logs traced him to the launch port. Associates assumed he was working with the crystal radiance generators on the flight deck.

Upon hearing this, Ju-bilee immediately rushed to the launch deck to check out Yaw-iyn's new test Orb, the professor's prized innovation. Yaw-iyn had developed the new drive for the fleet, using his Orb as the test module for the experimental crystal radiance generator. And his private lab would be the logical place to start her search.

The dome flashed away and Ju-bilee appeared at the Helandian's main docking station. The professor's new test Orb was moored at the shipyard which was set among boulders; framed against the ocean.

The fleet yard guards, however, had refused to give her access, so she had insisted they authorize her clearance with the Professor. When he could not be found, they were obligated to call in a security alert.

"We can't let you in without permission."

Ju-bilee narrowly restrained her fury. "Get it!"

She was not interested in polite discourse. All she'd wanted to see was the Professor's docking bay. And more importantly, find Adt or Sarleni.

The baffled men stared at one another, not wanting to create a scene.

"And now!" she demanded.

They reluctantly complied by calling in the fleet commander, who rushed over immediately, tapped in the access code, and then commenced with a full yard inspection.

Much to their chagrin all guards were questioned, just because of this annoyingly persistent HanJahn doyenne.

Sure enough, as she had suspected, the dock was empty.

She guessed that from his control room, a remote device had operated the hatch, so the Orb's departure would have avoided detection by the flight-tower.

Ju-bilee knew the Dean's reputation. Under his influence, and her son's determination, it was easy to guess where they might have gone.

Ju-bilee was outraged!

Is Yaw-iyn insane?

So what if he's an expert pilot!

In fact, a man in his position should have known better!

He may be a clever inventor, but he is not thoroughly trained to confront the Kaminaeans. He's not even an expert navigator. Any number of things could go wrong.

Sure, he's created some startling inventions for the war effort. But that is no excuse.

The audacity of professor Yaw-iyn luring them into uncharted territory with his, undocumented, unqualified untested, ideas.

I need to find those young fledglings.

How irresponsible of them to run off, before their training is ratified.

Back within her own secluded dome, she sent mental probes over the hemisphere, after first securing a frequency safe from unwanted intrusions. She systematically investigated possible flight paths between Helandi and Kamina; ignoring predictable routes.

Ju-bilee's arms spread wide and with a howling screech she darted straight up into the starry night, scoping the ocean between Helandi and the castle.

II. Illysæ Ad Mördi Tăłi

Adt, Yaw-iyn and Sarleni did not relish the idea of running renegade but under the circumstances, they could no longer delay their search, so they had quietly worked out their plan, collecting whatever additional specifics about the other missions they could obtain without raising suspicion.

The week's joint summit reported that the updates had worsened. Top command canceled further missions and escalated the Armada's readiness. When Adt and Sarleni saw the altered schedule, they'd protested along with the other academy teams who'd expected to be sent into Kamina. The HanJahn council heard their arguments and advised against it. Moyi was particularly concerned about sending Sarleni at all, because her brother was listed among the missing—for the second time.

The first time, HanJahn probes had located him several days after the Raiders' crash. An Orb was sent to transport him to the continent. It had succeeded in delivering Mahzit, except that the Orb and pilot were tragically destroyed by Kaminaean Gatherers. But he was again, out of contact; lost somewhere on the continent.

Torlo Hannis' unit was responsible for the continental relay station. The base was in its initial stages of preparation, when they had made their quick decision to move inland due to the sighting of Gatherers. Shortly after, connections were lost.

To date, a dozen units were completely destroyed. Those who had made it to the continent had shut down communications for security reasons.

Adt and Sarleni suspected serious problems and did not want to wait any longer to be involved. Adt was certain they would have a far better chance of effectively penetrating the continent. And their personal experience could be vital to the cause.

The only problem was the current ban on all missions which prevented them from officially moving forward. And they could not discuss the details of their plan with Yaw-iyn. Nor would they seek advice from Ju-bilee or Moyi. Their decisions had been secretive, under heavy mental cloaking.

Once they were ready to act, they shared partial plans with Yaw-iyn who had volunteered enthusiastically to pilot his experimental Orb into Kamina. He then taught Adt how to program flight plans, since they had cooperatively agreed he could not know their precise destination.

Sarleni mulled over the disastrous failings of the missions.

Torlo had been lost: Mahzit missing.

Most units like the Raiders, had lost contact.

Sarleni watched Adt set their course for the *Illysæ Ad Mördi Tăli*. They wanted to find Kinelian, master of this hidden sanctuary. For here was where sad, desperate Mutis from Kamina had come, seeking their final refuge. Sarleni and Adt hoped they could find clues from the caretaker before they approached their next destination: the Castle of Doom.

"Look!" Adt suddenly yelled.

Sarleni attention riveted to the view screen.

Two unmistakable silhouettes hovered.

Adt warned: "Gatherers!"

Yaw-iyn's hands flashed across the control panel. Bright light beams shot from the Orb, on target, penetrating the lurking Gatherers. There were no explosions. The targets shifted from shape to dust, silently; one blink and gone.

Adt stared, amazed.

"Ah yes! One of the weapons I've devised: simple really, although it uses up the Orb's energy sources. We can take no chance of discovery."

Sarleni instantly merged in Zygo with Adt as he absorbed all her essence. Neither of them wavered while drawing into singular unity. Immediately, they cast an invisible energy field around the Orb.

The professor checked the low engine settings on the control panel.

"I'll need some time to get them back to full power. Do you think your field can hold long enough until I get the cloaking shield operative?" Their voices could not be distinguished from one another through their combined force in responding to Yaw-iyn's question. "It should hold without difficulty," they replied.

You're obviously serious about Gatherers. What can you tell me concerning them?" The professor had adjusted the gages and now hoped to learn more about they knew.

"We were captured by one of them, off the coast of Bel-loniea and delivered to the Haknords. They are constructed spies engineered by the Kaminaeans: half animal, half machine Ersatz creations; flying marauders. The Kaminaean Mutis also produce half human, half machine warriors. We met one by the name of Skurals; a vicious fighter."

The duo sank into silence, drained by the Zygo field.

We should have united sooner; Sarleni rued, solidly holding up the Zygo force with Adt.

She felt a sharp separating chasm. All Helandian communications, including Ju-bilee and Moyi, were now lost to them.

* * * * * * *

When they'd sighted the island, Sarleni and Adt withdrew the Zygo. Yaw-iyn brought down the Orb, and they concealed it within a dense grove.

The welcoming dock and the mountains towering over the

strip of beach had not changed, nor had the familiar winding path. Adt and Sarleni eagerly ran towards the quaint sanctuary, all the while chattering about the strange things they had discovered on this island. They told Yaw-iyn about the eccentric old man and his dedication to this place.

The prospect of speaking with the kindly caretaker gave them hope. Kinelian was the meticulous supervisor of the island's activities and the archives maintained there. Certainly, he would help them contact the Mutis who had fled to the sanctuary. They would have brought fresh news; especially about the Kaminaeans.

Kinelian would surely let them speak to the council of Mutis. Important questions needed direct answers.

When they drew nearer to the settlement, a pang of disbelief dug through Sarleni. Stark changes were evident and disturbing. The conditions of the once grand buildings had dramatically altered. Formerly crisp and tidy huts were now badly weathered; the gardens, overrun with thorns and weeds; as if an evil had befallen the island. The proud structures had crumbled, and lay in ruin and decay.

Sadness mingled with concern. *What had happened to bring destruction?*

They stood for a long time, surveying the stark emptiness of the place in shocked silence. No birds murmured, no chirping of living creatures. A vile emptiness filled this lifeless place, with nobody in sight.

A quiet serenity had once radiated from neatly trimmed gardens, nestling their colorfully adorned cottages. What had once been so peaceful, now, reflected dismal bleakness.

A cold chill ran down Sarleni's spine. The gateway into the Sanctuary's gardens hung on a broken hinge. Suddenly, a sharp crackle drew their attention to a battered sign dangling from a rusted chain. It twirled in the bitter cold wind. Engraved on its charred side was ancient lettering, giving title to this once proud settlement:

Enatöræ Illysæ Ad Mördi Tăłi

Before them, in the broad open yard stood the obelisk: its vibrant, shimmering pinnacle; had previously pointed boldly, straight to the heavens. Now, it was scarred and mangled, like a dying giant twisted, and barely able to stand.

The path stretched along a straight line from the forest to the oval grounds of the monumental obelisk. All the buildings were boarded up: not a door or window left unsealed.

Lovely hedges bordering the walkways had now been hacked to brittle gray stumps.

What monstrous event had brought such destruction?

Kinelian, the Sanctuary's manager, had been so proud of his charge. He had told how the staff was shy of visitors, dedicated to their work, spending all their time keeping records, and caring for the Mutis that come here, to their final refuge.

The Helandians silently explored the hills, where the ancient ruins overlooked the sea. Sarleni wandered through the graveyard, down the stony path, and among the markers.

The caretaker and his odd stories had been a puzzling memory until Andon had decoded Talni's message, detailing the Kaminaean expansion. Now, she needed to find him and learn what Kinelian knew about the Prophet. Their host had delivered them to a group of Mutis led by one, who was dynamically responsible for directing them to the Castle of Doom.

They were coming around an outcropping rock, when Adt pulled her aside. "Someone is here!"

She had detected a similar connection.

Sadness has ravaged this place! The despairing thought equaled her anguished emotional state.

Before them, stood a peculiar miniature Muti; half normal size. Its cloak was a dazzling hue of sky blue, draped with vines of ornate flowers. Its face peeked out at them, adorned with tiny blossoms. It beckoned to them and quickly darted behind a rock.

"Hello!" Professor Yaw-iyn brushed past Adt, towards the Muti.

Sarleni grabbed him by the shoulder.

She spoke gently, sensing the Muti's shyness.

"We are looking for Kinelian. Can you tell us where to find him?"

To their dismay, the little Muti raised its chin and let out a long wail.

"*Lade meha, lade meha Kinelian. Lade meha Kinelian, Kinelian!*

Tears ran down its cheeks. Its soft blue eye-sockets filled to the brim, like tiny crystal clear pools.

"He is gone," it whispered, as if the very words were sacred, "Gone!"

"Gone?" Adt demanded, "Where?"

"Gone," the Muti shook its head sadly.

Sarleni stepped forward, feeling its sense of longing sadness. The strangely, haunting, little Muti seemed like a small child, seeking its mother. She had to control her impulse to sweep it up into her arms.

Do not touch it, Adt warned.

I won't. She uttered silently to him. *It looks so lost.*

The Muti's face tilted upwards; leaning towards her, hopefully.

Gently, she asked: "Can you help me? Where can we find him? We need information only he can give us!"

The Muti cringed. Its face drooped; pinched and forlorn. It shakily pointed to a stone up the path from where they stood.

"You will find him. There."

They thanked the little Muti and hurried over to the stone. The Muti followed. A mound of fresh dirt had recently been piled around it.

The little Muti stared at the stone.

"He was sad and tired. His struggle failed." Its voice was soft and frightened.

"Brave and greatly beloved, he was. In his final days, the Kaminaeans had come. The Prophet's legions spread ever closer to the Sanctuary. We saw him once during the last days, when he said the time had arrived. He never explained, just requested to be placed here."

Sarleni could read the many questions in Adt's head, all reflecting her own queries. He wanted answers.

"Exactly what's happening? There must be reasons."

"The mainlanders were banned from our island. Few remained at great danger. The locals fled into hiding. Mutis warned them to avoid the Sanctuary. We waited for the destroyer to pass. It came in a malicious wave, burning everything. See what was left behind."

The little Muti stopped abruptly, looked around and shakily pointed with its tiny dart-like fingers from beneath its cloak, jabbing towards the ruins. Crumbled walls, broken roofs and windows, unnaturally open rooms exposed to the naked storms of Noomas.

Sarleni tried to probe into the Muti's mind.

Cold silence answered.

She could not penetrate into that blank well.

The Muti whispered: "Not here. Not now. You must listen and learn, from the depth of the source. The *Guardians of Haldolen* tell of the seedings."

They stared at the delicately flowered Muti in amazement. Its eye sockets sparkled as if precious gems were embedded upon its lavender cheek bones. The leafy vines on its face laced down its temples to the curve of its neck and then toppled down both sides of its robe.

It began to hum a haunting tune while leading them among bold tombstones down the steep hillside.

The Muti came to a stop at a sharply arched ledge and rolled a large stone to one side, exposing a passageway. Once they were inside, it pushed the rock back in place and they stood in pitch-black darkness.

For a startled moment, all seemed threatening; dangerous.

What kind of trap have we allowed this little creature to lead us into?

Adt and Sarleni blended their minds.

See with your thoughts, came a gentle instruction into Sarleni's mind.

Heed the essence. Seek the Guardians of Haldolen.

Sarleni closed her eyes and instantly their surroundings glowed. Awe wafted through Adt and Yaw-iyn as they adapted to the illuminating space.

Experimentally, Sarleni opened her eyes and discovered only darkness. Closing them again, she could easily see the Muti trotting along a rough hewn shaft slanting dramatically downwards.

The branch of the vine gains strength from the root.

The Muti continued to send odd messages into them while they dodged tubers jutting out of the earthen tunnel.

Adt and Sarleni collectively tried to interpret its meaning.

Yaw-iyn had not said a word, though the man appeared curious enough, despite his puzzlement about what was happening.

The smell of rotting vegetation made breathing difficult. The Muti's humming had settled into a monotone. Fleshy stems loosely entwined, first yielded to their passing, and gradually thickened into tangled knots of particularly dense tubers, eventually blocking their path, completely.

The Muti pressed its face between the twisted tendrils and chanted unfamiliar words in its singsong voice.

"Lazu Rupa enre Muti en tal mundai....."

The rest of its lyric was muffled. All at once, the knot snapped open, snaking its long tubers along the sides of the tunnel and pulling them forward among the tangle of roots, allowing barely enough space to squeeze through the mass of vegetation.

She was startled, though not frightened or even threatened. Sarleni ran her hand along its smooth tendrils that flexed; opening into a single steep shoot. Suddenly, they were descending at an alarming speed. Without slowing, they came to a jarring halt and dropped through an open slot onto hard packed soil, tumbling unceremoniously over each other.

The flowered Muti guide sprang to its feet, bowed to the tuber behind them, and sang out loud.

"Lazu Rupa...."

And the tunnel dissolved into the soil.

The Muti's head cocked sideways, almost smiling. "You have arrived into the world of the Rupa. We are in the Wombura. Come. I will show you."

III. Life Source

They followed the Muti down a widening corridor to the entrance of a cavern. Soft, amber light bathed through this chamber. A soothing medley of voices came to them from the adjacent tunnels.

"The assembly has been called in your honor," it whispered. "I will take you there when all have arrived."

The Muti led them onto an entry overlooking the vaulted hall. Young Mutis, all flowered and sparkle-eyed, entered from various passageways and seated themselves on the ground,

They had never seen such youthful, appearing Mutis. Their flesh was lighter in color and smooth, unlike those commonly seen throughout the world. The eye sockets were deep, glimmering, clear bluish pools; not empty, black shells. Clear, bell-like, tones echoed in the cavern.

The melodic humming of the Mutis gradually ceased as the last citizens arrived. A single Muti stood, from amidst the throng and began a new chant, alone. When it had finished, another stood and continued.

Sarleni, Adt, and Yaw-iyn listened in amazement to their light, musical voices as they began telling a mystical story of the Muti beginnings and journey.

They sang in poetic phrases, about the natural cycle of life: About the wisdom of the ages and mystical purposes, not easily understood. For the Muti had always spoken in lyric symbolism and these were no different from the Mutis they had known, whose prophesies often included a connective force with regenerating stars and rooted beginnings into the depths of the world.

We and all are part of the whole.
We are the beginning,
Brought forth from the bloom of creation,
Divided yet joined through original birth.
For life forever dwells in time and space.

And living and dying are one and the same.
The mystery is unfolding.
The natural turning of the seed;
The universal space we share,
Spans less than the distance between the elements:

We are each one segment of the whole.
The turning is without end.
We seek and discover.
We begin again from the Wombura
We remain the original pulse,
The eternal rhythm binds time and space.

The chamber filled with their unison voices repeating the chants:

"...And the way was prepared for their rebirth...."

The voices had dimmed until the last echoing sounds had ceased. In stark silence they sat, for an eternal moment. Not even a whisper of sound could be heard.

All rose to their feet and faced the back of the chamber. Through the passageway, came a tall, majestic Muti, richly clad like themselves only twice their stature. As it entered the chamber, the young Mutis all bowed and shifted to make a wider pathway, as it strode through their midst towards the head of the hall. The tall Muti greeted the young ones as they were seated.

Its booming voice orated about the island and its provisions for the Muti.

"The sanctuaries had been the Muti's refuge for all time on

Noomas. Rupa provides protection beneath. It guards against many dangers. But now, the sanctuaries have been desecrated by the Kamina, and we cannot bring attention to them until that danger has past. Keep watch that their spies do not penetrate the shield of the Rupa."

A unison chord chimed throughout the hall, resounding in long waves until the words of the Muti could no longer be heard. When their voices diminished, the tall one continued speaking.

"The rebirthing of a vile seed caused a tragic calamity to befall our beloved Noomas. It has taken root and it grows with a speed beyond our natural control.

"Mutis are now rising up against this atrocity. We abandon our most cherished ethics, uniting with a vengeance against our brethren, the Muti of the Kalinis. We cannot allow its venomous creation to spread its poison. It must be weeded out. And all elements of it, completely eradicated."

It then shouted: "We shall stand on wisdom!"

The words resounded against the stone rafters. And the assembly rose, all shouting in solemn unison:

"Wise is your word!"

The wailing echoed throughout the chamber for a long time. When it subsided and the room had settled into stark silence, the tall Muti faced the Helandians.

"These scions recite events rooted in their generations. They are the seed of the new life: the living continuum of the past, even as you are to your people.

"What you must know is this: the Sanctuary guards the hope of the future, not only for the Muti, but also, for the people of Noomas. The seed of the throne awaits the cradle of the *Wombura*; for Rupa has sealed the crypt and will prevail until the power of Kamina is diminished.

"KiNal is your destination. You are needed. All will be clear after you arrive there."

Sarleni recognized the tall spokesman as the very one who had met them on their previous visit to the island when Kinelian had brought them to catacombs beneath the Sanctuary. Her memory flashed back to that meeting:

The Messenger you have been brought to meet is waiting. To find him, go to the mountain and enter the castle. Once on Kamina you will understand that instruction. For the moment, he has remained undetected. Serious attempts were made to kill him. Receive his message and take it to your Proctor. All I can do, beyond making sure you get there, is to warn you: beware.

The Muti laughed, softly.

You are right. We have met before.

It was speaking into their connected minds.

Adt instantly exclaimed, "You drugged us!"

"Yes. We needed to get you to the Messenger without risking any chance of detection, for I could not foresee all that would happen here. The brutality of Kalinis has jolted the foundations of Noomas. This transgression against the Sanctuaries had been heavily veiled from our visions. We had no warning against the spoilage of this sacred place."

Sarleni's probe only found a hard shell blanketed over the Muti. She had never experienced such a rigid block.

Seek the central source. The castle holds a single connection. Mahzit is on task as is Torlo. Great challenges face you. Prepare.

Remember my name: Sziat.

It felt as though Sarleni had shut her eyes, only for a moment. When she opened them, Adt and Yaw-iyn were standing next to her, and they were back in the Orb.

CHAPTER THIRTEEN
THE WITNESSES

Question: What have you to report?

Answer: I have seen horrors. And feared I would never escape. I have witnessed unspeakable suffering. Most have not survived. My village was overtaken for their benefit. My home was confiscated to serve their passions.

Question: Your home? How did you come to own your home?

Answer: We built it upon my family's land with our own hands. We had raised our children and our children's children, for countless generations, long before *they* arrived. Our home was torn from us when the *Voice of the New Truth* spoke. At first, we welcomed and honored the Muti as our ancestors had always done. And the Muti's benevolence blessed our people with sound wisdom. So it was, with the great Muti powers. We gave them the best of our stock, though we were confused by their interest in carnal materials. And thus, they demanded possession of our abundance.

Question: Did you support the Prophet's plans? Have you no loyalty to their grand vision?

Answer: How could we not support? They promised prosperity. And who would dare to question the decrees of a Muti? Yet, in time, we began to question the *New Truth*, and doubt its validity. Our community was no longer our governed town. They changed the name. Ou-wella on the Lake had been our roots, our heritage, and our place in this world. They banned the name, calling it Marfsu Park, demanding all markings and signs reflect the new name, destroying our family name and wiping out our landmarks.

Question: How did they come by the name?

Answer: They called it a country spa. They came from central Kamina: members of the Marfsu Court. Muti judges wielded great power. What they did to my people was appalling. Any excuse would bring their hideous punishments onto anybody who might have broken some edict of their *New Truth*. They only wanted a little diversion, they said; at our expense. And so, they would pick any person out of a crowd.

Question: By what means did they punish? Were they justified?

Answer: Beatings! They flogged. They gave no reason. Inflicting pain was their passion. The rest of us screamed until we could no longer make a sound. They called it a feast. But it was nothing of the kind. They wanted only to hear us suffer through their gruesome methods.

* * * * * * *

Different witness:

Question: Give me your report! What have you to say?

Answer: The inner circle of the Muti governing clans seized our homes, polluting our properties with their disgusting pleasure pads. Every night someone would be selected to be presented for the Muti pleasures. I stood among the appointed witnesses who were forced to watch their rituals. The flesh was cut off a man's arm with one sweep of a blade, while they laughed through drooling jowls. For the main course, men and woman were torn to pieces, skinned and beaten. They were still living, and screaming. The Muti would set them on fire.

* * * * * * *

Different witness:

Question: What do you know of the Kaminaean Muti?

Answer: Mutis used to be expressionless but not anymore. Not since the *First Voice to Speak.* Oh, I can tell you, *they* have changed! I became quite intimate with their ways when they forced me into personal service. These Mutis had ways of expressing great emotion, when it came to power over their human slave population. I had been picked to serve because one of the judges happened take a liking to my father, who had served him, as a young man. I was favored, as *Steward of the Home of Hadi.*

Question: What do you know of this place?

Answer: It was once a lovely, sprawling mansion on a small lake nestled in a secluded valley surrounded by the Oe-gana Mountains. My family had lived here for generations before the Muti banished us. They said it would serve a greater purpose, now. A resort, they call it. Bah! No, it was a wretched den of vile, corruptive seduction and torture.

* * * * * * *

Different witness:

Question: And what is your story?

Answer: They had requested my transfer to the valley, at the turn of my maturity. My tutelage prepared me for servitude. I fell in love with a young woman. She had also been favored as maiden to the House Master. She had caught my eye and won my heart. I felt great love. Ah, my downfall. I would have been better off to have been blind and unattached to anyone; to have been born without heart, without feelings. Alas, I suffered the worst of all pains because I chose to love.

Question: Why is that?

Answer: She will never again leave the valley for she was lost in the budding of her youth. I will tell you of her life so that she may not have lived and loved without purpose. She told of the valley before the Mutis came; a time when she was young, raised in her cherished home town. She was happy among her people in their lovely valley community.

Before the empire took possession, our lives were happy. Once they arrived, our village life died. For them, it became a popular Spa for Muti consumption. We served as required, and for some reason, the Muti masters took a special liking to my woman, lauding her with sweet compliments for her excellent service. My master would flatter me with high praise.

How well I had provided service. How quickly I had learned. What a wonderful human, to be so dedicated. And they would applaud our airs when we spoke adoringly to one another in their presence.

They even let us quarter together in a corner behind the manor house. Nobody ever went there, for it was in back of the kitchen pantry. To us, it was paradise because it was ours, alone: our little hideaway. We shared our deepest secrets in our special place together. For, we felt safe, and when we were alone, our greatest joy blossomed from our private intimate love-making.

"Take your leave and enjoy the afternoon, my dears," they would say to us. "You have served well and you deserve your time together. We shall not need your services again, until tomorrow morning. Go and be well."

But they had *lied* to us! This was no private place. It was a specimen room! A laboratory! They secreted spy devices in the place, broadcasting our most tender romancing at their grotesque feasts.

Our Muti masters had made a spectacle of us: a laughing joke of pleasure. Their Muti gawkers, drooling over fatted bellies, howling, jesting that twisted our sincere devotion into an ugly mimicry.

Yes, we were their pawns, nothing more. They ridiculed us behind our backs—deliberately deceived us.

We were taken for fools.

The deceitful monsters: the whole lot of them. How I despise their putrid, lying faces. How I would give anything to smash their scrawny purple hypocritical lips until they bled.

How they make me sick, sick, sick! The wretched Muti beasts recorded our love-making, and used it as an entertain-

ment, and even scientific study. We were merely one of countless couplings, kept in *their* private collections. When we
discovered the Monitors, we sought to dismantle them. But they
were replaced, at once. We no longer wished to be part of their
capers. So when we were dismissed from duty, we would make
excuses saying we needed to go to the town for supplies; or to
the fields for fresh herbs. The Muti Masters soon tired of our
absences and insisted we return to the room.

When my woman objected, the Muti master struck her with
a backhanded blow across the face. It was horrible. Her nose
and lips ripped off. Blood gushed everywhere. The other Mutis
roared with hideous laughter, as my love was callously brushed
aside, like rubbish.

Question: Your story is tragic. How did you survive?

Answer: When I wanted to object, I was restrained by a
friend. I meekly complied by remaining unresponsive. Silence
saved my life. And I could not change what they had done to
my woman. That is why I have come to join the Resistance and
become *One with All*.

* * * * * * *

Another witness:

Question: What can you say of the methods used by the
Mutis?

Answer: I gave details in my written report. I handed it to
your superiors.

Question: The Mutis?

Answer: They had no limits, if you want specifics. Brutalizing
beatings happened daily. People were compelled to fight each
other. Even to death. And they forced us to believe it was righteous. Like animals in the arena. Others were forced to engage
in sex while the Mutis feasted. Then, a coupling man and woman
would be beaten to death once they had ended their erotic tryst.
And they preached righteousness.

Question: What did you learn about the *Dens of Malis*?

Answer: The Dens. Pleasure houses for the Mutis. Nothing humans would call pleasure. Some said they were conducting experiments; testing methods for pleasuring humans and Mutis. It was disgusting. The Mutis raped and mutilated humans. I wrote my report. I no longer wish to talk about it.

Question: What is your personal experience?

Answer: Too much to speak clearly. My eyes and ears carried their pain to my loins, in witness. Some friends survived by serving the Mutis who kept them alive. For their business was in human trade, supplying them new legal captives.

Question: Explain.

Answer: The Mutis use their influence to possess man and animal alike; living chattel. There were regulations. Even within the Muti anarchy, standards compelled certain restrictions. Certain daily routines permitted some sort of ordering. We watched, attempting to discover their patterns and thus design our behaviors to warrant the least amount of possible violence. We raised minor objections, and the method worked, but not for long.

Their need for ever increasing passion thwarted our attempts to regain control. We backed off into a position of subdued submission. They continued to target the most emotional, energetic characteristics our people displayed. We played the game. Some legal boundary made our hopeless situation, livable. If you followed the accepted path, you could survive. If you stepped off that path, brutal and fatal punishment came directly through the Kaminaean Muti legal system.

* * * * * * *

Another witness:

Question: And you escaped in what way?

Answer: Friends, who had connections with the underground, helped me. They saved my life and brought me straightway to you, through many days and nights. I lost my left arm. By the grace of Nuja, I am alive. I will serve with all the strength that is left in this body, mangled as it may be. I'm willing to offer the rest of my flesh, if it can take one Muti's life.

* * * * * * *

Another witness:

Question: You must remember: service with us may demand a self-destructive act. Are you prepared?

Answer: I am. Living without purpose, means little to me. If I must die, let me do so with honorable vengeance, for all those innocent victims they have slaughtered. As they showed no mercy, so will I sacrifice *my* life; for their death. Make use of me as you have so many others who have served the cause so well.

* * * * * * *

Response to all:

The record of today's hearings is already filed. You will be notified.

CHAPTER FOURTEEN
THE SEDUCTION OF MAHZIT

I. "They Call Me Efre-Ah"

Mahzit stood in the dense underbrush, terribly shaken after watching his rescuer suddenly blown out of the sky. He was in a strange land without any connections.

His instincts automatically kicked in as he tried to reckon with the surreal series of events in recent days. Relying only on survival skills, he focused on the surrounding terrain. At least an animal track would most likely lead him away from the brine to fresh water. He knew how to live in the wilds and in a very short time found a rivulet; tracing it inland. His instincts proved correct.

A rambling ditch, for it could hardly be called a stream, led him out of the arid scrub-lands, winding through grassy plains. Occasionally, he would pause, and concentrate on a search for any sentient energy. But each effort brought disappointment when he found nothing. No hint of human habitation. He must find civilization. From there, he could search for a Resistance group. That was his mission; his duty. Nothing else was important.

Mahzit was determined to succeed.

Perhaps, the emptiness only reflected his limited training. Or his people did not want their connection traced to him by the Mutis.

Survival training had interested him most at the academy.

Hunting came easy; harvesting roots and fruits and nuts from the plentiful land was automatic.

After several days, the thin waterway connected to a sizable stream which sprang from a split into two larger channels. He chose the branch to the right. It curved around a rise in the land. Here, the terrain made a steep drop, cascading down over several large boulders. The water was running clear and fast, as it passed a small shelter. Outposts were common in civilized territories. Storms came hard and fast on Noomas and travelers needed places to hide or rest. It was the first sign of civilization and especially inviting.

He didn't feel quite as lost.

Roughly fitted stone steps led to a door on one side of this small stone shelter that was apparently there to be used by hunters or travelers.

I wonder who had built this. It looks ancient but maybe it's still used by local populations. But where are they?

While he replenished his water flask at the foot of the falls, renewed hope sparked through him. But his musings were interrupted by the sound of running feet coming from behind him.

Instinct drew him into a battle ready stance. Behind him, a young woman raced down the hill towards the hut.

The look on her face was pure terror, for swooping directly towards her was a jagged-toothed scavenger, talons flaring and long beak wide open, screeching hungrily.

This was the loathsome Kuknal.

He'd seen these blue-black marauders more times than he cared to remember, always on the prowl to snatch up any hapless victim within range.

The hulking menace haughtily flapped its leathery wings, gaining speed towards its coveted target.

Mahzit dropped his flask. With sword in hand, he rushed to engage the flying beast, shrilling a war-cry to attract its attention.

The aviator instantly shifted course in mid-flight; evil eyes glaring hate at this new intruder. Its long black beak snapped open, exposing a double row of jagged teeth.

Mahzit confronted the bony vice, well aware that it was wide enough to lop off his head in one hasty bite.

Automatic reflexes placed him in lethal proximity. He had never done battle with this kind of adversary. Impulse was his greatest weakness and most powerful weapon.

The shadow of a broad wing darkened Mahzit's vision as he thrust the sword point up towards its body, hoping the blade would penetrate a vital organ. Its breath flashed hot on Mahzit's face as the beast's jaws whipped past the sword's razor edge. He quickly swung again. This time he got complete satisfaction. The bird shrieked in outrage when the blade clipped across its beak, slicing away teeth and bone.

Mahzit pressed his advantage, diving in closer; fully focused. They were almost touching, breathing one another's air.

Now dangerously near, he took a split moment to aim one brutal thrust through sinewy flesh and brittle bone, entering the giant bird's small brain.

When the body crashed onto the ground at his feet, rocks exploded into the air around its bulk.

The bird was dead.

Mahzit turned to see if the woman was safe, only to find her kneeling in front of the shack, head resting on the stone pallet, arms outstretched as if reaching towards some godly idol.

She was ignoring him and the fallen bird.

The scene was odd. Aside from noting her delicate shape, he found her prostrate position startling. And what puzzled him more, were the eerie tones arising from her, in a faintly musical chant:

"*Yabuo Botannai. Yabuo Kahn—Ah nai. Efre-Ah nai.*

Oh, Holy of Holies, I praise you!"

It was obviously something mystically religious, though he had never heard anything like it before. He wasn't a devotee of any idols or deities.

More twittering and guttural mumbles rose in pitch, from her singsong lyric.

He resisted the urge to laugh out loud.

Even less logical was when she began banging her head; bouncing it on the pallet, as if she were trying to burst her skull open.

"*Yabuo Botannai. Yabuo Kahn—Ah nai Efre-Ah nai.*

A loud thunking of forehead against wood, audibly accented her repetitious lyric chant.

"*Yabuo Botannai. Yabuo Kahn—Ah nai Efre-Ah nai.*

"*Yabuo Botannai. Yabuo Kahn—Ah nai Efre-Ah nai.*"

He wondered if he needed to rescue her from her own self-destruction, when the ledge disintegrated, shattering in vibrant colors. An arched doorway opened to a murky hollowness.

Instantly, the woman was on her feet, staring at him, apparently unhurt by the head banging.

She shouted, "Warrior, to what tribe do you belong?"

The woman stood there saucily challenging him, hands on hips. Long blonde hair streamed around the fringed outfit hugging her delightfully compact frame. She was beautiful and not in the least, modestly dressed. Her garments barely covered her torso in snug ripples.

It was impossible to avoid staring at this stunning young maiden. Without shame, he held his gaze upon her, with open admiration. If his boldness bothered her, so be it.

And he couldn't help grinning, as he wiped his blade off on the dead carcass of the bird and slipped the weapon into its sheath.

"What's so funny?" she demanded, hips cocked to one side.

A soft twinkle in her eyes seemed to say: *I know what you're thinking!*

She frowned prettily at him. "Well?"

"Well...what?"

"I asked a question. And I *require* a response."

"*Require?*" he mused, brazenly cross-examining her with his eyes.

There was something puzzling about her attitude.

She tilted her head slightly to one side as if patiently awaiting an answer from an underling.

More bitingly, he repeated: "*You* require?"

Her eyes burned with careless mockery.

"You must answer. After all, politeness is a part of the honorary exchange between citizens. Unless you are an enemy, in which case, you would not have saved me from that beast over there. I am willing to accept your acquaintance." She purred from deep in her throat. "And you can stop stripping me naked with your eyes."

"Yours are stripping back!" he snapped.

Without missing a beat, she abruptly changed the subject. "Are we going to debate, like two dumb stone brains and...and argue? Be polite and answer! Or did you forget the question?"

"Who asks?" he demanded, bluntly avoiding her question.

She hesitated. "They call me Efre-Ah. You can do the same, since I owe you my life."

She seemed to change her mind. "Wrong answer; Botannai will punish. You have come as his servant. And for that, I am thankful."

"Serving who?" he replied arrogantly. "I don't even know your master!"

"Where do you come from? Your attire is extraordinary. Strange, at the very least: enough so to surely be sent from the god of all gods. Yes. I do believe that is a logical explanation."

He looked down self consciously, wondering what she found to be so unusual.

"Gratitude is in order." She made a gesture towards the hut behind her. "Botannai provides admittance. Look! The storm is soon coming and it will grow very cold."

Mahzit could see storm clouds emerging on the horizon. The cooling air gave support to the woman's warning.

"Come inside" she said firmly. "We shall make atonement. Kuknal shall be sacrificed to Botannai, so the gods may calm the winds and reward us with a feast from its savory flesh."

Efre-Ah had spoken matter-of-factly. She boldly pranced to the dead fowl. Withdrawing a waist knife from its sheath, she decapitated the bird, cut off its wings, and trimmed the talons and tail in a splendid display of proficient agility, determination, and amazing self confidence.

She tossed its bony claws at him, causing him to leap back in order to avoid their needle sharp points.

"Take them," she insisted.

Her eyes dared him to do otherwise.

With an awkward look of puzzlement, he wanted to question her further but thought better of it. He picked up the claws and latched them to his belt.

She grinned with smug satisfaction. Grabbing its thick thighs, she threw the meaty carcass of the Kuknal over her shoulder.

Mahzit stood; watching her with amazement for the fowl was nearly twice her height, even without the head and wings.

She could not have been any older than a girl, yet obviously strong and surely one delightful flowering vision. As she stepped up to the building, boldly passing through the open archway, disappearing inside, he could not ignore her delicate curves, or the carnal feelings they aroused.

A frigid gust of wet wind blasted him into the archway after the young woman. The storm had descended upon them with a vengeance. Lightning and thick hail angrily exploded from the black clouds. Storms were insidious and major ones especially terrifying. Angry weather patterns had become more and more threatening since the tri-lunar phenomenon.

To Mahzit, there had always been something basically horrendous about the natural planetary events demonstrating their power beyond human control. He could barely tolerate even minor storms, let alone a tempest of this magnitude. And though badly shaken, he was grateful to be inside the shelter. Roaring thunder, crackling lightening, and pelting hailstones shook the temple room. He knew all too well, that exposure to these savage elements would indeed, have been deadly.

Efre-Ah had dropped the carcass when Mahzit collided with her and his arms instinctively wrapped around her. She seemed like a lost waif, leaning towards him, needing the safe enclosure of his arms. Her body was soft; warm.

We are safe, he reasoned. *This girl is quite capable. And the storm could not have frightened her.*

Yet she said nothing. Neither of them moved. Time seemed to thicken as the storm outside raged on.

What was she thinking? He wondered. He was torn between reckless desire and noble protection for this fascinating girl.

The hailstones hammering maliciously at the shack seemed to beat in rhythm with his throbbing heart. Her limp warmth in his arms caused a mad rush of male passion to sear through him.

They were alone. None would know, except himself. Temptation begged him to kiss her. He resisted. Integrity defined his next actions. It seemed impossible.

Gradually he relaxed, allowing the flush to gradually dissipate. His musing was interrupted as he noticed a change between the outside world and the inner portal of Botannai. The thunder had stopped. Silence had fallen. A misty dimness illumined the cabin. But the girl was not there!

The flesh he was holding was no more than the breast of the fallen Kuknal!

Panic flooded over him, and he threw the carcass to the ground. *Where did she go? What terrible trap has she sucked me into?*

Mahzit searched for balance. Nothing was stable.

The space transformed.

The smooth walls narrowed, slipping, twisting. Frantically, he tried to push them back. The sheer walls slid by faster and faster. He lost all footing and abruptly collapsed, spinning, freefalling into a dizzying void.

At length, the gray swirling slowed, faded, and walls once again emerged around him. *Have I been hallucinating?*

A bulky personage dominated his vision. A deep voice was speaking. "Is this the man?"

"Yes. He saved me."

"Then he is spared and must be restrained."

"But Father...."

"*The Rule of Botannai* shall be strictly enforced. We reward valor. He has not been tested, yet. He is not prepared for acceptance. Until then, he will remain in custody and restricted."

The words held no logic for Mahzit. He reached toward the man but could see nothing. A heavy sleep clouded all thinking and he felt his body crumble to the floor.

* * * * * * *

"He's awake!" a sharp male voice was saying.

"Yes," the girl answered, very close.

Mahzit tried to sit up, but straps at his ankles and wrists prevented movement.

"Let him be free. Where can he go?" she pleaded.

"Botannai will judge him."

Their voices whispered softly, fading in and out. He tried to understand the muffled words. Their agitated behavior, however, indicated a sharp disagreement about something.

Fool Korda! He cursed himself. *What a blind idiot I was, to have trailed after her seductive behind. Idiot!*

"Food will come. I'm sorry about all this."

Mahzit looked up from where he was sitting.

Efre-Ah was standing before him holding a small torch. "It's not my fault. Father wouldn't listen."

Mahzit had an irresistible desire to strangle this lovely young woman he'd chased into the hut to escape the storm.

What kind of dangerous trap had she sprung? What kind of creature was she—friend or enemy?

When he said nothing she anxiously added, "Are you comfortable?"

"As a prisoner? I'd sooner have taken my chances with the storm, if you think I find comfort here!"

"You aren't captive."

"What do *you* call it?"

"Subject to classification—held in safekeeping."

"That's unacceptable. You have no cause!" he snapped, glaring angrily at her.

No more ridiculous diversions. I am on mission. Nothing else counts.

"I'm sorry," she admitted, taking a step closer. Her tone softened when she spoke again. "Truly sorry; I owe you."

A guard entered the cell, placing a basket of fruit on the floor. She took a yellow-knotted fruit, and pressed it gently to his mouth while continuing to apologize. "Duty alone would require I repay my debt!"

Maybe he was misjudging her. He certainly didn't want her as an enemy. More importantly, he was hungry. And he thankfully bit into its sweet soft pulp and gulped down half the fruit.

There was warmth in her voice.

"Consider this a start...a friendly gesture. It isn't the kind of reward I wish you to have for saving my life. You made an impression upon my father. He recognizes that you were very brave to save me."

She turned away: "Well, not that I need protection, you know. I'm quite able to care for myself and...."

"Except from birds of prey," He chided her, allowing his mood to lighten; hunger satisfied and humor returning. The food had provided amazing revival.

Tension broke.

"We *can* be friends. I'm sorry. We *will* be friends. That's a certainty!"

"Friend or not, why have I been held prisoner?"

"We fear the threat of the Kaminaeans and cannot trust anybody."

He let her words sink in, thinking about what all this might mean for him.

Can these people be part of the Resistance? Or are they wary of all outsiders? Perhaps that was all there was to their demeanor.

Caution certainly dictated a reasonable restraint against all strangers. "Tell me about the Kaminaeans and your people."

"Life is dangerous here. We used to trust the Muti."

Her brow furrowed. Her lovely golden eyes squeezed shut.

"We are safe as long as the...as the Botannai protects us."

"From what?"

"I told you! The Muti! Surely you know."

"I do *not* know." Mahzit hoped the lie was convincing.

"Do you come from outside Kamina?"

"Perhaps: what can you tell me about the *Kaminaeans*, Efre-Ah, and about your people?"

"We all have secrets. They are a part of survival. Don't you think?"

"Yes, secrets are sometimes critical," he replied patiently. "What more can you tell me?"

"We dwell here. We live. We wait...."

Suddenly a door burst open and the guard entered.

"Bring him! The *Court of Judgment* awaits his presence! Botannai has spoken."

II. In the Land of Botannai

Mahzit was brought before the council. A dozen tall, sour-faced men sat upon a long, narrow bench. One stood and spoke.

"You have been judged worthy. Your bravery with the Kuknal will not go unrewarded. We welcome you to meet our people. The council of the Trap-zet will summon you again, before complete illumination is bestowed."

Mahzit imagined the judgment must have had something do with the Kuknal talons he'd strapped to his belt shortly before the storm fell upon them at the waterfall. All he knew for certain were the sharp commands he had received from the council.

The chief nodded towards Efre-Ah, who was standing next to him.

"Our daughter of the Botannai has spoken for you. We have listened to her witness and we have seen her gift of the Kuknal. She, alone has the right to speak for you. You shall be in her charge. You have heard our fair judgment. While you stay among the Trap-zet, she must accompany you, constantly. "The law is simple. Bring disaster unto our lands and all suffer. Her fate is linked to your deportment."

They were dismissed.

Thusly the elders had given the girl custody over Mahzit. Efre-Ah had explicit authority to check his actions every waking moment; in effect, his jailer.

He hated being hounded by a female; it grated against his manhood. On the other hand, it wasn't exactly the worst situation, being so closely guarded by a lovely maiden. She was pleasant at times, even flirtatious.

Imagine her yielding seductively as a willing partner in a Pleasure Palace suite....

Sweet, momentary flashes were quickly overpowered by reality.

At least she cannot read my thoughts!

He could not bear to think of her eavesdropping on his secret fantasy. She dominated; she controlled; she totally possessed his attention. Damnable female!

* * * * * * *

Efre-Ah wasted no time showing Mahzit how to navigate among the lofty trees.

Her people had built their homes in their upper branches which served as passageways interwoven across the sky to connect the dwellings of the Trap-zet community. The trees had colossal thick trunks plunging endlessly into the dark, dense depths.

She told him about their journey and the nature of this amazing world.

"My father spoke often of his father who knew the world before the Kaminaean Mutis claimed ownership of our lands.

"I know the story by heart. My people had studied under the teachers of the world who had travelled far and would bring back wonderful knowledge. Our Muti foretold the turning of the seasons so that our harvests would be plentiful. Our families dwelt in peace. We adored our wise Muti. Father tells of the splendid seasons when the Muti came to live among the Trap-zet and teach new wisdoms to the people. The Muti had grown fond of the people and tender with the children. How they adored the sage Muti of the splendid season.

"After one such season, the Muti came when the moons did not shine. The kindness had drained from their hearts, for they forbade the teachings and burned the scrolls of learning in a great heap. A heavy gloom was cast over the Trap-zet. And the people grew fearful. The teachers and elders met in hushed secrecy. They agreed to send the children away before the next season, for fear the Muti would do harm, although they knew not what that might be. But they sensed a disturbing shift in the world and the Muti was changing.

"My father and the others were young when they were sent here to the land of the trees. That was before the people lost their identity; before the Kaminaean Prophet came to rule. Many people were destroyed. Here, Botannai protects those of us who escaped and the Prophet's Mutis have never penetrated our sanctuary."

To Mahzit the densely wooded canopy was a breathtaking tangle of purple, yellow, and red blending into a wild pattern of shapes. This world was unlike anything he had ever imagined possible.

She led him down to the lower branches and away from the community, towards a bower of flowering branches. And he followed, constantly wary, for he did not know where this lovely guide and official warden would lead him.

Efre-Ah scooped up a delicate vine covered with blossoms, twinkling like tiny star lights.

"I love coming to this magical place, full of delights and perils. For beauty often mates with danger."

Would mating with her be all that dangerous? he wondered, amused at his own imagination. He couldn't look at her without feeling the persistent pleasure he had experienced during the storm.

Just as suddenly, this fantasy was stabbed through with his perverse memory of their first encounter, when he thought he was holding Efre-Ah, but instead had discovered the dead Kuknal, limp in his arms. He shivered.

Why did she have to say it in that way? He shook the bizarre image away and focused on the woman.

She was pointing to a lavender vine, winding around a gnarly tree limb, covered with fuzzy yellowish cones. "Keep away from the Nikta creepers. Its spores will cause fever. We call it the Dust of Illusions."

She turned towards a velvety cushion of bright red fronds. "You can smell its intoxicating scent, very distinct; but you must not touch it. Even a small amount of its oils can put you under its narcotic spell."

He was on edge. Her scent alone, was taking him to the limits of erotic lust.

"Dangers lay all around us," she whispered.

A taunting fragrance lured him closer to her. He was dizzy. His mind left his body—detached—as if watching this scene as a different person. He felt lighthearted, very happy. He wanted to press that lush body against his own—how lovely, how desirable, she was, how wonderful.

She leaned against him, giggling.

He weakly tried to fight her enticing cheerfulness.

She took his hand and led him over broad flat branches naming her favorite plants, describing their healing properties; which ones were edible, which were not. For every beneficial quality she warned him of an alternate peril; often deadly.

"Be careful of thorns. They bring sickness. Seeds rain from the Wpishe blossoms when they mature and can burn your flesh. The ignorant are not welcome. You are safe with me to guide you."

Everything was so beautiful to Mahzit. He listened and watched.

All I want to do is touch her, feel the velvet texture of her flesh, to brush my lips against that lovely cheek.

Her voice was hauntingly alluring: "Be aware. Some potent spores might probe and distort the mind. I will not take you into the dangerous zones."

Oh, if you only would. Just ask and I will tumble into you arms, without hesitation. I just want your body blending with mine.

Mahzit opened his mouth but no words came forth. He could only nod, and smile, and follow this delicious creature.

Efre-Ah's eyes twinkled dreamily. "I will teach you how to avoid the madness. I owe you my protection. You are my personal responsibility."

Again Mahzit tried to focus. Slowly, the lustful imagery faded. The waves of insanity ebbed. *Is she aware of the confused state I'm in?*

She had stopped on a thick knoll and tugged down two sturdy vines and handed him one. "Come, I want you to see something special."

Feeling more clear-headed, he smiled to himself and admitted the fantasy was not without its charming elements.

Efre-Ah swung across an open pit, landing gracefully in the cleft of a moss covered trunk. It looked like a simple feat; but when he looked down into the gap, his legs froze in place.

Dark, shimmering webs crawled with insects, creepy beetles; most likely poisonous vermin. One slip and those creatures would have been scampering all over him.

Mahzit clenched his teeth. *After all, one leap could not possibly be too difficult.*

Sweat beaded his brow when he swung after her, clinging desperately to the vine. His feet barely caught the next branch.

He was still shivering when he heard Efre-Ah calling. "Down we go!" She had jumped into a thick layer of ferns.

Gulping hard, he followed. With a sigh of relief, he landed safely on another limb which proved to be a hollowed slide cut into a thick trunk. This took him down to where his sprightly guide stood, waiting.

Where is she taking us? Into some secret den, where she can ravish me? What a delightful idea. I would willingly surrender fully to such a possibility. Mahzit laughed out loud at that very idea. This was insanity.

She frowned prettily. "What's so funny?" she asked.

"Nothing—nothing at all;" he was embarrassed; glad she couldn't read his thoughts.

She plucked a small twig covered with tiny blue buds and handed it to him. "Here, take these. I'm afraid you might have been affected by the passion grove. These will help."

Her arm brushed against his cheek.

She was so close that he could smell the tantalizing scent of her skin. And all at once, he wanted to smother himself in her hair and taste her soft lips.

How easy it would be. We are alone. What could stop us?

He quickly bit into the berries and nearly choked on the tangy juice that squirted down his throat.

"Come!" she commanded, leading the way along a narrow corridor that cut through the walls of gnarly roots. She had sunk beneath another thick veil of feathery ferns.

Drugged or not, he had been shaken, uncertain of his footing; hoping to keep on the right path.

"The mysterious songs of Botannai whisper secrets of the Ancients. Very few people venture this low. The fathers brought me here to learn of the prophecy."

What prophesy? He wondered. When he started to question her, suddenly the vines lashed out and whisked her elsewhere. In that instant, she was gone.

Leaping forward, he grabbed at the edge of the murky pit and stared into the dark abyss, down which, even a Korda could have disappeared.

Where is she?

"Efre-Ah!" he called out.

Brusque silence followed. Not a sound. The cacophonic jungle of lively choruses had, all of a sudden, ceased.

He heard nothing. Saw nothing.

Confused panic ground at his heart. He searched the surface of the trunk, finding dents for foot or hand holds. Mahzit slipped down several layers of limbs, determined to rescue the girl from whatever vile monster had taken her. He blindly rejected the possibility that she might be dead.

A seething, rancidness hungrily churned in his body as if a beast had sucked him into its gut.

He could hardly breathe. Moving solely on instinct, he grasped the hilt of the sword strapped to his side and furiously slashed out; hacking at the unseen attacker. The blade sliced into inky blackness that suddenly covered his vision.

He was floating in a translucent bubble with Efre-Ah and pulled her close. Her whole body was clinging to his.

How quickly she yielded. Her lush, supple skin, shivered intensely. He had never wanted to be so completely absorbed by a woman.

Something is tampering with my mind.

A bewildering stream of emotions plunged him into a seething swamp of longing, of need; trying to drain attention away from the immediate danger. Ecstasy burned hot, with pain.

Help, I'm dying!

A voice wailed in his head.

Submit, embrace, enjoy!

Hypnotic voices drew him towards a whirlpool of self-destruction. He could not discern pleasure from pain, for both blended into a single throbbing continuum.

Fighting blind, his sword swung at the invisible fiend.

Love me. I'm yours forever.

Blinding light blistered the air. Sparks flashed white and exploded into a multitude of colors. A wail pierced his ears. Venomous eyes glared into his: black and ringed by white fire. Wide jaws spread and spat pale liquid, burning like hot acid, against his flesh.

Mahzit's sword aimed at the demon. Something snapped down on his weapon. He feared the blade would shatter.

A low moan broke through; followed by a heavy clunk.

A weak voice called out.

"Mahzit, are you alive?"

He recognized Efre-Ah.

The night sounds faintly returned.

Something very powerful must have possessed him. And a vital part of it was his very real desire for this woman; exposed and misdirected. That monster had perverted it into a horrid, death trap in its attempt to destroy both of them.

"Are you okay?"

Real concern for her safety, flooded over him.

"Just bruised—Botannai has helped me. I must pay tribute."

The annoying mention of her favored god was dulled by his joyous relief.

"What we experienced in there," she whispered solemnly, "was terrifying...dangerous...real, in a way...."

The amazing strength of her voice countered the delicate fingers gently connecting with his arm.

"I did not expect that thing in our sacred glen. That was *not* our Botannai." she shuddered. "Let's get out of this nasty pit!"

"You know the way out?"

"If we climb along the tendrils, we might find a natural path."

He followed close behind her until she abruptly stopped. Their bodies crashed together and his hand automatically curled around her waist.

"Yes," she whispered.

They clung to one another for an eternal moment.

"You're so beautiful."

"How can you tell in the dark?"

Reality snapped his mood to the conscious realization that they might not be out of danger.

Reluctantly, he slid his arm away from her. He was on a serious military mission, assigned to duty as a spy in alien territory. He was not here to have romantic interludes with strange women; no matter how desirable.

"You'll have to catch me, if you can," she challenged him.

Efre-Ah was well beyond his reach.

"Climb!"

He scrambled up the rough wall. Cold determination drove him upwards. Duty or not, Mahzit was human and she was very lovely. Her words flamed brightly:

"I owe you my life. It is yours and has been from the beginning."

III. Ceremony of the Holies

The test was Mahzit's—to fail or survive. Failure points to a bleak future; success promises challenging opportunities.

He had felt empowered ever since rescuing Efre-Ah; twice. First, from the monstrous Kuknal, its talons still secured to his belt. And then, from that creature in the deep hollow, whose mesmerizing imagery had bewildered him.

Then one morning, as they lay next to one another, she leaned back, a twinkle in her eyes.

"The time has come."

She sat up, taking his hand.

"We are invited to the retinue of Trap-zet."

For days, she had been telling him to expect a special meeting with the important leaders of her people.

He followed Efre-Ah along the swaying boughs, grasping on to anything steadier than the wispy path beneath his feet. She shifted easily from rope ladders to hanging bridges looking back constantly to check on him.

"Hurry or we will be late!" she sang out, her lyrical voice light and breezy, and not at all impatient.

"I'll catch up," he answered, clinging uncertainly to a sturdy knot in a vine. After he'd planted his feet on a steady branch and secured the vine on a hook, Efre-Ah grabbed his hand; pulling him under a layer of lacy fronds and into the meeting hall.

In truth, it was not a hall at all. Rather a sort of gallery among the tree branches. The platform was strewn with soft thatched twigs and leaves. Above, the tree limbs created a gentle wave of woven branches and hanging garlands of delicately scented flora.

They had arrived earlier than expected so he watched, as others were assembling. Soon the Botannai worshippers had filled the broad terrace; young and old alike. Their slim, limber bodies impressed Mahzit, who had been proud of his own physique and agility. He now felt challenged by this race of acrobatic tree dwellers. The people were taking their places, cross-legged. Half of them floated slightly above and in back of the others, who were seated on the mat, creating a second tier. He felt uncomfortably awkward, seeing them freely levitating and chatting among themselves. Not shaken, but envious, for the ability to hover was a highly specialized practice among the most experienced HanJahn students back at the academy. He had not yet reached that level.

Mahzit shook off his annoyance as he took his place beside Efre-Ah. After the last people arrived, an anxious silence filled the air. The hushed assemblage began to chant in a soft, rhythmic harmony. And then a strange thing happened.

The trees rustled loudly, shaking the entire space.

Mahzit instinctively reached for his weapon. Efre-Ah placed her hand firmly across his shoulder, as all eyes turned upward.

The hanging vines stiffened and began whipping back and forth, weaving in and out until they had lashed a solid covering over and around the gallery so tightly, that the whole space fell into a shrouded twilight. Silence once again reigned.

After an eternal moment a soft light edged its way through an opening and a solemn procession of tall, elegant figures glided to the front of everyone, their slender shapes casting long shadows over the audience. These were the elders of the council.

Mahzit recognized the man in the front. They had met at the temple lodge before the storm and Efre-Ah had called him father.

Facing them, the man's voice resonated strongly.

"Let the ceremonies begin!"

Instantly the people began singing, accentuating their hypnotic chant with a steady rhythm.

"Yabuo Botannai. Yabuo Kahn-Ah
"Wimati nai Nitra-El."

The elders stepped forward, one at a time, and bowed before the people. They all rose to their feet as the elders led the next verses.

"We praise you, Oh Holy of Holies.
"Oh, Botannai, you have blessed our people,
"With the bountiful treasures of life;
"You have led your followers to high places.
"Still provide secure dwellings for your worshipers."

The people chanted their responses back and forth, with the elders leading the continuous cadence.

The verses revealed a chronicle of mythological histories and prophecies; bygone legends passed down for many generations. They recited the testimonies of long wanderings through parched lands; of starvation, death and of brave survival through legendary battles with enemies; of ancient tragedies, and of their own tribal victories.

Several people wept when hearing of the Mutis, who had once been their beloved mentors. The population had been attacked and many died horribly at the hands of the evil powers of Kamina. The survivors narrowly escaped the Muti forces by taking flight into the trees. It was here where they learned the secret of the Botannai. Then they sent select scouts to round up the remnants of their people, bringing them to the lofty refuge of these amazing trees that now enveloped them with a protective shell. The outside world believed the Kaminaeans had destroyed their race. Here, in their jungled refuge, they remained well hidden within its uncharted domain.

Their voices rose in passionate reverence.

"Yabuo One. Yabuo Kahn-Nah
"Wimati Nah nai Nitra-El."

Mahzit marveled at their rich history and their bravery to have survived such tragic ordeals. The elder, speaking solemnly at the head of the platform, captured his attention.

"Our youth are strong and have trained well for the Resistance march. Soon the unified forces will join our valiant teams to take a stand against the Kaminaean oppression; for so it has been prophesied."

'And one shall come to lead them all.'

"New hope has entered our domain. Word has come from the east that a mighty power will be sent to help us. The continents of the world shall rise to our aid. One of their numbers is among us today as proof of this promise."

The elders all stared towards Mahzit. And people turned their gaze on him.

Efre-Ah stood; pulling Mahzit to his feet. She stepped forward and pressed through the crowd to join the elders. He had no choice but to follow.

He jostled through the people towards the elders, his mind filled with uncanny images of tormented victims; arms stretching towards him, fingers clutching at his tunic.

As if standing outside his body, he saw himself clad in a shimmering golden mantle, a crystal scepter in his hand. It was an illusion that refused to fade away.

The people's chant rose to a high pitch until the whole space vibrated with thunderous rhythms striking like lightning bolts against his ear drums. The din was deafening; intolerable.

He could not determine whether the shouts came from the illusion or from the actual crowd.

He just wanted it all to stop!

Mahzit attempted to regain control over his senses, stripping the nightmare elements from reality.

A shadow loomed. Light reshaped the visual elements. Chanting narrowed until it completely ceased.

Each elder laid a firm hand on his shoulders, sinking deep into their own ceremonial trance. They resumed their hypnotic drone, coaxing visions around the edges of his mind; a beautiful panorama beneath a pale sky.

A chill covered Mahzit's body and he pulled the mantle tightly across his chest. The scene clouded, shifting shapes swarming with armed men and women.

He was not amongst strangers though he had never seen this army before. It felt very familiar.

And it was he who led this legion of warriors onto a battle-field smothered in cold, wet fog. They raged forth against an onrushing enemy veiled from sight by a thick haze.

These were his people, his army, and he was compelled to march them into battle. As the fog cleared he witnessed the foe: hordes of armed soldiers rushing in from the hills. He lifted the sword in his hand and with one swift downward sweep, commanded the attack on the enemy lines.

Two massive armies clashed!

He was engulfed in madness with the crush of metal against metal, the scent of blood and sweat, the sounds of agonized voices in horrid terror and death.

The vision then faded.

And when Mahzit opened his eyes, he was aware of the gallery: no fog, no armies. It had all been an illusion, yet he still felt the cold chill on the back of his neck. Instinctively, he wiped his brow and was puzzled to feel his hair actually damp.

Another shock hit him as he looked around. The people had left. The place was empty; wide open. The sun filtered through the loosely hanging vines. He frantically checked his tunic, relieved to discover his own familiar garments.

The illusion had been so real. As if he had reached into a future framework, Muti-style, and glimpsed things yet to happen.

Efre-Ah stood close.

He stared straight at her, bewildered and angry. For even reality had failed him. Or was this some kind of different illusion?

"What happened, Efre-Ah? Where is everyone?"

They were alone, high among the treetops. Only the whisper of the wind dared to break through the silence.

Mahzit stared at Efre-Ah, as if seeing her anew.

"What was the chant all about?"

She looked calmly at him ignoring his words.

"Well?" he persisted, voice sharply edged. "What happened here?"

Then she finally spoke.

"Botannai will be your guide. No need to question. It has been decided that you will go to the *Dens of Knowing*."

"Come," she whispered. "They are waiting for you."

IV. The Dens of the Knowing

Efre-Ah had lifted a panel in the floor of the gallery where it wrapped around one of the supporting tree trunks. Mahzit could barely make out the subtle notches she was using for footholds to descend into the blackness. The panel dropped down above him blocking out the last rays of sunlight. Once again, he groped into the depths of the nightmarish roots.

He climbed further and further down, fully trusting this tenacious woman and her mythical Botannai god, who supposedly protected these people of the trees.

The entire concept puzzled him. His limited exposure to legendary gods had not included any true beliefs. The HanJahn teachings were purely based on logical reason and scientific studies.

In the darkness, the footholds became harder and harder to find. The walls were warm, and damp, and slippery. He tried to reverse direction and climb back up. It was feeling too dangerous. The wall buckled as if it were alive, completely engulfing him in a wildly compressed tube. His whole body slipped against the smooth surfaces. He imagined himself being swallowed by an enormous Finissine. That giant beast always crushed its victims with its coils. He expected to feel powerful, contracting muscles gulp his life down into an acidic belly.

But it did not happen.

This clenching tunnel dragged him downward in a gentle spiral. After a long unbearable descent, his body dropped onto a hard surface. He quickly came to his feet in a defensive position, scanning the immediate area for an enemy.

Only Efre-Ah was there on her knees, hair forming a soft halo around her head as she thumped it again and again on a golden pallet. She was singing out in a clear voice:

"Yabuo Botannai. Yabuo One. Kahn—Nah.

This time Mahzit was not alarmed by her crazy head-banging ways; or bewildered when the wall broke open into a passageway. Frustratingly unanswered questions nagged him.

He quickly scrambled after her and grabbed her arm as the entrance sealed behind them. "Stop, Efre-Ah."

She stared blankly at him.

"What's going on here?" he begged, "talk to me!"

Her shoulders shrugged, eyes fixed on his.

He stared back, not knowing where to begin. "Well, for one thing, that tunnel....

"It felt as if it was, well, not just a tunnel. Almost alive! Was it?"

She nodded. "Botannai can be fierce and strong. With the chosen, Botannai is gentle. You need not fear."

Mahzit swallowed hard. "You mean that thing really is alive?"

Mahzit shook his head with disbelief. "Okay: Nevermind. What happened up there in the gallery? Those people, half of them were floating!"

"Mahzit, Botannai is all." Efre-Ah smiled with gentle amusement. "In the assembly, Botannai prepares for the people and they sit where Botannai places them. They reside in his power during their worship ceremonies.

"You didn't think they could float all by themselves, did you?" She laughed out loud. "Only Botannai has power. Only Botannai can elevate people above the level upon which we live. Trust me!"

Efre-Ah pulled him by the hand. "We must hurry."

Now Mahzit began to sort through some of his confusion.

Efre-Ah obviously did not know that people certainly can have power over the elements through extensive discipline of the mind. But on the other hand, she had introduced him to a life form he had not known existed before, which she seemed to attribute to her Botannai god. This tunnel had flexed and responded almost like a living creature. Clearly he still had much to learn.

Voices sounded from up ahead and they ran through an arched entry into a low ceilinged room. Groups of young people were crowded around several long tables, examining scattered charts and documents. When Mahzit and Efre-Ah came into the candlelight, everybody looked up. Silence followed. Several older men rushed up to them. Their very presence seemed to take precedence.

Efre-Ah quickly introduced the tallest man standing next to a young woman.

"This is Councilor Wulak."

"We are honored to be first to engage you! We've been preparing for the expedition, charting the course, and planning our new strategies. Your help is needed, now. We've lost most of our best fighters to the Kaminaeans. We can't afford to lose more on this trip."

Everybody in the room was staring at Mahzit as if he were some kind of authority figure.

A man standing next to the Councilor stepped forward.

"Mahzit, we have waited long for a leader. And now you have arrived. Your help is vital to us."

Mahzit let his eyes sweep the room; then moved back to Wulak. They expected a response. Instinctively, he decided it would be best to not disillusion them at this moment.

"I'm willing to assist," he responded in a carefully polite tone.

A uniformed silence followed as if they expected something more from him. Glancing at Efre-Ah, hoping to get some sign from her. He was miffed by the fact that she merely grinned.

What do they expect from me? he puzzled.

After several awkward moments, the councilor began to explain.

"We are actively involved in disrupting the Kaminaean Mutis, when possible. Our actions have been costly. Weapons are limited. Our methods have, thus far, been protected from detection. But we shall increase our level of attacks on specific critical targets. We will engage with a united Resistance army, once the arms and forces have been centralized. Our resources are expanding. We must move soon before their spies discover our strongholds. Your arrival comes none too soon."

"Yes," Mahzit nodded, as if he understood the plan. Perhaps they were right to consider him an important contact. "And you are...?"

The man coughed, with self-conscious embarrassment.

"I am Ro-Nah, chief historian of the Trap-zet people."

He gestured towards his lanky, young companion.

"And this brash fledgling is Havli-Ah, my assistant."

She nodded, graciously. "Welcome to the *Dens of Knowing!*"

Mahzit noticed that the walls were honeycombed with cubicles. Each niche contained scrolled parchments similar to those spread upon the tables.

Councilor Wulak picked up where Ro-Nah had left off, following the Helandian's gaze.

"Archives, Mahzit; and valuable maps: strategic plans we've been accumulating for our missions."

Ro-Nah moved from table to table, summarizing the layouts and strategies for each unit huddled around each sector. Mahzit had attended war conferences often enough to understand the implications. He had seen several similar chartings during the mission briefings from the Messenger's files. None had contained the details being revealed here. The historian paused only briefly at each table before he urged Mahzit to follow him.

"Notice the maps here. We've recently obtained vital new information, which we will need in order to gain access to the Kaminaean central core. Timing is crucial. And all nations must be of one accord at the time of attack in order to succeed in our conquest."

The tall scholar paused as he turned squarely to Mahzit.

"We are on a deadline. Botannai has spoken. You are the *One* we have waited for; the *One*, who has come to lead our expedition safely to the Meeting of the many. Botannai has made it known that the time is soon arriving, to act. Our duty is to disrupt the empire, as best we can. And we are ready."

Mahzit stepped back, several paces.

"Wait, just one moment. What are you claiming?"

He was alarmed at the scholar's directness.

"Are you assuming that I am some kind of special envoy with special powers? What is it *exactly* that you think I can do here?"

He paused, and then added. "I assume you speak for the Resistance. Am I right?"

Councilor Wulak saluted. "To the Resistance! The *Sacred Promise* is now answered, and we are most honored to have you among us."

Ro-Nah shouted, lifting his fist high.

"*Yabuo Botannai! Yabuo One. Trap-zet Nah!*"

Then before Ro-Nah answered the question, everyone echoed his words, with raised fists. "*Yabuo Botannai! Yabuo One!*"

A reflective silence accented that chant. Then, the man said: "Yes, Mahzit. Help from the East has reached our lands. Through you, we will be released from the Kaminaeans, at last!"

Again, the people chanted. "*Yabuo One!*"

Ro-Nah said: "The Great Prophecy has finally come to pass and we are most honored to have you among us. For, our Prophet has spoken."

"*Yabuo One!*"

Mahzit stood there, stunned and uncertain about what to do or say. Was he destined to play this kind of role? They expected him to respond or at least accept their definition of what he was to them. And he knew he had no choice.

"You are the *One*," Ro-Nah continued. "You will lead us to victory!"

He needed to accept this position for now, in order to guide them into the fold of the Armada's ultimate thrust against the *Kaminaeans*. Surely that alone, would justify his making use of whatever sense of power they wanted to bestow on him.

Again, everyone cheered and chanted, making him feel foolish and very uncomfortable. They obviously considered him a special emissary or leader.

In a way, this was roughly what he'd been sent here to accomplish: in one manner or another. He was here to learn, and discover, and report back to his superiors in Bel-loniea. These maps and information would be vital to Bel-loniea and the Armada.

Still, he felt somewhat uneasy. He was not a god or super human. Yet, they seemed to think him to be just that.

He glanced at Efre-Ah and realized that she accepted this as viable and authentic, and nodded reassuringly to him.

Mahzit considered the odds. Perhaps his predicament was not so far-fetched. A leadership position for a HanJahn officer of the Armada could conceivably turn out to be an advantage for both the Resistance *and* the Armada in fighting against the Kaminaeans.

He remembered legends about heroes in ancient times, performing all kinds of strange magic and ending up in awkward situations. It represented a sampling of what drove the fanatic to blindly believe in false gods, based on mythological tales. Yet, great powers had many times, done tremendous good under selective social triggering. Some for good; some causing terrible results. Sometimes fantasy gods and goddesses were useful tools to bring control over the masses.

Am I a symbol of hope to these people?

Mahzit had to carefully think it over. How was he going to navigate this situation? To be worshipped as some kind of divinely designed champion, or Holy Personage was completely out of the question.

How did I get myself into this mess? What do these people see in me? If they only knew my JaJa routine—ha!

He thought about the irony of their intense determination and figured: just maybe he could redirect the implications by following *their* lead.

Mahzit did some quick calculating: *If I agree to their demands, they'll teach me the ropes and I can, in turn, apply the HanJahn skills without having to couch my sources.*

Hey, this could prove to be a great set up after all!

And so, he decided, it might be wise to take advantage of their misguided vision. And that's what mainly counted.

In jubilant submission, he raised his hands.

"Alright, I hear you believe that I can help you with this fight. I am glad to be here. Let's find out what we can do together. Though, I'm hardly more than a connection between you and...."

He hesitated; then quickly continued.

"I speak for *Proctor Romos*, the power that speaks through me!"

A cry of devotion sounded, in response.

"Yabuo One! Yabuo Trap-zet Nah!
Praise to the Proctor Romos!"

As Mahzit had hoped, they would now accept Romos as a god-creature, of some sort. In Bel-loniea the man's status was certainly nearly that powerful.

All eyes leveled on him.

"Yabuo One!" they chanted, in unison.

"Praise, be *Botannai!"*

"Yabuo One! Yabuo Trap-zet Nah!"

They expected him to respond.

Reluctantly, though hiding his uncertainty, he nodded.

"Yabuo One! Yabuo One!"

They shouted again, but Mahzit raised his arms again, to

calm their zealous enthusiasm.

"What must be; is so."

He had no idea what that meant but hoped it offered the correct response. From the expression on their faces, they approved. And thankfully, didn't break into another round of *"Yabuo"* chanting.

Mahzit studied the faces of every person around him before he spoke directly to Ro-Nah in a very business-like manner.

"First, you'll need to fill me in with the details. Tell me everything you know, everything you've done and who it is, that we're going to be meeting."

The historian agreed: "We are honored."

With that, the Trap-zet historian led him back to the first great table and they dropped into a heavy discussion concerning the material: historical, as well as their current strategies. The picture that the man's words depicted was stunning.

Mahzit was truly impressed, hardly noticing that Efre-Ah had left the room. These people were exceptionally confident about confronting an overpowering enemy.

They had experienced near annihilation, and understood that serious peril was intended for all human communities at the hands of the sadistic Muti monsters. They knew that the Kaminaean Empire would ruthlessly crush all threats made against their edicts. That meant all the peoples of the land.

He needed to learn all he could. And fast.

CHAPTER FIFTEEN
THE MUTI NEW
ORDER OF NOOMAS

The woman stood near the front of the crowd, hardly breathing, dazed with anticipation; bordering on fear.

She repeated the quoted words over and over silently beneath her breath: *"We have more to gain in death than we do in living"*, thus blotting out the unison chants from the crowd crammed tightly into the assembly hall.

The execution ceremonies raised excitement and fear. This would be her third and last time she would attend.

The Muti stood on the stage with arms spread wide.

"Give allegiance and total submission."

"We give absolute loyalty to the *Holy Muti Mandate*!"

The unison response rose from every throat of those in the audience.

The Muti spoke again. "Anything less is wicked."

The throng obediently answered. "We believe in the Muti Law!"

A bitter hush settled over them before the Muti continued.

"Weakness of character causes defiance and poor judgment. Neither are reasonable alternatives to death."

It pointed to the row of battered humans chained together on the platform.

"These creatures dared to enter the forbidden grounds against our edict. Rejoice with gladness at their painful punishment!"

The crowd cheered at the Muti's command. The woman

tremulously raised her voice with the others. She felt no joy for her convictions were in angry conflict against her obligatory duty.

"They dared to defy the law. They dared to enter the library of ancient documents. In the city of the Ancients, we have protected the treasured Mhyo dialogs. Ancient truths, designed to be transcribed, only through Muti authority. Insights from the past shall be handed down to the people. Miracles are many; recorded within these libraries of detailed historical records filtering back to the Time of Origins and beyond to the beginnings when Mother Planet gave birth to all life. And so these men and women are condemned, for they dared to desecrate that which is the holy body of all wisdom!"

The Muti's arms pointed skyward and it lectured the people.

"Remember! The *Holy Muti Mandate* spoken by the *Voice of the New Truth* hails from the Master of Kamina.

"All else are lies. Take heed of your elders. For man on Noomas is the newest of all creatures. Yes, this world housed others long before the human arrived.

"The Muti predate all!"

The audience uttered their obligatory consent. To many of them, the Muti could not lie. Only a few chosen ones shared her truth. The woman knew of the evil in the Kaminaean Muti power. She knew, deep in her soul, that this Muti was cruel and dangerous and all it spoke was in contradiction to the universal life force. Its words pained her to the core. She could barely tolerate its insidious speech with its contaminating deceptions.

The gnarled Muti droned loudly above the captive throng. Its flashy jewels glistened in the high noon sun:

"Believe my words and you will survive all that comes to you. The essence of human purpose in Kamina relies on obedience. Follow Muti Law.

The Muti deliberately scanned the faces across the hall.

"Fear death. And submit your flesh to the wheels of pain. Thus, the pleasure of the Muti is served, as decreed by The Prophet. You deliver *our* ecstasy."

She did not fear death! Revenge would be her moment of restitution; her final act against the Muti.

Death would be less horrid than her unrequited painful memories.

Only one season ago, she had witnessed her father's murder. She had watched his body swelling under the infusions jolting through his limbs, before death had finally offered release.

When her two older brothers refused to ravish her, the Muti used electro-whips to rip the flesh layer by layer off their bones. Then family friends were commanded to rape her. They submitted to these demands, rather than surrender to that alternative of agonizing death.

The following day her mother committed suicide by leaping at a Muti who silently brushed her aside. Its open hand broke life away from the enraged woman, in one swift moment. Her mother's body had piled at its feet.

The Mutis had abandoned her and she was left behind as a living reminder of their absolute power.

Shortly after, the Resistance came and nurtured her back to health.

Now, was her moment to sing the glories of the radiant moons.

Her time for retaliation had come.

She needed only to await the signal.

And then, the word rang in her ear: "Act!"

Sound burst forth, loud and violent. She automatically yanked the cord at her waist, and waited.

People screamed.

She expected pain. Where was her pain?

Where was embracing death?

The explosives strapped to her body had failed, terribly. Everybody was running in shocked horror, away from the burning wreckage; but she remained quite whole.

Dazzling relief spilled over her. *I'm alive!*

Not disappointment. Not shame; only sheer joy that death had not claimed her; not swallowed her into oblivion.

Emotion overwhelmed everything.
I live!

CHAPTER SIXTEEN
"WE BOW TO OUR MASTERS!"

I. Qon

Unquestioned faith restricts survival.
Beware the snares of untested faith.
Beware the folly of absolute doubt.
Either concept without wisdom inflicts tragic suffering.
—Koris School of Healing Arts

Consciousness returned by degrees. I remembered battling some gladiator. My body ached; throat parched with thirst. There was a forced march.

Sorla, in Kanns. No, it must be Kamina.

My thoughts were fractured, attempting to piece events together into a logical sequence. Barely aware of my surroundings, I recalled the locked cell engulfed in darkness; thankfully blanketed by sleep.

The door suddenly sprang open. A blinding sea of light flooded my cell. Callused hands grappled me to my feet. A Muti lurked in the corner. At first I believed it might be Sziat but it looked smaller, bulkier; and remained very quiet as brawny guards yanked me down a narrow corridor.

"Where are you taking me?" A hand slapped my face. The message was clear. I knew my question had been foolish.

The Muti answered, "You will entertain our hosts with a bloody fight to the death!"

Laughter echoed from the pack of guards.

"You will die handsomely!" another voice scoffed with a dare: "Unless you survive the duel!"

They hauled me around a corner through a gate onto a field filled with scores of Mutis seated at long tables. They feasted from overflowing platters jeering and pounding the tables with clawed fists. Hoods flapped away from gnarled faces brightly marked in vivid colors. Glittering jewels laced their wrinkled necklines.

The flamboyant attire and bombastic attitude of these Kaminaeans alarmed me. Their robes with flashy patterns, matched their facial markings: amplified by glistening rings on long, bony fingers and bejeweled chains draped across naked chests.

To one side on a low stage sat a corpulent Muti upon a gaudy throne: most likely the overseer, entertaining members of its court and guests with a lavish banquet.

Human slaves mingled among the Mutis. Scantily clad maidens served over-laden platters around the tables.

My weapon today, was a club with a metal hook on the end. The guard who shoved it into my hand had tried to test the hook against my thigh, but my dagger intercepted his attempt, with a thin slice across his wrist.

From the corner of my eye, I saw a Muti pointing towards me and snickering; shoulders held back, mouth rippled in a black-toothed sneer. Others cackled at random. Human companions at the table chattered among themselves.

The guards had shoved me through a side gate onto the field and I stumbled forward several steps. All eyes turned my direction, but trained on something directly behind me.

I whipped around in time to face a grizzly beast of a man rushing forward, arms extended, as if he intended to toss me up in the air with one full swing.

Right away, I recognized Qon. Further back towards the far end of the grounds loomed four gladiators, armed with clubs, locked in combat. I swung wildly and ducked, racing past Qon to engage one warrior behind him. My hook caught his foot in mid-stride. He toppled into his opponent, just as his weapon sliced across the man's skull. Blood spattered the dirt.

One swift death brought on a roar from the packed tables, followed by instant silence. The arena guests seemed spellbound; riveted on the spectacle before them. They had anticipated my quick death by these savage fighters.

Instead, I had survived—for the moment.

"Didn't recognize you," said a gruff voice close behind me. "I'll help you!"

I did not glance at Qon who glared towards the ogre extracting his bloody blade from the corpse.

"Kill them!" he hissed.

I charged the other two combatants.

The third fighter awkwardly lunged but was stopped when the blunt end of my club came in solid contact with his midsection. I swung again, ramming up into his groin. He doubled over. My club popped loudly against his head. The skull exploded, splattering its contents in a hideous mess of blood, bone, and brainless gore. My heart raced. Juiced by the victory yet sickened by the slaughter, I could not afford to hesitate or think. Survival had demanded an irrefutable toll.

Qon lifted his victim high over head with one heave, smashing him into the last contender. My hook snagged through the neck of his body on the stone floor. Nobody moved. Even the audience was paralyzed by the rapid volley of violence.

Then Qon leaped at me. His muscular arms snapped around my body, wide face dominating my view, though he was only squeezing lightly, feigning a death grip. His fierce performance conned the spectators, which roared their approval.

"Die for *them*, so you can live!" he snarled.

Qon's code of honor and morality splintered reason.

"I don't want to kill you," he insisted. "Die for *them*!"

I did not like the idea and butted the giant with my head, throwing him back several steps. The two of us faced one another, just within reach; not touching.

"We can refuse to fight!"

I had confidently suggested he alter his plan.

"Fight—fight—fight!" screamed voices from the tables.

The Mutis had fallen into a stupor, groaning and gasping in unison, awaiting our next move.

Qon squinted for an excessively long period and then addressed the grossly bloated Muti at the head of the table who had been glaring intensely at us the entire time. The giant warrior broadened the suspense unbearably long before he finally spoke.

"We bow to our Masters. We declare ourselves winners!"

He pointed to the four dead warriors.

"Let it happen!" Unexpected shouts rose from the spectators. "Let them live! Let them live!"

"They can die tomorrow, or the next day."

"Hurrah for the victors!"

"Let them live!"

Who could possibly guess at the perverse twists of the Muti mind? Yet, the spectators had decided to back our play.

Then, the massive Muti on the throne stood, flesh vibrating as it breathed heavily, glaring hatefully at us. It stepped to the edge of the stage, surveyed the room, and then lifted both arms.

"Enough!"

And the crowd stopped mid-sentence, falling into a dead calm. A cold edge of mockery colored the Muti's voice, as it turned towards us.

"Fight now: and the survivor wins a choice slavegirl. Refusal to fight gains no reward, except your cold, hard cell. "Decide."

When Qon stood his ground and did not budge, the Muti waved its arms with unconcealed disgust.

"Take them away," it sneered.

The audience stamped their feet and bashed their mugs on the table. As armed guards rushed us out of the hall, I heard that Muti scream. "Bring on the next match. I am hungry for blood!"

Thus, we were dismissed. A new group of gladiators entered the arena, as we were escorted down a corridor to the cell block.

And the door slammed behind us.

"Welcome to my cell." Qon sauntered across the sparsely furnished room like a country gentleman: "They provide champions decent quarters. You can make use of that bunk."

He pointed towards a corner where the rafters slanted low. I noticed a short cot around the corner, set back in a semi-private space.

"Few of us last longer than others. Me? I have managed several seasons. You are the first to best me in combat. We are both lucky to have survived tonight. Perhaps, we should be friends until we compete again."

The man beckoned me to join him at a small table against the wall. I slumped into one of the chairs, suddenly realizing my fatigue.

"What is your name?"

I spoke my cover name, "Jan Sorla. I'm from Kanns and do not ask me more."

"Accepted," Qon drooped tiredly onto a leather-strapped chair. "It is our time to celebrate! Food will come soon. But tonight there will be no women; a minor punishment for not having sated the Muti."

"Enough talk, for I am hungry."

The gladiator clapped his hands and roared, "Bring food!"

The door flung open and two slavegirls brought in platters filled with steaming dishes. They placed these on the table before us; then went to a side shelf to fetch wine.

One woman leaned very close, lifted a goblet to my mouth and pressed her soft lips against my cheek.

"Some day soon....," she promised softly.

Then a guard rushed the girls out.

We dug into the Porshi, fruit and meat.

"The one who served you is especially gifted at pleasuring a man."

Under these conditions, captivity took on a different meaning. Playing champion gladiator as dinner amusement for the Muti Masters of Kamina was far more desirable than confinement in a darkened cell or instant death.

Deep within where my Torlo Hannis identity was safe, I longed to return to Bel-loniea and possess the only woman who would ever mean anything to me.

Sorla's outward response was different, however.

"Men need their women," I muttered.

My priorities towards Youi and Bel-loniea and Torlo Hannis withdrew to the folds of the blocked inner core.

Slavegirls were common in pleasure palaces and a natural outlet for warriors like Jan Sorla who would unquestionably accept full favors for services rendered.

As a professional mercenary turned captive, I now faced a perilous future, performing for a caravan of savage Mutis. And if I proved lucky, I would have ample information to report to the leadership of the Armada. My primary

duty was survival, at all cost. Very little else mattered.

The caravan trekked from one settlement to the next, led by a long line of mounted Mutis. Behind them came the ranks of warriors and prisoners; then the gladiators with Qon and me at the fore. The human slaves brought up the rear of the march, outnumbering Mutis by more than two to one. They hustled among the wagons and domestic herds. We camped in clustered tents and when the sun went down, guards kept a lookout over the perimeter throughout the night. Nobody explained our destination.

The journeys were long between villages, thankfully keeping down the number of obligatory combat feasts and consequently; fewer slaughters.

From each settlement, men were forcefully added to our band, replacing those who died. The Mutis demanded their strongest warriors to compete with our ranks. Quite simple: human life had no value beyond the ability to outperform the next combatant.

When they met a certain quota of newly acquired survivors, the warriors were divided and shipped out. Word had it that they were destined for the Ersatz installations to be reprocessed for the Kaminaean army.

Qon's attitude about duels was blunt.

"Someday we will again be matched against one another. The champion wins fortune, and fame, and perhaps freedom. It has happened to a few lucky brutes."

Such a speculative goal was not what I favored. Imprisonment among these unpredictably irrational Kaminaeans was a disaster waiting to happen. Whether we stayed in the arenas or were shipped to the rehab installations, neither prospect was encouraging.

All roads lead to Deathwall. Andon would often quote this as his favorite line he found somewhere in the Mhyo Legends. Right now it seemed rather appropriate.

The Mutis passionately excelled at savagery. They would order a victim stripped naked and strapped out on a table. Then, surgeon masters of butchery trimmed their living bodies as if they were the dead meat of a hunted animal. Their goal was to keep them awake as long as possible, screaming in agonized terror. First, they were skinned slowly; then the outer appendages torn away, one at a time. The Muti butchers managed to keep these victims alive and writhing for a prolonged time, while the audience salivated and sneered, smacking their purpled lips, groaning louder and louder in a savage frenzy. They grappled for the severed limbs that were tossed at them, all the while begging for more.

Demonstrations of this kind motivated gladiators and hostages alike, to favor quick death in battle. Warriors in the arena were known to intentionally plunge onto their opponent's sword point in order to avoid the slow torturous death ritual.

Battle was a mercenary's way of life. But this degree of brutality made it barely palatable, even for a hardened warrior.

In an arena, on a stage, or in a field of battle, the score was quite basic. In the end you either died or survived. In fact, men like Qon and me were in a choice position, as long as we lived. Jan Sorla was a master at survival, however, we could not maintain our status indefinitely and we knew this truth, all too well. We were doomed to die sooner or later. Nobody could last forever with volatile challenges. A slight mishap would definitely be fatal.

While I gained information concerning the empire, confinement restricted my ability to deliver it to the Armada's command.

For many days we traveled through a hostile valley; scorched and barren. One evening the caravan stopped in a charred village square. Cinders floated in a choking cloud of blackened soot. The village must have been torched days ago, but the embers still smoldered and reeked of burnt human flesh.

We stared at the dismal wreckage in absolute silence. And then a Muti spoke.

"The unfortunate wretches have been exterminated because a few common villagers rebelled against the Kaminaeans. It is a warning to all, that the empire's demands must be obeyed without question."

We left before day break and our captors rushed us through the rocky valley as if anxious to get beyond it.

Captivity is not uncommon; though seldom as disorienting as I now experienced under Kaminaean control. My sense of timing and direction became greatly diffused. I could hardly manage to track when a day began, or ended, and found it difficult to determine the direction, in which the caravan was moving.

Food pellets and water were rationed out when we stopped to rest at odd intervals when no settlement was available to provide us with lust banquets. Like a herd of wild beasts, we halted midday or midnight, collapsing and falling into a fitful sleep. We never knew how long we'd be permitted to rest. Just as unstructured, the march would begin again. We quickly learned to reserve our strength.

It was a winding journey, struggling through heavy brushwood and ditches; scaling deep hollows, pressing through dense forests; then across open plains. Sometimes we entered villages.

We tramped down solid stone roadways along ridges, overlooking valleys. Within their treeless plains, we generally came upon sizable townships. Light flickered in windows; smoke drifted up from chimneys. We'd pass a few lone dwellings before reaching the town gates. Usually two sentinels would step militantly aside, allowing us entrance.

At this particular gate, however, their stern faces did not offer hospitality. We soon understood why.

The wailing met our ears from a distance. A cracking snapped and another agonized cry erupted. It grew louder as we entered the outer ring of huts and low brick homes. Our route took us to the inner plaza.

The Mutis dismounted in a corner of the open yard while our troop of gladiators slowly circled around a cluster of villagers. Nobody took notice us; not even one head turned to acknowledge our arrival.

Eleven men were strapped naked to posts and people were pelting their bodies with stones. Mutis with whips, stood behind the throng, whipping any who refused to throw a stone. From a short distance away, our hooded Mutis watched, approvingly.

Blood spattered when bigger rocks smashed human flesh. Some of the slumped bodies were already unconscious, or dead. The still living were either whimpering or screaming in pain.

We, too, stood in horrid silence, watching and waiting. None of us dared to comment, even among ourselves.

When all of the victims had fallen mute in death, the tired looking villagers simply disbanded. And our Muti leaders remounted and roughly herded us through the plaza out of the town.

They hurriedly picked up the pace as soon as we had passed the last building. We didn't slow down until sunset, when we set up camp.

During these travels, the Mutis continued to engage in their nightly parties. We would be brought before their tables where they slurped from metal goblets and gorged themselves out of foul smelling buckets. Long benches bordered the arenas where we were pitted against men and beasts.

I figured out how to be popular, despite their open hatred for humans after I'd participated in enough of these events to polish my winning maneuvers. I played with my opponents, dodging their attacks and faking my lunges so they fell short of causing unnecessary bloodletting.

The Mutis would rage with lust. They wanted to see blood and to hear the victims cry out in pain. I would appease the spectators by dancing around any opponent. I'd cut the air within a breath of naked skin, bowing with derisive mockery. The Mutis found my game amusing. I noticed them reveling to any stimulation that would bring them higher emotional release. It was a narcotic to them, slobbering their approval with noisy, belching grunts and squeals. So I sustained the scam, taunting my opponents; I continually pushed their weapons aside with my own sword or club.

I had learned how to plan out my combatants, measuring time and steps, doling out the final fatal blow to each, when they could no longer hold any reasonable defense. I managed to prevent at least a few lives from ending, during these bizarre competitions. The longer I could keep the Mutis entertained with a single live victim; the sooner they would be sated: and then close down the arena for the night. My charade worked and its showy style evidently impressed the Muti mind. Right now I was a favored competitor of these lethal sports, but the Mutis were savage to anyone who made a blunder.

One morning we were awakened quite early. The darkness was broken, only by a ring of torches. Two Mutis stood in the light: one holding a naked man by the neck, feet dangling above the ground. The poor fellow was screaming as the other Muti smacked his face and body, over and over, with an open hand until they'd ripped the man's head off.

They tore his bone and flesh to shreds after his body went limp. Then the Muti simply released its bony fingers, dropping the lifeless shell into the pool of blood on the ground.

"Just punishment," the Muti raised its hollow eye sockets to the crowd.

"Similar consequences will be dutifully imposed onto those

who would disobey our laws," it warned loudly.

"A better death for this *broken* champion would have been witnessed within the arena tonight.

He has made his weaker choice. You are less than the Tedasect, creeping uselessly to our annoyance. There are enough of you to go around...and around and around. You breed with the stupidity of insects."

The Muti waved sharply at the humans standing nearby, who immediately stuffed the dead man into a sack and took him away.

I overheard a guard and Muti muttering, quietly:

"Nothing personal; this one got lost and stumbled into our hands. The fool was attempting to return to the village; instead, walked right back into the camp. We would not have bothered searching for him otherwise."

Thus, I had made a refreshing discovery, possibly a loophole to the Muti dominance. Since human chattel had little value, the Mutis did not waste time or effort, searching for an escapee. Lose one; grab another.

Escape was possible.

Nonetheless, it was a difficult challenge. And recapture was something one did not want to happen; even to a hated enemy.

II. Escape

Wise council advises discernment when seeking wisdom.
When strong voices boast, take heed.
The louder the opinion, even stronger should be the doubt.
For, true wisdom requires open eyes, and untarnished experi-
    ence.

—Teachings of Moyi

The towns and villages we had seen were small and their people provided resounding appreciation for our matches. I couldn't help feeling that their enthusiasm was only designed to impress the Mutis. To me, the villagers didn't appear to be enjoying the duels as much as their actions indicated. Blood spilled daily in the arenas and humans cringed with real pain and disapproval. It was in subtle contrast to their loud accolades: but the contradiction was obvious to an alert observer. The Muti paid no heed to human body language any more than people could distinguish the rigid expressions on a Muti's stone-cold face.

And the Kaminaean Mutis had made no effort to understand their human population other than to brand them as less profitable than quickly breeding insects. Toys and lowly animals of little significance beyond forced labor, to enslave, torture, dominate. And in due course, eat their chattel. Humans provided a distraction from their ordinary routines.

Once I understood some significant weaknesses in the Kaminaean Muti character, I began to devise serious plans.

I could not possibly continue this life indefinitely. Nobody could survive long as a combat prisoner.

Back when I was a young cadet eager to prove my worth, I had been fortunate to avoid the prisons that were filled with fierce gladiators from all over the galaxy. I had escaped that trap, then. And I had no desire to undergo that experience on Noomas.

My inner thoughts lurked behind the outer aggression of the Kanns mercenary.

Sorla continued to practice survival while my shrouded Torlo compiled clues and data. And I needed to make a direct connection with the Resistance or at least gain information that would be of use to the Armada. This captivity restricted my chances of successfully returning to Bel-loniea. My Jan Sorla persona continued to revel in the limelight as a fighting star among the *Kaminaeans*. Meanwhile, my inner core of Torlo Hannis distanced to another realm and calculated multiple escape plans.

I had to be careful.

I didn't intend to end Jan Sorla's career by fighting dismal death duels. Therefore, my exit plans had to be perfected. And

I hoped to include Qon, since we were closely partnered. My only alternative would be to eliminate the man if he tried to stop me. A regretful idea, since I had grown to admire the fighter. I needed to convince Qon that his life expectancy in the arena was surely limited and that my plan offered a better choice.

It would not be wise to allow these thoughts to surface. How could I communicate my ideas to Qon without the Muti intercepting my thoughts? Assuming they were tuned in. Even if I had strong telepathic skills, utilizing them might be dangerous. The enemy might intercept my message. Nonetheless, I had to experiment.

I tried to think commands without speaking.

Qon, can you read this?

I tried sending simplistic thoughts his way. Nothing succeeded. My experience was limited to connections with Adt and other Helandians. I had no experience in such matters; most frustrating.

Another idea occurred to me.

The Mutis in Bel-loniea, dedicated to families as sages, customarily gleaned human thoughts, using physical contact. They would approach and place their hands upon the human skull.

I attempted subtle, physical contact with Qon while pressing thoughts in his direction. Unfortunately, this Muti-style connection produced no response.

In conversations, I'd *think* my reply toward him without speaking. That failed.

I never studied under the HanJahn Masters of Helandi. I had used the experimental telepathic machines but I had no telepathic aptitude; nothing worked. I gave up the useless exercises, frustrated and resentful of my limitations.

Still, another idea came to me when I remembered something Sziat had said:

Mutis have better things to do than examine human thoughts.

The Kaminaean Mutis were callously indifferent; highly controlling; brutal. The gladiators were treated like wind-up toys, programmed to perform death battles.

Humans on the other hand, are able to communicate a tremendous amount of information through body language and facial expressions which Mutis seemed to neglect. I had already observed their indifference to nonverbal communications with humans. What I needed to learn was whether or not they were basically ignoring our thoughts.

Late one evening, as we were escorted towards the arena by Muti guards, I quietly lifted my battle shield, covering my face with it, thus, protected against a reactive blow from a Muti.

I cautiously projected my thought towards the Muti closest to me:

Muti, you smell foul.

Braced for a retaliatory beating, I waited. The Muti seemed utterly deaf: or merely disinterested in my commentary about its body odor. To test them further, while still holding the shield for protection, I deliberately stumbled against the Muti guard to my right.

Bastard beast! You stink of Korda!

Its reaction was instant. The Muti twisted, right hand lashing out across my shield, knocking me into Qon and throwing him against the wall. The Muti then turned away, saying nothing to me. We were expected to stand and follow without commentary; which we did.

Qon angrily muttered: "What's wrong with you? What happened? Why'd it hit you?"

"An accident; I stumbled."

I tried various hand motions and silently mouthed words towards Qon. Presently he picked up on my signals.

These experiments taught me two things: For one; the Muti was not intercepting my mind. For two; the Muti showed no interest in my gestures. Plus; I had succeeded in getting Qon's attention without alerting the Muti.

That evening when we were alone, I began to explain my plan to Qon and he quickly adapted to the idea. Qon had been captured from a southwestern island during a battle with

Haknords who sold him in the Kaminaean slave markets. Qon wanted to be free, too. Neither of us wished to continue this bloody charade, designed for the Mutis' entertainment. He had no doubt about his doom; believing there was no escape. Thus, he'd opted to make the most of his lot.

We had exchanged a few furtive strategies, when a noise outside our door caused us both to look up. It was enough to alert us to the potential danger lurking everywhere. While various warriors continuously guarded us, we could never be certain who stood outside the door: friend or foe; human or Muti. Safe communication with Qon was critical. We would need to develop a silent code.

We agreed to carry on a ridiculous discourse about our future fame and fortune while, silently developing our personal sign language and mapping out our tactics on the dirt floor.

So, I opened our dialogue with a blatant boast.

"If we ever win our freedom, I would throw the biggest feast ever imagined, in honor of our benevolent Mutis."

"What?" Qon winced, quite puzzled.

I made a face contrary to my words, shaking my head, rolling my eyes to each side, as if watching for a spy. The man studied me; then nodded.

I raised my voice, spouting outrageous fantasies, to distract guards outside our doors.

"We could build a life parading through the world. Two companions, making a career as mighty warrior entertainers! We would be rich! We would be a famous team. And the women would flock all around to satisfy our desires during the long hours of the night."

My words rambled on with nonsense about the two of us becoming a Kaminaean legend. Nonverbally, we established our own pattern of physical codes. It started with facial expressions; then hand gestures. Within a short time we had created enough sign language to silently communicate basic commands between us.

Occasionally, we heard rustling and muffled laughter outside the door and knew someone must be listening in on our pseudo-private talk; probably thinking us to be pompous fools.

As we continued shouting acclamations of fame and fortune, Qon sketched a rough map of the camp into the dirt floor of our quarters. He outlined the corridors around the caravan tents, banquet hall, and arena.

I marked down side paths I'd noticed. He nodded, crossing out several and circling others. Our plan was nicely taking shape.

We sat up all night scheming.

In the early morning hours, we were whispering last minute plans; both of us somewhat excited, by then.

"We turn on the guards and attack...we disappear into the streets."

"They execute escaped slaves!"

"They will let us kill each other. What's so different?"

Qon, hardly a fool, caught on to the scheme.

"A good point; they pay us with slavegirls, and this!" He waved at the food. "Perhaps, you are right. I'll listen."

"I agree," I loudly proclaimed. "The food is adequate. Imagine the fine feasts and prime women we gain, if we worked as a diabolical team. Together, we may win several *every* night! And luxury; if we convinced them of our combined strength! What a team we'd make!"

Qon and I strategically acted like stupid buffoons who only wanted to kill and eat.

By demonstrating our combined entertainment value, we soon had, indeed, created a distraction.

Meanwhile, I took advantage of our bouts and kept testing the Mutis further, trying to determine whether our minds were actually being observed. My insulting thoughts slammed towards the Mutis each time I bloodied my blade on the ignorant, hapless ogres they had pitted against me.

We would exchange a few blows and when the opponent was fatally wounded, I would complete the death ritual, deftly knocking the challenger unconscious; and then, noisily toy with the lifeless body until the Muti masochists salivated hungrily over the mashed gore I produced from their victims. The lesser gift that I could offer was a quick death for the victim before dissecting the warrior's limbs.

This kind of brutalizing was savagely immoral but the alternative was a non-contender. I either pleased our captives or tempted them to deal harshly with me.

Qon would frequently grouse: *They had a perverse sense of humor.*

The Muti crowd roared, lustfully. I purposely swung my sword so the blood dripping from its blade splattered into the faces of the nearby Mutis. Furious grumbling spouted from those who had been splattered while their companions laughed, hysterically.

I mentally screamed: *That'll teach you, Korda dung!*

No response or retaliation came from them.

Several days later, while the caravan was still within the enormous city, we decided to make our move. They housed us in the standard set of cubicles.

Guards were posted outside our door, when we began our premeditated ruse.

Qon was reclining and I stood over him, complaining.

"I think you're boasting too much!"

He glanced up while I continued the feigned quarrel.

"The next slavegirl of yours stays out of my space! You can have her in *that* corner; not in the same one I'm in!

"I'm not interested in sharing. Not with you or anybody."

"Why not?" he roared back at me. "I thought you enjoyed watching...."

"I want privacy!" I hollered.

"I'll let them pleasure me when and wherever they wish." His voice didn't miss a crusty beat while his face brightened sharply.

"And you better enjoy it, or I'll bash your head in!"

"Bash my head in?" I growled. "You can't even bash a skulnal with *your* oversized head."

The grin on his face broadened He pretentiously stomped toward me, causing the walls to shake. Anyone actually witnessing the scene would have believed he was about to attack with lethal force.

"I can do more than that!" he bellowed. The muscles of his body swelled dramatically, accenting this man's power.

We now faced the door so that the guards could hear our mock-quarrel.

Qon and I both slammed hard against the door.

Fights like this one, occasionally burst out among prisoners so we expected the guards, in due course, to intercede. When the door flew open, five human guards stormed in, swords drawn. We were locked in a body grip. The guards pulled us apart just as Qon's fist puffed the air in front of my face, barely missing contact.

"You die!" I cursed, leaping at him.

"You want to fight? You can save it for our masters!" a voice ordered.

Guards wrestled both my arms behind my back.

"I'll kill you," Qon screamed, straining against the guards who had pinned him back, as well.

We could fool a Muti with visual code. But *human* guards would easily realize we weren't seriously fighting unless we threw our full weight into the charade.

"I'll shred you to Fiza strips, you putrid Korda dung!" I raged, pretending to struggle and taking care not to break free of the guards. They needed to believe we could be easily restrained.

Qon managed to swing his right fist out at my face. The last guard prodded him away at sword point.

I spat profanities at Qon.

"Shut up, you two!" one of the guards snapped, shoving the butt of his sword against my collarbone. The sudden blow knocked the wind from my lungs.

"Save your hate for the death duel. The survivor wins his slavegirl *alone* tonight."

Our ruse had brought quick results. We would be taken to the

Master Muti judges and forced into a death duel.

The human guards took us through the narrow streets towards a central plaza.

Night had climbed down onto the world and Clinsolnosn was edging up rapidly behind the towering buildings, casting long shadows between the torch-lit alleyways.

Our guards didn't seem to suspect that we might try to escape. Utter compliance was expected. Any suspicion of rebellion would evoke excruciatingly slow death. No sane person would openly challenge the Muti authorities.

My plans relied heavily on the guards making this assumption.

As we were pushed around among the escorts, they exchanged jabs, joking at our expense.

One of the guards poked at me and jeered.

"He is stronger than he looks. Iron meat. You better fight hard if you want to live."

"Qon is favored by the slavegirls," his companion added. "Tonight I place my wager on his head."

"I doubt that!" I scoffed against the insult.

"I'll cut out his heart and toss it at the nearest Muti to devour! He will die tonight!"

Qon rammed his face at me.

"I'll chop your feet and arms first; then slice your chest wide open. Your screams will please the ears of the masters! And my slavegirl will moan and groan in ecstasy tonight. At last I'll be free of you!"

I growled another threat back at him as the guards grabbed both of us.

"Save it for the banquet hall!"

"You are champion. I have a week's wages at stake on your victory over Qon."

"You'll win it!" I swore. "I will break him slowly! Cut by cut!"

Another guard laughed, obviously taking sides against the other man.

"I don't think so. Qon is a monster. And this is personal."

"*Very* personal!" Qon echoed, as we were pressed through the narrowed streets towards the middle of the town.

"I'll feed his meat to the banquet hounds as he slowly dies under their ravenous fangs."

The guards were openly amused by it all.

Luckily, no Mutis played escorts on this night.

"Listen to them!" one said.

"What spirit!"

We continued to attack one another in this mockery of words, all the while studying the nearly empty streets lined with towering buildings. They were taking us along some back route, almost devoid of patrons.

The guards were so convinced of our mutual hatred that they paid little attention to our subtle signals. Intent on raising their bets about which one of us would survive, their wagering had heightened until they hardly noticed more than the challenges we exchanged.

One of the guards cried: "Look, they can't wait!"

I believed they were hoping we would start attacking one another.

Their lust for bloodshed and action had created a fracas and we were the main attraction.

I waited until we were in a particularly dark, deserted alley.

There was *no time* to waste; our next actions came swiftly.

We lunged at one another, arms grabbing, flinging, and thrashing through the air. Then we stumbled against the guards, on purpose, twisting rapidly into the guards. Each of us knew what must be done.

I snatched up one of the guard's daggers, so fast that the poor fool couldn't react. Before he realized anything was wrong, I'd plunged the blade into his heart. With my other hand, I found his sword and swung it free. The sharp blade sliced through the mid-section of his companion who crumbled to the ground. I let the blade slice across a third man's neck. Without waiting, I twisted and drove the sword's point into another guard's chest.

It happened too fast for them to know they were dead. Qon had attacked in much the same manner. And within a few fatal strokes, it ended. The guards lay dead: all six of them.

Quo leaned over and collected pouches from the dead men; weighed them in his hands as he cut them free, and stashed them into his garment. I grabbed their weapons and two capes.

"We might need these!"

He agreed with a quick nod and without looking back, we rushed down a narrow, twisting alleyway; then stopped to slip into the capes, thus concealing our stolen armaments. Rounding the corner to an open street, we immediately dropped to a casual pace in order to avoid attention. We were ignored.

The precinct was riddled with narrow winding streets. More trees and fewer lamps lit the empty roadway. The spaces widened: the buildings sprawled further apart. Finally, we found ourselves entering a densely wooded forest.

"Freedom," I gasped; then, quickly moved ahead of Qon, leading the way into the thick foliage. The moonlight was nearly blotted out, casting us into shadowy darkness; silently groping from tree to tree. There was not much to see, until we noticed the moonlight reflected in a stream up ahead. Water was a necessity. And suddenly I realized just how thirsty I had become. We greedily gorged ourselves and then collapsed with exhaustion on the bank.

There was no hurry, now that we had finally escaped captivity. What I planned on doing next, was unclear. The future, at the very least, looked hopeful. Freedom never felt so wonderful.

For the first time in days, I thought of Youi and Bel-loniea. I longed to be entwined in her arms, to feel her soft body close to mine; to know her loving intimacy. I loved her so deeply that I let this fantasy lull me until I drifted into a heavy sleep.

* * * * * * *

Dawn was breaking when I awoke. Qon must have risen earlier, for he seemed refreshed and alert. We were not certain where we were or how long we had slept. We assessed our surroundings. Among the underbrush and trees, we had few choices. We headed upstream for a short while when the rivulet spilled over at a brick embankment beneath a bridge and the thick forest abruptly ended. And in shock, we stepped out onto a tree-lined avenue of shops and taverns.

Dumbfounded, we stared back into the forest, and then, at one another. I, for one, was feeling embarrassed and foolish. I had seldom experienced city-enclosed woodlands on Noomas and never one of this immensity.

We must, at least, try to appear like native residents," I said, quickly taking stock of the situation.

Qon patted the pouches he had taken from the dead men. "We shall purchase city garments.

"And I want food!"

Qon and I were not dressed appropriately for the open streets. A tailor shop had displayed tunics, so we discreetly pulled two off the rack, dropped several coins on the bench and hurried down the alleyway, before the shopkeeper noticed. Next stop was an open bakery for a morning meal.

With full bellies, we now felt more energetic and less conspic-uous. Cautiously, we strolled along the lane, trying to appear casual while the place was quite deserted. Once the markets had awakened, we'd be able to blend into the natural crowd of people going about their morning activities.

The buildings were set in a rigid pattern of metal and finely ground stone facings. Entrances were trim but clearly bolted shut, probably to prevent thievery. Decidedly unfriendly and not at all welcoming; more like warehouses and industrial districts.

The main road twisted and snaked through the maze of wood, brick, stone, and metal structures. After a time, the neighbor-hoods shifted. Colorful awnings shaded wide windows. Flowers adorned porches. It was a splendid display of warmth, which boldly suggested a cheery population. A few shopkeepers were out, sweeping their stoops.

Here in a workman's sector, I guessed that we might avoid

the dreaded Kaminaean warmongers and even find contact with the Resistance. All of this was quite questionable. At least we were free.

The euphoria of escape quickly altered. The streets were soon populated. Indeed, not by people. More and more Mutis were coming out! We dodged into side lanes, trying to discover the places where people would be more prevalent, finding it harder to blend with these towering purpled Kaminaeans.

The populace was Muti dominated; there was no question about that. They congregated in numbers with brash authority, attended by frazzled human servants.

Very few *people* walked the streets, and none were armed. We quickly realized the need to hide. Sneaking swiftly down a side lane, we managed to squeeze between several stacks of empty crates, scarcely before a group of lively Mutis approached. They were laughing and jostling one another.

By midday we had purchased boots and proper cloaks to better conceal our identities. The urban sprawl of monoliths, colonnades, monuments, and all manner of gigantic structures tightly woven together, spiraled skyward, tenfold higher than any I had ever encountered anywhere in my galactic travels.

We must have reached the heart of the empire; a colossal metropolis, designed for Muti comfort, and Muti society.

III. Into The Streets

We are not helpless we are merely blind.
And, when sight is wasted, we must create perception.
When control is dead, then reality needs reinvention.
What the universe denies, we create.
            —*Teachings of the Night Voices*

We hung in the shadows of the alleyways, avoiding the streets populated by Mutis. Frantic human slaves flanked each lavishly decorated Muti, desperately determined to obediently anticipate their masters' whims.

Keeping ourselves discreetly pressed to the narrower alleys, we eventually spotted a steep, narrow staircase between two storefronts leading to a covered alcove on the roof that was facing the open turf. Climbing it, we found a vantage point from which we could look down over the square and watch the bustling Mutis, undetected. They seemed to be heading towards a structure on a plainly clipped lawn of deep blue grasses. The cloaked throngs were in a hurry; human slaves trotting to keep pace with their masters. Wave after wave of Mutis rushed by and into the pyramid. After a while, fewer Mutis arrived, and then none at all. When the central square was virtually empty, we descended the staircase and once again, entered the street.

Everything was tranquil, now that the Mutis were absent. Finally, we discovered a district built to the human scale. Here we felt more at ease passing shops and markets serving people. No Mutis seemed to be present but it was a rather meager municipality that didn't cover much territory. Gradually, the structures again, rose before us. The city seemed endless.

A remarkably steep pyramid stood in a lovely fenced-in park. We avoided the armed guards patrolling the gates, by skirting the plaza. The next corner was suddenly noisy. Qon and I slipped behind tall shrubbery to watch, as a procession of Mutis, led by an entourage of music makers paraded across the plaza toward the mammoth pyramid.

Following directly behind them, was an amazing crowd waving banners. A figure near the front looked startlingly like Mahzit.

Before I could be certain, the man disappeared and the parade came to a sudden halt with a loud explosion, followed by another and another, in quick succession.

A dozen grav-disks descended from the rising smoke, firing Kay-pellets into the park. It all happened so fast that we could only watch in fascination. Kay-bombs detonated upon the procession of Mutis. We saw mangled body parts scattered in the flurry of these explosions.

A woman raced out towards the fleeing Mutis. Several grabbed at her. She ignited herself, blowing up the Mutis who had intercepted her. Charred limbs scattered in all directions.

Resistance! Something whispered: *Be witness!*

It took only a moment to recognize the voice of Sziat. I didn't have time to question or think, beyond that recognition.

We were mobbed by armed people carrying sticks and clubs. And only a few wielded swords and knives.

Where had they come from?

An attack on the Kaminaean Empire turned unexpectedly brutal in its intent, right at the heart of their central territory.

The grav-disks showered the plaza with Kay pellets. Gatherers descended, zapping high energy beams at them. Disk after disk burst into vivid flames of deep purple, red, and yellow. They incinerated every last one of them. None had escaped their doom.

A command sounded in my head. *Come this way, fast!*

I looked around; then stared at Qon. More words repeated demandingly in my brain.

Sziat? My mind raged, *the betrayer!*

In the same instant, I caught the glimpse of the familiar Muti darting down the alley behind us.

Hurry; don't hesitate! Don't delay! You've seen enough!

The Gatherers had left.

I darted after the Muti; Qon followed.

More explosions echoed back in the square, as we ran down a twisting alley thickly packed with floppy huts, cages, tents, and vending stands.

Some kind of festival must have been going on, and a Resistance attack probably had been scheduled to disrupt it, head on.

Another explosion came from the adjoining street, and that voice persisted.

Quick, time is short.

Qon muttered something behind me.

I focused on that voice, speaking inside my head.

Take the lane beyond the markets.

A louder explosion shattered in my ears; too close.

The shadowy cloak appeared a short distance ahead. I saw Sziat's face briefly, before it melted into the onrushing crowd.

Unreasonable anger flooded through me at seeing Sziat. I truly wasn't sure what my feelings were, concerning the Muti.

Why should I trust someone who had betrayed me?

Yet, I did.

The street was zigzagging through dank, dusty alleys, cutting between the tall angular buildings.

We turned yet another corner in the road. Men and women sobbed, in horror. Smoke dusted the air, where a huge hole had been blasted away, in the street.

Sziat hastily urged: *Enough! Come; hurry.*

The scene before us was one of indescribable horror. Mangled bodies scattered everywhere. And screams mingled with raging yells of anger.

I watched people clutching one another: some clawing at empty air. Others just looked blankly into space. Dead, crippled body parts were strewn among those of the living wounded.

Moans chanted a death song with its own frightening tones of anguished pain. Empty eyes mirrored the shock of death.

Blood stained everything; flesh and muscle dangled from splintered bones. A man clung to his detached leg, embracing it as if it were a helpless infant. Children lay in shocked wide-eyed wonder, as their last moments of awareness faded.

The tragic cost of war lay before us.

And among the casualties, even the ugly indestructible Mutis appeared pitiful in death. Purpled bodies scattered among their shredded cloaks.

I wanted to shut them all out.

"Come!" a strong voice ordered. A large hand grabbed my arm.

Sziat stood there.

Without thinking I said: "Qon! This is a friend."

""You must not be seen." The towering figure pushed us into a nearby alley. Find this tavern; the one marked by the sun-shield banner: the Inn of Tions. You will be expected there."

The Muti shoved a small bundle into my hand. "Pay for a room."

With that, Sziat turned and departed.

"I can't explain. For now we're safe."

I tapped the coins the Muti had given us as a positive reason for trusting it.

"You are a strange outlander!" the gladiator laughed, nervously: "A Muti...*friend*?"

"A friend; yes," I was as staggered by my open admission as he was.

"You *trust* it?" Qon was perplexed, and I tried to process the chaos we had seen in the streets. I couldn't come to terms with the stark horror of the pure madness; inexcusable slaughter.

In battle, the warrior seldom thinks of the blood or the destruction. It is kill or die. We wipe away the details and survive from moment to moment. That is the only route to keeping one's sanity. War is savage brutality.

People don't die easily. Death comes in slow degrees. In battle, the mind is blind. The warrior sees only the glory, the survival, and the ecstasy of victory. Anything less is insanity.

In the aftermath of such a battle, all are guilty. None are innocent.

We had witnessed a brutal massacre, exploding a peaceful day into shards of terror.

The suicide attacks had been doomed from the beginning; a mixture of sophisticated grav-disks, sending Kay-bomb explosions, coupled with intimate human bombs, mingling among the Muti crowds and detonating randomly.

What chance did they have against the Mutis' cumulative power? What desperation drove them? What kind of organization made it possible to assert this type of bold, reckless attack?

From a distance, I had witnessed whole planets obliterated, stripped of all life supporting elements; wiped out completely.

It evoked no real effect on the warrior. Seeing it up close under these conditions, had a stronger impact; threw me off-balance.

In this traumatic state of anger, we entered the tavern; hardly aware of slipping into a secluded booth.

A server was leaning close. "Will you please accept a guest?"

Qon's thick eyebrows arched. There were several unoccupied tables, so this was obviously, not a request of convenience customarily made, in a fully occupied establishment.

I agreed—with suspicion, scanning the room, cautiously.

The fellow returned a few moments later with a man and woman. Even in the dim light, I recognized the man.

The young warrior clasped my hand heartily, while he introduced the very young woman at his side.

"I am so glad to see you, Commander! This is Efre-Ah, of the Trap-zet. We're—"

"What are you doing here?" I interrupted, unable to contain my deep relief at finally seeing a familiar face. Torlo had suddenly surfaced within me and was strongly driven to glean all the facts this Helandian must have accumulated. I disciplined my anxiety and strove to maintain anonymity.

In order to protect Sorla, I must quickly make introductions that clue the Helandian into my situation.

"Who is he?" Qon demanded, impatiently.

"Mahzit," I said, with deliberation.

"Jan Sorla greets his friend with great joy. I have been worried, thinking that you had died in battle—"

Mahzit quickly picked up the cue.

"I did survive. As, I see, *you* also overcame...the enemy. I have since, made connection with the Resistance.

Mahzit had changed a lot, I noticed. His face was seriously set, with the controlled purpose of a toughened warrior.

"I'm mystified to find that *you* are that contact."

It wasn't difficult to guess the guide's identity.

Sziat; the infuriating creature!

I introduced Qon and briefed them on the Kaminaean camps we'd experienced.

"We both managed to escape captivity."

What followed was a long conversation during which Mahzit informed us about his position with the Resistance. They had mobilized dozens of factions across the plains. He reported; most had connected with other missions units.

It was obvious that the woman was enamored with him. Efre-Ah continually gazed into his eyes, captivated by every word he spoke. Probably not hearing him at all; worshipping his presence. The two were without question, lovers.

When she finally spoke, her voice was softly flushed with pride. "I just knew our captain had wide influence. Now that I've met you, Jan Sorla—and Qon, I am surer than ever, about my Mahzit. Thanks be to Botannai, who delivered him to lead us against the Muti. Mahzit will save every one of us. He is our hero!"

He looked uncomfortably embarrassed, flushing notably.

"The Trap-zet elders enrolled me in this position as commander for the Quadrate Project, Sorla."

I stared hard at the determined young man. Mahzit was no longer a youth. That much was clearly evident; branded with the maturity of a battle hardened warrior.

Mahzit pulled a leather wrapped packet from his cloak, quickly passing it to me. "The guide said you'd know what to do with these."

I absentmindedly whipped the packet beneath my own tunic in one smooth move, still puzzling over what he had said about the Mutis strongholds.

"While Qon and I championed the Muti arenas, we witnessed the growing campaign against human settlements."

I detailed their locations and populations. Mahzit and Efre-Ah listened intently. Qon provided additional sites he knew about and confirmed the increased uprising against the Muti.

We had instantly bonded on the common cause of revolt.

"Our escape seems to have been provident, Mahzit."

Periodic explosions echoed in the background, mostly muffled from a distance. Several shook the inn; the weary occupants reacting with nervous shrugs and snickers.

Mahzit unexpectedly stood once the server had left, pulling the woman up next to him. "We must go. We have not finished our mission here."

Efre-Ah furtively glanced around the tavern. "Others await orders. We cannot stay longer."

Tucking their heads deep into hooded cloaks, they swept out the door and vanished into the thick smoky alley. I regretted the interruption only wanting to continue our discourse.

Qon and I ordered a meal, downed salty ale and then I told Qon to pay our tab. We stood to leave when another man approached our booth.

He was handsomely dressed in a long tailored cloak, subtly concealing a belted Kay-gun at his side. He sat without hesitation.

Peering at Qon he queried, "Are you headed north?"

"North of what?" Qon snarled.

I cautiously replied.

"I won't mask the fact. We both are."

"Are what?" Qon was visibly alarmed.

The stranger's face remained stoic. "Danger abounds. The journey will reveal true courage."

Qon demanded: "What is he talking about?"

The man leaned close to me, his narrow features quite serious.

"The guide spoke highly of you, Sorla."

Then he glanced at my bewildered companion.

"My friend, Qon; we're together."

I winced at being recognized by this stranger and wanted to even the score, quickly.

"And you are—?"

"Ponat: courier for City Ops."

The man bit his lip. "Bring Ka!" he hollered to a passing server, who immediately turned on his heels.

"This establishment caters primarily to the human servants and is not particularly favored by Mutis. That works to our advantage. But we cannot stay here long. The raid is liable to be squelched by the Kaminaean authorities."

The Ka was quickly delivered to our booth. We silently stared at one another, slowly sipping the hot refreshment before he spoke again.

"Seven slayers sacrificed themselves in order to eliminate a considerable hoard of Kaminaean Mutis attending the celebration. Their primary target was the Honorary Exultation at the Holy Temple Ceremony. We destroyed the most prominent Mutis today.

"However, it cost too many innocent people. Killing even one Muti is a victory. But, it will win no war."

Another explosion rattled the table. He steadied a wobbly lamp and continued: "Many good warriors are on task at the central square. Their operation is now completed."

"We have lost a number of grav-disks but not without compensation. The city arsenals are under fire as we speak. The raid shook up the city forces. And we're blasting their munitions reserves throughout the city right now."

"Our numbers are growing by scores each day; some large enough to recruit whole settlements. Armed and trained units are equipped for battle. Know that our manpower is no match against the Kaminaean warrior clones. Once they unleash that diabolic army, we will be no match.

"We are in dire need of equipment, if we are to have a fighting chance against this tyranny."

"Agreed," I said. "Qon and I will assist the cause. Where do you need us?"

Ponat leaned in closer, pulling a parchment from his tunic, unfolding it just enough for us to see the crude map in the dingy lamplight.

"Here. I can get you past the city barrier. At dawn you must seek the Calisa Station. Mounts will be waiting. It is arranged."

He folded the map and gave it to me; stood, and left us. "Be safe."

I tucked the map in with the bundle Sziat had given me. Drained by the violent events, we retired to a room on the third floor of a nearby inn.

After settling in, Qon and I unfolded the crude map. A small X marked 'Tilans', as our present location; an arrow pointed upwards, and a line passed through patches labeled as forests and plains.

According to the map, we were supposed to travel north. I lay awake, retracing the devastation we had witnessed.

Nobody wins in a war.

Everyone is a victim.

Only the dead find peace. The survivors will always be haunted by the memories of what could not be avoided.

This conflict was different. This world was technically not at war. These people had not declared an outright enemy and yet, out of nowhere, seven terrorists caused mayhem. An irrevocable fear had been cast over a people who were already too oppressed to help themselves; tragedy upon tragedy.

* * * * * * *

Early that morning, we'd located the stables of Calisa Station, beyond the district, hidden in the folds of a narrow ravine.

A man was working on a fence post, as we approached. I decided to be direct and without ceremony.

"Where can we hire someone to take us *north*?"

He studied my face; then looked out across the gulch: "Trails through those hills are well-*masked* during these times."

I formed my words carefully around the code.

"We're willing to pay the price if you can *reveal* the route."

The words felt awkward but the message got delivered.

The man dropped his tools and led us behind the stables. Two bucks stood saddled, packed with food, water, and supplies. They were similar to the breed ridden by the desert tribes. As I mounted the animal, it stiffened.

"The steeds are specially trained; keen of eye and ear. Their purpose is steadfast. They know the masked course to the north; may the gods speedily reveal their purpose; safe journey."

Now, we faced an unknown trek into the heart of Kamina. Picking up the reins, I coaxed my steed forward but it balked and circled around to the back side of the stable. Qon's mount followed. Both animals stopped in front of a low booth where we found two heavy cloaks, boots, and harness belts equipped for warriors. Qon and I looked around; seeing no one in sight we dismounted and put on the gear.

Wasting no more time, we remounted. Evidently needing no command, our hoofed transports trotted sprightly towards the snow-capped mountain peaks.

IV. Uncharted Course

Approach the new, with colors of honor.
For there are no limits to virtue;
The valiant forge into dangerous zones,
Where, common propriety is not distinguished.
                                    —*HanJahn Missives*

We had been keeping a steady pace through open wilderness, no sign of human or Muti, stopping only to sleep, and allow the steeds to rest. The foothills were an easy climb but the journey became more difficult as the terrain steepened. We labored along an angular ridge until we finally had to dismount and climb by foot, with the bucks leading the way. They ascended each new rise with agility; then waited patiently for us to catch up. When we had reached the summit of the range where the path smoothed, we could once again ride.

Late one afternoon, our mounts unexpectedly came to a halt. They stood alert. *For what?*

It didn't take long to gain answers to that question.

A hooded figure came around the bend and we both recognized the rider.

Sziat!

Our steeds cantered towards the Muti who turned and led

us down the far side of the slope, where a rushing waterfall plunged into a narrow gorge.

As always; whenever this elusive specter emerged; my anger would seethe. I could not understand this highly esteemed luminary who continually ran off, leaving me in one catastrophic predicament after another, to fend for myself.

This obstinate creature posed as a companion, a teacher, a guide. It had rescued me from sure death. At other times, it dropped me amongst the vilest of the Kaminaeans, without recourse. Its treacherous behavior was a demoralizing puzzle. And I no longer had the fortitude to contain my bitterness against its duplicity.

"You have reason to lack trust," Sziat admitted, candidly.

I guessed it had read my mind and knew exactly what I thought. I felt violated and tormented.

"We are battling a common enemy," it continued. "I, too, am determined to destroy the Kaminaean Muti tyranny."

Sziat's words heightened my rage.

Isn't it one of them? Is it trying to confuse me? Or test us? What does it mean?

The Muti had paused, shifting its weight on the mount. "Your aura spans realms beyond the present, Jan Sorla."

I puzzled over those words I had so often heard from a number of wizened leaders and sages. And I loathed hearing them again, as we negotiated a narrow track leading down towards the ravine.

Any words, at that moment, would have been swallowed by the roaring water crashing into the steep gorge.

The challenging trek twisted through gnarled roots, hanging vines, and slippery boulders. I clung to the bristled mane with both hands.

Stiff branches swept at my face, threatening decapitation. Juggling this onslaught, while trying to remain astride at steep, jarring angles, was nearly impossible.

I would never again rely on this warrior Muti. I swore to myself, firmly. *It had deceived me, too many times.*

Fury and confusion infused my reasoning. I wanted to respect Sziat who had rescued me; had guided me. But its unforgivable betrayal countered my ability to understand this baffling Muti.

Gradually, the rugged terrain slackened and we could ride upright. Our sure footed stallions fearlessly scrambled along the slimy ledge, showered by the icy spray of the cascading river.

Our hooded companion spoke silently:

Life rushes us onward like this river. Look up above. See how it sweeps over the edge, never to return again.

That is the past.

Here is the present moment, churning and swirling among the choices yet to be made.

And beyond, the waters divide, ambling along uncharted channels; rushing or stalling, wherever it must go.

The paths are many; the choices, variable.

Put out your oar. Bend your rudder with the current, Sorla.

You may choose a course. Its fate remains fluid, until the journey's end. Just as any leaf floating downstream, we are compelled forward into the developing destination.

Pay close attention to what I am telling you.

Our steeds had stopped on a flat shelf overlooking the panoramic beauty of the gorge.

We dismounted and watched the splendid scene. Steep rocks rose high above majestic trees to snowy crests. Rushing currents dashed against stately boulders and danced along many divided rivulets through the belly of the gorge.

Sziat's voice rose above the thundering torrents, as they splashed frigid foam over the smooth rocks upon which we stood.

"From this vantage-point we see from where we came, and where we now are, and where we are going.

"The Muti explores multiple parallels. We're guided along alternate paths, any of which may lead to a desired goal. Like the rivers, each one chisels its own path, predictable at some points; indecisive at others. At these junctures, its destiny is variable. Once a path has been chosen, there is no returning.

All currents shift with the tide."

Sziat dramatically swept its arms high, raising its rich, melodious voice.

"I don't know with certainty, what will result from our efforts. We will proceed together. Though, I may aide our endeavors with insightful wisdom, I cannot, nor will I, divine what is to come."

The Muti sounded as if the universe had known the mysteries, all along. As we climbed onto our mounts, Sziat then spoke directly into my mind.

Your arrival here on Noomas is one of those junctures. Therefore, you are feared by Kalinis. Your destiny has been told within the circle of the Prophet.

I was deeply troubled.

What did he mean about my destiny being spoken by the Prophet—which prophet and why?

I remembered conversations with Andon, with Romos, and the palace Mutis. They'd all alluded to implications that I created a disruptive effect over the future of Noomas.

Mutis often claimed my shadow dangerously loomed over the future of this world.

Qon glanced at me, mumbling something illegible.

Sziat, lightheartedly, shifted the conversation toward Qon.

"I have also seen your future. Fear not."

The gladiator scowled.

"Fear is not within me, Sziat. And I do not give heed to the makers of fortunes. My days are marked by duty well done. And this day, I expect to be no different from any other."

We had reached the bottom of the gorge and followed one of the meandering creeks to where the waters ran shallow.

Crossing the stream, we followed Sziat through the forest, in silence.

The Prophet knows your effect and fears your presence.

That voice in my head faded, as if a silent storm had swept it away.

Sziat just continued to lead us through the forest and beyond.

This is when I began to realize I considered Sziat male, almost as if *he* were human.

What a stark change in my own perception!

He had taken on a meaningful personality; which I now accepted. The shift within my reasoning was swift, powerful, and solid; as if some internal switch had been activated.

Our relationship had altered in these few moments.

Muti or not, Sziat was a warrior.

When I wondered if all Mutis were male, Sziat intruded my mind, once again.

If that suits you, consider me male. We may be female, or both. Our process relies on unified energy, combined as a constant, sustaining whole. Whereas, humans rely on division of powers brought together through power struggles and compromise. I think of myself as Sziat, Muti; Custodian.

This day, I am a warrior. As long as we must engage with Kalinis' tyrants, the warring nature will prevail over all others, within the Muti that is me. Until an end is brought to the empire, we must all fight.

The Ancient Mysteries that were unleashed must be severed and completely dismantled. Its cruel embers of hate will continually cast a curse across all of our lives until it is smothered.

The mental connection closed, like a sliced cable.

I knew it was useless to question him further. Our travels had taught me that. Once Sziat was finished with a conversation, nothing would reopen it until *he* desired a continuation.

Sziat led us between the towering mountains into a valley, where we made camp for the night.

He disappeared before dusk and reappeared after the last rays of sunlight had faded, holding the fresh carcass of a skulnal! The fat creature, rarely captured, had a succulent, meaty tail coveted as a special treat among the warriors of Bel-loniea.

We had built a small fire, and over this, Sziat roasted the skulnal. When it was charred on the outside, he yanked the tail off, broke that in two parts, and handed one to each of us, tossing the carcass into the forest behind him.

"Not for me. I had a serving of raw...." Sziat hesitated.

"Its mate satisfied my needs for sustenance. The body of this one will sate the night scavengers. And thus balance things in harmony with nature."

Wisdom from Sziat often soothed my worries. And in such moments, I nearly forgot the heavy load of his betrayals.

Qon and I rolled up in blankets. The camp was secure. Sziat was a hooded shadow, standing over the warming fire flickering against the black shadow of his hooded cloak.

What a puzzle this Muti was. He had betrayed me severely, yet here I was, once again accepting, trusting, even befriending this enigma of my present quest. Deep within me, Torlo knew that Sziat was crucial to the mission. Yet Sorla fought against insane odds, that Sziat could ever be trusted again.

How can I know for sure?

The Muti had behaved like any ordinary, human man, hunting with zeal and providing for his comrades.

My integrity ached for answers to many unasked questions reeling, over and over, through my mind.

Reasoning intermingled with stressed quandaries. Sziat was inside my head, as Adt and Sarleni had been. I had not previously experienced this, even in the Galactic Federation; only on Noomas.

Andon had spoken at length, about this phenomenon, when I first encountered the Mutis. Questions wandered in wistful, disjointed ramblings, through my semi-wakeful state.

At what point did consciousness arise in any living entity, be that animal or vegetation—or, perhaps rocks?

Calling it mere instinct diminishes self-importance. Each living creature certainly understands the universe at a different level. The thoughts blurred and then re-shaped themselves.

Without a telepathic connection, how can we know what other species might experience? Or think? Mutis have the gift of reading minds. What did they actually know?

We humans assume superiority over those we know nothing about. We rarely relate to a plant or a micro-organism that may contain a different way of understanding the universe through its own living experience.

I pondered these and other abstractions until my eyes slowly closed and I dropped into a troubled sleep, choked by a dark phantom, beckoning me to follow it down into a deep abyss.

"Your fortitude whirls against the tide. Tumultuous storms churn; confounding The Prophet."

A foreign whisper had pierced my brain.

I reluctantly submitted to the unwelcome thoughts. Repeated, horrifying images had returned, and once again, I succumbed to the rising terror within.

Where did this come from? Something alien invaded my dreams. In nightmarish desperation, I reached for Sziat. I needed his advice, interference; even protection. No answer came.

* * * * * * *

Crashing dissonance, blinding flashes, frigid tempests tore across my mind as invisible fingers kneaded my flesh.

Youi hung suspended in emptiness, her gown swaying, as if she were riding an invisible current. She turned and saw me, a pleading expression on her face. Her lips spread wide, but I could not hear words. Then her body stretched outwards, in all directions at once, merging me into its very substance. The throbbing of her heart, pounding faster and faster, was over-whelming.

* * * * * * *

Suddenly, I sat up gasping; sweat pouring from my brow, fully awake.

Blackness shrouded the camp. Things were as they had been before we curled up in our blankets. The camp fire had diminished to glowing hot embers, shedding little light.

Shaking myself free of the blankets, I strode to the fire pit, tossed in a few stray branches, and stirred it just enough to rekindle the flame. Then I emptied the flask, quenching my dry throat before returning to the sleeping pad. This time I sank quickly into a dreamless sleep.

When Qon shook me awake the next morning, I felt quite refreshed.

We continued our trek through the forest which slowly rose into rocky terrain. Sziat pressed onward some distance ahead of us. He slowed only after the sun had dropped to the horizon and light dimmed from the world.

"Our destination is near."

Sziat pointed to the narrow canyon. Qon was splashing in the stream. As he leaned over, scooping a handful of clear water, I dismounted and joined him.

Qon gazed beyond me and shouted in shock, "Where'd it go?"

Sziat had ditched us again.

At that very moment, we heard the thundering pound of hoofs coming from the canyon.

Before we knew it, armed warriors had surrounded us, weapons drawn—betrayed again.

CHAPTER SEVENTEEN
PROPHET OF LIES

From: a document discovered in caverns on Kamina

Some have thought me to be a dreamer and even called me Prophet of Lies. Those who were sensible have wisely accepted my teachings. My purpose was to translate writings. And this one, of particular significance, dates back to the Ancients.

How I came to be selected to be among the scholars transcribing tomes is a peculiar tale, of its own. For in that day, the people zealously sought after the knowledge to be gleaned from newly discovered Libraries of the Ancients. Myths, legends, historical accounts abounded, within a stockpile of urns and cave niches, containing untouched scrolls and documents, buried in catacombs within the sleeping mountains and below the sifting dunes of the desert. Wisdom; carefully preserved over the ages.

Among them we found many accounts relating to *The Epic Dialogs of Mhyo*. My duty depended upon gleaning this very legend from wherever it may be found. And as quickly as I could transcribe their meaning, the authorities of the day snapped them up and distributed them among the scribes. They in turn, provided copies of my translations to scholars who had been consigned to teach their message throughout the territories.

Ah, yes. Truly, it was a great season of awakening for the peoples of Kamina. And that is sufficient validation to support my reputation.

I present the following as evidence of my findings on the

matters of Origins that came from numerous Historic Scrolls.

The scribes had penned the legend from memory in the earliest transcripts, for it seemed to have been of oral tradition, predating the written word. I had traveled to countless excavation sites and compared nearly identical text, recorded across many generations.

Herewith the following essay will speak for itself.

THE ORIGINS

I was a wandering minstrel, traveling from town to town and making acquaintance with local tradesmen. As yet, I am an unknown foreigner, for fame would not come to me in my lifetime.

In a particular valley, I came upon a hospitable village and there I shared a tankard with an old man at an inn. The valley of lush Chilso trees and grasslands specialized in brewing particularly potent ales. The elixir had loosened his tongue and he spoke freely, boasting of the recent influx of scholars and scientists into their quiet community.

In short order, he had told me of a certain rare and beauteous urn which he had unearthed and hidden away in the days before the discoverers came to his valley. And that evening, under cover of the clouded night sky, he had led me to a grove. There, beneath bountiful vines, sat a low-lying shed where he'd stowed the relic.

I have not yet recognized the culture of origin; therefore I am not entirely certain about the significance of its meaning. Here, I will present its expressed ideas within its original complexity.

Upon that day long ago, the Mothers came out of the heavens in a plume of fire, so bright, that it blinded any who would gaze up onto the skies.

And they did hail glory and laud upon all, singing joyously. "We are of the origins!"

They brought with them, many great vessels, generously laden with gifts from above. And we welcomed them to become the foundations of our tomorrows.

The Mothers remained constant, caring in equal measure for the people and the lands. For it was a time of blissful parity.

Mighty cities sprang up and people thrived from generation to generation. Many were the peoples and wide did they traverse over the fruitful lands.

And the Mothers encouraged the Seeker to go and increase in learning. The origins remained with the people and the people cherished their root beginnings.

Upon that day, was the coming of the Slayer.

Warrior Father came down from afar, upon fiery dragons and besieged the cities.

The Valley of the Living, was then, cratered with devastation, and all those who had been, were no more. The Mothers were trampled when the Warriors came to rule. And the Law was written, thusly:

All will bow to your God of Law.

All will laud the Man of War.

All will be purged with Dragon's Fire.

All will toil, forevermore.

The script reflects a defined shift from the origins. However, the following portion had been significantly damaged. I have reconstructed this portion, to some degree:

Lo, the Gods forbade the birthing...the first replication.

Locked in frozen crypts...the Southern Stars....

Lo, the second and third variants of saintly form....

One to foster...of paradise

The other...seeks...and wisdom.

The damaged portion at this point was too shredded to decipher. At length this much came clear in a fairly readable piece:

...Understands and thus...the living roots of the land....

The birthing...guiding torch to seek wise....

One will be a dedicated servant.

The flawed...would dominate...the natural order.

And, the final glory was a gift of rebirthing....

Favored this last, as the Observer, who must seek all that is...

The end of the scroll appeared once more, in lyric form:
Destruction freed the land.
And the people obeyed the New Order.
The Discovery, the Bright seed: new Birth!
And the first has been restored.
Brought forth by the second cast;
No longer lost for the ages have re-found.
Given to resurrection the Great Order has become.
The new powers bore fruit worthy of the New Truth.
The Kingdom arrived.
The Mighty Voice of New Reason took shape.
New lands of the empire reformed.
Unto the name of the New;
The God of Order was....

The last portions had been tattered. A few salvaged bits pointed to serious clues. I hesitate to suggest alterations. However, if one were to substitute the 'Muti' for 'mothers', a revelation may occur. Perhaps, it may even apply a different meaning to some of the lyrical words of our treasured Legend: *Three Moons of Noomas.* I believe this change might be also applied, to other ancient text.

I dare not say more.

* * * * * * *

The Discovery came countless years ago when I journeyed as a minstrel in my youth. Its influence changed my life. From that day forward, I sought answers, while keeping this scroll secret, as I had pledged to my friend, though the old man has long since died.

This is a tale of the Origins and not of my quest. My fame follows me, not as minstrel, but rather as a teacher of the ancient legends. Shortly after this wondrous encounter, I became a master scribe and scholar of Mhyo legends.

Alas, my original quest was never completed. My search for the Origins was brought to an abrupt halt when the New Order banned further excavations. I imagine that the new empire, of which the Ancients spoke in lore, has reawakened. I believe it to be the Muti Empire of Kamina.

Today the people called me a Mad Man; or sometimes the Prophet of Lies. I continue to write for any persons who dare to question the Muti purpose. Those who prefer to discount my works, call me a fool, a charlatan, a babbler of fables. It is up to others to decide the value of my words.

CHAPTER EIGHTEEN
MISSION COMMAND

I. Diano Flight

Captain Darmond's regiment had been directly involved with the peace resolutions between the two formerly contentious nations of Bel-loniea and Diano. His commanding officer now presided over the integrated Diano forces.

The situation actually hastened to secure the newly formed bonds, particularly between the Diano recruits and those from other nations. So, when the Captain's application for mission duty was approved, his briefing with Torlo Hannis had produced favorable results. He was assigned the standard grav-disk unit with ten top men from his region. The one foreign addition would be their Helandian pilot: Verss, by name.

The unit had undergone intensive training with Helandians, Bel-lonieans, Raiders, and other multinational forces. They were educated in the latest Helandian technology, interwoven with ancient practices. It included cross training for the international troops, many of whom had formerly been enemy combatants.

Darmond proved to be an outstanding instructor during the transnational exercises. And his men proudly coached the mixed troops in the explicitly specialized Diano tactics which would be incorporated into the Armada's campaign, though it had been difficult for them to disclose their unique methods to outsiders.

By the time the training was complete, he and his men had gained remarkable competence in a wide variety of survival and combat techniques. In addition, they had grasped a fair understanding of the Helandian tools and the operations of the grav-disk that would carry them on their mission.

* * * * * * *

His unit was activated shortly after their flight exercises with the mission fleets. The Diano had never ventured beyond the coastline before and Darmond was thoroughly enjoying the privilege of being among the first officers selected for the secret missions.

The captain mulled over his next steps. He was not comfortable relying on a pilot for his orders but this mission was different. Instructions would be transmitted only through a thought-transference held within the pilot's mind.

Unlatching his harness, he approached the helm.

"What coordinates are you reading, pilot?"

He bit his lip, realizing he had spoken a bit harshly. The Diano rarely addressed women by rank which would normally have been fine, since they were subordinate by nature. However in this case, the Helandian pilot was in fact, his chief assistant officer. He reminded himself to be more attentive to her position next time.

"Sir, the flight plan had been coded for routine operations when we first took off. It has been altered."

Officer Verss skimmed over her panel, systematically checking each control.

"No errors, sir. We are activated. West southwest is our heading: destination, Kamina: estimated arrival, as yet undetermined. "

She swiveled away from the panel looking calm and expectant. "I will inform you when Helandi sends further instructions."

In theory, it was a reasonable plan. In practice, the whole idea of a pilot, let alone a *woman* pilot holding all the cards in her head, was unnerving.

"Very good, pilot...Officer...Verss. I will await your report."

With that, he settled back in his booth and stared at the endless ocean, his thoughts methodically reviewing the directive.

Search and discover. Report all findings through pilot. Accumulate information related to the Kamina. Collect data. Make contact with Resistance, if possible.

The mission was dangerous and secret. And they might not even return, at all. Central Command repeatedly drummed this fact into their officers. Their survival training had been lengthy because their grav-disks were not designed to make the return journey. The units would need to remain indefinitely on the continent, and hope for rescue, only if and when the Armada arrived.

Captain Darmond weighed the stark possibilities as he went to the pilot's booth again. Verss said that the message had been short. Helandi exercised caution against potential interception from Kaminaean sources. One menace they had been warned to avoid was the Gatherer-flying creatures, resembling the Kuknal. They were reported to be nearly indestructible, half machine inventions of the Kaminaeans.

Helandi had not stated their specific location. It would be somewhere on the Kaminaean continent.

"How soon do we land, Officer?" He was anxious to be on solid ground.

"My scanner indicates a shoreline. No sign of established settlements in the vicinity. We will land before daybreak. Hopefully we'll remain undetected, sir."

A sharp rush for adventure spurred him into personally making the rounds and waking his men.

"Make ready. Collect your gear. We are near our destination, men."

Strapping his equipment together; then buckling in, he marveled at Verss' expert piloting as she smoothly brought the craft down.

They had landed in a shallow knoll among low trees. Off in the distance he barely distinguished a hazy range of shadowed ridges in the predawn mist. When they disembarked, several men quickly went about picking up broad branches to camouflage the grav-disk while others spread out to scout the area. He was not fazed when they reported no findings. Wilderness spread out in all directions inland beyond the shore.

The captain made his choice: straight west.

They packed their gear and rations with unhurried discipline. These were tough, hardened men. Each warrior carried a remarkable load, chatting among themselves in good humor. They were a mix of men with different specialties; yet, all had a common dedication to duty.

Their trek was quite natural, following rough terrain with no difficulty and the Diano traveled a solid day without incident or any sign of civilization.

From their briefings, they expected this continent to be every bit as broad as their own and paced themselves for a lengthy journey.

Each evening shortly before sunset, the men engaged in their customary sport of Barinos. Verss watched the group of players with interest. She studied the ground before the men as they arranged stones for their next match.

The standard rules required a player to stand in a ring of ten stones. He would then toss a blade straight up into the air. The goal was to toss it high enough in order to enable him to collect all ten stones and pile them into a central mound in the exact spot where he expected the blade to land.

The pilot often watched the men shoot several rounds of Barinos, their excitement heightening. The popular game was designed to sharpen their aim, agility, and coordination. Each player in turn, tossed his blade skyward; then dashed madly to collect his stones and pile them where he expected the dagger to land.

Most of the warriors had a keen sense of direction, accurately assessing the mark. So far, not one of them had positioned more than six stones before the knife plummeted to the ground.

It's similar to a sport played in Helandi.

She'd sorted the general layout of the game by now and decided she wanted to try her skill at it. On this particular evening, the game had advanced rapidly into a tense match. Sasni was beating the odds for the first time and all eyes were riveted on his actions. He raced like lightening from stone to stone, collecting them into a single pyramid. His blade had soared upward in a glimmering spiral. Just as he reached for the eighth stone, his blade twisted, falling straight into the circle and slicing into his lower leg. He yelled out, furiously. The men chided him for foolishly placing his leg in the way of the dagger's fall.

"Take the blasted dagger for all I care, Forusl. You couldn't beat my score if your life depended on it. And someday, it just might be the death of you!"

Forusl's otherwise jolly face sobered, staring at the wound. Everyone went mute while the warrior wrapped a rag around his bloodied shin, cursing. The mood among the men was souring, quickly.

But when he held out the palm of peace, Sasni heartily gripped his hand, shaking off his anger which had only moments ago, nearly spiraled to a deathly threat.

The Helandian was thrilled to be watching this powerful display of competition among the Diano warriors.

Her spirits were on edge. She desperately wanted to participate but she had held back. Three strikes against her: rank, gender, *and* race placed her too far to the outside of their game.

Yet she wanted to be accepted as an equal and guessed this might be an ideal opportunity to impress them; earning their admiration and acceptance. Such games, she realized, could prompt powerful kinship and possibly develop mutual bonds. It could also back fire and goad nasty tension.

She decided to risk it.

Officer Verss stepped forward.

"Would you permit me to play a round?"

The men stood back, puzzled. Games among the Diano were reserved for men, only. At any rate, the toss required strength, speed, and accuracy. Few men ever succeeded at this sport.

They stared at her, baffled. No woman had the power to send a blade high enough to accomplish that feat.

She stood her ground.

Darmond sensed the tension rising and decided to quickly break the mood. He personally, marched into the ring and laid out the stones for her.

Nobody had taken her challenge seriously. Even the captain was reticent in a minimally polite fashion. The Dianos expected her to fail. How could a woman do otherwise in a man's game?

She studied the playing area as they gingerly stepped aside. Verss reached into her belt strap and whipped out a dagger. She knew that if she botched things, the men would most likely, alienate her. It was a risk, either way.

The Diano barely saw her swift toss of the blade as it flew straight up, hissing nearly out of sight.

The pilot focused on one thing: collecting the stones. She sprinted from one stone to the next; then in one rapid sweep, arranged them in a balanced pyramid.

A cry of ridicule rang from among the men.

Liftuj laughed out loud: "Wrong...place!"

All at the same time and with a dull thud, the knife smashed into the rock pile, scattering the top layer as it slid into the hardened dirt, up to its hilt.

The laughter stopped, abruptly.

Officer Verss swept up the knife, holding her dagger high in jubilation and turned to the men; face bright with winner's pride. Her raw enthusiasm faded sharply as each man lowered his gaze, refusing to look, directly at her.

Darmond immediately strode into the ring and firmly brought a halt to the game.

"Time to get needed rest: I'll be expecting you all to be up early."

She must learn, the hard way, that an outsider must earn

their approval over time. He thought to himself.

After the Diano had retired the captain, sensing the pilot's disappointment, spent some time talking it over with her. "The men will follow your orders if you stand firm. Never doubt yourself when taking charge over the unit."

He cared about her desire to be included; however, the hard fact remained. The Helandian was on her own, ignored and excluded from their camaraderie.

* * * * * * *

"We will break camp and immediately move out." Darmond announced. "Tvolte, Eldrik. Pack light. I want both of you to cover ground quickly. Run ahead, straight west. We'll follow. Report back when you find anything: the rest of you double up on your gear."

"Let's go," he ordered.

The terrain soon began lifting slightly by late afternoon and Forusl spotted the scouts jogging back towards them. Sweat poured from their brows. They hardly caught their breath.

"We found only a sea and cliffs as far as the eye can see."

A dull silence dropped heavily on the unit.

Darmond nodded. "It's nearly night fall. The plain seems tame enough to trek by starlight. What say we continue to that shore?"

They reached the seaward ridge under the light of the moons and settled down for the night.

When dawn broke, they breakfasted to the sound of steadily lapping waves crashing against the rocks far below. An ocean spread out like an endless void.

With their choice of direction narrowed to two, Darmond decided to explore north but they had not journeyed long before the barren plateau ended at a sharply, cutting gulch. The unit was forced inland a good bit until the land gave way to more navigable ground.

Several days later, when they were again trekking along

the high cliffs above the sea, it suddenly broke away from the ridge, giving a clear view of an inlet below. They gazed upon a C shaped lagoon with one angular opening to the ocean cut between jagged rocks and lined by a narrow beach.

A massive ship was moored within that cove. From its size, Darmond estimated it could hold a dozen military units, complete with artillery. Several small boats were hauled up on the beach with men busily working in a make-shift camp.

The pilot pointed to the flag at the rear of the ship.

"Haknords!" she reported, "And those flying monsters; they're Gatherers."

Two towering black silhouettes were perched on each side of the flag.

"Gatherers," Sasni asked?

"I know nothing of them. But about Haknords, I know plenty. They hang around harbors, particularly the taverns; gambling and carousing. Mostly making trouble and not to be trusted."

The captain agreed. He knew the type.

"Common for many traders; and you are right about the Gatherers. They look fearsome. I would think the Haknords have some sort of control over them.

"If *those* hustlers can handle the flying beasts, then surely, we'll have no trouble with them, either."

"Not so quick!" Forusl was saying.

"I've heard that Haknords are ruthless. No fear and no respect for life of any kind. They grab what they want from those too helpless to defend themselves."

Officer Verss seemed to be on equal footing with the unit, on this issue.

"Very bad reputations follow them even in Helandi. They loiter around seedy taverns that cater to any unscrupulous vices!"

Liftuj laughed at the idea of Verss encountering Haknords in a seedy joint. He'd stayed out of the discussion, until now.

"They enjoy the drink and the gaming and quickly fight any bold enough to challenge them. They rob rich and poor, alike.

Mostly making trouble, they attack at the slightest provocation."

That, Darmond realized, *could easily describe a number of malevolent Diano he'd known in the past.*

Darmond chuckled.

"Typical for many traders: my family did business with them. They are wild; on the fringes of society and gullible for wagering on contests and games of sport. Gambling fools.

"One must be alert and tough-willed in dealing with these people. If anyone succeeds in outsmarting one of those scoundrels, watch out! They don't give up easily. Jealousy is widespread."

The lore surrounding them was colored by long sagas; tales sung in markets and port cities.

Apparently this particular crew had business with the people of Kamina.

"They are profiteers, pure and simple," said Tvolte.

"Yes. Profiteers; *not* pure or simple," he pointed out. "Dangerous or friendly; no Haknord likes to be bested in a trade!"

The warriors considered various tactics, intending to approach the pirates.

The captain didn't like anything they came up with. Most of their ideas seemed less than practical. A direct assault would be disastrous. The Diano were out-weaponed and out numbered.

Then Verss reasoned: "Perhaps we *can* make use of their gaming spirit."

The Helandian was smiling sprightly. "I have some ideas, sir...they are neither cowards nor stupid. We're an armed fighting unit and not easy bait for captivity. Otherwise they would make slave meat out of any luckless victim."

She then quickly detailed a plan that unexpectedly appealed to Darmond.

"Are you suggesting a bluff?" he asked her.

"If we approach with aggressive boldness, I doubt they would guess the truth."

He brightened at the idea. "Remind me not to bet against

you."

Turning to the men, he ordered: "Stow the gear over there! Respect the Haknords. Do not give in easily to their demands."

After a short rehearsal of their plan, the men were ready to go.

They scrambled over the rocks towards the harbor, creating as much noise as possible, making a loutish pretense of being intoxicated and argumentative in order to attract the attention of the Haknords.

Verss had stripped off her officer bars and torn the uniform to make it appear ruffled. Now she looked the part for her role as captive of the Diano. When they reached the beach, the Haknords, having noticed their loud approach, had prepared a welcoming committee of over twenty burly crewmembers, all holding Kay-guns and swords pointed threateningly at the newcomers, approaching their camp.

The unruly Diano stumbled recklessly over the rocks lining the beach, initially pretending they hadn't noticed the Haknords. The men put on the deception of being easy targets, teetering carelessly.

The Haknords had prepared a hostile welcoming party, mouths hanging open, eyes gaping. Darmond faked blundering ignorance when they reached the beach as he dug his heels into the sand and stretched out his arms in exaggerated alarm. The unit tumbled awkwardly into one another behind his one-man barricade, looking like a bumbling band of buffoons.

"Hello, there!" Darmond slurred at the Haknords gregariously. He'd swung his arm sloppily around the pilot as she feigned panicky cowardice. "Looks as if you have just what we need to resolve a bothersome problem, here."

He liberally, shook the woman.

"What might that be?" one of the Haknords growled back.

"We discovered this lovely morsel climbing around those cliffs and can't agree on what to do with her. Maybe, you can help us. I'd guess you know the art of profitable exchange. What do you think? Could this female fetch a good price on the open market?"

He waited for the Haknords to reply, half doubting that even a brainless Korda during its mating season would swallow those lines.

The Haknords just stood there, gawking without comment.

Sasni complained rudely, tugging at Verss' arm.

"*I'm* not through with her, yet. When I'm finished, you can sell her at the open market. By then, she'll be well seasoned."

Snarling at Sasni, Darmond raised his dagger.

"You're done, if I say so. And I say so. These men look as if they know a good deal when they see it."

Whipping around, he spat straight into the midst of the Haknords.

"What do you say?"

The Haknords had taken the ridiculous bate, beguiled by the presence of a woman and goaded into their insatiable addiction for gambling. The gnarly crew instantly sprang into action, grumbling bids among themselves. The Haknords had begun shouting insults, each one trying to out-bid the rest.

Darmond saw his chance to take advantage of their emotional state and pressed them into an ever heightening frenzy.

The Captain impatiently demanded, "What is your best wager?"

Voices had risen to a fierce pitch, both Diano and Haknords quibbling price and finder's rights.

Just then, a tall, muscular warrior stepped out from behind a rock in the cove and strode sharply into the midst of the Haknords, clearly not of their race. He was perfectly proportioned and handsome.

"Enough!" He swept them all to silence with a quick wave of his arms.

The Haknords immediately froze, all eyes glued on the powerful man in hushed silence. This was one detail the Dianos had not anticipated. The armed soldier towered over even the tallest of the unit and he clearly did not appear as easy to fool as the witless Haknords.

Fortunately, the Dianos were prepared with plan B in dealing with the pirates and now was the time to act fast.

Darmond and Verss both turned to face the unwelcome guest, glaring intently at him. Using the same intense tone as the warrior had used, the captain demanded: "Speak."

"I am Aminoa!" the warrior boasted, "Overseer of the Eastern Charting Commission."

He executed a steady examination of the Helandian. That steel-cold, deliberate stare did not miss a single detail. His eyes slowly drifted from the top of her satiny hair, over smooth curving shoulders, running all the way down slender legs, to her half-laced boots.

Then, he sneered at the Diano. "*You* have nothing to bargain with. This wench is *my* sole property."

As he spoke, the Haknords stepped up next to Sasni, who had deliberately shifted the pilot behind himself.

Aminoa aimed his sword directly towards Darmond. "As for *you*, identify yourself. What is your business?"

Leaning forward, a sneer tracing across his face, the Diano captain did a quick double switch, no longer swaggering as a drunk.

In fact, he rose to his full height and began shouting insults at the Haknords. "What fools are you to question authority? Do you not recognize the Proctoress?"

These words roared out from deep within Darmond, echoing loudly against the cliffs above, as he continued to shout even more threateningly: "We have been patiently watching your use of *our* waterways. We granted you enough time to settle your load on *our* shores. Do not keep us waiting for your payment of the toll. It is late! We have not been paid, and our patience has run out.

"Pay the fee for your intrusion, *now!*

"You know very well, that we own all that you see, and will stand for no intrusion without tribute!"

II. The Tide Turns

The Helandian had slipped behind Darmond. She had scanned the Haknords, bending their thoughts to believing the captain. Now was the time to take control, even if it seemed a long shot.

Defiantly lifting a dagger from her boot, she bolted forward, and yelled with wild arrogance:

"Behold! My power sings with the flesh of the dead! Provoke me not!"

The Helandian's melodrama had taken on a rather surreal texture.

Aminoa backed away, as did the men behind him.

They're buying my ridiculous threat. Amazing!

A flush of excitement shot through the pilot.

This is actually, rather fun. Silly creatures are so gullible.

She decided to press on even stronger with the ruse by shouting thick, venomous contempt at the Haknords.

"Why have you defiled our shores with your foul stench and that rotting barge out there? You insult our lands! Dare not threaten my powers; release your weapons!"

The gaping mouths of these Haknords revealed their bewildered reaction.

The Diano sprung into action, wielding their weapons and surrounding the Haknords, their blades flashing menacingly in a powerful appearance of confidence.

All, except the tall rogue who seemed to be their leader, dropped their weapons which clattered against the ground, as they raised their arms in bewildered surrender.

The leader's ugly face contorted in anger as he haltingly responded.

"Well! With what kind of witchcraft do you threaten us?"

"Pay or I strike! For *my* royal bidding is the spirit of this land and the cove. I *am* the ruler of all you see before you. Do as I order!"

"We beg pardon for any disrespect we may have shown your mighty Proctoress!"

The man made a gesture to the others and one of them fumbled with a pouch, shuffling quickly up to his side.

The Haknord now tossed the small bag to Darmond. The sound of coins rattling together, revealed its contents.

"This will hardly be enough. You have bloodied the price with your flagrant delay." Darmond spoke with measured authority. "You have stayed too long. Petty tokens of polite beggary will not suffice."

He paused, pointing towards the ocean. "We take the ship!"

"The ship?" Aminoa sounded confused though he spoke quickly in response. "What would you want with our bulky old craft? We can make you a better bargain than this old battered and leaking barge of ours; for we dare not insult the goddess."

"What could you possibly have of worth beyond your shabby ship?" Darmond scoffed, dramatically glaring at the scoundrel.

Officer Verss echoed his demand.

"Waste not another moment of our time. We've seen enough. You have nothing of value to us and that piece of junk would serve better as fish bait kindling."

She sneered at the leader and then strode deliberately towards the others, shouting.

"Men: Prepare to blast that barge out of the water."

Darmond watched, catching his breath in shock at her brazen threat.

Aminoa was decidedly shaken by her words.

"No! Wait!" he sounded desperate.

He paused for a moment as if thinking hard. Then spoke in a resigned tone. "Perhaps you will find our cargo of interest?"

His voice hastily lowered to a near whisper.

"The ship is not what you want. You need not destroy it! The cargo is valuable." Then mysteriously added: "For you are correct in noticing its paltry condition. On the other hand, it transports a highly treasured cargo."

His dark eyes narrowed. "We have certain items you would

find suitably appealing."

"What would that be?" The pilot made her demand without moving. Her dagger was still pointed directly at the throat of a quaking Haknord.

Darmond stepped closer to Aminoa, positioning his own dagger in the beguiling warrior's ribs and demanded, "Produce these riches so that we can decide for ourselves, whether your words ring truth or lies."

The overseer flinched as he hastened to explain.

"We have charted the oceans and the shores of every island. The ship carries detailed *maps* of the shoals and reefs, even of these waters. Of course, the ancient elders of Kamina hired them for a price. Truly this will honor your demands. And make *her* great profit...if she chooses to bargain with the Kamina!"

Verss was suspicious of Aminoa.

Why was this man so willing to divulge these charts? It must be a set up.

"Kamina, you say?"

The pilot demanded.

"Prove their worth or we blow that lump of wood rot out of the water."

"Believe me; those charts will bring a grand price. I'll show them to you. My men will row us out. You can see for yourselves."

This was precisely what Verss and the Diano wanted. Once on board, they could learn what they needed for the mission.

"If they are so useful, I may spare that tub. Take us out, immediately!"

Darmond kept his dagger lodged sharp against Aminoa as he spoke. The other Diano followed his example, guarding each of the slavers who would row them out. The rest of the thugs had been left behind, tied in a bundle on shore.

* * * * * * *

The Helandian had been scanning the Haknords, mostly

getting mixed emotions of fear and confusion from them; nothing discernable. They were obviously dimwitted mongrels except the tall one, Aminoa, who was not readable at all.

She broadened her scan of the ship. Almost no life energy was evident on its deck. The Gatherers emitted no force as if they were purely mechanical; odd.

When they had rowed closer to the ship, Verss picked up several large pockets of mental activity emanating from below deck. Sitting next to Darmond in the launch, she squeezed his arm tightly to get his attention but did not want to alert Aminoa, who was sitting on his other side. Darmond's knife was still wedged against the man's ribs.

When they reached the hull, Darmond ordered his men to board first. After they made a clean sweep of the deck, they returned, reporting that the deck was clear, except for the statuesque winged Gatherers chained to either side of the aft cabin. The black sentinels lifelessly loomed over the deck while the Diano climbed onboard.

Captain Darmond and Verss, both armed, hurried Aminoa towards the aft cabin.

"Let's see those charts, Aminoa."

Darmond's eyes bore solidly on the tall warrior as the man, showing no sign of resistance with the Diano on his heels. Inside the cabin, Aminoa unlatched an ornate box, pulled out a scrolled parchment and spread the detailed map open on a wide table.

The pilot recognized the borders of the Northern Territories from her navigational training. A section of peculiar markings along the Kaminaean shoreline caught her attention. Most likely this map was a valuable find; and it would be especially useful for the Armada.

Her speculations were suddenly interrupted by a loud racket coming from outside of the cabin. Aminoa turned sharply towards the noise. Verss, unnoticed, swiftly hid some of the smaller charts in her vest. Darmond had also snatched up the open chart and was securing it under his belt while jabbing his dagger hard against Aminoa's rib. The Diano shoved him out onto the deck, with Verss close behind him,

An unruly mob came towards them waving weapons, screaming nasty threats.

Darmond's eyes swept the crowd,

"Tame your crew, Aminoa—now!"

Amazingly, the chaos instantly stopped. But it had not been the warrior or Darmond's command that had stalled them.

The mob backed away as a grotesquely fat Haknord stepped out from the hold, flanked by two armed Haknords.

"Aminoa, I am not pleased!" He screeched. "Explain your-self."

The pilot overheard Aminoa whisper to the Diano captain. "Put your dagger away, before you get us all killed."

Darmond hesitated only a moment, before slipping the knife into its sheath.

Verss shivered. *That creature is evil to the core. I can feel it.*

Aminoa stepped forward cautiously. "Your Magnificence, Lord Belay-toh, we have brought guests."

He sounded fearful, as he addressed this large mass of flesh.

"These clever men entertained us with a little test on shore. I brought them onboard for your pleasure. They are quite clever, I assure you. I am sure they would be delighted to engage your hardy crew in sport."

The ugly Haknord glared at the Dianos and then a toothy grin split his sour face.

"Yes; sport!" he heartily stomped his boots on the deck with gusto. "You've done us a good turn! We appreciate the games. Particularly games of challenge."

Aminoa hastily hissed in Darmond's ear.

"They will play *anything*. Be quick about it. Challenge him. He won't be able to resist."

Darmond remembered enough about Haknords to know this to be true. Still, he was uncertain about trusting Aminoa. At the moment there was little choice.

He strode forward and made a deep bow.

"Lord Belay-toh, allow me to demonstrate a sport for your pleasure. I shall call on my men for assistance. With your permission, may we borrow some items from your ship for the game?"

The grossly large man nodded his consent as the captain went back towards the cabin where he had previously noticed a stack of rigging rings. He picked up a dozen of them, while grandly announcing: "Prepare for the Barinos, men!"

Captain Darmond held up two of the metal rings and boastfully challenged the Haknords.

"Not one of you can defeat my men at this game. You can bet on it!"

Harsh grumbling mixed with eager shouts arose as the Haknords smelled another chance for gaming and gambling.

The creature stood between his guards like a chieftain holding court.

"I will judge who wins and who losses," Lord Belay-toh blurted out, "as most pleases my coffers."

Domineeringly dangerous though his words were, they held an edge of amused interest. Yet, the man's authority over the ship was obvious.

On cue, Darmond's men began reciting the customary rules in a noisy clatter of debate. No one could understand what they were saying; but it was not intended to make sense, except to display a lame attempt at gaming rule courtesy. In truth, their pre-game exchange was designed to baffle the competition; showy nonsense.

Darmond watched the Haknord crew react with intense interest.

They probably had never seen the Barinos.

"Demonstrate!" Darmond ordered his men.

He glanced at Belay-toh, his voice bleakly serious. Impatiently, His Lordship bellowed.

"Name your terms—be done."

"You're ship; if we win."

The captain had placed the bid simple enough to intrigue a

rock.

"And what do *we* gain if you lose?"

"My men's service, of course," he replied and bowed again.

"And the woman?" Belay-toh stared fiercely towards the pilot who had slipped to the back of the Dianos, trying to remain unnoticed. "She will be a spicy addition to my property." The obese leader was actually drooling." Until I become bored. Then perhaps I may toss her to the crew for their amusement."

The Haknords cheered at their leader's offer.

"Fair enough," Belay-toh sneered.

All turned to stare at this Haknord leader while he wrung his hands with rapt anticipation, his beady eyes flaring greedily.

"His Magnificence is a gambling addict." Aminoa whispered, "Accept his offer. Tell him it is a worthy prize."

Darmond hesitated long enough to make any ordinary person begin to squirm. He wanted to make the Haknord gag on his own lecherous lust.

With measured words, he casually conceded: "What else could we expect? Of course, she will be honored to pleasure you upon call, any time you might wish to be so serviced."

"You speak for her?" Belay-toh's eyes narrowed and slowly turned towards the Helandian, silently demanding her to respond.

"You will find me complex." she responded without sincerity.

He leaned back frowning in puzzlement; then asked the captain.

"Is she worth the trouble?"

"More than you can imagine. I promise you, if we lose and you win, she will be a worthy reward, for she is soft and supple; a soothing prize for a hearty man."

Darmond watched the hulk salivate messily all over the deck. *The slimy Kdula is most likely envisioning fantasies about the sexual favors he was going to extract from my Helandian pilot.*

"She will please me." The Haknord was visibly excited, shivering like a Jilio in heat for its mate.

"Will you accept the challenge?" Darmond pressed his words

brashly. "Before your men here, will you honor this wager?"

There was a short silence and then the Haknord nodded. "Why, of course. You have your rules, we have ours!"

"We agree, then. The ship, staked against the service of my men, and the personal attendance of this woman."

"The win will be ours. Of that, I am confident."

A roar arose from the Haknords.

"We never lose!"

Their repeated chant grew into a frenzied howl, continuing like wild animals until Belay-toh raised his thick arms, silencing them.

"Enough: show us your game. If you win, we will listen to your demands."

At Darmond's signal the men began the game, arranging the rings. When Forusl raised his dagger for the first toss, the sniveling mob whined and backed away. The unit held a tight circle.

Forusl scored six rings before the dagger slammed into the stack, lodging its blade solidly into the deck.

The Haknords cheered. Their leader snapped them to silence. He then placed his fat hand on the slaver standing to his right and pushed him towards the rings.

The Haknord fumbled for his own dagger, his mouth gaping wide. The Diano skirted around him, resetting the rings in the circle.

Nasty grumbles spilled over the Haknord crowd; a few shouting at the gaming slaver.

"Toss your blade high, Smukri!"

"Pile the rings faster!"

The slaver nodded several times, coughing hard, then winding his arm round and round and round loosed his dagger up towards the mast. He grabbed four rings and threw them into a pile before the dagger fell. He was faster than the Dianos would have guessed.

It was a noble attempt. Clearly, he lacked the ability required to beat the Diano's score.

"Well done!" Belay-toh boomed, glaring with cold confidence.

Darmond bowed very low, "We are honored by your games-manship."

The creature snorted an unintelligible response, waving his arms in a peculiar pattern.

The Haknords had begun to nod, steadily increasing the pace of their bobbing heads; grinning and swaying.

The warriors were baffled, not knowing what this gesture meant. Darmond cautiously let his fingers grip his sword. Verss had lifted hers part way out of its scabbard.

Tension heightened so thick, one could almost smell it. Haknords and Dianos hung in suspense, like a tightly coiled spring ready to snap.

And then, Darmond's sword swung—too late.

In a single bound the entire Haknord crew leaped past Belay-toh and mobbed the Dianos.

"Disarm them!" the leader screamed.

Their unified tactic was so sharp, so complete, that the unit had no chance. They were outnumbered by a mass of sword swinging crazed slavers.

Darmond's sword point slipped readily into the gut of one Haknord, but five others crushed into him from the sides. Hands grabbed at his left arm. He whipped around to slash at the man. Two others yanked him bodily from behind, forcing him to the ground.

Verss sliced down one of the slavers who struck the captain on the back of the head. Somebody grabbed her shoulder. A knife thrust against her throat. There was no recourse, except to surrender.

"Drop your weapons!" Aminoa demanded.

With the captain unconscious, Verss recognized their dilemma and ordered decisively.

"Do it!"

The clatter of weapons, hitting the deck, noisily mingled with the Haknords' hostile derision.

The Dianos were dragged to an open hatch and tossed into

a dark pit, like grain sacks. A slamming crash, followed by the clank of a heavy bolt, left them in dead silence. Presently, one, and then another Diano, called out his name. Darmond, too, responded; thankfully, unharmed.

The room tilted. A swish of water on the hull of the ship signified that they had sailed out to sea: but where?

III. The Ship

On occasion, the Dianos were permitted on deck to air out and allow the Haknords some amusement. They would batter them with insulting crude remarks.

For Officer Verss, it was a different experience. She was brought up separately—alone. And the loathsome Haknords had relentlessly pawed at her.

Hands off! She mentally warned them. Each day on deck she'd planted messages in the Haknords' minds, convincing them to leave her untouched in order to reap a better profit for the slave markets. In her weakened condition it was possible to sustain control enough to generally dull their actions; though not their words.

Then one day, much to her relief, she was brought out, accompanied by several Dianos. And for the most part she was ignored. The guards were too busy managing all of them, to pay any special attention to her.

The Dianos had not been idle during their dismal captivity. For they had been devising escape plans. Some were wildly impossible, but all were based on one special fact: Kay-pellets stashed in the lining of their tunics had been overlooked by their captors; and they would provide a key advantage for any engagement against their captors.

Successful escape depended on perfect timing, and perfect organization.

Never would they be more ready to activate their plans.

The ship was approaching an island. They were quite close

to the rocky shore and she could actually see a busy harbor off in the distance.

Swimming to the beach and escaping captivity, she calculated would take less than an hour but she instantly realized her thoughts were ridiculously irrational.

It was broad daylight, and the sun pained her eyes to near blindness. She kept her face covered, exaggerating her discomfort, and listened intently to the idle talk among the Haknords who were bickering among themselves.

"What is that?" one said, peering through a spyglass and pointing at the seaport. "Interesting!"

The slaver next to him grabbed the cylinder and aimed it in the same direction. "They've built new stockades since the last time we were here; expanding the slave market."

The other yanked the cylinder back and took another long look.

"I'd wager we'll be paid richly for our bootie this round," he pondered, squinting towards the Dianos.

His scrutiny stopped at Verss; fat lips drooping into an awkward leer.

A slippery chill raked over her body as his gaze swept over her.

"A shame we can't keep this pleasure toy for ourselves."

She repulsively protested: "Better the slave market than this Korda barge!"

"You'll soon wish you were back here! Even in my arms!" the man laughed, nastily.

"Never!" she snapped back, immediately annoyed by her own lack of control. It would be smarter to remain silent.

"Slavegirls are popular trophies for rich buyers."

He lurched aggressively towards her and stroked her neck. "Yes, you will bring us great profits."

Verss cringed with disgust at his touch, slyly confronting him: "Your captain would slice those fingers off if he caught you handling the merchandise."

With that, the man shoved her away, snarling: "Shut up!" He

grabbed the flask from his companion, lifted it to his thick lips and gulped. At sea, the crew had been gaming and drinking continuously; even the officers were carousing. They were all in a perpetual state of drunkenness.

Provoking the Haknords when they were so close to shore, would be unwise. Time was short. She did not know how long they would stay and they needed to make use of every second on deck if they hoped to hit upon any chance of getting away. She made a mental note of everything that might give them an advantage.

Once back in the narrow, dark hold, she discussed her new ideas with Darmond and the others.

Meanwhile she busily unraveled fine wire which was attached inside her tunic, threading Kay-pellets along it at intervals. The Dianos, who had not yet been on deck, would then attempt to subtly run them between the wooden planks above the hold. All the while she was imagining the unthinkable: this might be their last chance to take action together, for soon they might be sold off to different owners.

"Get these on deck the best way you can. Be sure to keep the lead lines within my reach; any other ideas?"

Darmond came up with a thought.

"Well, we could just knock a hole in the side of the ship and start swimming!"

That brought on a chuckle from several men. But in fact, that was exactly what they planned to do.

They spent every minute completing the work they'd begun at sea; quietly chipping holes systematically into the ship's hull. This time they drilled deeper until the water began to trickle in.

They were hurriedly loosening every plank, hoping to allow their entire unit to escape into the sea, at once. There would probably be only one slim chance for all of them, when the planks were broken from the hull; for the narrow cargo space would quickly flood.

All they had to do was to wait an agonizingly slow period of time, filled with frighteningly tense anxiety. This risky plan could easily be defeated; everything depended on perfect timing. Even then, their chances of success seemed slim, at best.

It was deep into the night when Verss finally gave the signal. Several Dianos grabbed hold of the loosened, leaky planks; the water already rising slowly beneath them.

Verss ignited the first line, watching the flame leap and sizzle under the barred hatch above them. They listened. As soon as the first Kay-bomb blasted up on deck, she lit two more strands. Then things happened fast and the Haknords were yelling and screaming, all racing up to the deck.

Now the Dianos worked feverishly in unison, yanking and smashing at the planks; water gushing in hard, forcing them to the back of the hold and flooding the space quickly. The men braced themselves, gasping in their last breaths of air. Nobody could move against the heavy weight of the sea rushing in.

It seemed like an eternity but finally the water pressure stabilized and released the Diano.

They scrambled, pulling themselves out as fast as they could swim away from the ship.

Verss struggled against the frigid torrent, her lungs aching to burst. Pitch-blackness gave no clue which way was up or down in the open water. She knew that struggling would only waste resources.

Releasing control to the sea, she permitted her body's natural buoyancy to guide her to the surface. The turbulent sea granted no mercy. Bomb after bomb echoed through the murky depths, each blast sending churning turbulence through the ocean. Every nerve strained to release the spent air trapped in her convulsing lungs. She was being propelled furiously along a watery path that denied escape. The pressure was too strong and anguished lungs began to exhale a last, life-giving breath of air.

Relax, do not struggle; came a foreign thought. *You are not alone.* Something about the sea felt very close, very familiar. *Yes, I am with you for the moment.*

She felt no fear. It had to be illusion, even though she sensed something swimming near. Her air had been spent, her lungs craved to inhale. She fought the urge.

Calm, you live! The thing swooped in and shoved her upwards. It shimmered in the dark water.

Suddenly, the surface broke and cold air filled greedy lungs. She had succeeded!

Pressing her head back, chest high, she drifted on the sea, thankful for the cool, fresh air.

Oh the blissful joy of air.

A strong conviction filled her mind.

Your mission must succeed!

She embraced the thought, clinging to it with total dedication before she realized it was not her own.

I've survived.

At that moment the ocean seemed to roll in from all directions with heavy waves.

Eyes opening, Verss stared at a most awesome sight. Swimming within reach was a lovely creature; its shimmering copper fins pressed against Verss, guiding her along the choppy waters.

You made it, Verss. Now, you must find the others.

Then it flipped away, glimmering bright copper fins against the background of the burning ship as brilliant flames shot into the sky.

The burning deck puffed smoky billows, casting light and shadow over the open waters.

Blinking in astonishment, she turned away. The shoreline was closer than expected.

With a few strong strokes she was in the shoals. Here, she crawled very low against the sand in case the Haknords or any one might notice her.

She sensed others scrambling along the beach at the waters edge, but they were too jumbled to tell which was friend, and which was foe. In her exhausted condition, it was near impossible to sort out the details. Normally, the detection of life was easy. But in this horrific chaos, the various strange breeds scattered on the shore made it difficult to determine a precise location and identity of each Diano.

For some moments she lay flat on the sand, dazed; feeling like a beast wanting to shake itself dry. Controlling rapid breath, calming it down; Verss focused on grounding herself.

Prepare for anything! She struggled for confidence. And that definitely was *her* thought. In the ocean everything had seemed dream-like; disorientated.

Facing near death is horrifying. I could be hallucinating.

The Helandian felt uncomfortable being exposed on the beach. The craggy cliffs, lining the sands, would be a good place for cover. She ran from the water's edge to the nearest boulder, and then to next, keeping low, creeping nearer to the rocky refuge.

Her senses had cleared enough to feel grounded in reality again. She recognized a Diano crouched behind another rock near her: it was Tvolte.

"Officer Verss! Over here," he whispered scarcely loud enough for her to hear. "We were afraid you had died."

Quickly, she darted towards him.

"Me?" she managed with a bit of humor. "I don't just survive, I conquer all!"

The warrior smiled, speaking softly into the darkness behind him, "She's fine!"

Three other Diano were with him.

Surveying their immediate surroundings, she knew what they should do. "Being in the open isn't a bright idea," she said.

Tvolte nodded towards a ledge higher up on the cliff. "There's a shallow cave up there, sheltered from the beach. It's a fairly easy climb and I think it will be warmer. Perhaps you should rest there while I look for the others, alright?"

It was clear that Tvolte meant no disrespect in making the quick decisions and the pilot was in full agreement. They each moved one at a time, up into the cave. He waited until she was settled before disappearing into the night. It seemed like only a short time had passed when the Diano returned.

"Any luck?" Verss asked as Tvolte huddled close to her.

"Two more of our unit made contact. One is badly injured; can't be moved."

She pulled pack of tablets from the pouch at her side and pressed some into Tvolte's hand.

"Get these into anyone who is injured. They'll restore energy and accelerate tissue mending."

Tvolte took the tabs and slipped back out into the night. She adjusted the flat service pouch that was strapped tightly to her body under her uniform. The material was waterproof. It felt uncomfortably bulky, made twice as thick, since she had stuffed the Haknord charts into it.

Verss closed her eyes, slowly chewing on a tablet she'd kept for herself. Almost immediately, the strength of the meds revived her enough to mentally probe into the dark for Captain Darmond but she found only a vague haze of indistinguishable human energies. She probably needed more recovery time to restore her inner senses. The spreading warmth cut through the frosty chill air, lulling her into overwhelming fatigue and sleep.

* * * * * * *

Suddenly a stiff, bony hand clamped over her mouth. Verss instantly struck out blindly at whatever was attacking her.

"Be still. Shyiln is sent for you."

A crackling voice sparked her into full consciousness. It was impossible to move under the stranger's powerful grip.

"You must come."

A peculiar fellow was directly in front of her. His face looked pleading, even kindly, in a strange way. He pulled her upright. It was still dark.

"Who are you? What do you want with me?"

More startled than frightened, Verss looked around and saw that the Dianos were just waking.

"Meetin' strangers says Shyiln. And fetchin' the lady. That's what Shyiln must do!" The wry little man grinned. "Bring your men. Hurry: no time."

He had jumped to the cave opening, peering out furtively.

"What are you talking about? Who are you? And who is Shyiln?"

The Diano warriors suddenly sprang on the little man, rendering him helpless in their grip.

He squirmed frantically under their grasp; eyes wide with fear.

"Stop! Don't need to fight Shyiln! Friend sent me. Says he's awaitin': name's Tvolte."

Upon hearing that name, the Diano released him.

Leaping to his feet, the strange fellow laughed and swept a quick bow to her.

"Shyiln is your guide; knows these hills better than anyone. Come!"

There was no mockery or insult in his action. The stranger was sincerely trying to reach out, to reassure them. He grinned, and then let his eyes level with hers for an instant before he turned sharply, climbing up the stony embankment. They were forced to follow him.

The wiry fellow was fascinating and a bit questionable; dangerous perhaps. Difficult to tell: hard to read.

What a strange looking chap he was, too. Small, thin frame; aged in a way that didn't suggest age so much as experience: rough experience in the downside of life; survival in the dank, seedy areas of raw, underworld society. This male-thing felt more like an unpolished sage. Scattered, distracted and hesitant and yet grounded.

He was a confusion of so many conflicting elements, that she couldn't make sense out of him. Their guide led them up a stone path away from the cove, continually muttering to himself.

"Shyiln is no fool. Strangers and treasures floatin' to the beach from a burnin' ship; all for the takin'....

"But no! Shyiln cannot collect. No huntin' with the scavengers. No!"

Suddenly he stopped his rant and cocked his head.

"Shyiln must go. You will find your friend there."

He pointed hastily up the path; then disappeared back down the hill.

Verss scoped her surroundings. At long last she sensed familiar Diano not far ahead of them. They quickly found Tvolte and the others.

One of them was leaning against a rock, a rag wrapped around his head.

"Liftuj, you've been hurt!"

Verss knelt down, pulling out energy tabs from her pouch and handing them to him.

"I'll be alright. If it hadn't been for Tvolte, I'd not be alive." The men quickly exchanged details of their escape.

"Well, we're free. That's important," she said.

What next? She wondered while anticipating the men's obvious questions. They expected leadership from her. Verss was about to suggest they begin making plans to find the others when a booming voice cut in:

"I see you've all survived!"

It was Darmond.

The captain stepped closer surveying them to see who was accounted for and who was not.

"I am very glad to find the lot of you in one piece."

His voice was brisk and attitude in total control of the situation. He glanced towards Sasni who waived back reassuringly. "You're right about that, Captain."

Verss was especially relieved to shift control back to him. In the secondary role she was in a better position to make use of her own specialized abilities, without being distracted.

Darmond was not alone and they all recognized the little trader trotting up behind him.

"Shyiln knows the hills. You will follow Shyiln. Much to show you; time is short. Shyiln will lead you to special places."

The cadence of his words was almost hypnotic. His eyes raced over the Diano. Something was radiating around him like an invisible field.

Shyiln was saying, "This island is full of legends. Shyiln will tell you."

IV. Follow the Peddler

It was Darmond who cut through Shyiln's excited talk about the island.

"This peddler found me on the beach with Eldrik, who had been hurt badly when the ship's hold flooded. One of the planks floated us to the surface. He was unconscious. We managed to reach shore with the plank supporting him. I tried to revive him, but Shyiln here, came along and convinced me to do otherwise."

"Nothin' to worry about," Shyiln interrupted the captain. "Shyiln saw. Nothin' else to do: better to leave a dead soul to find its own peace. No time to waste. Many men drowned. Shyiln told him: not safe out in the open."

The captain continued his report, restraining his heavy emotion.

"I found Rudjih, dead on the beach. This man standing here is—"

"Shyiln the thief, if you wish; profiteer, by trade: seller of information. Shyiln lives by the work of hands and words. All for sale to strangers like you."

The little man pulled at his ears. "What is Shyiln sayin'?"

He looked puzzled, stamping the ground. The expression on his face shifted; shocked. Then went on; as if having a conversation with some invisible stranger: "You *do* as you're told, *creature!*"

Frowning angrily, he screeched.

"No! No! No!"

His eyes were darting left and right, back and forth, feet stamping faster and faster and then he came to a sudden stop, standing perfectly still.

The Diano looked at each other dumbfounded, not sure whether to laugh or take this odd behavior seriously. Darmond fumbled with his supply pouch as if searching for something important; then moved away to a rock, working quietly alone.

An odd field of energy surrounded the babbling street trader. Verss could not identify its source.

Shyiln continued his melodramatic display, mumbling to himself, rambling on about urgent situations and secrets and other cryptic nonsense. His gaze drifted aimlessly, "What do you want; advice...? No, you seek guidance."

His eyes went wide with excitement, head nodding anxiously, bony hands rubbing together.

"Great wonders. Secrets few know about."

"Why such generosity?" Verss asked.

Shyiln frowned, leaned forward.

"You think Shyiln is dishonest? Smooth; slick on all sides? You think Shyiln is crazed."

Bony hands flew high, eyes continuing to study Darmond.

"Shyiln's a mere peddler of goods and information."

His head bobbed and shook

Where'd that come from? The pilot sensed an aura lace over his body for a flickering moment.

His voice had faded into a whisper. "Shyiln's as honest as they come on Kasiisi. A trader and...Shyiln has plans; many plans. Shyiln can do all the plannin'."

Forusl had been watching closely and now looked hard at the sneaky peddler. "You've expended a great deal of effort to bring us here. Obviously, you want something."

The little man looked as puzzled as those around him. "Shyiln knows what Shyiln knows! Shyiln delivers on promises made. Come. Follow and discover!"

Tvolte stepped up, closing a circle around him.

"You could be leading us into a trap, for all we know. Why should we trust you?"

"Does Shyiln lie? Never! Shyiln's words are bound beyond the roots of this island; to the core of Noomas."

He sounded desperate to convince them. Looking skyward he paused, as if checking whether his words were acceptable to some invisible god.

Then, he timidly stared at Verss.

"Doubt not Shyiln's promise. Over there," pointing to the expanse of hills. "You will find amazing secrets."

Why was he directing his message to me? Verss wondered.

He rattled on, but she was no longer listening.

It was some time before he stopped his strange behavior and then Darmond took over.

"Enough of your boasting: daylight breaks soon. Tell us what to expect from this place! Information is what we need."

A crafty expression crossed the little peddler's face. "Shyiln lives by trade."

"You may not survive the next hour if you don't cooperate!" Darmond warned, measuring his words.

Shyiln slowly turned, shaking his head from side to side. "No no. Shyiln's fair. Shyiln deals...make deals."

"Look! The sky brightens with the dawn. It is safe to go. Come and see for yourselves."

Shyiln's not shy—follow Shyiln."

They watched the spry little man as he ran ahead of them, doubled back a few steps, and then scurried off along the well-padded trail of sod and sand. They passed beneath stone archways, winding through tall hedges partially concealing broken walls.

The morning sun played against their world, creating long shadows along the path.

When they came upon a steep staircase, made of perfectly fitted slabs, they spied Shyiln looking down from the top, impatiently waving for them to hurry. Climbing the oversized steps gradually drained their tired, aching muscles. Each worn leg dragged laboriously up to the next level. Verss fought against the fatigue, lagging further behind as one, and then another Diano stepped past her.

She chewed on an energy tab, handing out the last of them to men. Wiping a hand across her forehead, she focused on the rising trail.

At last, she reached the top; a long flat rise of pure white stone. Several men had grouped around an oval rock, nearly as tall as Darmond.

Their guide was pacing back and forth, impatiently annoyed by their fascination with this monument. "Come, no time."

He pushed aside a clump of hanging vines, exposing a narrow passageway.

"This way: come, come! Time is fleetin'!"

Shyiln moved quickly into a narrow passage which opened to a slit of sky, far above. The bulky warriors labored, often turning sideways to squeeze through the passage.

Verss was directly behind Darmond, occasionally probing forward. Ominous vibes drifted back through the narrow gap, but she could not get a uniform reading. Even Shyiln's shimmering aura had stopped. Something felt terribly wrong.

She whispered very softly.

"There's someone or thing up ahead; a very weak life form."

Darmond immediately grabbed Shyiln, catching him by the neck. "Where're you taking us? Who's up there?" He rasped harshly into the thief's ear.

"You are chokin' your guide!" Shyiln coughed, pulling at Darmond's hand. "Quiet; almost there: you'll be needin' Shyiln for bargainin'. Guards watch the digs. Keep marauders away. Shyiln knows the way."

"I will break your scrawny neck if you cross us."

Darmond kept his hold on the thief while listening for any sound up ahead.

When the passage opened to a broad space, Shyiln tried to bolt forward but Darmond had tightened his grip on the guide's neck.

"Over there, behind that rock."

Shyiln was squirming to get free, voice husky as if the words were stuck in his throat: "The guard house. You'll find weapons. Beware. Stay strong."

"Forusl, Tvolte check it out." Darmond pushed a small dagger into the latter's hand. "Here."

The scouts crept silently along the jagged stone wall towards the boulder Shyiln had indicated.

Verss anxiously watched them, mentally reaching out for any signs of life. After a few minutes, she detected a sudden change in Forusl.

"Captain, something is wrong."

No sooner had she spoken those words, than their scout reappeared, motioning for them to follow.

"Brace yourselves. We found a man bound and badly tortured. It's gruesome. There's an arsenal full of weaponry. This appears to be a guard station, like Shyiln said."

They entered the cleft rock and in the far corner there was a heavily built warrior shackled by arms and legs. The poor fellow's half stripped body was brutally slashed, slouched over a spreading pool of blood.

Verss realized she must have sensed the last of the warrior's life energy drain from his dying body. Locked in her own emotions, she stood there, unable to hold back tears. Darmond stepped close, gently wrapping his arm around her shoulders and protectively guiding her to the back of the grotto where they had found a sizable stash of swords and other arms.

"Whoever did this cannot be far," Darmond commented, as he chose a sword and strapped it to his belt.

The other Dianos did likewise and Verss selected several daggers and a short sword for herself.

Shyiln backed into the shadows, wringing his hands.

"Dangerous times; dangerous places...," his crazy monologue rambled. He evidently, was no longer willing to run off without them.

"Shyiln," Darmond sternly admonished without malice. It was clear that the little guy was deeply stressed. "Calm down. This is not what you expected us to find. So, be quick. Speak clearly. What have you brought us to see? Where are these legendary discoveries you promised?"

The little man pointed a shaking finger across the opening to another of the grottos, but he did not move.

Darmond was not going to let the thief stay behind. "And you will show us the way."

He roughly pulled the man by the shoulder in the direction indicated. Shyiln nodded, quickly obeying like a puppet, once again leading the unit into the open space.

Several of the warriors had spread out, ready to fight anyone who might be waiting in ambush. Tvolte, who led them along the edge of the grotto, suddenly pulled up.

"There's an ash pit still smoldering; bones and flasks lying around. We'll probably find others like him in these caves."

They hadn't searched far when several rowdy warriors bearing weapons, suddenly ran at them from out of another grotto.

No words were spoken. They moved instantly.

Darmond took the lead, when the warriors fell upon them. He was quick, sword swinging an arc, slicing the air, just missing the man's chest.

They reacted sluggishly; most likely half drunk. The flask in the last man's left hand, said it all.

Darmond gave no ground as these men counter-attacked with brutal intent, one in front and two at either side, creating a half circle around him.

The captain didn't budge.

The other Dianos rushed forward, forming a full circle around the four combatants.

In all the confusion, Verss saw little from where she stood. The flashing of swords and sound of metal slicing against metal echoed among the rocks. A scream of agony was followed by a dull thud.

The Dianos pulled back, revealing four bodies sprawled on the ground before them.

No one in the unit had been harmed.

"Drunken fools," Tvolte rued angrily.

"Apparently," Darmond observed, wiping his blade on one of the dead men.

"This area here; these caves...whatever their purpose...at least these sots won't be engaging in any more crude amusements."

He turned and noticed Verss watching.

"They weren't the ones who killed that man," she said somberly, visibly shaking. "They didn't do it. He was one of *them*."

Darmond frowned. "What are you saying?"

Just then, a loud screech echoed throughout the chamber as a dark shadow swooped from above. The broad wings of a Kuknal soared up, spiraling higher, until it reached the peaks of the cliffs, and then disappeared.

All the Dianos suddenly, ducked behind boulders, staying well hidden from the birds until the last of the screeching echoes had ceased.

"Men or beasts: all dangerous: we must be alert," the captain cautioned

Shyiln, who was still groveling beneath an overturned shield, whined. "Much drinking and reveling...the army of Kamina is swarming with low life; Shyiln knows."

His voice quivered with each word.

Darmond gruffly drilled the guide.

"Can we expect to find more of them?"

Shyiln was already beginning to rummage around one of the dead bodies. In moments he had stripped several pouches that jingled.

"Thief!" one Diano snapped; disgusted.

"That, Shyiln is. Every man survives as he can. These... *things*...will never be noticed. Many fights up here; strip them of the weapons, if you need to. Take coins; make it look like a robbery."

On one side of the fire circle, several torches lay scattered, which they collected and lit, before entering the next grotto. A high ceilinged vault cut deep into the mountain, veined with several tunnels.

They had entered the caves.

Shyiln chose one of the branching corridors, without hesitation.

It was not a pleasant journey; the walls were peppered with a series of nasty side niches, only a few were empty.

The horrors they found in the chambers were ghastly, and Verss felt revolting vibes cascading through her. Skeletons were chained against blackened stones; the bones hanging with strips of dried flesh turned leathery. This appeared to be a series of torture chambers. The implications were unsettling.

"Ignore. Ignore!" Shyiln angrily shouted, trying to sound strong. "Plenty of that; ignore!"

He urged them to hurry on.

Nobody objected.

V. The Blade of Death

In the adjoining room, they discovered a crudely drawn map, half the height of a man, chalked along the corridor with black ash. They could see the noticeable form of a continent with one name slashed in the middle.

KAMINA

The map had a rather desperate look about it as if swiftly drawn. Verss broke the silence.

"Could it be a dying man's last message?"

Shyiln looked mysteriously at them, glancing from one to the other.

"Did Shyiln not tell you? The maps you seek: plenty here; hurry. Shyiln knows the dangers. This place is not safe...."

The voice faded, as did Shyiln's thin form, running back out through the tunnel.

They had barely begun to decipher the Kaminaean map when their guide suddenly, came rushing back toting a bulky sack. He tipped it over, dumping the contents on the ground, and speaking hastily in his choppy style.

"A passage goes downwards. Shyiln will show you. You will go there now...yes. Shyiln must not wait. Go now! Take them to the passage."

The Dianos wasted no time collecting the rations of Mio

sticks, fruits and flasks, doling out the supplies to one another, as Shyiln kept talking.

Darmond bit into a succulent bluish rod, its sweet flesh speckled with tiny black seeds.

He listened impatiently, to the wiry peddler: "Just where do you intend for us to go?"

Their guide's eyes narrowed.

"Do not delay. Shyiln don't have all day for foolin' 'round; must get on with important duties."

He broke off, again looking mystified by his own words.

"Come, follow Shyiln!"

The Helandian discerned a foreign energy; almost alien.

Dropping her mind block, she quickly probed further into the caves which seemed to respond to Shyiln's anxiety.

A multitude of voices cascaded:

...*Beware the blade of death.... Flee! You will be found out.... Do not stand against the monster.... Get out of the caves... trapped.... Escape.... Don't wait....*

Voices kept driving grave warnings of danger. They came from all sides, flooding the cavern. She could barely tolerate the pressure of all that sound: all those words, blanketing, smothering; pulling tighter and tighter around her mind. Breathing heavily, eyes shut tight, Verss dropped to the ground, covering her ears, blocking, to stop the voices.

Captain Darmond instantly knelt down beside the pilot, staring firmly into her eyes.

"What is it? What did you hear?"

She barely whispered between clenched teeth.

"Do as he says! Hurry...no time."

She didn't need to explain, for at that very moment, an unexpected visitor announced himself.

"Well, Shyiln. You've succeeded in bringing me to these scoundrels.

Aminoa swaggered into the chamber, grinning smugly, casually swaying his sword back and forth around the space between himself and the Diano.

"No! No; never did!"

Shyiln had scrambled behind Tvolte, pulling the empty sack over his head.

Darmond was instantly on his feet, as were the other Dianos, swords drawn and aimed straight at the intruder.

Aminoa moved like lightening, slicing two swords out of the Dianos' hands and pointing his directly towards Darmond, who stood fully alert, determined not to back off.

An arrogant grin twisted Aminoa's thin lips.

"You cannot stand against my challenge!"

The Haknord's warrior had lowered his weapon.

Darmond lunged without hesitation; sword flashed at the rogue's bare chest; aimed to land right on target—the heart.

Aminoa's weapon had blocked; casually brushing the officer's weapon aside at the last instant, slimly preventing it from cutting flesh.

Once more, the captain parried a swift circle around the man-machine's extended blade, counter-thrusting. And again, it was thwarted.

Aminoa moved gracefully without effort, like a slick Tian sliding through each elementary act.

The weapon attacking Darmond was razor sharp; blade tapered to a needle point, creating a blur of near miss.

The rogue displayed extraordinary precision, designed to illustrate extreme accuracy and demonstrating clearly that Aminoa was enjoying an effortless game of swordsmanship.

Their swords danced out this continued pattern several more times before Darmond stepped back, observing his opponent with amazement.

Aminoa smiled coldly, revealing no emotion. "As you can see I played easily with you on the Haknord ship. Here I will finish the work. You shall be no challenge to me."

Darmond suddenly felt the tip of the man's sword-point touch his shoulder, then it lowered to skim across his stomach, and tap each thigh so swiftly, that it was impossible to see the blade's movement.

No blood was drawn without purpose. It was a nasty exhibition of control and contempt.

"You're too simplistic with the sword—a stumbling child."

And the blade tapped the top of Darmond's head, came around and touched his throat.

"How easily you will die. Right here under my carving magic," he gloated with no intention of humor: light, airy, and yet lacking any thread of sentiment.

"My Kaminaean masters gifted me with immortality," his voice boomed. "I serve them with my supreme skill." He paced arrogantly through the cavern. Hollow of genuine emotion, eyes glassed over, he paid no notice to the Dianos; totally dismissing any danger coming from these outclassed combatants.

This display of callous scorn enraged the captain, who instantly lunged.

Aminoa swiftly struck the sword to one side with such violent power that it threw the Diano off balance. The warrior smugly glared.

"I played the gentleman and let you live a bit longer, and *you* *attack*, when you *think* I'm not looking! What a cowardly act! You're death will be slowed to a lingering series of bleeding wounds until you collapse in a writhing, crippled heap. Wonder at your fatally miscalculated ruin!

"We are many mighty men; specially designed by our Muti masters: more than mere flesh, muscle, and nerves. We have been re-mapped, re-designed from weak and clumsy humans into impermeable excellent *machines.* And you can never defeat us!"

The man-monster's voice blasted so loudly, that the rocks audibly cracked above them. "Indestructible metal has replaced bone and our hearts are shielded against any deathly thrust!"

Mockery gleamed on his countenance.

"No matter that I tell you the ingenious machinations of the Prophet's Mutis. You cannot do harm for you will all die by my blade. Man by man, body by body, cut by cut.

"Witness the masterful art of my makers. And let it be known that I am only *one of a legion of the Kaminaean warriors.*

"As I speak the Mutis of Kamina, the Prophet and its legions, are completing the most powerful and invincible army every conceived! And we shall dominate or crush every last one of you.

"The wise ones among you, who sensibly surrender, shall be the lucky ones. And if selected to survive will dwell among the subjugated that are swallowed into the fold. And they will taste the sweet righteousness of serving the mighty Prophet Kalinis.

Brazen, foolish scourge like you will be devoured into their bottomless bellies of death!"

Without hesitation he snapped his blade towards Forusl: the point drawing a red streak down the brave warrior's side.

"You can see how easily I range my blade to the very edge of his skin. The next will pierce clean through bone with one thrust."

The fiend's blade again, darted directly towards its target. Forusl stepped to one side, sword lifting to cross against the attacking weapon. The move obviously astonished Aminoa, who would not have expected any counter play.

"Well, he breathes a moment longer! That's all. He can watch, as I cut another down; a little here and there!"

The man-machine's weapon swiftly circled and cut down Liftuj's arm as he dodged in the nick of time.

It was all done so casually, demonstrating Aminoa's superior ability to destroy them.

"All of you are dead men," he scoffed.

"Be reasonable, Aminoa," Verss said, stalling for time.

She had unsuccessfully tried to probe this monster's mind but failed; drawing a blank.

Her only possible conclusion: he was not human—an Ersatz; just as he had describe. Thus, she decided to attempt to reroute the villain's concept of purpose—challenging its computed rationalization.

"You're just a puppet for His Magnificence and the Haknords. The Kaminaeans created you for their own purposes: a stupid servant. Is that what you want to be?"

She was playing on a hunch against his arrogance. Blank mind or not, there was an element that suggested a blatant human ego underlying the warrior's cold emptiness.

The warrior turned to her, icy rage marking his face.

"The Kamina promise great honors. Aminoa serves no Haknords."

A distinct pause separated his words. His voice showed emotion, as if a switch had been flipped within him. Something human registered inside. She guessed that she might have reached a self-reasoning segment containing some remnant of his humanity.

Verss pressed a challenge: "Think about it, Aminoa. If you join our cause, you can be a free man and win genuine honors.

"What have the Mutis done for your good? They are using you to *their* advantage. Not to *yours*."

The towering Ersatz warrior hesitated and did not reply immediately. But when he did, his threatening words were noticeably wavering:

"I will survive. You will be dead. I alone will live!"

The pilot persisted with her attempt to convince Aminoa to reconsider:

"You are destined to be a petty killing machine with no life of your own. And you will be thrown on the scrap heap when they are through with you; nothing more.

"Is that what you want?"

Aminoa trembled with fury at her words but he did not shrink back. Instead, his voice raged with mechanical tenacity; no hint of human sentiment.

"I—am—*immortal*."

The Helandian had failed.

He stepped forward, sword raised to strike.

"None of you will leave here alive. Which of you brave heroes wish to tempt me?

Tvolte suddenly leaped at the callous warrior, from behind. Sasni closed in to his left and Forusl aimed his blade, ready to cut in from his right. The fiend spun swifter than any of the Diano could parry, striking all three Dianos' sword against the stones.

"You will die first," he snarled, now face to face with Tvolte and with that, Aminoa's sword had plunged clean through Tvolte's chest.

"Who will die next?"

Rage echoed from the Diano warriors as the others stormed at Aminoa, all at once. Metal clashed against metal resounding bitterly, within the stony crypt.

Aminoa's blade lashed out with lightening speed, whipping left then right. Swords flashed against stone and flesh.

The chamber was too small for the men to gain advantage around the Ersatz-monster, who systematically hacked at them, fatally striking each one down, until only the captain and the pilot remained standing.

Few blades had penetrated Aminoa's defense. But from the streaks of blood glistening down his glossy muscular body the perfect machine showed evidence of his flawed humanness.

But he was despondently unaware of his own mortality.

"How easily you fall before my skilled fingers. My bland extends from my thought. I think, and thus, the sword's point finds my chosen destination."

Verss, with her dagger in hand, had watched all of this, with astounded disbelief.

At that exact moment, the cavern suddenly turned bright yellow. A smoky black haze coiled into the space in front of Aminoa. It grew in brightness, and then constricted into a thin spiraling rod.

Everybody froze, stunned.

The shape pulsed, bloating into a giant scaled serpent. Two fiery eyes rampantly fixed on the terrified warrior, who stood paralyzed; sword not moving. The warrior's mouth opened wide. All sound froze in his throat, as the bulging striped head swayed.

The serpent wove back and forth, its coils billowing, winding steadily towards the man-machine; its jaws snapping hungrily.

There was no escape possible for Aminoa. His sword arm lifted, and with lightning speed, thrust at the serpent that instantly whipped around the warrior. Its coils clamped down hard until the sword splintered. Then wrenching the captive around, the serpent crushed Aminoa's face down against the stone floor.

Aminoa shrieked with terrorized pain. The serpent slithered down the tunnel, dragging him noisily after it, brutally smashing him back and forth against the rocks.

The captain and pilot witnessed in disbelief.

The danger is past...for the moment!

Verss was too dazed to even try reasoning out the source of that voice.

Aminoa's swift demise was followed by a long, shocked silence.

Shyiln's stammering was barely audible.

"Go, go, go. You...you...must go fast!"

Turning, Verss saw the trader quivering in a corner of the cave.

He raised one arm and pointed the opposite direction of the way the serpent and Aminoa had left.

"Go—there—hurry!" was all he could manage to say.

The little peddler had regained some of his courage, frantically pushing them down the twisting corridor. Verss stumbled, slamming into something she could not see, for they had plunged into darkness.

CHAPTER NINETEEN
FRIEND OR FOE?

I. The Hidden City

You may wonder: What about God?
I ask: Of which god do you speak?
You answer: The only one that is.
I wonder: Another, names a different god.
If you then say: There is one God.
Would you have your answer?
                              —*Moyi, in a Singular Debate*

We had been dumped, once again, by the infuriatingly difficult Sziat and now, as before, we were surrounded by warriors. I had grown quite weary of repeatedly landing in these predicaments.

Qon pulled his sword from its sheath, ready to defend us. I did the same. However, the army did not advance.

One warrior raised his sword slowly, holding it parallel over his head with both hands. The rest of them sheathed their blades and backed away a few paces. They gazed steadily at us, unflinching.

I guessed, from their manner and dress, that they were not connected to the Kamina, and that we were probably not in any real danger.

Nevertheless, my anger held strong against Sziat, and not in the mood to be overly polite.

The leader's stony features were framed by sleek black hair. His gray eyes scrutinized my body with damningly brutal judgment. One word pierced me like an arrow.

"North!"

I didn't hesitate: "Mask."

The man's face remained unreadable as he countered: "Reveal!"

My anger quickly subsided.

"The Messenger has sent us. We seek knowledge."

He turned his mount and addressed his men.

"At last, these are the comrades we have been expecting. Welcome them!"

The warriors closed in, forming a tight ring around Qon and me. Each saluted, as he passed by. Then they galloped off in a double column. When the last warriors had passed by, the leader beckoned us.

"Follow."

That was all; simple and direct.

We rode through a twisting passage, along a narrow gorge that split through the mountain.

Jagged rocks hung close. The gap was barely wide enough for our steeds to traverse. We finally came to the end.

Before us lay a crimped fold of land, strewn with clusters of sod-covered huts, interspersed among patches of woods and fields. Even the connecting paths were cleverly carved along the natural cut of the shadowy ridges, sheltered by high rocky cliffs on all sides.

Our escort had stopped and dismounted.

"See and observe!" His arms proudly swept over the valley. "This is KiNal.

"Note the natural protection of the terrain; well concealed from travelers or aerial spies. Each structure mimics the wilderness; every precaution is maximized to ward off intruders or traitors."

Qon and I had found our destination at last; the central stronghold of the Resistance. I drank in the amazing details, as

I studied the layout of the community. An odd configuration of dwellings, in various shapes and heights was cleverly designed with native growth and stone. From above, the natural materials would obscure any sign of civilized life.

Some structures were ovals, standing in random order between scattered clumps of trees. Here and there were flat-topped buildings, several stories high. Bright purple foliage covered the roofs. Various camouflaged tents spread out in scattered patterns; similar to those of nomadic tribes. The layout cleverly obscured an amazingly complex city under its canopy.

The cliffs themselves were undercut by hollowed slices, masked with fine netting to hide their actual curvature. Even from this close proximity, most of the city was effectively camouflaged to appear to be natural crevices and folds in the boulders. Only upon careful study, did one realize these openings provided accesses to vast caverns, internal buildings carved into the rocky mountainside. Our host scrutinized at me with disarming intensity.

"Your arrival has been expected for a long time. Everything is altering at an accelerated pace. The tyranny is spreading wider by the day. We cannot keep our location secret for much longer. It is only a matter of time, before we'll be discovered. Without help, we're in danger of being crushed. Limited weaponry, connections and tools prevent us from realistically combating the Mutis. Your assistance is critical to our survival."

His words fell heavy on my heart, having witnessed the horrific conditions in Kamina.

"Getting here has been a struggle."

He agreed.

"Quite understandable. We were concerned, knowing only that somebody would come from the other side. You're arrival is deeply welcomed.

"Pockets of Resistance fighters are struggling against this foe with self-destructive methods. Their tactics have remarkably impacted the Mutis, at a tragic cost. Too many excellent fighters have been lost. We try to maintain contact in order to

coordinate actions against the Muti. Communications are difficult. Our scouts are not always...."

He broke off; then said: "For now let's get you settled."

As we continued on through the obscure streets, I noticed
a unified dress code among the people; modest tunics and
breeches. No rank, craft, or station marked status beyond that
of a mere citizen.

"Where are the warriors? The military?"

A solemn look creased his stern face.

"Everyone is a fighter; all committed warriors. Discretion is
paramount, of course. Spies are everywhere and, if given the
chance, they will strike without warning. A civilian community
is less important to them. A military one would instantly be
destroyed.

"You will be told more by others. Tonight there's a banquet
celebrating your arrival."

We rode through a corridor cut into the sheer side of an over-
hanging cliff. The archway ended at an awesome cavern, filled
with ferns and flora of all kinds. A natural waterfall misted
into a lake where men, women and children busily went about
their activities. A team of youth raced across one sparkling pool
while others cheered them on from the sides. Several women
corralled a dozen toddlers in the shallows. We were ushered
around the back of the falls onto a spacious veranda, attached to
a cozy room, stocked with food and garments, similar to those
of the others we'd seen.

Qon's eyes were wide with wonder. "I thought you were
jesting when you promised we'd be living in luxury!"

We both laughed heartily and I said: "This place rivals the
resorts of great cities, don't you agree, Qon?"

He mused good-naturedly: "Yes. The only thing missing are
the slavegirls!"

The guide replied seriously, even annoyed. "We have no
slavegirls here in KiNal."

"What about Pleasure Palaces?" Quo pleaded, clearly
distraught by this response.

"No need for those here. If it is women you want, well, they will be there at tonight's dinner."

"My body is hungry for more than food!" He flexed his arms and the muscles bulged hard as rocks. "They need pampering."

"You can expect liberal attention, for many women will find you attractive. So...enjoy."

Qon was about say something I suspected would make him look foolish, so I clamped my hand over his mouth.

"Interesting," I calmly replied, winking at Qon, who had reluctantly given in to my constraint. "Tonight we feast."

"Later then; the event schedule is posted near the pool on the public board. I'm sure you'll easily find the banquet hall."

When the man was out of sight, I filled myself a tankard from a small free-flowing fountain and then bit into a succulent fruit. Qon did likewise.

"Very nice amenities: and if he's right about the women; well then, I can't wait to meet with those lovely ladies tonight!"

The boorish gladiator of Jan Sorla was just as excited as Qon about the prospects.

The Torlo Hannis in me had no wish for female companionship; other than Youi. I had to fight down a sudden pang of longing for her. I had no emotional desire for any other woman. How long, before we could be once again, together?

Qon's words teased my impulsive instinct for female companionship. The male beast has no moral restrictions; regardless. My love for Youi had not blinded me to other females. And Jan Sorla was clearly prone to seek out women.

After a short rest, we were headed towards the banquet hall, when a cloaked figure approached us. It looked to be a mini-Muti, but as the face came into view, we saw a very aged woman, features crumpled in wrinkles; an uncommon sight on Noomas. She rushed up towards me, eyes, intensely bright. "You came, at last!"

Her direct manner and urgency shook me, as if she knew me personally, yet I had never seen her before in my life.

The old woman clung to my arm, in wild desperation. "I have

words for you," she rasped nervously. Then she stretched up to whisper frantically in my ear. "Be wary of the Southern passage into the lands of white. The miracle, hidden beneath the vaults, will sing the song of madness. I was there long ago when...."

Out of nowhere, armed guards pulled the woman away, as she screamed back: "Beware of them that say different. Be alert. I have seen the annals among the ice tomes. I know...."

Her last words faded, for she had been carried out of sight.

Regardless, I had made no sense of her words.

One of the young guards apologetically ran back to us. "I hope she did not alarm you. A few damaged souls among us, like this one, can't always be avoided; a sad product of the horrors caused by the Kaminaean rule. The unfortunate woman is possessed by the madness. We know her as the *Mad Crone of KiNal.*"

I listened and said nothing. The words she spoke seemed significant. Her eyes seemed too clear to be labeled insane. She had believed in her odd cryptic tale.

Qon seemed to shake the whole incident off by bluntly saying, "Crazy she is! I agree! What has a southern warning got to do with KiNal?"

"I can't answer," I replied, trying to sound casual. "I have no idea what she means, either."

The young guard laughed. "Where are my manners? Let me introduce myself to you."

He extended his hand, "I am Hahdasee, regional sentinel of the Central Guard. We heard that two new Messengers we've been waiting for had arrived. And here you are! May I accompany you to the great hall?"

We talked openly with this eager young warrior and soon were engaged with this vibrant community

Hahdasee was very easy to talk to and full of many opinions: "Some would toss their lives away for a chance to destroy a Muti!"

I understood his point. "The sword can be dull against their rigid flesh. No question about that."

"Mutis move too fast to be easy targets. I witnessed an entire unit wiped out by just one Muti, single-handedly."

Qon added his experience, "One of them bashed a human's skull with the back of his hand. Only bloody pulp was left in place of that head!" He demonstrated this by swinging his own arm, almost knocking me over. "One sweep of a Muti's arm can be lethal."

"That's only a part of what we're up against," Hahdasee confessed. "The Muti have massive factories producing mechanical clones. They've been using beasts, mixing biogenetic parts with some sort of artificial intelligence; the Kuknal replicas. They call them Gatherers. The human clones are even worse. No telling how many warriors they've afflicted, altering their brains and physical make up into a half machine sub-human army of nearly invincible strength."

In the Muti arenas, we had witnessed other gladiators pitted against a few of their viscous man-beasts. Through luck alone, Qon and I both had avoided those fatal monsters.

The young officer was describing them quite well.

"It is impossible to distinguish a human warrior from one of these synthetic creatures, until you see them in action. They are coldly calculating monsters, without any concept of morality: beasts ruled by their masters by design; loyal only to their Muti Masters. We've been developing our own prototype, but as far as I know, they are not yet tested.

We followed Hahdasee as he wove through the milling crowd, gleaning more information from him along the way.

"As I said, our resources are limited. We've sometimes resorted to using everything within reach, as a means to combat the Muti. A rock or a boulder or, in some cases, our fighters become human bombs, determined to over-throw their powerful dictatorship. I miss my friends who've chosen that route."

He stopped.

Neither of us spoke. I instinctively wanted to seek vengeance for the horrid anguish the Mutis were causing these people.

A jovial group was coming up the path towards us. Hahdasee

quickly introduced them, bending our conversation to more pleasant topics. Qon and I especially enjoyed the company of the lovely, light-spirited women in the crowd.

At the Great Hall a short line led to long, lavishly decked buffets, laden with hearty varieties of fruits, meats, and breads. We'd overfilled our own plates until they could no longer hold another morsel, causing Hahdasee to laugh at us juggling this bounty.

Looking around, I noticed how much this assembly differed from those of the Kaminaean Muti banquet arenas we had so recently survived. No musicians or dancing ladies were in this place. In fact, even the table servers were absent.

The festive atmosphere, with its colorful sights, sounds and bright conversation all competed for our attention. More food was generously piled on platters; then passed around, from guest to guest. Plentiful pitchers of ale adorned all the tables. We quickly relaxed, being sated and refreshed, and soon became engrossed in dynamic debates about political gossip. Most interesting was the latest news about warring outbreaks.

Introductions casually came our way, and I made quick mental notes of several names, though foremost in my mind was the image of that crazy woman and what she had said.

My attention skimmed over the conversations as Sorla the mercenary; uncertain whether these people understood my mission or whether they expected me to be like Qon; a common warrior.

A particularly attractive woman flirted with Qon, dazzling him with her alluring smile. She'd clearly won him over when she came to his side of the table and slid in next to him.

Even Torlo enjoyed watching Qon take advantage of this delectable gem.

The women on either side of me had been sharing bits of light conversation. A lovely lady across from me heightened my intrigue even more. Her intelligent eyes and slender body tempted dreamy thoughts. I noticed that she had been watching me from the beginning.

"You're the new celebrities, aren't you?"

"I didn't think it showed."

"Strangers are not common here. Your reputations preceded you. We've been advised. You must be the warriors from the Resistance forces, right?"

At that point she was pulled into an intensely whispered conversation with the man on her left.

While I strained to hear, the woman to my right interrupted.

"Are you taken for the evening?"

"Taken—where?"

Her candor amused me.

"Where would you like to be taken, love?"

As I hesitated she almost apologized and asked, "Have I shocked you?"

"No; only took my breath away for a moment." I had not intended to insult the woman.

"How could a man refuse such beauty?"

The woman, on my other side, lightly chimed in.

"She's not the only friendly lady around."

I turned to find myself face to face with a charming blond; shimmering hair flowing over her bare shoulders.

"Are both of you a working team?"

"It could be," she grinned brightly.

"Who knows what we might do. Why not make us an offer?"

The first woman tapped my back.

"What a nice idea. I enjoy sharing."

I considered the notion of slipping away with them. For certainly Jan Sorla would play this game with abandon.

Just then, a foot nudged against my leg beneath the table. The lady opposite me did not look up but simply concluded her conversation with the man next to her.

"Not tonight. I have other plans for the evening."

When the gentleman had strolled away, she turned her gaze on me.

"I do believe you are being pestered. I apologize. We were talking about the political situation."

She smiled warmly, raised her right hand and waved away the flirtatious women, who promptly left the table as if I had turned to poison.

With the flip of a wrist, she had taken command of the situation. Sorla's intrigue was short-lived, for her beauty had captivated his attention.

"KiNal has been here for a very long time. The designers built the original structures during an amazing era. But since then, it has been abandoned; probably many generations ago. At about the same time that the Mutis were shutting down the digs south of the central city, a team of explorers came upon it quite by accident. Nobody guessed what an ideal find this would turn out to be."

She glanced around the room.

"We are proud of our achievements here in KiNal. I mean, it is absolutely perfect for our activities."

The tone of her voice became less conversational and more authoritative. This was no light, flirtatious commentary.

"Some of our scientists speculate that its inner avenues may have spread throughout the entire continent. We'd dug deep enough to discover evidence of an even earlier inhabitance. We've been clearing those areas beneath the mountain to house refugees from different territories within the Kaminaean Empire."

She paused for a moment, as if considering the impact of those words on me, and then took a long sip from her chalice. "I always find it difficult to be trustful of strangers. I certainly would not freely share this without Sziat's introduction of you and your companion."

I absorbed the depth of her information, with an air of detachment.

"You must have been aware of the renowned archeological excavations that had sprung up all over Kamina long ago?"

"I have heard. Surely that isn't proof."

"Long experience has given me some insights." she had lowered her gaze. Then continued with a more determined voice: "That will be the topic for later conversations. We need your help."

What followed covered much of what I already knew, though her fresh perspective shed new light on these facts and filled in many gaps for what was known in Bel-loniea.

"Something mysterious must have been found. Like wild fire, word spread to shut down all the instituted libraries and study halls. It could have been about a dangerous development, perhaps.

"Our people were among the first archeologists who encountered the change in the Mutis. We were warned to hide ourselves away. Then our benefactors silently disappeared."

The tension in her voice left little doubt that she meant to convey some underlying meaning beyond casual dinner conversation.

"Most of our settlement is located within the mountain, thoroughly hidden from view. But we suspect our cover will not last much longer, for the Mutis continue their rapid expansion. They must be brought to a stop or we're doomed. Our central operations cannot be discovered."

I keenly focused on every word.

"Luckily, for us, Kalinis has not yet learned about KiNal. We are determined to elude their Monitors and spies for as long as possible."

She stopped suddenly, as a gentleman approached.

"Commander Dunai, may I have a word with you?"

I watched the man respectfully lean over to whisper something in her ear. Then, he straightened and sharply saluted.

She stood while tossing me a quick, formally commanding smile.

"Come. We are requested."

A marked change in her attitude unmistakably implied that I cooperate and I followed her out of the crowded room. Her gait was militantly aggressive, feet snapping on the stone floor with the hard rhythmic beat of a marching warrior. Our clomping boots echoed along the empty tunnel, until we reached a cross corridor.

"This way, please."

We passed through an obscure portico into a compact office. The walls were bare. The seating composed a ring, facing one another. Men and women who were engaged in hushed conversation immediately ceased as we entered the room.

Commander Dunai nodded and all sat. She pointed me to an empty chair and then settled down in the one next to it.

Every person in the room was alert. Nobody spoke. All awaited her next words.

"Bring them in!" she instructed. There was no doubt as to who was in command. Everybody sat frozen; all eyes fixed on the door through which the man had disappeared. The silence seemed to last an eternity, until the sound of running feet echoed from down the corridor.

The officer returned, breathless.

"They are missing!"

"Missing?" she demanded. "You had them under guard?"

"Yes!"

"Explain!"

"I can't!"

"You are responsible!"

The blood drained from his distressed face.

Before she had even finished her statement, a dim light materialized in the middle of the ring of seated people. It brightened, and then burst outward revealing a man and woman, both of whom were unquestionably familiar. They quickly scanned the room; then faced me, brightly alert and warmly amused.

A shocked gasp jolted through the room.

I, too, could hardly catch my breath.

"Adt...," I cried out, "Sarleni!"

There they stood before me, in this foreign room, surrounded by officials of KiNal.

Adt greeted me with dry humor.

"We were hoping we'd find a friend here." *I suppose you'll fit.*

Sarleni's thought cut him short.

Sziat said you'd be here.

Adt acknowledged the senior officer at my side.

"Commander Dunai, I presume?"

She nodded.

"We are responding to your request for arms against the Kaminaean Muti domination. Our coalition is assembled and preparing for full activation. In fact, the Armada is at this very moment, approaching Kamina. This man must return to Castle of Doom when your business is completed."

"Thank the gods, you've finally arrived!" Dunai stood and sighed heavily. "Once we've exchanged all vital information it will be done."

"Good." Adt said.

"With you permission," I asked, "may we have a few moments alone?"

"Of course," the Commander replied. "We will continue our talk later. Go with your friends."

II. Midnight Raid

Doubting one's strength against an untamed enemy breeds self-defeat. Drown not in self-doubt, nor bloat self-confidence. Expand the scope of possibilities. Never assume superiority.

—*Wisdom of the Ancients*

An officer ushered us to a secluded room. Adt and Sarleni followed, as if they were physically in KiNal. Nobody would have guessed they weren't there in the flesh.

Adt curiously examined me.

You seem different.

"I'm a professional gladiator," I boasted.

He winked. "Have you been sampling the benefits of your victories?"

The implication peeved me. I avoided responding directly to it. "I've met required standards."

"Ah, the life of the warrior," Adt needled with typical humor.

Seeing them together intensified my yearning for what I had left behind in Bel-loniea.

"Tell me, how are things in Bel-loniea, and Youi?" I asked.

Adt answered: "She has been—"

"Active!" Sarleni cut his response short.

"I hope not *too* active."

I had meant to sound casual, but it was far too edgy. I damn well missed her. War claimed a terrible price from everybody, tearing apart families, lovers and friends. This was my longest separation from Youi.

Adt brooded: "These times make painful demands on all of us."

Sarleni probably noticed my low mood and intervened. "We cannot dwell on sentiments...."

Silence! Youi is secure and protected!

Both Sarleni and Adt looked startled.

Sziat sat perched on a stool in the far corner. None of us knew for how long. When we turned, the Muti had risen to his full height.

"Just listen!"

He was not prone to social politeness or idle words.

"Kalinis is on the move and we must act quickly. The natural shielding within these caverns is dangerously narrowing."

We clustered around him, sitting close, while he outlined what was expected of us. Adt and Sarleni had learned a great deal at the HanJahn Academy. They brought me up to date on the progress of the Armada. I shared my discoveries in the Kaminaean arenas, and about Kalinis' hold on the inland communities.

Sziat confirmed all of our information.

"Kamina is quickly changing and it is time for action. Open conflict has already begun."

Then he turned to me.

"You will soon join with the Armada. It has been fortressed

at the Castle of Doom.

"Your spy missions secured the northern seacoast. Others have connected with the Resistance inland. They've compiled a communications web across the plains effectively coordinating many of the outposts.

"Not all have been brought into the grid, yet."

He paused, glancing towards Sarleni.

"Your brother was able to work among the Trap-zet. They've conducted multiple raids against the Kaminaean forces. He's been extremely successful."

I stared hard at Sziat, wondering how much he would divulge. He said no more on the subject. He turned back to me and continued:

"The Raiders located a tribe actively rebelling against the Mutis. The Armada will find that useful.

"Many of your Zygo primes are active now under the HanJahn support. Sarleni and Adt, of course, have advanced significantly, as you can see. Most of the others are already positioned with the ships and infiltrating the outposts and Resistance groups, in this same manner. The word is spreading quickly that the Armada has arrived.

"Be prepared for the unexpected."

With a wave of his hand towards Sarleni and Adt, he added, "You two and the professor are needed at the castle. Torlo has his duties."

I faced Sarleni with a questioning look.

Up until now, I'd experienced Sziat as a guide, a rescuer; a traitor; not easily defined. I had not anticipated his authority to extend this broadly; and certainly, I would never have guessed that Sarleni and Adt knew him. Their remarks astonished me.

"Sziat has been a magnificent counselor among our leadership. Even our own Muti highly honor his guidance." Adt noted. "War has been waged upon the coastal regions. The Armada is completely mobilized. The flagship has reached the castle, as he said."

I turned to address the Muti, but he was not there. This time

I was not distressed: only annoyed. Meanwhile, they told me all about the Helandian conference, The HanJahn Academy and especially talked, at length, about Professor Yaw-iyn's advancements on the Orbs and the vast fleets in the Armada. "He's s a brilliant scientist and an exceptional warrior, Torlo."

Adt was beginning to fade.

"His inventions have strengthened the Armada tremendously."

Sarleni's voice waned, her form splintered into transparent fragments.

"We're actually with the professor in his Orb. When you reach the Castle, we will talk again."

I walked alone down the corridor, thinking about our talk. So many questions were left unanswered.

Back in my quarters, Qon lay sprawled across the floor, smugly laughing to himself.

He was plainly drunk and it was not difficult to know what he'd been doing.

"The women in this place are amazing," Qon blurted out.

"I mean, she took me to her place."

He giggled like a schoolboy. "What a gladiator's dream! She handled me as if I was her last chance at ecstasy."

He smacked his lips like a fully satisfied Korda and then collapsed into silence with a ridiculous grin across his smug face.

Wild beasts often take a very long time with their courting rituals. Then they fall unconscious, sometimes for days, before recovering. And Qon was categorically behaving like one; totally wasted.

I gave him a shove with my boot to make sure he was still conscious.

"They're living on the edge of death," I said matter-of-factly.

"I'm certain you'll survive the ordeal."

It was the kind of comment expected of Sorla.

"You can bet on that one."

He mumbled some half audible details that involved far more

than I wished to hear. I stopped listening, since he was off in a fantasy world, and soon passed out in a deep sleep.

My concentration lingered on Adt, Sarleni, and Sziat.

Memories of Youi always dwelled in my heart. Sometimes I forced myself to submerge them deeply in order to avoid painful distraction. Right now visions of her flooded my imagination with threatening melancholy. I tried in vain, to press them out of my head.

I needed complete focus on duty.

* * * * * * *

Later that evening, Commander Dunai took me to their operations sector, where we pored over maps and records. I watched a dozen of her staff members collecting a steady stream of incoming data and marking the positions of active attacks on a wall map. It seemed to be the busiest spot in the hall, couriers bringing in news every few minutes.

Other charts recorded hits on the empire in recent days. They had been tracking the locations of factories which were producing massive stockpiles of their weaponry. Important compounds housing secret military machinery and supply warehouses had been marked, as well.

Dunai pointed to a particular chart, showing regions southwest of the castle.

"The desert clans in this region have stepped up their actions. Our agents reported that ever since a new tribe, led by one named Kal-Nor, joined forces with them, they've succeeded in numerous sabotage missions against major installations.

"Our people have accelerated their campaigns against the Kamina at a remarkable speed. Latest report has located them in the dunes south of KiNal."

I didn't try to cover my blatant pride.

"Yes, Commander Kal-Nor leads one of our finest units." I said, "A hardy lot, as you have noted."

A courier approached Dunai, interrupting our exchange and

handed her a message. She stared at the memo.

"Gatherers were spotted near one of our outposts. We've got to get to them before the enemy does. I want you to join us. We can deliver you to the castle directly after the maneuver."

I followed her out of the operations sector, while getting briefed on their emergency attack protocol.

"Our plan is to raid a crucial target. A major factory was discovered. We believe it to be their largest mass production installation of Gatherers and Ersatz warriors. It's been under heavy surveillance. We are not yet ready to stage a sizable attack. With limited resources, we've aimed for smaller vital targets: mainly transportation routes, storage facilities, assembly plants.

"The Gatherers watch every move, bent on discovering our base operations. We lack sufficient weaponry; therefore we plan each attack immediately after we've successfully stolen the Kaminaean equipment. This method has been tremendously effective, considering our limitations."

Dunai and I marched at a fast clip to collect Qon. And then we joined an intense crew of some twenty men and women, all heading in the same direction along a mountain corridor. When we stopped, it was not evident at first, where we were, until the crew systematically cleared away bundles of netting. They had exposed a tarmac and small fleet of grav-disks cleverly disguised as boulders. We had reached a flight station.

"There," the Commander pointed, "is the natural opening, facing the lake. From above it resembles a solid mountainside. However, they could break the illusion any day, as the empire expands.

"Thus far, their Monitors in this region are disabled. In fact, our outpost fighters have been systematically destroying spy towers around the central city. The Mutis were rebuilding them almost as fast as we took them out, but of late, it seems the Kaminaeans aren't keeping up with our clever fighters. We've blasted down at least a dozen in the past month and all of them are still out of commission. The Resistance units continue to attack their transmission stations, gradually dismantling their network across the continent. As you know, we're running out of supplies. Now we're depending on your people to back us up.

"Tonight, the stars are hazed by high clouds; no moons. It's a lucky break for us. If we prevent detection, we should be able to take a direct route. That will get you both to the castle before daybreak."

She led us to the nearest grav-disk, designed to carry five warriors. The machine was similar to Bel-loniean vessels; perhaps a bit smaller. Compacted around a central cockpit were four mounted Kay-guns, easily swung into position from under the slim ledge of the ship; obviously designed for tight maneuvers. The compartments were extremely cramped, designed for the thin, wiry frames of flight specialists—definitely not fitted for full bodied gladiators. It was heavily armed and ready for action. Bel-loniean ships usually contained only two Kay-guns, in front and back.

Dunai took the pilot's seat, indicating Qon and I should man two of the guns.

"We've altered these ships for night raids. The weapons stay out of sight, so that during normal flight, they emulate simple transport vessels."

As she leaned forward, activating the ship's controls the grav-disk shot out into the black night.

"Raids need to be carefully selected, aimed for major effectiveness posing minimal danger to ourselves. We can't afford to lose a grav-disk. The Mutis confiscated all vessels decades ago. We've gradually stolen some back, and then re-equipped them with the necessary weapons for this kind of attack. Tonight, we'll track a caravan carrying men and supplies to a major weapons factory."

The air was chilly as the grav-disk soared through the night sky. Stars flickered in the moonless cosmos.

The flight triggered a flashback; instant memory of a familiar scene.

My galactic unit had been engaged against some military post on some unnamed planet, during a war between rival factions determined to destroy one another. It seemed the same story, everywhere. Humans continually battled for their personal territory, against anything that might threaten them. It sadly reflected the nature of the animal.

We are an aggressive lot. No matter where we go in the galaxies.

Yet, we are tiny specs in the universe. Our values impel us to act no better than a pack of brainless mutant cells, waging battle against a spreading plague. We behave like a rapidly breeding species that takes over territory from any weaker creature.

Perhaps there are other places, other times, other galaxies, containing intelligent life that might operate with different agendas; beyond our imaginations, and probably unrecognizable by the barbaric standards of humans.

I scoffed at my own musings.

Creatures large and tiny, even micro size, may contain greater complexity than we allow ourselves to believe. Where does life begin? Are plants conscious? At what point between a one cell entity and a magnificent thinking human, does self-awareness become alive?

Annoying, random questions like these, summoned many past conversations I'd shared with Youi's father, Andon Janis. They were more in keeping with his continual argument that life and intelligence may very well, be far broader than our human scope of understanding.

'Is a rock aware of its existence? And if so, could a world itself be a living being?' Andon had often challenged me with such puzzles.

The Commander's voice abruptly cut into my thoughts.

"We're nearly on target. Prepare!"

I shifted my attention. We had mounted the Kay-guns and tightened our harnesses just as the grav-disk began its dive towards a clump of shrubs, an oasis between the barren dunes of the desert below. Tents huddled around a sparse camp fire, whose tiny flickering flame created an easy target in the night.

The ship swooped down on the camp and attacked. We

aimed our Kay-guns, loaded with highly charged shells, and fired, demolishing everything within range. Nothing could have survived.

I didn't doubt that women and children had been wiped out, along with the planned target. The brutality of war is so robotically delivered. The violent destruction we inflicted sickened my gut. An entire community slaughtered, with that one sweep over the encampment.

The ship made one final pass across the ashen sands, for that was all that remained—blackened soot.

"Well done," the Commander said; then shot up into the open black sky, leaving no trace of its path behind. "Our target was successfully destroyed."

"Was it a military unit?" I asked, hoping for some, small reconciliation for our raid. Her answer only deepened my regret.

"No," she replied, "a Muti, and its immediate followers."

I don't know why it annoyed me so; yet the act seemed callously impersonal. "That included everybody?"

I knew war demanded killing anything that got in the way of a successful mission.

"Yes: everybody. They had captured one of our posts and we needed to make certain no one would be alive to tell about KiNal!" She sighed, "We couldn't take the chance. Our attack mission was to obliterate everything there, including the prisoners; who were our people."

"I would assume—"

"Need there be another reason?"

That was all there was to her explanation, though she did add: "At least, this was not a suicide mission."

No, I realized. What's the difference? The guilty and the innocent, enemy and friend, had been wiped out.

All war was, by necessity, without moral ethic, beyond destroying the perceived enemy. And this war was no different. Its only agenda was to end the Kaminaean Empire, at any cost to anybody that might get in the way; innocent or not.

There was little need for further conversation. She had given me an opportunity to participate in a raid. Though, I'd become less certain whether to consider it a privilege, or a curse.

Turning back to the instruments on her panel, her words had a softer tone. "The other ships will have struck the factory, by now. The divergence will serve us well tonight. I have a chance to get you to the Armada safely under cover of darkness."

She throttled the ship, due north, towards the Castle of Doom.

CHAPTER TWENTY
THE PROPHET OF DOMINANCE

The Prophet stood rigid, looking across the hall packed with hooded Mutis. It ignored their anxious prattling. Instead, its mind scanned the eastern seacoast of Kamina, pleased with what it saw in these current boundaries of its magnificent expansion; its domain spreading rapidly across the oceans. It would soon encompass the entire world of Noomas.

Slowly, it sank back into the cushioned seat, nearly engulfed by the ornate throne towering high above the churning throng of Mutis pressed tightly into the dark chamber.

Here, it felt smugly secure, for it eagerly lusted after the empire that would ratify the full extent of its predestined rule. Since the extraordinary discovery of the buried libraries, it had reconnected to the mysterious lab; a structure designed by the Ancients many millennia ago. Within those walls, it had discovered the origins of its purpose, undistorted by the feeble, misconstrued doctrines commonly disbursed among the populace.

It had delved deep into volumes of archived history, back to an earlier age. It had learned of those terrible days, long forgotten, when the vat of consciousness had abruptly darkened.

After the fall of the ancient origins, the planet had altered until only crumbled ruins remained as a tragic symbol of a once powerful civilization. The Ancients had long departed, along with the secrets to all that they had so carefully built.

Kalinis sighed heavily, pondering the current conditions of

Noomas. Perfection could have bathed this world, if only they had endured, as it was meant to be. Because of the unforgivable error long ago, Noomas had been severely damaged; nearly ruined. And its pathetic condition was only worsened by the insidious migration of those despicable *humans*.

And, even more appalling to its kind, was the drab, nomadic Muti; the only breed which had survived the vaults of the ancients. It alone, lingered through the ages, as the only living remnant from the Ancients. It had generated into no more than a weak Muti variant: inept; without the prime force, lost for too many lifetimes. That flawed branch had, from generation upon generation, tarnished Noomas with its depraved lethargic apathy. They cast futurological projections of bogus guidance upon the human sheep through their untamed pathways.

Kalinis burst into rage. It held a deep-rooted disdain against the plain robed Muti of Noomas, glad that it was not one of *them*: Glad that it had risen above their lot, with its superior passionate ideals.

It could not restrain its abhorrence of these Mutis, and continued to brood.

Without source, without purpose, the lone Muti roamed aimlessly among the humans. For it knew not how to execute its dominion without the ecstasy, the joy, or the insatiable Muti passion. Their power is futilely lacking the essence of the missing seed.

Prophet Kalinis stomped its boots heavily on the stone pallet, then pulled its shoulders back; smoothing the cloak and bejeweled chains across a bony chest, as it continued to reflect on the growing empire. For soon it would attain the fullness of its coveted prophecy.

The new birthing spawned in ancient times, had been reawakened. The Kamina had broken its petrified status and released the rooting seed. And the new fruition was almost completed.

Reactivation had ignited the elements previously lost within the dim memory of another time and place.

Kalinis, the Prophet of the New Order, had emerged.

The Kaminaean Empire had ascended unto its empirical Muti rule.

Human infestation was doomed to be obliterated; their self important spirit would be squelched and they would fall under submission to their rightful Muti overlords. Any creatures who failed to comply, reaped brutal punishment. For their very existence must be diminished to incontestable servitude.

Along with them, weak Muti advisers who failed to assimilate into the perfect power within Kamina would also die. Any who defied the Prophet and its word were expelled to the graveyards of the vanquished. Unfortunately, a number of the old spineless Muti breed had proven stubborn, and thus needed to be beaten or destroyed, as ordained by Muti law. The work was demanding but persuasive actions eventually succeeded, enlisting more converts; expanding the empire's boundaries.

The Prophet gloried in this escalated growth and hated the past limbo.

Then, remembering that it was not alone in this cavernous place, it returned its attention to the central core and addressed the minds of the loyal Mutis awaiting its message.

We merge. Our minds transmute a protective shell over our revered Kamina. We must never forget our divine destiny. Combine with the links throughout our land and unite in ecstasy. Destroy the hateful forces that pit themselves against our powers.

Remember the promise.

Our history began before the loss of the Ancients.

We labor for one common goal: a complete consciousness in unity. And I am your voice: the word; your core.

For this is our preordination.

It was permanently embedded among the loyal Mutis awaiting exact guidance.

Power sprang from its mind, spilling over the empire's landscape and beyond to the coastal outposts. Though distant from its present location, Kalinis scanned the regions occupied by its minions who were scattered among the human populace. The

Prophet penetrated their minds searchingly, until it settled on one Muti, located within a sizable, bustling community.

Come forward!

The underling immediately responded to its probe; trembling in submissive homage and was lifted by the invincible power of Kalinis' very thought, from the coast directly into the chamber.

Express yourself!

Kalinis glared at the terrified Muti.

"Speak if you dare."

The gnarled, plain-hooded Muti wrung its hands anxiously.

"They are here in vast numbers!"

Kalinis condescendingly discounted the quivering vassal.

"I'm not concerned."

The Muti worriedly persisted.

"But you must be."

Kalinis scoffed, enticing its victim to say more.

"They are limited."

The coastal Muti continued to argue, unable to control its rising fear of the encroaching enemy.

"They are strong and bonded with the *Muti Watchers*."

The Prophet was growing more impatient with each pathetic argument for it had no tolerance for such weakness. It decided to provide one more chance to the pitiful serf. This would be its last.

"They are helpless against our powers. We are prepared. We control the continent. They will be drawn into our clutches and demolished in crushing defeat.

"The creature, Torlo Hannis will disappear from Noomas, along with all the foul beasts that threaten to breed the disgusting human race."

The Muti minion visibly shivered and shrank beneath its dull cloak, ashamed to be seen by all who witnessed the interrogation; its voice, barely audible.

"We are frightened. They are many against our few. And our bravest warriors have already fallen."

Prophet Kalinis billowed, nearly doubling its size. Its words reverberated in the lofty arches of the chamber. And the hall fell silent as Kalinis sang out for all to hear.

"Blessed be those who have honored my unification.

"Blessed be the Muti that follows the path.

"Bless those who worship my word.

"Forever, they will honor my power.

"Upon my word, you live.

"Or die."

In unison, the loyal Mutis joined Kalinis.

"The Ancient Powers cannot be defeated.

"We are a single fusion in unity; as it is written."

It was time to mete out the prescribed penalty on the one who defied his dictates.

You are a coward. Quake not, for those who have left us.

The Muti groveling before Kalinis instantly recoiled, as a fiery white bolt engulfed its prey. In an instant, the wretched creature had crumbled into a heap of ashes.

The Prophet slowly eased back to its former stature. And, after a long moment had passed, it began once again, to orate silently, to its devoted followers.

Prepare to crush the Armada.

Soon, their shadow across Noomas will fade. The promise given to the Muti will be complete, once the creature, Torlo Hannis, has been trampled along with the Sziat, and swallowed into my belly.

CHAPTER TWENTY-ONE
THE ARMADA

I. The Crossing

Kigor Dorta and BerJahn were examining the latest incoming communications from central command when the Muti approached. The hooded emissaries had been actively present ever since the Elite Force was established. Kigor had never adjusted to their eerie ways of making an entrance.

The Muti placed a gnarled hand on each of their shoulders. *We will soon be arriving. Make note and prepare for the silence. Look to your inner strength. Be not swayed from the goal.*

Then it strode smoothly out of the room.

Kigor shook defiantly, shedding an edged annoyance. BerJahn hastily swept his hand over the panels, shutting down the transmitters. The lights dimmed, leaving them in a blue pallor cast by the stars sparkling through the control room's transparent roof.

Neither officer spoke. They were both members of the Elite Force on the flagship for the Armada, Kigor holding a command position by the Proctor's order.

Officer BerJahn had a quiet way about him, yet Kigor had witnessed his aggressive expertise when they had met at the sports arena. The HanJahn master had taught him a few new tricks with crystal shards and Kigor, likewise, had given the officer useful pointers in swordsmanship.

Now they were facing the real world, not the gaming fields.

BerJahn turned away from the viewing screen and moved toward the door.

"Shall we join the others?"

Kigor nodded and followed him down the corridor, towards the forum of the Elite.

"Did the message for Adt and Sarleni get through in time?" Kigor asked.

"I believe it did." The Helandian officer replied.

BerJahn always insisted on thorough details. They would have to make their preliminary moves based on updated reports.

Qui Shan greeted them as they entered the forum.

"Sit. Let's get on with the reports."

All were there, except for Ju-bilee. Kigor acutely missed her. She had attended most meetings but lately, communications had been reduced to emergency functions, so he would probably not hear from her again until after the Armada reached their destination.

General Shan turned to the staff, requesting all officers to present their latest information. BerJahn was speaking.

"Sarleni signaled briefly then locked down communications. The frequency came from central Kamina. We assume they made contact with KiNal. We expect further news within a week."

The round table discussion went long into the night with animated debate. All the while, the Armada, in formation, soared across the ocean, approaching the halfway mark.

The force had suitably integrated multinational top level experts, personally handpicked with calculated precision by the General. And his charismatic confidence still influenced the entire staff; they operated smoothly as clockwork.

Commander Dorta and General Shan tirelessly worked long hours moderating difficulties between the varied national forces.

* * * * * * *

After this particular meeting Kigor and Qui relaxed over a

hot mug of Ka in the General's quarters.

"Sir, I admit, without modesty, that we've done well! Not even a quibble from any level of my own staff."

"True. Although I still have to deal with you!" the General laughed, patting Kigor's lean shoulder. It had been a hard won command victory to have rallied all the nations into a combined war machine.

"No problems there."

Dorta raised an eyebrow. It was good to release a bit of tension. Then Shan spoke.

"Our Muti contingency has communicated regularly with me and several others, more than ever before."

The Muti ability to read into the future, along with their sheer size and strength were factors that had often cowed many leaders and placated the multitudes. Mutis had always provided a solid backbone for human society. Never before had they been questioned.

"How have you managed to deal so *well* with them?" Kigor grew thoughtful. "I have yet to feel at ease in their company."

Qui knew this had been a sensitive spot for the swordsman. "Do they intimidate you, my friend?"

Kigor sipped his Ka without responding directly.

"So, back to my point." He was avoiding the question alto- gether. "As leader of this complex Armada project, you shine like a nova lighting the galactic heavens, Shan, You've succeeded magnificently. Few could have handled things better."

"What—a compliment?" Qui exploded with an edge of humor.

"You've proven to be a master statesman!" Kigor insisted on remaining fairly serious.

"Could you expect less of my diplomacy?" the General studied his comrade carefully. "We're dealing with a Muti war: one group passively honoring their non-violent ethic; the other, without ethics of any kind. A passive community threatened by an aggressively murderous one."

He was so right about the dire situation. World views had

shifted with eminent threats from the Kaminaean Empire. No longer could anyone stake unmitigated faith on any leader or Muti.

"An unprecedented uprising by an unknown nation on an unknown continent challenges all of us. Moreover, our Muti population faces an aggressive enemy culture of their own kind: Muti against Muti. And worse yet, the Kaminaeans intend to eradicate us all! "

Kigor saw the tired lines around the man's eyes and again praised his efforts.

"Sir, you've done a grand job."

"Between you and me, we could use a long, long vacation."

The General chuckled only to return to his solemn tone.

"I do believe the Muti warrior is our most powerful factor against the Kaminaeans."

"On that, we both agree!" Kigor remarked.

* * * * * * *

When the Armada neared the coast, General Shan activated the plans for engagement and the fleet shifted to preliminary battle formation. Gradually, the distance to the shores of Kamina shortened. Tensions and excitement spiraled upwards.

Then they arrived.

The Armada spread across the sky like a solid chain of jewels stretching along the coast. All the ships patriotically unfurled their flags from every nation—a clear statement of united purpose. The flagship held both the Helandian and Bel-loniean colors. Each massive ship synchronized perfectly executed formation with the next, not quite touching.

Guard ships flanked front line Orbs above and below core ranks in tight spear-point patterns, ready to penetrate enemy lines.

The fleet spanned the horizon. Warriors locked in sharp readiness; unmoving.

They had come to do battle, determined to defeat a ruthless

enemy, an empire controlled by Mutis who threatened to dominate the whole world.

Silence moaned across the expanse before them and a steady wind swept along the ocean's surface. Countless clouds drifted by. Stillness prevailed. Nothing dared breathe life into the scene, suspended in petrified balance. And they waited.

No enemy came forth to challenge the Armada's invasion. Only the perpetually lapping waves beckoned to them.

The Castle of Doom stuck out like a spindly thorn pricking up through the smooth thicketed forest.

Slowly, in uniform order, the Armada bedded down among the forests, the rivers, and countryside along the coastline. The flagship positioned itself upon the northern cliff.

Here, they cast their battle front, the castle equipped to house the command hub. Quiet greeted them. A tranquil scattering of meager fishing villages dotted the shore. Somewhere beyond, lay the unseen enemy: the Kaminaean Empire.

II. Masked Truths

Professor Yaw-iyn bent over his control panel to adjust a new rod which still needed to be programmed into the central brain of this magnificent machine he had so proudly developed. He fully understood its importance as the principal model for advancement of the Armada's Orbs.

He finished the last adjustment; then turned to the screen to test the results. It seemed to be working! The Armada's efficiency would be boosted tenfold with these improvements. If his hunch was right, he could pass the adjusted rods to the fleet within a few hours.

Meanwhile, he was keeping a steady watch on his friends, Sarleni and Adt. They had beamed somewhere out there in enemy territory while their bodies rested in his Orb. Few of the HanJahn duos had accomplished this unprecedented level of the Zygo.

He recalled that day when they'd persuaded him to join their risky adventure. Even he would not have defied the HanJahn pundits like they had. For to do so would surely have invoked their Helandian wrath; something he preferred to avoid. They had landed at the castle, only to be met by the HanJahn Empress herself, awaiting them in a flaming rage. The look on Ju-bilee's face was enough to blast an iceberg out of the sea. And she nearly did just that when she'd unleashed her fury into the ocean, causing immense waves to crash upon the cliffs in a show of power.

Yaw-iyn was terrified. Adt had convinced him to wait out her stormy rampage. When her reprimand calmed, Yaw-iyn had noticed an undeniable twinkle in her eyes; a spark of devotion she silently focused on her son, even while issuing strict orders. Within that hour, they had been off on assignment, their bodies berthed under Yaw-iyn's care on the Orb.

Sarleni's voice behind him snapped his attention back to the current moment.

"We will talk again later."

Turning, he saw Sarleni and Adt beginning to stir. Consciousness slowly returned to their bodies as they gradually opened their eyes. Stressed by the transmission, the duo revived with considerable difficulty.

Yaw-iyn fixed hot mugs of spiced Ka and soon they were busily talking about Torlo's journey and about KiNal and the Resistance movement.

Sarleni stretched her stiff joints while they talked.

"Torlo looked alright, though a bit hardened from his mission. He has a friend, a fellow warrior. It was rough for both of them but they finally made it to KiNal.

"Qon will be coming back with him and you'll have a chance to meet them."

"How did he react to the news about Proctoress Youi?" the professor wanted to know.

The two furtively glanced back and forth. Then Adt spoke up.

"We didn't have an opportunity to talk about her disappearance in Helandi."

Sarleni was more specific.

"Sziat actually cut us off and told Torlo that Youi was safe. Besides, the Muti changed the subject to other matters at hand."

The professor solemnly weighed Sarleni's words.

"Perhaps it was smart not to tell Torlo that his wife is missing."

Adt looked worried.

"That's the only logical conclusion. I hope Youi is not harmed."

The Professor shifted the conversation by showing them the latest improvements on the communications system. Then Adt joined Yaw-iyn at the ship's control panel, intently listening to the professor's explanations.

* * * * * * *

Sarleni felt conflicted as she watched the men. They were accomplished warriors, though driven by different agendas: Adt—a man of action; Yaw-iyn—a man of invention. Yet they complimented one another. She was pleased by how their personalities blended.

Still, there were concerns about Torlo and Youi. Her anguish over Mahzit was no less painful. The fact that he was heavily engaged with Resistance operations granted little consolation. Sziat's vague allegations were annoying. Mahzit's location was unclear. What did it actually know about her brother? Or even about Youi's abduction? Was Sziat hiding something?

No, she reasoned, *surely there were other pressing issues that prevented the Muti from revealing more.*

A wave of mystifying energy constantly surrounded this particular Muti. Sarleni pondered the reference it had made about Youi.

Why does it bother me so much? It's all so awkward with no explanation. And I just can't handle the fact that the Proctoress was abducted in my own country!

She was with child, who would be a forthcoming ruler of Bel-loniea. Nobody had an explanation for where or why she was missing.

Why wasn't there an all-out search endeavor for the Proctoress?

Sarleni churned over the facts until she was completely discouraged. The silence around her was deafening. How long had she been tormenting herself?

Adt had left the professor and was fast asleep. Yaw-iyn seemed self-absorbed, focused on the Orb. It was his invention from top to bottom and he seemed to continually be making refinements. The man apparently had unlimited energy.

The meeting with Torlo had been draining to both her and Adt. She desperately needed rest and snuggled up to her man; closing her eyes.

* * * * * * *

Yaw-iyn poured himself another hot mug of Ka from the thermo—unit and smiled to himself.

At least this corner of the operation is secure tonight. Programming complete: files transferred without a hitch, and my good friends sleeping soundly.

He sat down at the screen systematically scanning his assigned sector of the Kaminaean borders and checking updates on flights in and out of the encampments.

General Shan had positioned Yaw-iyn's Orb north of the castle. From here, his scanners covered the shoreline and inland Kamina. At the same time Yaw-yin's single Orb was capable of shielding the flagship, including the castle. It could achieve all of this without being detected.

Along the coast, military insurgence of the Armada pressed inland and advanced steadily into enemy territory. So far they had made substantial progress in overtaking the coastal towns and pushing back the Kaminaean warlords, though they had met with a significant amount of resistance. Standing orders declared every community to be set free from Muti control, annexed and protected in an expanding arc under the Armada's control. Meanwhile, the bulk of the Armada nested offshore, their presence making a bold statement of power.

The Kaminaeans had not been passive. They fought back, engaging in battle with fierce vengeance. Reported casualties seriously raised caution among the Commanders. All front-line troops were heavily at risk, despite their remarkable advancement under hazardous circumstances.

Yaw-iyn scoured the territory in his range, systematically tracing each sector on the graph, skimming randomly over the grid then repeating the scan. When the blips matched his current list of authorized maneuvers, his shift would be complete: nothing unusual to report.

III. Ambushed

Kigor was on the communications deck when an odd dispatch from a local village was brought in by a courier.

Request counsel: Please send able advisor for guidance.
Help needed: Esteemed Magistrate of Neh-Duhn.

It had come from the northern sector, not far from the castle borders. The swordsman considered the implications, perplexed by its brevity and decided to personally inspect Neh-Duhn.

He could use the break. This would give him some respite from the confinement of the flagship and he'd use this opportunity to personally visit the situation directly on the ground.

Besides, the next forum was scheduled within the hour; a perfect time to discuss this with the Elite Force.

* * * * * * *

General Shan greeted each officer entering the forum. Kigor

handed the memo to Qui who highlighted its content 'top priority' when the meeting commenced.

They mulled over the irregular missive after various other dispatches had been shuttled out among the units. A Muti raised suspicion about the irregular dispatch from Neh-Duhn.

"This northern community was within our annexed range. So why is a Kaminaean Muti requesting aid from the Armada?"

Everyone talked at once, quoting statistics and debating casualty lists which included a considerable number of damaged vessels. The front lines were currently successful in their engagements with enemy forces and had advanced another full day's journey inland.

Kigor listened.

The lone Muti standing by Qui aptly called for order.

"Decide wisely. Discretion within must prevail over impulse."

Consensus soon settled around the table. A unit would be sent forth to secure this community. But no ground combat officers were readily available to meet the request for counsel.

They unanimously agreed that Kamina had probably not unleashed its full capabilities. Therefore it would be strategically unwise to break down their reserve flanks for this minor incident. Not yet.

"I suppose you'll want to send a seasoned officer to check this one out, Kigor."

Qui Shan held up the list of available officers that a courier had just presented.

Master Dorta accepted the list, glancing over it twice and then passing it across the table. His eyes scoured the room, studying each of his colleagues around the table: a magnificent force, these chief commanders of the allied nations.

Five eminent Mutis paced slowly along the outer fringes around the forum. Moyi and Ju-bilee had beamed in from Helandi. They held persuasive positions representing Helandi's governing seat.

For the most part, Ju-bilee remained tacit and watchful though Dorta had noted that things rarely happened without her approval. Her presence alone made a dynamic statement.

For the sword master, the Helandian woman significantly diminished his resistance to passions best forgotten. She was visually just as he had always remembered her. Instinctively, he wanted to possess her, for it was impossible not to desire this woman.

Was this feeling only a shadow from the past?

Kigor lowered his eyes and cleared his throat before speaking.

"General, it seems our senior officers have their hands full. I hesitate to reassign any one of them away from their posts. What do you think?"

"Valid point," the commanding general surmised.

"I suppose you have other ideas, Dorta?"

Memories were one thing. The present was now. They had no window to any tomorrows. His concentration was on the current affairs, but another, strong chunk of his mind was elsewhere.

One thing the swordsman knew in his gut: the love-affair with Ju-bilee had never died. But neither of them wished to reopen old wounds. The woman was a super Korda in any room. He was uncertain, confused, for sure: desirous, naturally. Reasoned logic spoke against any move towards emotional territory.

In war, the human animal's mating urges rise dramatically.

One last fling, each man tells himself, *before I die*.

Preferably in a lover's arms; a fleeting escape.

Oh, for a local pleasure palace, he mused, with an irony that brought on a silent, self-mocking laugh.

"I'll deal with this, personally."

Kigor had always been driven to participate in personal combat. And here was an opportunity to lead the team in answering this requested contact.

Nobody objected.

Even General Shan agreed.

"Very well, Commander. Select your team. An Orb will be prepared for you, at once."

After the forum ended, Ju-bilee came to his side.

"Take care. We can't afford losing a man of your abilities."

"No worry. This isn't a very dangerous job."

There was something troubling in her eyes as they swept up to meet his and he felt irrationally close to her.

Is she actually here, inside my head?

Imagination; he wanted to withdraw.

He wanted to touch her but dared not move.

The inner conflict was infuriating.

She smiled with tender understanding; perhaps as a friend to a friend; a long time, old friend.

Intimate warmth threaded through him; a longing.

Illusion!

Ju-bilee exhibited an enigmatic casualness.

"I think you need the diversion. It will be satisfying, I'm sure. You always were a man of action; a valiant man with the sword."

Her hand swept the air between them. Or had it actually touched his shoulder?

He resisted the impulse to accept this friendly gesture. A touch was not the proper response right now.

Nothing was. Then her fingertips brushed down his arm.

Reality melted as a universe of sensation cascaded over him. Ecstatic pleasure blew away all resistance and fantasy mated with memory flooding him.

Kigor was overwhelmed with mixed emotional responses; impossible for any logic to sort through. For an infinite instant, confusion pierced him with kinetic force.

Then it shattered.

Was it a moment or an eternity?

He could not tell. True or not, intimacy always happens within. Thus it is real enough.

We don't need complications.

Were those her words or his? He could not tell.

Then her voice rang softly in his head as she faded away.

Be safe.

Kigor's daze slackened when General Shan broke through his trance.

"Enjoy this perilous bivouac, if you must!"

"I'm expecting a low risk on this one, Qui. Once the troops settle in, I should return to the castle within a few hours."

Kigor calculated his plans as the General came to his side.

"I envy you. Sometimes I'd like to be engaged in the heart of action. Shoot off on some jaunt."

There was humor in the General's voice as he warmly gripped Kigor's shoulders.

"You never know what to expect."

"That's half the sport, isn't it?"

Kigor laughed. As career warriors they had both come to their present rank through actual combat duty rather than political or royal family persuasions.

"Still, take special care!"

The warning was not as serious as it might have sounded to a stranger observing these long term friends.

"I'd hate to lose my co-commander!" Qui said on his way out the door.

Kigor waved back and headed for the transport deck.

* * * * * *

The mission's destination was within a small valley, marked on a map as a remote community which had puzzled them when the dispatch had come in.

By mid-morning he was strapped in the Orb, surveying the village. His small squad of grav-disks surfed above the valley. Then one by one the ships lowered to the ground.

Kigor watched for any unusual movements. The place looked peaceful. Soon some locals banded together in an open plaza within the village. From all appearances this seemed logical. They had no reason to suspect any danger.

No sooner had his own ship landed than explosions rattled the air and the sky was abruptly clouded by a trio of Gatherers. From nowhere, they'd surfaced; too fast for Kigor's crew to defend against their vicious attack.

The welcoming committee was a ruse. Instead of villagers they were met head on with lethally armed warriors. Mounted forces pounded in from the forest at the same time as the Gatherers swooped down from the sky, spreading cinders of death, devouring the village structures in their wake.

Kigor's flank ships immediately lifted from the ground and fired highly charged Kay-shells at the Gatherers. Kigor expected great damage to be inflicted. However, the shells exploded before they reached those monster's gleaming wings. They must have been protected by an invisible shield. Nothing could get through to harm the Gatherers.

Sharp beams bolted from the half-living creatures, destroying four Armada grav-disks.

His ship was grounded. Kigor and his crew fled the Orb just seconds before it, too exploded. Surrounded in wide open territory, his officers and crew immediately engaged the Kaminaeans now running in their direction.

Kigor's brave unit was being crushed by a deadly barrage of slicing metal blades. The mere volume of combatants attacking them was cutting away these dedicated men, one after another.

As he leaped forward in their defense, dead bodies on both sides collapsed in bloody piles. The enemy hoard continued to surge over the corpses in a murderous attack.

Mind and fingers automatically directed his sword in a netted pattern of lightening parries, saving him from death over and over again. Even then he was nicked several times. These half-machine soldiers were immense, extremely agile and threatening even against his defenses.

The wave of pseudo-human fighters was practically slaughtering his entire unit of highly trained Special Forces as if they were babes without weapons.

It was impossible to survive long.

Crackling energy engulfed his body.

Away! A familiar voice whispered.

Ju-bilee loomed like a giant, wickedly weaving a pattern of *thrusts and parries.

Nothing could touch this astounding female warrior, sword in hand, fighting like a demon. When the flat blade hit metal, sparks darted in all directions, striking out to the left and the right. Flesh and metal mingled in violent red hot lava waves.

What kind of weapon is that? Kigor wondered. *The Armada could make use of this device.*

Ju-bilee's thought snipped back. *It responds only to a HanJahn mind.*

The Helandian woman dashed with lightening speed hacking at a man-machine who instantly fell. Her weapon's sizzling ferocity swept into the next attacker; who exploded upon contact with its blade. A third and fourth opponent fell, all within a single breath on top of the growing mound of tangled armor and bloody flesh.

Kigor's men leaped into action against the foe alongside Ju-bilee, cutting down fighter upon fighter. The machine-warriors clambered over their blood-soaked comrades seething feverishly to slay the combatants. Kigor's sword sliced straight through an arm, exposing metal; not bone. The poor creature crumbled on top of the gory debris, exposing the same metallic tissue combination.

What are these...things? he demanded.

Ersatz creatures: Dangerous; like the Gatherers.

Ju-bilee explained; then swelled menacingly to titanic proportions causing the Kaminaean forces to fall back in shocked horror.

Electric fire radiated from Ju-bilee's hair slashing down the foe. Blazing tentacles rippled over the enemy, each strand tearing their flesh. With howling screams they writhed into their ranks. Gasps of rage spilled over the Ersatz army. They crushed forward ravenously, pushing away their dead to get at the Armada team.

Again, they were surrounded by a mass of determined blades. The sting of sword point touched Kigor's chest, which he swiped away with an instinctive counter-attack.

A Gatherer swooped greedily towards them, purple beams

flashing alarmingly close.

Ju-bilee's form pulsed into a brilliant starburst. White light-ening streaked out, forcing the Gatherer to burst into the Ersatz army.

The Armada warriors fell back in awe when the Helandian woman was again visible but had not diminished in size. Thick strands of red hair lashed out wildly as she shouted: "Stand strong—grab hold!"

The warriors clasped at the ruddy coils and were whisked up away. The master swordsman watched this amazing rescue operation; then immediately engaged two Ersatz warriors who doggedly clambered over the wreckage, like mindless machines, lumbering robotically forward. The Commander's sword cut a pattern of swift thrusts into the enemy.

Keen, compassionate eyes swept the dismal, sickening field. From out of the tree-line, more soldiers advanced. Any prob-ability of surviving this massive assault was painfully dim. Suddenly Ju-bilee returned, pulsating in dim bursts, face pale.

Can't last—we must go—now—

Kigor caught the limp woman. Strands of red hair snapped powerfully around his fingers. An electric shock twisted up about his wrists.

Hold...me! Arms weakly draped over him.

Need your power. Open completely to me.

The Commander was instantly immersed in a whirling shapeless void; empty silence. Immobilized. Blackness dulled all senses and then absorbed both their bodies, channeling them through a roiling vortex.

He felt light and saw sound; barely sensing the fragile Ju-bilee trembling ever so slightly as they clung together.

All at once an unfamiliar space became visible. A transparent dome encircled the place, surrounded by ice covered mountain peaks.

Ju-bilee lay motionless on a mat covering the open floor. She was the woman he had fallen in love with long ago; the mother of his son. Not a mere materialized image. But she was breathing far too shallowly; barely alive.

Kigor accepted the domed room as real; situated somewhere in the midst of a barren, frigid wilderness.

This must be part of her private world. Why had I never seen this place before?

Splintered portions of Ju-bilee's life had always remained private. Even during their most intimate season, these secrets were unapproachable.

Was this where HanJahn studies had been pursued in such depth that blocked out all personal ties?

She'd ultimately decided to dedicate total attention to such studies. Memory of that terrible day was still painful.

Since then he had been solely responsible for providing the protective care, and training of their son.

These sharp memories were jarred away by a sigh from Ju-bilee and a smile that formed a silent, mental whisper:

Welcome to my sanctuary.

A thin voice spoke trembling words:

"I'm sorry to bring you...*here*." A hint of humor weakly sparkled from those lovely eyes.

"You required protection. Before being hacked to death."

"My men," was all he hoarsely managed, remembering the horrid battle; the brutalizing defeat. The loss had caused terrible pain and guilt.

"You are here now," Ju-bilee weakly soothed. "And we're safe." Her head sank back on the mat, eyes slowly closed.

This woman who had risked everything in order to save him now needed urgent care. And the swordsman vowed never to leave and would personally attend to healing his beloved Ju-bilee.

Your duty is with the Armada.

An uninvited reproach pierced his thoughts. Moyi's image appeared beside her mat.

I'll take care of her, Kigor.

Moyi could be most invasive. But the man was right; and probably was the best defense Ju-bilee could hope for under these conditions.

"Keep me informed!" Kigor gruffly instructed.

"I will," Moyi promised, waving a hand.

With no additional comment the dome faded, replaced by a foggy shaft which opened to a corridor leading to his stateroom on the Armada's flag ship.

* * * * * * *

The defeat of Kigor's squad was a serious setback.

The council frequently deliberated over the Armada's progress and this particular forum was no less strained than the previous ones.

Hot Ka and Porshi loosened the debate to a more fiery level when Adjutant Vejir remarked: "The defenses we've come up against have been weak and disorganized."

Kigor angrily snapped to his feet ready to challenge the young assistant but Qui was just as quick to pull him back into his seat, speaking with directness.

"Do not forget that Master Dorta's men fell into a well conceived trap. The survivors are apprising our units of their experience with those Ersatz warriors. We all know the danger of underestimating an enemy."

"My apologies, to you, Commander," The adjutant nodded solemnly to the elder.

"Quite alright, Vejir, carry on with your analysis."

True to his form, Kigor's voice rang smoothly as he brought the meeting back to its focus on the war's progression. Tempers and nerves often flared unexpectedly among this multicultural lot. None of them had ever participated in so complex an environment.

The swordsman strode quietly across the room to refill his mug.

"I have been detained, as you all know," he said. "I'll want complete details on all battles right away. What is your assessment of our current situation?"

Vejir summarized the movements of the fleet, detailing each encounter and listing the annexed territories.

"Since the campaigns began, we have occupied the beach-head and significant territory inland with quite manageable resistance."

"So far," a Muti cautioned. "We cannot afford to be fooled again. They control the continent through an array of surveillance devices and military installations."

The comments continued on speculation as nobody had anything new to report this night.

When Moyi stood, the debate ceased. "We must prepare to meet a serious defensive attack when it comes."

That brought an end to the forum.

CHAPTER TWENTY-TWO
OPENING SALVOS

I. Plunged into War

The purpose of all life is to die. All things are born for dying. It is that simple. All roads lead to me one way or the other.
Deathwall

— *From Deathwall: the Epics of Mhyo*

My head was reeling as we sped through the night sky, Commander Dunai at the helm of our grav-disk. We had wiped out an entire desert caravan in order to destroy a singular desired target.

When the target was an impersonal dot on some screen without any apparent living individuality, it seemed less horrific.

The Commander turned away from the instrument panel and spoke softly.

"The other ships will have struck the factory by now. The divergence will serve us well tonight. I have a chance to get you to the Armada safely under cover of darkness."

"Avoid surveillance." I warned. "Our people would ruthlessly attack any suspicious craft; just as your fighters slaughtered that caravan."

"I am taking the flight path Sziat gave to me yesterday."

In silence she sped east towards the Castle of Doom slowing when the grav-disk approached the outer fringes of the Armada.

During this flight, the effects of the KiNal raid persistently hounded me. Innocent women and children slaughtered. This night the act of anyone's child unscrupulously murdered struck me personally. Coming fatherhood was changing my world view.

"We're almost there," Dunai cut into my thoughts.

The hint of dawn tinted a patch of open meadow as she hovered the grav-disk. I had expected her to join us, meet the proper authorities and arrange connections with the leadership of the Armada. The KiNal pilot only pointed westward as we climbed out.

"I'm needed in KiNal. We'll be in contact soon. Tell your people our story. Make arrangements for arms shipments to KiNal.

"Tell your command that we are prepared and will serve your Armada. Our people are well organized and ready to attack the empire, head on. We can increase the pressure from within. Combined with your Armada's forces we shall bring an end to the Muti dominance."

Brave words, I realized. Her people were dedicated and zealous, and would surely prove a vital force to overpower the enemy. Even if successful, the aftermath would be horrific. Rebuilding a defeated nation would prove to be far more complex and time consuming than conquering its territory.

I realized the hard work required a life time dedication of many people, world-wide.

The grav-disk had disappeared by the time Qon and I reached the tree-line. Hoisting our gear over our shoulders, we took a narrow pathway through the matted brush. The woods gave way sooner than I expected and the familiar silhouette of the castle took shape.

Almost immediately Bel-loniean guards challenged us. Without ceremony I introduced Qon and myself. They escorted us directly to the officer in charge.

* * * * * * *

At the castle we discovered an array of aircraft hovering over the beaches and cliffs with more forces arriving daily, wave after wave. The flagship loomed over the ring of battle terminals, dwarfing the castle itself. The Armada had taken possession of a broad band of coastal territory.

The direct exposure of the fleet was a major concern until Helandian security forces assured me that no enemy ship could approach due to the outer reflective barrier and the inner cloaking shield radiating from Yaw-iyn's Orb.

My official position among this international militia was highly esteemed. Romos, the Bel-loniean Proctor had instated me as his official spokesperson for Bel-loniea. My word was as good as that of the Proctor.

The staff immediately apprised me of the Armada's status. General Shan had effectively established a solid command post at the castle and then expanded our control inland. His calculated precision and charismatic confidence continually influenced the entire force.

Very early on I discovered that Sziat was widely accepted as an equal among equals. Helandians, commanders and Mutis respectfully pulled back upon his entrance. Even the Elite heeded his words as statements of policy, if not direct orders. When he attended meetings, Moyi and Ju-bilee as well, respected his counsel.

My first days on the flagship flew by in a whirlwind as the Armada advanced solidly upon the continent of Kamina, condensing its battle formations and their position across the coastline.

Our initial spy missions had connected with an amazing network of Resistance pockets. During my brief visit to KiNal I had witnessed the detailed complexity of their connection with the underground organizations throughout Kamina.

Thus was created an interlinked cooperative engineered between the multinational forces, administered by the HanJahn which effectively transmitted communications and supplies among the fleet and annexed regions.

BerJahn pointed to a blank sector on the transmissions screen.

"We've been waiting for KiNal's location. That spot's been a vital link on all strategic schemes. Until now, we've been unable to complete the vectors. Thanks for your work, Torlo."

After I submitted the additional defining coordinates that Dunai had specified for KiNal, Commander BerJahn and I took a short break while the technicians completed their work.

By the time we got back to the communication station, the KiNal grid was lighting up like fireworks. Fleet control had dispatched cargo loads of supplies immediately on first contact. Timing was crucial.

A dispatcher handed BerJahn a sizable list of memos previously exchanged with the central hub in KiNal.

We both looked over them carefully.

"What do you make of this one?" he asked, pointing to a message near the end of the list.

It was a broken note, apparently truncated during transmission; both the source and sender had been cut off.

> *...Reported significant findings beneath the complex: Team retrieved one tablet. Deciphered first lines: Haldolen Speaks. Referred to vault within. Trans stopped.*

A few days before, I had received a personal message from the Janis Foundation.

> *Torlo,*
>
> *Compare the enclosed information from the Messenger with our research. If we look at the Ancient's logs from a galactic perspective they seem to closely match the description of civilizations disbursed by early Federation colonial ships.*
>
> *– Andon*

A particular graphic layout showed ruins spread out across a valley with most structures semi-buried depicting an earlier civilization; possibly advanced, though unidentified as human or otherwise.

Maps matched the current terrain of the planet. The major continents were marked with titles we had read only in legends. Sziat had spoken of the *Vaults*. One called *Lopn* was marked on a land mass labeled *Haldolen*. Attached was a scribbled note from Andon.

According to our research, cloning experiments had gone awry. The bio-codes which melded imperfectly were destroyed. Certain variants apparently produced aggressive strains.

I wondered if it connected to the Lopn reports. The remainder of the notes took me much longer to decipher. Studying this mammoth puzzle in Kamina left me with very little sleep.

I rose early the next morning, facing a more familiar challenge. A summary of the Kaminaean spy missions had been delivered to my quarters, along with a hearty breakfast tray. I could barely keep my burning eyes pried open, ruing the ominous task staring at me like a cantankerous Korda. Ironically, I had ordered the reports myself on the previous day, thus subjecting myself to this abusive ordeal.

Swallowing half a mug of Ka in one gulp, I stared at the numbers. Poring over each set of tragic statistics, brought back dark memories of my own perilous journey I preferred to forget. It had been a long, grueling trek through Kamina as Jan Sorla, and tortuous gladiator rings left permanent bodily scars. In addition, my brain was fried to a pulp from all the bouncing back and forth between two personalities.

After draining the last drop of Ka, I chomped down the meat pies which had turned cold, and then returned to the reports, sorting through the piles until I had managed to absorb most of the data.

My next task was to organize a unit directly under my command; its duty; yet to be determined. I had offered Qon his own crew, but he insisted on staying with me as my number one guard and assistant.

II. The Wall

Curtains of decision cloud solutions.
Creating puzzles toward progression.
Do not be confused.
Divide that which is before and after.
Clear the mind and penetrate illusions.
Wisdom and understanding follow.

– Teachings of Moyi

When the blasting alarm horn brashly terminated my sleep, I automatically ran for the bridge and by the time I reached the command deck, Qui Shan already stood staring at the wide viewer, speechless. Our startled eyes witnessed a barrier spreading between us and the continent on Kamina.

The glowing oblong structure shifted from yellow to red gradually bloating toward the Flagship. When it deepened into burgundy hues the mass flattened and spread from left to right, dropping down into the forests beyond the castle and upward into the outer reaches of space. It suddenly solidified and we now observed a clouded Wall between us and the Kaminaean continent.

General Shan sprang into action, ordering probes forward, maneuvering our battery of flanks back and away from its expanding perimeters, utilizing every Helandian Zygo power available to determine its nature.

"Commander BerJahn, open all communications to the Armada. Transmit all probe reports directly to the flagship. I want immediate details on this force. How far and how fast is it spreading?

"Tell Officer Yaw-iyn to boost all force fields to full power.

"Commander Dorta, ready all pilots and crews to battle alert, but hold steady. Report any sign; any movement—immediately."

I watched and listened, realizing that we must be up against a cunning enemy.

"General, I've seen opaque force fields before, though they were rare during the Galactic Wars. Never had one been used within a planetary atmosphere. If this is what I think it is, we are in grave danger.

"Any force field of this size is potentially aggressive. Not protective, if my guess is correct. It could demolish everything along its path with insurmountable destruction."

We both turned to the screen just as Kigor commanded a test of power, releasing a series of Kay-shells, but they disintegrated short of reaching the surface of the purple Wall.

"The space between the Armada and the Wall has become an abyss which nothing can penetrate."

It was a Muti who spoke those words.

A second flurry of explosive charges hurled towards the Wall was gulped into oblivion. Kigor Dorta ordered one last round of fire at the monstrous barrier, to no effect.

The General issued the command to retreat and the crew leaped into unwavering action.

"Cease fire! Pull back!" he cried. "Direct all resources to your shields. Preserve munitions. Cut communications down to emergency lines, only. Do not move until further notice."

Once we had stopped attacking, the Wall hung there; staunchly unmoving, unyielding.

This was instituted by no common foe.

The crew clung stoically to their posts while the Commanders withdrew to a forum.

The Wall was both real and mysterious. We all experienced its daunting density which stopped the entire Armada dead in its tracks.

Nerves were cut raw during the continual standby alert. The dismal silence drained everybody's stamina as flagship crew tore apart all the available files, pored over every detailed map, chart and document sent from the Messenger.

And found no answers.

All annexed territories were out of contact; any communication attempts with our contacts in Kamina were stopped short by the Wall.

Nothing worked.

Our Mutis were conclaved, combining their wisdom. Everyone worked, frantically trying to figure out what to do next.

Every person in the fleet was on emergency alert. Probes periodically tested the Wall. All communication stations applied double shift, searching for any signals. Engineers, technicians, every crew member with any idea, worked continuously at trying to breech that impenetrable barrier.

Endless meetings ensued. Eventually I retired to my quarters, baffled and tired, trying to sort through volumes of incomplete information. From time to time a specialist would furnish some new details to be evaluated. I lay on my bunk wracking my brain over this Kaminaean puzzle. No solution would surface. Our invasion had been stopped short before it could begin.

It was difficult not to feel utterly defeated. We all worried about our forces beyond the Wall; for the Resistance and the KiNal operations who were urgently depending on our support. And here we sat; dead in our tracks; crippled.

But not beaten. It occurred to us that we were, in fact, unharmed, undamaged, for the most part. If the Kaminaean forces had been capable of destroying us, wouldn't they have done so immediately? Strangely, that was not happening.

There was hope, if only we could find a way to breach that Wall.

* * * * * * *

Days passed in stifling deadlock. Tempers flared on nearly every shift. We were emotionally and physically wearing out.

Qui Shan spoke with me, gravely concerned about the condition of the fleet.

"We have plenty of armed power; however, the morale of the

fleet is suffering badly. The units are beginning to splinter into ethnic and racial fragments. The officers notice a growing lack of confidence among the units.

"We need to reassure the entire fleet of our singular cause, bring their focus back to the prime directive.

His thinking was a radical divergence from the traditional hierarchal order of our governments. Nothing else was working and he was a man of solid practicality. I actually liked his idea.

The General chose several particularly skilled youth to present their ideas to the Elite Force. They discussed their ideas openly; then the team settled on a joint plan incorporating the new design.

He called all systems commanders to the main deck, to listen to a young HanJahn cadet selected to address the leaders.

"Our units are stressed beyond limits," she began, mincing no words. "We would like applicable duty assignments. Inaction strips our senses. Permit our teams to carry out investigations. Perhaps we will find some weakness in that Wall if we act against protocol."

After she had finished speaking, the HanJahn cadet nodded respectfully and began to step down when Moyi strode to her side, catching her by the arm.

"Well advised, Kailet," he said. "Indeed, we must choose progressive action."

A few commanders grumbled disparaging slurs.

"We cannot afford to permit inferior technicians to be instructing their elders!"

General Qui Shan patiently held an open forum for seniors and juniors to join and voice their opinions during these open sessions. No decisions were intended to be finalized, thus each individual was at liberty to speak freely without judgment.

Moyi's strong, steady voice reinforced this principle of equanimity.

"All views shall be considered thoroughly here. When a problem of this magnitude surpasses even our mastered abilities, people will tend to extend unreasonable blame. It is to our benefit that everyone puts forth effort to combine our intelligence and express possible solutions from all perspectives."

But not all of the scheduled forums followed the prescribed guidelines. The severe doldrums caused by the Wall, had challenged this diverse multi-cultural assembly and rekindled unsettled rivalries among former enemies.

This particular meeting was attended by several strong-headed commanders who had become quite agitated with the confining impasse resulting from this suppressive Wall.

I worried that sitting here doing nothing would only fuel their anger. The room rumbled with heightened agitation until Kigor Dorta and Adt stepped forward. Standing back to back, they unsheathed swords and crossed them overhead creating a sharp clang.

Kigor shouted, "Silence!"

"Adversity among our ranks is poison."

They lowered their blades before the subdued officers and the sword-master continued speaking.

"You are all aware that we, in this room, are unquestionably on the same side of the conflict. Never doubt this fact."

He stared into the eyes of every man and woman present with the same keen aim he practiced when engaging an opponent in battle. Such a penetrating glare from Commander Dorta was enough to silence even a Proctor.

Then he repeated: "Never doubt this fact."

Stepping over to Cadet Kailet he continued: "This woman has sensed a very important flaw in our response to that Wall. And we shall remedy the error."

He ordered the ill-tempered troops to be separated into teams; each under the supervision of at least one HanJahn specialist. "They can vent their grievances by scouring the castle inside and out, looking for any useful evidence that might further our campaign against the formidable Kaminaeans."

Kigor instructed the remaining officers to group their units in shifts.

With that task under way, he then turned to Adt.

"Both you and Kailet assemble all inactive personnel. Prepare them for shore duty shifts.

When my team had first landed at the castle we'd explored the grounds and building from top to bottom. Very few corridors beneath the entry level had afforded us access due to major structural damage. I did not have high hopes for new findings. At least this assignment would keep them occupied during this immense lull.

As Master Dorta methodically assigned each duty, the meeting gradually lifted with an air of purposeful unity.

He then addressed Commander BerJahn. "May I have a word with you?"

The Helandian commander looked up; nodded then quickly dispatched his orderlies before returning to Dorta. After they'd been dispatched, the two officers dropped into deep conversation.

"The enemy forces we'd encountered prior to this blockage, had appeared limited," Kigor was saying. "Once this fog of a Wall lifts, we'll implement those plans of yours."

"I remember Neh-Duhn. Your unit met with a remarkable army there," BerJahn countered. "You dealt with a near fatal trap. Their metallic warriors nearly wiped out your entire unit."

Since my discussion with Moyi had ended I overheard the Commanders' conversation in reference to the Kaminaean strength.

Kigor's stern features winced slightly. He had never discussed it, so I supposed that the incident must have been a painful blow to his personal military standards.

I figured it wise to change the topic after I took the liberty to express my concerns.

"I am less optimistic about our ground operations," I said. "As I told Shan yesterday, I had seen force fields before. I cannot say this one is or is not what I have experienced.

"If I may, I'd like to share an event I had once witnessed. I was commanding a fleet for the Galactic Federation, when a dense smog field, something like this one, had been reported on a colonial planet in my sector. My team was immediately dispatched to investigate and protect our colony because they had recently been assaulted by an authoritarian neighboring settlement. But when we arrived, within the hour of the notice, we were shocked by what we found. The mass had lifted, but not one sign of life could be found. Whole sections of that continent had been utterly stripped."

I decided to spare details of that nightmarish incident and the war that ensued, for it had occurred a lifetime ago. I basically let my two comrades consider my words in silence.

* * * * * * *

Meanwhile the Wall posed an impenetrable obstacle. Communications beyond our fleet were lost.

The Muti cautioned against sending probes into this colossal barrier until the HanJahn could establish verifiable access. We sat frozen for days on end.

No action.

No word.

No sound.

By now, the teams had examined every stone of the fortress from the ramparts to the dungeons. Ancient relics turned up among the ruins, mostly broken down equipment apparently cast aside in the hidden nooks and lower cells. They detected passageways that had caved in and were blocked with hardened clay and rock. Other cells were quite empty; possibly stripped clean a very long time ago. It appeared to be a dead end.

Despite the renewed vigor among the crew, I still felt thoroughly discouraged by this intense lull.

* * * * * * *

I was poring over a stack of reports in the officer's lounge one evening when all mayhem broke loose. A search probe had reported a change in energy emissions. One of the HanJahn officers notified me and we headed straightway for the command deck. In moments, all personnel were at their stations.

The fleet and all crewmembers were recalled to battle formation, leaving the castle hastily secured. Yaw-iyn inspected all force shields and then we waited and watched.

All was quiet for several hours.

Then suddenly a portion of the Wall shimmered. We watched as a slit in the Wall spread directly in front of the flagship. Vision was suddenly impossible as black vapor foamed out through the slit. Engineers adjusted the screens and gradually we saw what was happening.

Before we could warn our front ranks, the sky was crammed with hundreds of dart-shaped ships all firing at us at once. Two of our grav-disks fell before we could fight back. The tiny ships had cut through our shields.

General Shan wasted no time activating the fleet and we immediately targeted all approaching enemy vessels. Great explosions shattered the foe but their numbers were astonishing. The destroyed ones were replenished with more ships pulsing bolts of deadly energy into our fleet.

Several of our front line Orbs crumbled into the sea below. Those that survived the opening moments of the conflict effectively counter-attacked.

Qui Shan remained calm as ice.

Our flanks held. Orbs and grav-disks shifted forward to replace those that had been destroyed or disabled.

Both sides were determined to annihilate the opposing fleet without mercy.

Waves of energy beams merged with the fury of wild starving beasts ravaging one another. Our Orbs fought valiantly despite crippling damage from the darting enemy ships. The battle raged with non-stop showers of streaming death bolts.

Then, in one swoop, the enemy ships turned and dove back into the slit. The Wall dulled; the opening shrank shut.

We were neither defeated nor victorious. The enemy was hidden behind their purple screen.

It had all ended swiftly.

Now only the wind sweeping along the ocean surface brought any presence of life to the scene. The battle had turned icy cold—deathly quiet.

Our ships stood silently, awaiting another attack. And nothing happened. The long silence pronounced the end of this onslaught from the bowels of the Muti Empire. We had prevailed. However, mere survival was not our purpose.

The Armada was determined to rout the Kaminaean enemy. Without access, we could not carry out our plan. Every known avenue was blocked by this impenetrable Wall.

* * * * * * *

All active units assessed damages and reported. Qui Shan reviewed the incoming data personally then ordered staff to make immediate repairs on the flagship and all the battered units. Every HanJahn specialist employed Mind Powers in search of survivors among the wreckage in the seas and along the shoreline. I summoned my special unit to initiate rescue parties.

Back in my quarters, I collected my survival gear and was about to head back to the launch deck when I ran across a tattered leather-bound case. It felt remotely familiar. The strap which held it together was embossed with an alien series of characters. I hastily opened it, spilling out a pile of very thin, fibrous parchment, several of which held well labeled maps of city streets and others of broader terrain.

Then I remembered. *Mahzit had slipped these to Jan Sorla in that tavern back in the city.*

I had forgotten about the pouch mainly because I'd been distracted by the other parcels Qon and I had also acquired within minutes following our encounter. That had been a coded map and dispatch which led us to KiNal. In our haste, I had forgotten about Mahzit's bundle.

At the moment I had no time to reflect, so I crammed them

all back in the case. I had to concentrate on preparing my crew for the search and rescue operation.

CHAPTER TWENTY-THREE
THE CITY UNDER SIEGE

I. Opening Challenge

The first weeks of executing the Resistance Revolt in the city posed an extreme challenge to Mahzit. The first strike forces had been very effective in disrupting the city guards and police force. Lookouts had watched their actions closely, identifying their hidden armories and munitions storehouses, tracking every Kaminaean military operation within the city grid. After the raid, strict orders sent every fighter out of sight to wait for the next phase of the plan. The city was in chaotic mourning, for the damage was not limited to the central square. It was a strike meant to rout out the city arsenals and manpower, which had worked perfectly. But now they would wait until all was ready for the major strike; the Quadrate Project.

His teams had worked among the secret communities nested in the outskirts of the Quadrates. Mahzit and Efre-Ah had organized the early units along the outer sectors of the city where various shop keepers went about their business while selectively streaming the incoming troops into their back dens. From there, out of sight and sound, they would be escorted throughout the dugouts beneath the city.

Fighters from all around the country side were gradually converging in small groups, mostly by night, to minimize drawing attention from the Mutis.

They managed to smuggle multiple parcels of supplies to

the thickly veined Resistance networks. By the time they were ready for their first hit; the Helandian had become very familiar with the city streets and intricate grid of hidden paths.

A number of days had passed since he'd met with Torlo and given him a complete copy of the master plan. He was certain that the Commander had, by now, reached the Castle of Doom in safety because KiNal had sent additional supplies along with Dunai's orders to prepare for the city assault. The coded message was hidden among heavy explosives, all concealed in a shipment of crude lumber destined for the slave quarters. Their cluster-teams were counting on the Armada to back them up, once the pyramids had fallen, which, of course, was their ultimate goal: to destroy the Muti Quadrates.

The plans progressed very well over the last several weeks while their field units cleared the outer perimeters systematically destroying factories and storehouses of the Kamina.

Warrior teams in the foot hills to the west had established themselves as decoys for the ever present Gatherers, by provoking aggressive moves against the Kamina. The bait had worked better than expected.

Resistance look-outs confirmed sightings of the dreaded Gatherers in units of a dozen or more flying westward, away from the city and thusly away from the eastern seacoast.

Now the last of these special units were converging on the city, one by one, to join the big battle.

Mahzit circulated steadily among the new arrivals, briefing them on their assignments, connecting with each unit leader, personally rehearsing the action codes and making certain there would be absolutely no mistake.

Every maneuver, every strike must be perfectly synchronized if they expected to succeed. Mahzit felt his blood run hot with anticipation. He was highly excited and convinced that everything was perfectly synchronized. They would soon find out.

Later that week the last of the expected troops had arrived, been armed, and instructed. In a few days he'd be wielding all of his resources and there would be no turning back.

* * * * * * *

On the day before action he settled in the bed-sling, hoping to catch some sleep, when the vision revisited him as it had from time to time.

It was he who led this legion of warriors onto a battle-field smothered in cold, wet fog. They raged forth against an onrushing enemy veiled from sight by the haze.

These were his people, his army, and he was compelled to march them into battle. As the fog cleared he witnessed the foe; hordes of armed soldiers swarming in from the hills and the skies. He lifted the sword in his hand; then with one swift down-ward sweep commanded the attack on the enemy lines.

And two massive armies clashed!

"Come on, Mahzit. It is time."

Efre-Ah pulled at his sling and woke him, whispering quietly into his ear. The dream instantly faded as Mahzit came alive and rapidly began reviewing the city plans.

"Duty calls," she whispered. "Today is the big day."

Mahzit fought his desire to linger with her one last time, for they were preparing to lead powerful units into a unified assault against the Muti City.

They embraced. Then he reluctantly released her and she left in silence. The woman was responsible for the western unit. From here on out they would coordinate only by strictly coded signals.

And the Muti Quadrates would soon fall, once and for all.

As he strapped on his gear Mahzit was pleased by his pecu-liar clarity of self-assurance.

Strange, how calm I feel.

Mahzit was leading a critical and complex operation and fully expected to reach a successful finish. It was a tremen-dous responsibility and Efre-Ah's people, now *his* people, had prepared him well.

Excitement spurred him towards the prospect of the day's promising engagement. He hurried through the underground dens, assuring each unit leader of his own confidence. Then he stood at the recessed portal and watched as the troops quietly slipped into the chilled predawn.

Checking the time, Mahzit calculated precisely when the 'Dawn-strike' clusters would be moving into position around the outer four corners of the city. The Mutis had designed each of the four Quadrate Pyramids so that they resembled the Master Pyramid of Kalinis which was located right here in the main central square. The major difference between the lesser monuments and this one was the great disparity in size, for the dimensions of the four corners were half the height and depth of the True Pyramid of the Prophet, Kalinis.

Precision meant everything. Each Resistance unit must be perfectly coordinated. The Kay-bombs must be detonated at the same time. Then the Resistance would expect the city soldiers to disperse towards the four corners in order to defend the exterior boundaries of the Muti Quadrates. The city would react in full chaos while the Muti overlords sent the bulk of their armies out to the perimeters, thus reducing the strength of the forces within the central city square.

Meanwhile, Mahzit and Efre-Ah's teams were expected to lie in waiting because these inner units had to tackle the largest and most heavily fortified target of them all.

Their unit was split in two parts. The teams held twice as many troops as each of the four outer corner units. They faced the colossal central structure, twice the size of each of the four outer Pyramids. And they expected a full army of guards. No communications could be risked. They relied on trust at this critical juncture. Visual signals would trigger the inner city attack. His team would invade the Kalinis Pyramid only after smoke and fire were evident from all four corners of the city.

According to the graphs he had studied, it was heavily catacombed with numerous subterranean vaults cut deep into the bowels of the continent. And it was there, far beneath the ground, that his team would go.

The toughest job of all was sitting and waiting.

The city is too quiet, he thought.

Mahzit slipped down a narrow alley to a stack of empty baskets. He deftly reached among them and located a lever. Pressing it hard, the plank came loose, providing just enough space for him to enter the back wall of a warehouse.

"Did anyone see you, *Yabuo One*?"

"No. It's dead still out there. Stay calm and alert. We don't want to move out a moment too soon."

He still cringed every time the young rebels addressed him by that ridiculous name. But he pushed that annoying thought aside and focused on his purpose.

The plans required precise leadership. And lead was exactly what he would do. He strode through the ready troops, their eager faces glowing with long awaited anticipation. There was no fear among these brave fighters. Today they would claim their rightful place among the legions that fought for freedom.

And they were many. Standing in this immense warehouse were two thousand ready soldiers.

Across the square on the opposite side of the Kalinis Pyramid would be an identical unit of Resistance warriors, waiting in a warehouse, equally prepped and ready to go. Efre-Ah would be leading them from the west side of the central square.

The plan was simple and exact: at the signal, when the fourth pyramid had been struck, both units would instantly converge on the square. The Resistance force would engage the enemy at the surface.

Mahzit's special team had a difficult assignment. They needed to clear the way for the units to escape once their task was completed. But it would be dangerous.

Their objective was to infiltrate the ground level and then break through the snares they had discovered in their stolen lay outs of the inner halls. There was only one safe passage that would lead to the lower levels. All others were heavily engulfed with impossible and lethal traps. Mahzit and Efre-Ah had memorized every detail of the map to the fifth underground level. From there, they would have to find their own way.

II. Await the Rupa

Silence loomed heavily over the lead group as they crept stealthily into the square. The mood was grim, all their attention zeroed in on the oval entrance to a cylindrical monolith offset to one side of the central pyramid.

A sentry paced back and forth on its flat roof. A rodent in the alley squealed briefly. Mahzit crouched in the shadows and waited. His heart raced but his head stayed calm. Timing was everything.

Then he saw it. The first signal flared in the far distance just to the right of the tower, followed by a second to the left.

The siege had begun and the pyramids were under attack.

He counted to ten.

Then he saw it. Barely above the cityscape; the third one flared, right on mark.

Mahzit whistled once to alert his fighters who were on standby, hidden in the adjacent alleys. Ten counts after the fourth flare, they would make their move.

The sentinel on the tower had seen the flares, too. From his post, he would surely have observed the burning pyramids in the four outer Quadrates.

Suddenly the heavy metal doors on the tower opened as armed soldiers flanked out into the square. And that was exactly what the Resistance was counting on. Mahzit's troops were ready, firing Kay-bombs into the square from all sides as they advanced towards the enemy. The front ranks fell dead as more soldiers ran out, firing Kay-guns into the city streets. The Resistance fighters were sharp-shooters, easily picking off the Kaminaean troops until they had routed the entire squadron.

And that's when Mahzit's unit made its move. They had lain low, waiting for a lull in the opening fight. Under cover of misty morning haze and smoke, they made a dash for the open door, turned immediately to the right and then ran several lengths down the hall. There they paused. Mahzit placed a tight pack of Kay-pellets in the hinged edge of a barricaded door; then ran further down the corridor, weapons ready in case they encountered any guards who might still be in the building.

Sure enough, three armed warriors met them almost head-on just as the explosives went off. Mahzit's men silenced them quickly; then dashed back to the opening which had revealed a steep staircase spiraling straight downward. They scrambled into the dark interior of the Kaminaean tower. The stairs stopped abruptly and according to the maps they had memorized, they were in the north tunnel which would take them to the third lower level of the great pyramid itself. Working in total darkness, the unit counted their paces weaving past alternate tunnels that would have been instant death traps.

They knew they had succeeded when a luminous portal shone through at the far end of the tunnel indicating that they had nearly reached the inner complex of the central pyramid. It was up to Mahzit and Efre-Ah to initiate the trail down to the fifth level. Every fighter on task had memorized these exact paths. Once they had destroyed the Mutis and the upper floors, each fighter needed to find this route on their own. It was their only means of escaping the city.

Mahzit heard a soft chirping almost immediately upon passing into the major halls beneath the Pyramid.

They crouched to the side and listened. The signal was faint, but it matched the code he and Efre-Ah had decided upon.

Gently he clicked back; three short, two long. The reply came from the left corridor. His unit moved towards it.

"Mahzit!" Efre-Ah unprofessionally threw her arms around him. He held her tightly for a brief moment; then quickly returned his attention to the units, making certain everyone was safely secured—all eight of them.

They would locate the passage down to the fifth level, as soon as their precise location within the colossal structure was determined.

He closed his eyes, relying on the Zygo training now made stronger with his new skills learned from the Trap-zet elders.

A vague probe reached into his core, lightly touched and withdrew. Some shadowy awareness was alerted to of their entrance into a Muti domain. This was something alien that seemed to be carefully observing from a distance.

Mahzit detected the Muti presence above their location. Scanning the corridor, he located the designated chamber which would give them access to the lower levels. The passage was simple enough, once they avoided several very well marked corridors which seemed logical, but in reality, if entered, would have proven deadly.

His senses had served him well. Soon they had scaled several steep and narrow tunnels, all leading downward. Then they wound along a flat corridor lined with several closed doors to either side. The Trap-zet unit quietly pressed against each one until they discovered one portal that swung open to reveal a cavernous chamber.

They moved in silence. Only the muffled sound of their feet touching the stone floor echoed against the narrowing confines of the corridor. They continued through to another room.

What now faced them was stunning.

The walls were etched with vivid pictures; panoramic scenes of towering needles, fat at the bottom. These were cylindrical ships, poised for lifting-off from a space field. In the foreground were oddly bloated multi-colored shadowy figures, strangely garbed in dark robes; neither human nor Muti. Slender tentacles dangled out in every direction, blending into one another. Beyond those limited details the images were ill-defined.

"These might be creations of some ancient artist," Efre-Ah gasped. "They probably represent the Rupa."

A thought edged into Mahzit's consciousness but he did not stop to question its source.

"The Rupa are here," she said.

Efre-Ah pointed at the middle door in front of them.

Without further consideration they followed her directly through that portal into a smaller room. A dull pit was in the middle of this chamber. It dimly pulsed, as if something alive was filling its space, though visibly the area was empty and hollow, like a silently whirling well. Mahzit stared at it, trying to decipher between what he saw and what he felt. When he closed his eyes, he was strongly aware that it was overflowing with some kind of nearly invisible liquid and it pulsed in a disquieting rhythmic beat, as if breathing.

Efre-Ah approached the pit. With her hands spread wide, she began humming something eerie and familiar. It was the same melody she had sung when they were deep in the Trap-zet tangles. Then she started chanting softly:

"Yabuo One. Kahn—Nah, Yabuo One. Kahn—Nah, Yabuo One. Kahn—Nah...," over and over between long, lyric phrases.

The warriors standing next to Mahzit pulled him aside while Efre-Ah continued her lengthy ritual.

"This is the Rupa in its raw, basic essence," Havli-Ah explained. She had studied in the Dens of Knowing and understood the Rupa more than most of the Trap-zet warriors. "We cannot hurry its awakening for it will speak to us when it wills.

"Let me tell you what I know while we wait."

Mahzit nodded, politely trying to be calm. It was somewhat unsettling to be instructed by this historian, which was her status back in their training sessions.

"Go on," he said, with disciplined tolerance. "I will listen."

Havli-Ah continued speaking very softly so as not to disturb the ritual. "We often see them lingering beneath our dwellings. They are peaceful to those who are friends. Throughout the planet there are boundless Rupa ports, fiber endings, corridors, channels, call them what you will. Here we can connect.

"The Rupa have great powers; and it transforms whatever niche it chooses. It networks throughout our world, some more vital than others. Even down into the core, it is an integral part of the planet; just as your heart is a part of your body. It manifests in many ways; threaded webs, sensory connections, transport vents, like this one. And its consciousness is a massive tangle of neurons within its brain.

"The Rupa tell of it in terms of matter. They have said that living matter and self awareness are a continuum from inanimate to animate. The elements of a stone and those that make up our bones and brains are not all that much different. The same material used in different ways for alternative purposes.

"We have been told many things that are beyond our understanding. It has been written that this evolved level of the Rupa is an assemblage of intellectual influence extending into the sinews of all matter and life forms throughout Noomas.

"Some scholars have studied its properties extensively and they believe the Rupa draws and deposits its creative force into the fibrous core. And thus consider the Rupa, or perhaps, more precisely, that a part of its totality, comprises the container and the contextual material from which the planet is fashioned."

That was the historian's entire explanation.

Just then Mahzit looked up and saw Efre-Ah slip into a ring of tendrils which must have emerged from the pit. She sank slowly into it, and then at the last instant was gobbled up in one simple swallow.

As another warrior stepped forward a huge bubble of energy swelled out of that well and engulfed him.

Follow the others, a melodic thought whispered.

He actually sensed each of the special troops being instantly submerged into an elongating shroud of energy. Then a sinuous vine rambled up through his legs and a moment later he was engulfed into a non-visual current which pulled him violently into a fast spin and then abruptly stopped.

Now he felt the enveloping material; slick, almost metallic. He was standing upright, on a softly cushioned vibrant surface of an oval depression in the floor.

"This is Rupa," he heard Efre-Ah say. Its shimmer surrounded them as she led their units down a corridor and onto a gleaming metal stairwell. Mahzit felt a coaxing tug as he descended. His feet seemed to be pacing the steps, but a strange sensation led him to believe that he was actually being sucked downwards. Behind him came the others who had dutifully followed them in this extraordinary journey through the Rupa passage. The entire unit was propelled through rolling channels that blended one into another as they zipped through illusion and surrendered to reality. And, for a suspended time, they slipped onward, neither slowing nor stopping, tumbling in a seemingly endless cycle of perpetual motion.

Mahzit was uncertain whether the trip had been real or imaginary. He was aware of leaning against a narrow hillock; the Trap-zet warriors scattered nearby.

Above the unit, the sky burst bright and they were near a stream which rippled down a cascade of boulders into the wild foliage below.

Mahzit did not attempt to rationalize their position, for not far above they heard a screaming cloud of birds flocking towards them.

The unit was about to face the most unexpected challenge since their invasion.

The threat was unquestionable as Mahzit prepared to engage in a brutalizing battle for survival.

Efre-Ah and the other Trap-zet had other plans.

"Come, Mahzit, this way," she said. The warriors nimbly slashed down several long, sturdy vines that were hanging from the trees near the stream and slung them around one of the trunks. Then one by one, they slid down the slippery stream and into the jungle, Efre-Ah and Mahzit following behind, long before the soaring marauders could reach their prey.

Once again, Mahzit was chasing this forest nymph through her safe Botannai haven, where the Rupa had deposited them.

CHAPTER TWENTY-FOUR
SPIN THE COMPASS

Mighty are the victories of God
And weak; those of Man;
The vats of the Ancients promise life.
Those who wisely choose, survive;
All else die.

— Universal Table of Truths

When we returned from the rescue maneuvers my unit escorted about three dozen wounded to the medic-pods. To my astonishment, an entire Kanns regiment was assisting in the restoration procedures and in-processing the wounded.

Turning to Qon at my side, I said: "It looks like there's still a lot of work to be done before we're finished for the day. I'd like you to take over and report stats to me this evening."

"I'm honored to serve!" Qon waved a stiff salute my way.

Before I reached the hall, he shouted after me. "You know, survival recovery is new to me. I have to admit it's refreshing to be on the healing side for a change."

I had to laugh as I rushed down to the launch deck. He was so right. Nobody ever tried to save a life among the Kaminaean Mutis; ever.

The bay buzzed like a nest of insects with mechanics racing in every direction in their effort to mend the ships. All supervisors were actively involved; working alongside their units.

Even Professor Yaw-iyn was deeply involved, hovering over

a damaged ship, shouting orders to the nearby mechanics. One glance satisfied my concern about the reparation progress so I headed for my bunk to get some badly needed rest.

That was not going to happen any time soon, for when I reached my quarters the first thing I noticed was the pouch from Mahzit laying on the bed, where I had tossed it.

Wearily, I reopened it and noticed one chart which sparked my interest, entitled *Haldolen Colony.* Several points were marked, including one labeled *Vaults of Lopn.*

My thoughts shot back to that incomplete dispatch from KiNal:

...reported significant findings beneath the complex. Team retrieved and deciphered first lines of one tablet.

"Haldolen Speaks. Refer to vault within."

Suddenly it seemed very important. At the time we had assumed the broken message was from KiNal.

What if it's from the Resistance elsewhere; maybe even from Mahzit?

I must get these to the Elite right away!

Not bothering to pull my boots back on, I snatched up the parchments and ran through the corridors towards the command deck.

Why had I not examined these sooner? I hurriedly retraced my memory of the meeting with the young Helandian. *What was it that he had said?*

Our brief encounter in the tavern had nearly slipped from my memory.

They had mobilized dozens of factions across the plains.

The charts in this pouch contained critical details including data about our own missing units. My thoughts raced through the implications as I rounded the corner heading straight for the communications port.

The workspace was very active with specialists riveted on every available console, continually re-examining the data banks.

At a cluttered table, I pushed a few scrolls aside and spread the charts out. Everyone immediately crowded around. Even the Mutis were interested.

We knew that KiNal had staged assaults upon principal cities throughout Kamina before the Wall went up. BerJahn had tracked their maneuvers and staff had decoded the incoming transmissions. According to their schedule, the main city would have been secretly infiltrated before the Wall appeared.

If our calculations were correct, KiNal would have launched their major strike at about the same time the dart ships had attacked us.

I examined the leather straps around the sheaf of charts, a very fine grain from an animal I did not recognize. And the binding was intricately sewn with the most translucent threads I had ever encountered.

Turning over a chart on the table nearest to me, I noticed an inscription on the reverse side. One of the HanJahn specialists decoded this for me. She said each parchment held such a message describing detailed war plans.

As I sifted through the contents of the pouch, I discovered a micro sliver similar to the one Adt had retrieved from the Messenger.

"Commander BerJahn!" I called, holding up the tiny chip like a trophy. He ran over to see my find.

"Let's have a look." The Officer examined it briefly; then headed straight for the communication console and slipped it into the reader. The view screen lit up, projecting a holographic image.

Mood was foreboding as we all watched the screen depicting the heavy metal doors standing partially open. We saw the towering needles of several early model spaceships.

Beyond the spacecraft was a stage rising in a series of tiers. A bright light emanated from above the platforms, casting a pale hue on a sparkling image of a robed figure. The light dimmed and a resonant voice spoke:

We originated from a galactic sector which was on the verge of exploding. Shortly after we had transported our people to new worlds, it burst into fragments.

Our generations were birthed here and developed a wondrous civilization. Over the ages our empires rose and fell then rose again. Our histories are recorded, but that is not what I have come to report.

Today we are in grave danger of extinction. While this young world of Noomas grows stronger, our people grow weaker. Our genes have been degenerating with each new set of offspring and our scientists have failed to find a solution to our lethal problem.

We are a dying race.

We have not given up hope. If you are receiving this message, then you will have encountered our replacements.

New Haldolen sought to produce life, using genetic tissue from various origins. Our purpose was always to preserve our weakening culture. Thus we fused our own cell matter with stronger beings which displayed a promising set of adaptive genes.

The image dimmed and ceased transmitting. The voice broke off. After a few moments we noticed half shadowy patterns of bluish light; then the voice was once again speaking to us.

The Genus Design manifested extraordinary results and soon we had developed a compatible likeness.

Our people gradually merged with the New Haldolen race. It flourished with vigor.

We watched with hopeful anticipation, intercepting minor errors. Eventually those errors became major problems. And we were shocked to discover the resulting creature to be self-disciplining and self-developing. Its autonomy was extraordinarily strong; however, it lacked any sense of morality. It was unable to feel compassion for any other being.

This was one defect we could no longer control. It expanded its own agenda and threatened to overpower our people.

The projection froze; then jerked forward.

We had not anticipated this possibility for it was flawed. With great pains and diligent work, we have managed to abort its production. The last specimens were sent to the southern vaults. The others were renovated using an experimental reversal formula.

We continue seeking the desirable gene. Time runs against us.

Our civilization is doomed.

The end draws near at an accelerated rate.

We have produced an alternate species we believe will survive our plight. The newly mutated gene has begun to grow. But our time is short. We will never know its final form.

If the Genus organisms spawn successfully, our objective will have been met. And if they seed themselves, the population may flourish. They are well designed, even if imperfect.

We had hoped to survive long enough to intermingle with the new race. As of this journal, we fear they will not be ready before we are dead. Time, alone, will be their witness now.

The Vaults of Lopn contain our heritage.

The animation collapsed. The display faded and receded into the screen.

Sziat stood silently with his back to us. At length, he turned, pulling his hood down to expose the bony purpled skull.

"He was talking about the Muti: my origins."

The mood in the room shifted. Nobody spoke. It was as if an ancient riddle had suddenly become crystal clear.

Sziat shrugged lightly: "Let's get back to work."

We immediately did so with renewed vigor. I glanced towards the contents of Mahzit's pack, now opened to maps of the Kaminaean capital.

"Could the *Vaults of Lopn* be secreted somewhere in the city—perhaps within one of the pyramids?"

"I don't think so," BerJahn said, pulling out a bin of ancient scrolls. "According to the Ancients, those vaults are in some remote sector."

He handed me one of these parchments retrieved from a spy mission that had actually connected with the Armada.

Everyone, including the Muti, was racing from one file to

the next, calculating, studying, and comparing. All the viewing screens flashed with Andon's library files, as well as those of the Helandi.

Sziat approached me with a scanner in his hand as I pored over a particular chart of a barren land mass to the south of Kamina.

"What about these notes from Andon, Torlo? He seems to be referring to a description of our world; collected before he actually landed near Bel-loniea.

I now remembered some details from my original flight to Noomas, also.

The ship's computer had identified three prospective landing sites for my ship. One was on the snow-capped South Pole; another in the middle of an ocean. The third near a highly populated area. This last had become my chosen destination.

Andon and I had, by chance, through our separate journeys, calculated similar landing sites in the same general region of Bel-loniea. Later Andon created the Noomasian library after painstakingly collecting various ancient and current documents from all over the Free Lands. The files from his ship and those from mine had contributed significantly to the archives. Collecting information from unfriendly nations about their various explored sectors of this planet was always a sensitive matter. And the Muti were most secretive about disclosing details to human populations. However, Andon persevered and gradually amassed an admirable amount of data which had served as the base for his international research department.

I hoped that somewhere among these materials, we'd find clues to aid us in stifling the Kaminaean invasion—and very soon. We were running out of time.

Adt approached my table and began studying a report that Sziat was reviewing. It dealt with a series of islands.

"The Muti Sanctuary we visited was remote. Are the vaults protected in those territories?" he asked Sziat.

"I really don't know, Adt. For a very long time they'd protected those sacred grounds from the Kamina. The place was safe until recently, when Kalinis destroyed the compounds.

"It will only be a matter of time before the fledglings hidden beneath its roots, are discovered. Rupa is a strong guardian and will continue to provide protection as long as possible.

"We still do not have answers. Even the Rupa's heritage remains a mystery.

"Odd," he paused, momentarily turning away. "The Ancients claim to have created the Muti in a vault, as a scientific experiment." Then he spoke softly, as if to himself, "a disturbing thought."

Sziat's mood instantly shifted, as if some internal switch had snapped down and he bluntly said to Adt: "Right now the Prophet Kalinis is our target. See what references you can connect to the vault."

Sziat pulled out a global map from beneath a stack of papers in front of us; then turned towards me: "What do you know about the South Pole?"

I suddenly remembered that strange woman Qon and I had encountered. The sentinel had said she was the Mad Crone of KiNal. Her words nagged at me.

"Beware the Southern passage in lands of white. The mighty miracle hides deep and sings the song of madness!" she had said.

I hurriedly flipped to another map I had pushed aside moments before. Perhaps this was the very thing I was seeking: a possible marker at the South Pole. Either an ice cap or small continent covered the region with few markings; mostly a wide expanse of empty space below the major continental coastlines. However, this one had a distinct inscription in some ancient writing.

I showed it to Sziat and Adt. "What do you make of this?"

Very few documents existed of the southern regions of Noomas.

"I have seen these characters before," said the Muti as he picked up the chart and strode quickly across the room to where the other Mutis stood, weaving together in silent communication. He spread it out on a table. Immediately the other Mutis began verbally talking over one another, a rare occurrence. They were obviously excited about the finding.

"*The Vaults of Lopn!*" several Mutis shouted altogether.

This information firmly solidified our decision. There was no debate. We knew exactly what must be done.

CHAPTER TWENTY-FIVE
PYRAMID OF KALINIS

I. Valley of the Seekers

"We are the Gods! We are the Creation.
"The Realm of Noomas is the Core of All.
"Bringing Birth to the Cosmos"
                        —*Words of the Prophets*

Sziat and I selected our lead team and we prepared a flight with a unit of troops to the South Pole. General Shan agreed to prepare a convoy of ships to accompany us. Professor Yaw-iyn would pilot his Orb—a fully armed war machine.

We made inspections. Adt and Qon secured the portal before strapping themselves in. Moyi and Sarleni strapped in behind the cockpit. Sziat sat in the cockpit, programming our destination as the professor reluctantly gave him control of his Orb, stirring us southward.

Our flight across the ocean sent us further away from the Muti Empire of Kamina. During this time we joined our minds. Sziat carefully enveloped us into his central Muti shell.

It was important for us to coordinate perfectly together, so we spent the majority of the flight in training. The unity would generate its power through the singular embodiment of Sziat who would transport the entirety of our unification. Each of us had to open a clear channel.

The Muti brought us all into a highly focused state.

Torlo's mind will provide the vital lens, through which you all pass. Respond to the word when spoken. Create the link.

Anchor!

An electrifying jolt shook through me.

It felt like I had been stretched clear across the galaxy.

The connection broke with a pounding headache and massive disorientation. I'd been flooded with an invisible substance, which then extended outwards.

For now, we were once again separated within the cavity of our own minds. The power was amazing.

Sziat continued the exercises until we had effectively disciplined our minds to expand in such a manner that our awareness mingled even without exchanging thoughts.

While we rested between sessions, I wondered why he had selected me as the focal point of our connection and Sziat explained parts of the process.

The core of the Muti uprising is honed against some foreboding omen you represent and Kalinis fears that. You are the vortex which provides faster access into my shell. Others will be anchoring at the same time in similar groupings.

If each person were to link individually, the timing would be too uncertain.

The strength of your thoughts stems from your origins containing elements of your heritage. Your advent on Noomas triggered the Prophet. We of the Muti have felt it from the time of your coming.

Later, Adt and I discussed it further.

"You are perceived as a dangerous threat to the Kaminaean Empire. Nobody has an explanation for this phenomenon."

Sarleni and Adt were continually connected as a unit in order to increase the shielding around the Orb with their Zygo. That's why it seemed as if both of them were speaking simultaneously. "We believe you did not arrive on Noomas by mere accident."

I pieced together my original objective, looking for some link to their theory, but it simply did not make sense. "I came here specifically searching for my father's roots, my heritage.

When I was very young my biological father died, so I never got to know him. Andon married my mother. I had hardly met my new stepfather, Andon, for they vanished while on an interstellar journey.

My last point of contact led me here, to Noomas, where I found Andon, alone. His wife, my mother, had died. Any information she could have given me about my father died with her."

From my point of view, we had two completely unrelated purposes for my existence on Noomas. I could understand how the Noomasians, with all their history and wisdom, easily fit both Andon and me into their historic expectations.

They had claimed I was the "Lost One", Torlo Hannis. At the same time, my personal living experience, born as the son of Dal Sorla was following the career of a galactic warrior as Jan Sorla. I had spent my entire life in search of my roots through my father.

I felt like two completely separate persons. Or were Torlo and Jan really all that different? Is it possible that they existed both together on identical plains in parallel universes?

Andon often spoke of the ancient theories that referred to complex Multi-Universal concepts. And others which were less developed that suggested the concept of parallel universes existing throughout the black empty matter of space and time.

At length, Sziat interrupted our discussion: "We are soon approaching our destination. Accept the fact that Torlo Hannis is your anchor and allow events to move to their conclusion, no matter where it takes us."

* * * * * * *

The voyage moved swiftly over a watery world below.

We were confident that the charts had given us perfect direction as Yaw-iyn's Orb descended through the clouds towards a compacted glacier. A pure white sheet of ice covered bleak patches of rock scattered across the landscape.

Imbedded throughout these frozen ice fields were amazingly

well-preserved ruins. Rubble littered the length and breadth of a grid of avenues marking the remains of what must have once been a thriving city. The Professor landed us on a relatively flat square beneath a line of broken towers looming over the forsaken city.

Semi-dusk cast an amber shroud over the land. A surreal jumble of rocks rippled through the sprawling metropolis over-shadowed by a singular massive mountain.

Yaw-iyn adjusted the range scanner until it had scoped the expanse of the territory. The viewer glowed as it completed its scan of the desolate field; frozen in time. An eternal feeling oozed from these ruins. It was easy to imagine this place crowded with millions of inhabitants going about their daily lives.

It all seemed strangely familiar.

Have I been here before?

The visage resembled scenes that had riddled my night-marish dreams. The wind whined mournfully.

As we left the Orb we were blinded by a frigid gush of ice and snow.

"The Prophet is here," Sziat said as he gazed intently towards the mountain peak. Its façade broken by a series of steep ledges and caverns.

Be alert.

We proceeded cautiously down the avenue and I realized that now there was no hint of the bitter cold. Subtle heat seemed to radiate from the shattered ruins. A warm draft crossed my cheeks like gently placating fingers.

Then Sziat's hand gripped my shoulder.

Anchor!

I instantly concentrated on the Muti. He was the vessel which would contain us all. Both Qon and Yaw-iyn instantly melded. Adt and Sarleni blended their Zygo; then slipped into the vortex within my shell which Sziat had prepared.

Focus.

My cohesive meld now morphed into Sziat; as the Zygo merged all of us with countless Muti minds within this unified

Sziat-mental fusion. It was a strange mating. We were all a part of one another.

He transmitted through my consciousness. Or so it seemed.
Peace.

I connected to all or perhaps all connected to me. The seamless conversion left no trace of individuality. We had access to a full global range of vision, like a single cell in a collective brain. In fact, our cumulative perceptions sharpened to extraordinary levels into and beyond the natural rock, ice and air.

Sziat now formed the vehicle through which we would confront the Prophet Kalinis. We stood on the icy ground as a solitary entity staring at the mountain.

A grayish mass upon its peak became visible. This vapor slowly constricted into the shape of a Kaminaean Muti.

Sziat stretched his arms, the cloak billowed as it transfigured into a blue shield. Then he marched boldly forward along the central avenue.
Allow nothing to touch us.

Kalinis floated above the peak. High above the Prophet a flock of marauding Gatherers blackened the sky. Then far below, at its base, a legion of warriors emerged, heading straight towards us.

White light shot out from the Prophet's forehead, driving directly into our shield. Pain throbbed in my extremities. For a protracted moment we were segmented like crystal shards.

Our unity was broken by its violent impact. I hung in splintered space for a fraction of eternity, severed from the others, spinning motionlessly without direction. Then the Zygo snapped harshly back and somehow Sziat held us together.

Fury sparked the space in a blinding series of explosions, each stronger than the last. We shifted into a tight wedge, forming a spearhead; and plunged a powerful bolt into Kalinis. Our shield sustained its retaliatory charges.

Adt and Qon fought to my left, slashing the soldiers down like playing cards. I parried a threatening sword and then thrust through its owner's neck in one sweep. Thick blood drenched my body.

We engaged the enemy warriors, fighting blow for blow, shield and spear repelling and assaulting simultaneously.

My body responded automatically within the Zygo and yet I witnessed it all from a detached space above and beyond— observing distantly, even as I fought.

Death converted energy drawn from the foe and returned it with greater force. Our determined courage increased steadily. My calm resolve strengthened. Our goal fortified with each volley; becoming surer; more defined.

Consume the weapon of hate.

Kalinis' fervor for hatred and death fueled our passion for love and life.

Dissolve its lethal fear with pure courage.

If the slightest doubt arose within our ranks it could weaken our bond and allowed Kalinis to slice Sziat into a million shreds.

Unified, we consumed its power into ourselves, then instantly sent it back from within our Zygo.

Focus!

That singular command narrowed my aim into a dense beam which intertwined with the others. My senses shut out all light, sound, and thought. We were one within the Zygo; splayed across the battlefield, darting from source to source; bolts of energy split into countless fragments.

Sziat pelted the foe again and again as if time had stopped. I became nothing more than a conscious awareness without thought, without memory, without name.

Numbness crept over my body, separating me from the others in a disturbing sullen solitude as the frenzied din of the battle abruptly stopped.

Silence lapsed over the battlefield. Dull pain dripped through my veins. My limbs hung heavily. Only my rapid breath and pulse pounded like a roaring current.

The next thing that occurred to me was that the others were no longer connected to Sziat. The team now stood on the icy ground once more, staring at the mountain.

II. Vaults of Lopn

Into the Universe flows our being
Herein we choose by which reality we shall live
Thus life defines the Universe of our birth.
　　　　　　　　　　　—*Mighty Words of the Eemel*

Suddenly the ground began to shake violently. The area between our Orb and the ruins swelled and tilted. A chasm fractured the avenue and spread across the land from one end of the valley to the other. Ice shattered, crumbling down into the widening black hole, splitting the land as if an invisible chisel had ripped it apart. The rumbling crash of ice and rock shuttered the air.

"Hurry, this way!" Sziat yelled. He had grabbed my shoulder and was leaping away from the trembling stones beneath our feet. Adt and Sarleni sprinted up one side of the avenue; Yaw-iyn and Qon followed close behind. The rubble slipped beneath our feet as we ran.

I momentarily looked back, stunned to see a pyramid lift out of the crater. Ice and rock swirled and crackled around its rising, spreading base.

We continued running away from the ruins as fast as our feet would carry us, not daring to stop during the thunderous quake.

Sziat was leading us up a fairly smooth hillside. He had stopped and waited as we caught up. The rumbling had ceased, but its echoes continued to reverberate through the broken valley behind us.

Amazingly, we had not run very far away from the ruins. A few lengths below us, the colossal building had settled in place, dominating the majority of the valley floor. The ruins were mostly buried within the now closing gap.

I stared in awe, at this magnificent temple. It must have been constructed by the gods, themselves, if gods even existed. It was a masterpiece to behold; exquisite lines of pure craftsmanship.

Its shear golden walls gleamed in the sunlight. An arched entry beckoned; leading into its shadowy interior.

We were all immobile for some time, motionless. A single cloud of blended ice and mist hovered on the horizon. The opening into this building brightened a little as the reflection of the sun radiated partially into its depths.

Adt said suspiciously: "A trap?"

I think not, Sziat answered. *I sense a quiet power within. Something very real is waiting. Perhaps something has been aroused by our arrival. We don't know what the builders of this place left here.*

As a unit we marched down the hillside into the valley and approached the majestic arch which adorned only one of the steep smooth sides. Like miniature insects we entered onto a monstrous corridor. The interior wall was equally as sleek as the exterior, with no visible markings. The width and breadth of the avenue was beyond our vision, drifting into a dim gray void beyond.

This wall identified a corridor of grayness. The arch faded far behind us. Somehow, collective knowledge dictated to keep going. Nobody spoke.

The corner curved to our right into a compact hall, apparently made of the same gray substance.

This corridor was short, ending at a vault so large that the ceiling lifted into infinity. It felt like a long dead place—without any sign of life. Words seemed useless.

A faint distant hum of machinery drew our curiosity. It gradually increased in volume. A softly glowing space covered by a low ceiling was its source; the walls pocked with numerous alcoves.

Deeply incised across the ceiling was an ancient scrawl. The message was clearly meant to convey great power which we learned much later, after the Andon Janis Foundation provided the following, detailed translation. Andon's note had stated that Noomas had not become at this time. The very name was yet unknown.

HALDOLEN SPEAKS

The Valley of the Living was smoothed into a flatland; all those who had been, were no more. When the Mothers were trodden, the Warriors were Law. And the Law was written thusly:
All will bow to our Gods.
All will be of male content.
All will breathe the dragon's fire.
None will hoe the ancient lands,
All will bend to toil in the new valley of our Lords.
The Vaults of Lopn within the pyramids were fashioned with thousands of stones lifting to the stars in honor of the Ancients. The last of the Mothers rose in their glory; as recorded by the Guardians of Haldolen. With the destruction came new truth and the name of Noomas was manifest.

The chambers through which we had moved bore an eerie element of neutrality; neither threat nor welcome. Another predominant droning beckoned us onward until it had centralized within a marvelous auditorium equipped with numerous mechanical devices. Long, flat tables ran in parallel lines. A series of mesh screens swayed above us, causing a gentle breeze to filter through the softly glowing space. We had reached the source of the droning machinery.

Our very presence must have tripped some automatic circuitry, for as we entered the room a bright light beamed and a sparkling creature appeared above us.

Sziat examined the apparatus closely and I heard his voice in my head:

It appears as a Muti for me and will seem human for you.

Whatever was in control of that image was forming its shape to fit our personal non-threatening acceptability.

Then it spoke.

"Life is a delicate balance. After many generations our race has dwindled, for we were struck with a sickness that has caused

severe damage to our genes. We could no longer reproduce.

"We fused our own cell structures with those of other beings; exploring sustainable matter in hopes of saving our world—our living species.

"All the information for their creation is grounded here in this protected vault. Not knowing who will discover us, or what the results of that action might bring about, we have left our knowledge in a manner that can be reordered to communicate with most intellects who might wander within range of our sensors.

"Our prime incentive urges us towards successful mutation of new life from old. The first version of our experiment was accomplished.

"Those of my class were involved in biophysical research. We structured chemical compounds in fluid cells. Details are recorded, of course. I will explain briefly here. In an effort to preserve life, we created a number of variations.

"My dedication involved the essence of living matter. I dealt with genetic design. We wished to devise restorative structures through the combination of our essential tissues with those of another race which was also dying out on our world. Their roots spanned distant planets far from this one.

"The first living species was flawed. We tolerated a certain amount of failure and therefore hesitated to destroy the very life we had created. Our compassion proved disastrous.

"Success came much later. We had developed basically differing personages. They are effectively thriving and multiplying slowly. We believe they will continue to be a part of our world, and will survive beyond our biological term. The brain capacity is fully intact. Most have a strong desire to expand knowledge. They call themselves Seekers.

"Several of the later models exhibit strong skills we had not anticipated—they have taken the role of Guardians of their species. They have an uncanny passion towards searching to new pathways through time and space.

"Alas, our numbers are dwindling. Many of our scientists

have died and we are rapidly depopulating. It saddens me that
we shall not witness this new race in their expansion.

"The world we had planted for our descendents is doomed. It
will end soon, in my lifetime or a bit later. What we leave behind
will be entombed within these vaults for we cannot allow the
new race to know what we have done. They must never know
how they were created, for this knowledge is too potent for any
inexperienced entity.

"When we complete the transition, the Vaults will be sealed
for one hundred generations. After that time this new race may
be ready to learn the truth. Their records have been care-
fully stored in a library which also contains our histories and
the legends and lore of many previous generations as well.
Hopefully you, too, will have wisdom and continue to expand
upon its volumes.

"You are welcomed to explore. Use whatever knowledge
gained with great care. The warnings are interlaced with the
data."

The creature, whatever it was, folded in on itself, as the light
that had given it birth blew out.

Sziat spoke slowly, hesitantly:

"The Ancients seem to have left this message with hope that
their work would carry on; as if they have been expecting us,
I believe. It will be up to you to decipher which truths you will
need in order to bring peace to Noomas."

We gazed around at the incredible display, staring at one
another in wonder with renewed strength and hope. It seemed
evident that the doorway which had given us entrance proved to
be the passageway into the Ancient Libraries of Haldolen and
the legendary Vaults of Lopn.

Just then, the rumbling began again. It felt as if the quake
was not yet over.

Sziat spoke with alarm: "It is not what you think. Kalinis has
discovered us. The battle is not yet over, friends."

"Anchor!"

In shock, we instantly obeyed and collected into the Zygo.

Before we completed the transition the auditorium rattled, like the sound of grinding stones against stones. Mist blotted vision. We feared another devastating quake was shattering the ground. Our team tumbled through a damp, murky cloud, jumbling together like grain sacks, we seemed to be falling and twisting through a borderless flume and then our feet crashed down onto a solid structure.

III. No Room for Error

To be inclusive is to say:
The wise are open to new insights;
Madness exists in pure devotion.
The healthy are aware of their limits.
— HanJahn Missives

Gradually the air cleared. We now stood in a group, tightly packed on the top of this pyramid. Our feet barely supported us along its sharp edges. The slightest movement would send any of us tumbling down the steeply inclined sides.

A booming voice echoed through the ruined city which sprawled far below:

Surrender unto my minions!

We watched in amazement as the streets filled with warriors followed by legions of armed Mutis scrambling towards the base of the pyramid. The imbalance of power was devastating. We were trapped on this pinnacle about to be massacred and there was no escape in sight.

More warriors and Mutis filled the plaza below shouting in unison:

The Prophet is your only protector! Embrace Kalinis as your omnipotent ruler!

A fiery red glow emanated from the pyramid's base and the warriors yielded to the shrouded Mutis who pushed their way into the blood-red beam. Then they mounted the steep ledges of the monolith, clawing at the stones like a cloud of venomous beetles.

Submit.

Breathe the perfect truth.

Escape is not necessary.

Surrender to your rightful destiny.

The Mutis were, by now, nearly halfway up the pyramid. They gouged into the ledges with powerful claws, feverishly climbing at an astounding speed, causing chunks of stone to tumble onto the grizzly warriors below.

The Muti silently raised his cloaked arms.

Anchor!

The single word flashed us once again into the Zygo.

The voice inside my head took a different tone now.

Resist! Sift past the illusion.

I recognized Moyi's steadfastness over the buzzing of the Kaminaean Muti's persistent swirl of luring voices:

Yield—release your doubt.

Succumb to your rightful nature.

Surrender unto me, for I am Kalinis!

Unreasonable panic challenged our new unity. My sight dimmed and I floated in a dimensionless space void of sound, color, or vision. I could not see the body of Torlo Hannis.

Feel it in your core and become one with us.

Utter pleasure surged through my veins and for an instant, the joy of that release melted all tension. Resistance was lost.

Yield to our embrace; let us have possession

Overwhelming confusion drenched my spirit; crippled my will. I struggled to move, to run; though we were trapped upon the pinnacle of this mighty pyramid with nowhere to run; no room for error. The enemy was poised to destroy us at any sign of weakness.

Hate yourself; hate the universe and enjoy pure ecstasy.

I was isolated within that smothering embrace.

Where was Sziat, Moyi, all the others who had been a part of our Zygo? They had vanished.

I desperately reached out for my companions, seeking the lost link to our connectivity. Almost instantly phantom shapes began to form in the surrounding darkness. My companions slowly solidified back into existence; then flickered to near invisibility.

Control: Sziat's voice soothed in my mind.

Anchor.

Focus: think!

The Zygo re-emerged, supporting me like an enveloping cushion. The murderous Kaminaean Mutis crushed in around us.

We instantly engaged in unrelenting attack.

I raised my arm and saw a Muti's arm, and knew it was mine. Sziat swung our sword in wild sweeps, cutting through bone, flesh, muscle. The Kay-gun in our left hand fired explosive pellets blasting away bodies as if they were made of dust.

Each destroyed creature was replaced by another. Shapes and faces shifted.

Arms extended hands, wielding long sabers. The bloody blades were cutting, lunging, snapping, and greedily churning in an almost invisible fortress of death.

Screams escaped from the throats of dying creatures. Snapping heads, mouths filled with razor teeth snarled in the agony of death. It was a delusional fit of madness seen through a twisted prism, undulating in convulsing shapes.

Die!

The line between illusion and reality imploded.

Voices thundered:

Surrender! Be One unto Me!

The universe dimmed, flickered.

Experience the rapture.

The Prophet attempted to breach our protective shell.

Sziat and Kalinis were wrapped in deadly combat, clawing at one another, pieces of flesh, bone, muscle, exploding, flying into oblivion. They were a part of me, even while I watched with out-of-body detachment.

Love me, Kalinis raged. *And live under my dominion!*

Sziat replied, as our right hand lifted up and rammed into Kalinis: *Rebirth must endure death!*

The two colossal Mutis compressed into one integrated pulsating image, each devouring the other.

The balance was too perfect.

Focus. Avoid the illusion; seek reality.

The only pathway to conquest was breaking that balance.

I must directly engage the darkness and personally affront Kalinis. There, inside the monster, we must make our thrust to defeat its supremacy.

Conquest demanded dominance.

I must slide in close, like hunting a Korda.

The mountain of Kalinis' face loomed. Dark canyons gaped where eyes should have been. This was the pathway into its living core.

It was there that must penetrate the nucleus of the Prophet's inner mind.

The full unity of the Zygo spun a thin trail of condensed energy around me, and I saw my companions band together behind Sarleni. She stood before them with a bow in her hands. I perceived every detail in slow motion as she quickly fit an arrow into her bow.

We were that shaft. Our combined essence formed the arrowhead. Strong fingers pulled back the string and I was the tip, the finite point, aimed into the Muti's eye-socket.

Her hands released the feathered arrow. The bow snapped the shaft forward in one swift driving force aimed at the Prophet Kalinis. Suddenly pulsing flesh of living matter completely engulfed me. I was in a shapeless pit; plunging into raw fat sinews, blinded by its very density.

I was falling, drifting, being brushed aside in one swift surge of unrelenting resistance.

Time froze. Then a broken rhythm of light and sound rose around me, only to be shattered by silent darkness.

Had we invaded Kalinis or had the Prophet absorbed us into

itself?

A faint moaning broke the suffocating silence. I twisted, straining to hear and to see the source. The glow faded to a desolate lifeless plain. A hollow voice lured me towards a distant glow, pulling me towards it through fragmented space. Then I heard the tiny childlike wailing:

"Wait—stop!"

There; standing naked before me, was a small Muti huddled and shivering on a windless, rocky mound. The horizon blended into the cold, gray sky. The Muti's face turned upwards, its azure eyes gazing sorrowfully into mine, tears running down its unmarked cheeks.

Its frightened plea intensified: "Don't!"

Tiny gnarled hands reached out, pleadingly.

"I want to live!"

I had never seen a Muti child. The concept was beyond my imagination.

And eyes attempted to envelop me in an overwhelming flood of emotion. I had never seen a Muti with eyes.

"Love me," a voice murmured.

I felt terrible sadness; a deep longing gnawed within for this forlorn creature. This was an innocent waif. I was fascinated, curious, overcome with protective desire.

How could I love any child if I could not embrace its longing plea? All living creatures deserved to exist, to enjoy a full life. That was all that was being asked of me. Do not deny its right to exist. Respect all life.

Those eyes holding me captive, intensely stared in bewildered fear. They gradually darkened, narrowed, condensed; dragging me into their overwhelmingly powerful gaze.

The Muti face became molten. The body remolded, the voice deepened with a hypnotic flow of words I could not comprehend. My thoughts discerned them to be reasonable, so pleasantly conversational that I simply stood there listening; yet I did not absorb its words. I felt bonded to it, determined to defend it with my life.

It had risen to the full height of a hooded Muti, its heavily creased face tilted downwards. My fondness had deepened as if it were my brother. I found myself powerless to question our kinship.

It shifted again, into Kalinis, the Prophet, draped in a glowing robe. Bright red and yellow ornamental markings covered its ashen face, giving it a smooth, timeless appearance. The depth of those two empty sockets drilled into me.

I saw the danger of an alien creature arriving on our world. Its shadow fell across our lives like a cruel monster. It would become a lethal threat to my magnificent empire. And this could not be.

The Muti's arms rose as one bony hand pointed directly at me and it spoke my name.

Here we stand; the two of us, Torlo Hannis; but only one may return to our beloved Noomas.

The paralysis holding me captive, melted. The world gave way to one sole image of Kalinis, frozen at a standstill.

Die.

Terror shuddered convulsively from the Muti's frame.

The long shaft of the arrow we had created propelled me directly at its skull, dashing violently towards this being that I had, only moments before, loved as if it were my lifelong kinsman.

My heart wrenched within me as the Muti turned and cried out one last time:

Spare me!

But its begging came too late.

Like the shattering of glass, light burst into cutting slivers, imploding towards where I had stood. I could not fathom the impact or rationalize the meaning.

It seemed like I hovered in eternity, plagued by insurmountable emotions, none of which relieved the wrenching pain in my gut.

The bitterly blasting wind had calmed but not even that silence was soothing. A faint light played odd patterns upon the scattered shapes around me.

Out of the dark void came Sziat's message to me.

This, Torlo, is where your shadow blends with the misted future. The pathway of your journey will conjoin with ours. Here before us, in a timeless zone, we are challenged with tangled elements.

Through this maze you must go. Choose your path.

Sound—shape—background; all materialized like phantoms emerging out of blinding oblivion. Jumbled disconnected scenes swirled like jagged shards of phantom mirrors shuffling in myriad possibilities. They blended, the edges interlocking, integrating into a billowing gray substance.

I gasped air into my lungs.

A man's form was floating cross-legged in space before me. *Collect your thoughts, Torlo, become orderly.*

That name surrendered identity.

I had been born on Noomas, without memory of my past; without knowledge of the world in which I found myself.

I was Torlo Hannis.

Slowly a vision of a woman's face appeared: Youi, Proctoress of Noomas.

"Take me to her!" I demanded.

A caped figure stepped out of the fog.

Focus. And become....

The finite point of my conscience expanded in all directions.

Light enveloped my body, creating patterns of the world in which I now exist.

CHAPTER TWENTY-SIX
AFTERMATH

I. Mysteries

Rebirth occurs in many shapes.
Intelligence extends beyond formalized learning.
Understanding only reflects in the light of solid facts.
– Words of the Prophet

It must have been a long time before I noticed others around me; Moyi, Adt, Sarleni, Qon, all of them.

We had fought an inexplicable battle.

Although our bodies seemed unscathed, our inner senses had been stripped to the bone. Each face showed the haggard signs of having endured an insurmountable ordeal; and we needed a period of healing.

The dead were entangled with one another; ignorant of their fate; oblivious of their alleged enemy. In death they became companions through their unfortunate sacrifice.

Lying upon the blood stained ground directly before us was the distorted, shredded form of the Kaminaean Muti Prophet, Kalinis.

A mighty killing had taken place, and I now stood amidst the aftermath of its brutality.

We had defeated the Prophet yet its minions still existed elsewhere on Noomas.

Our primary mission had been completed.

Professor Yaw-iyn deftly maneuvered the ship between high glaciers; a massive expanse of ice covered its frozen basin. He piloted the Orb towards the sea.

The immeasurable task, of integrating broken communities, leaderless armies and the Mutis throughout Kamina, was still ahead of us. This colossal undertaking would involve many years. With the Prophet vanquished, its influence ceased. Our work had only just begun.

* * * * * *

The impenetrable Wall had fallen when the Prophet was destroyed. And the Armada had immediately advanced in full force, upon the continent. Communications had been restored. Word came that the Central Muti City had fallen at a tragic cost. Its overpopulated districts made it impossible for people to effectively evacuate. Mass chaos ensued. The city burned hot for weeks after the invasion and those trapped within the inner boundaries had no chance of escape.

The backlog of data that poured into the communications banks was quickly compiled to make it possible for the Armada to infiltrate throughout the empire.

We were keenly aware of the enormous struggle still facing us.

The remaining Kaminaean forces were scattered; segmented from one another, doggedly following the dictates of their local leaders, determined to cut out every territory they could grab as a personal empire. And their loyal disciples fought vehemently against all whom they considered invaders of their homeland. These were independent armies, disconnected from each other; and strong enough to stubbornly fight for personal domains.

Cleanup projects were immediately assigned by General Qui Shan and Kigor Dorta. My tasks involved restructuring the Kaminaean governmental systems.

With the snake's head severed, the disconnected tendrils of militant communities clashed violently against foreign control.

These political and private military units and tribal leaders would rather die than surrender.

Killing off even the most powerful of commanders does not automatically create easy solutions resulting in peaceful governing bodies. Nation building is far more complex.

Time, however, was what we had in abundance. Patience and wisdom needed exactly that; until new trust and understanding permeated their war-torn boundaries.

These virtues proved to be our most effective tools. The surviving peoples of Kamina gradually gained confidence. Our newly established government assisted them, encouraging the tribes to section off cultural differences, and to honor them as a standard division of power.

In short, my main objective was to govern a supervisory system, distributing the bulk of the administration to the ruling classes of the people themselves according to their customary mores, not mine.

II. Last Meeting

Into the Universe flows our being
And in that reality we choose to live.
Thus life permits universal promise.
—Conclusions of Torlo

Sziat and I had grown accustomed to long journeys together. Once in a while he would invite me to walk with him through the Kaminaean wilderness for old times' sake and he would pontificate, as was his style, about deep issues of the world.

It was on one such wandering on a particularly lovely day, that we shared such an occasion. At the time I did not know that this would be our last.

And we discussed these genuine concerns; or more correctly, he did pontificate and I did listen as was always our style:

"Most cultures bring belief systems and special gifts to the table of life.

"You must allow the greater powers—those universally enduring levels beyond the scope of reason—to abide at the base of all reckoning; for they will inevitably influence your daily life.

"After all, every living consciousness is linked. We are all part of the greater scheme of things. On this planet alone, from plant to mineral; from insect to mammal; in flight and in sea; the Muti and human: we're all part of the whole, contained in an intricate network; a webbing of intelligent creativity and conscious awareness of the universal workings."

We walked in long silences between Sziat's wisdoms and I had no urgency to hurry him or question his words. Those black holes, serving as mysterious unseen eyes, inspired me with a peculiar comfort for I had discovered a bright element of adventure within them.

"As you know, I look far enough into the future to gain broad perspectives. My findings would, no doubt, make an impact on your friends Adt and Sarleni; even Ju-bilee and Moyi will revel in the evolutionary leaps yet to occur. The next generation, your heirs, are destined to develop ingenious solutions to the current complexity of social problems that plague our present world. Amazing intelligences: remarkable ideas."

He lifted his arms dramatically. "I will have to speak with Moyi. But that will be another time."

He didn't elaborate on the details, though I knew his oratory. My fine friend saw the world as an exciting setting for our descendents as he often told me in his unconventional way.

"Your children will make a fine contribution to the next several decades of your species.

"This, Proctor Hannis, is your life. You came to this world from a long distance seeking memory. And here you have found kindred travelers from the galaxies who have also made their home here over the millennium.

"I can promise you that liberating Kamina will be the greatest achievement of your life-time. Enjoy it with your woman, for she is none other than the wise mother of this next honorable generation. Youi stands strongly by your side; this I have seen."

Sziat was rarely specific, though I gleaned a great deal of understanding from his words.

"Perhaps we Muti were produced from a common vat, as described in the Vaults of Lopn. And perhaps our ancestors melded with the Ancients.

"I prefer to believe that we are, indeed, the native of this world, for I sense a deep kinship to the soil.

"One basic element binds Noomas that cannot be denied. That is the Rupa. It has endured through longer epochs than any of us can fathom. Its sinews bind the essence of the world. Their roots travel throughout its framework."

Sziat had always carried a high respect for the Rupa. As for me, I found it difficult to comprehend.

Was the Rupa created here or elsewhere? Or did the Rupa create Noomas?

The question seemed rather fanciful.

"During the decades, Kalinis had been wielding its power over Kamina; the Rupa had paid no heed to the quarrels among the surface inhabitants. It had thrived through many changes among the worldly rulers; none of which had ever solicited the assistance of the Rupa in the past.

"In due course, the greedy Prophet's appetite threatened the Rupa's territory. It then took an interest in the Muti's behavior. Humans and Muti experienced the Rupa with a new awe and respect, as you know. Those of us who have survived the Rupa's wrath will do well to keep out of its way on this planet."

Sziat's speculations were interesting. We had, on occasion, spoken with the Rupa; however the conversations were always cryptically laced with their complex voices. Still, we had benefited from their efforts after the conquest.

"We of the Muti are different from you." Sziat said. "We understand time and place in a unique way. Though, there are limits.

"I have yet to reach that outer boundary. Nothing short of

discovering all that I am, will satisfy my needs.

"I'm a seeker."

We talked many long hours together about various things. Sziat had wisdom and answers for nearly everything. With the exception of a few topics which will never be solved.

Was he one of many Sziats? Or was Sziat the last of his kind—the sole survivor of the Prime Muti variable?

I would not discover the solution to that mystery or enjoy another enlightening discussion with my Muti friend.

He walked away, as was his habit. I never saw him again.

EPILOGUE

We've had a good life, each of us creating unique designs towards happiness. Proctoress Youi and I are passionate about maintaining the natural equilibrium prevailing over our beautiful world.

Moyi continues to teach. Adt and Sarleni mastered their Nexus to a finer degree of unification.

Ju-bilee frequently visits the Dorta family, including Kigor. They've since discovered a rich balance of companionship that was previously denied them.

We see the Dortas often for our personal bond was intensified since their daughter and our son married. And with great pride, we are privileged to experience, first hand, the priceless achievements of our ever expanding descendents.

Kal-Nor and Linia share a vigorous life in the deserts of Kamina.

Qon astonished me most of all. He and Andon developed a multinational task force dedicated to the rehabilitation of Kaminaean cultures. His passion began when he had joined my rescue team on the Armada. He has been obsessed with healing and rebuilding people's lives ever since. The days of brutal killing are now a part of his past.

Mahzit contacts us from time to time. He has accepted his leadership among the Trap-zet and is thoroughly dedicated to Efre-Ah, who had captured his love.

One troublesome issue has arisen among the people of Kamina. Historians document important events with great care;

however the populace tends to embellish their own versions into legendary fables. Local loved ones who died for the cause become idolized war heroes: successful leaders praised as gods.

I generally pay no heed to their amplified chronicles.

However, since the name of Torlo Hannis has monopolized recent versions of historical events, it is impossible to completely ignore what is written about me. Even my sons and daughters sing the songs, embellishing these exaggerated odes with their personal twists. These fantasies picture me as a supernatural creature who may even have invented Noomas itself. And I have tried but completely failed to dispel these sagas.

Ju-bilee and Moyi seem to be perpetually fascinated by the puzzling phenomenon of humans always needing to create superheroes.

Religious masters, gurus, philosophers and scientists from all walks seek answers to the mystery of creation, be that through scientific, spiritual or mythological evidence. The HanJahn continue to expand their Mind Powers into such intellectual areas, as do the Muti and perhaps, even the Rupa.

As Proctor it is impossible to publicly subscribe to any such systems, mythological or scientific. I came to Noomas without memory of my past and now I have been immortalized with a legendary role in the Conquest of Noomas. When asked if I have found the answer to such questions, I simply say: "Not yet."

POSTSCRIPT

Shortly after he had told us of these events, communication with Torlo ceased. All efforts to reconnect have failed.

In fact, chances are that we will be long dead before he once again transmits to us from Noomas. One can only wonder: will the future offer another connection with Torlo Hannis or is his voice forever lost?

The silence leaves many unanswered questions.

—Charles Nuetzel & Heidi Garrett

ABOUT THE AUTHORS

CHARLES NUETZEL was born in San Francisco in 1934, and writes:

"As long as I can remember I wanted to be a writer. It was a dream I never thought would materialize. But with the help of Forrest J Ackerman, who became my agent, I managed to finally make it into print.

"I was lucky enough not only in selling my work to publishers but also ending up packaging books for some of them, and finally becoming a 'publisher' much like those who had bought my first novels. From there it as a simple leap to editing not only a science-fiction anthology, but also a line of SF books for Powell Sci-Fi back in the 1960s. Throughout these active professional years I had the chance to design some covers and do graphic cover layouts for pocket books & magazines."

His work on covers and graphics are a largely influenced by his father, who, as a professional commercial artist, had painted a number of covers for sci-fi magazines in the 1950s and later for pocket books—even for some of Mr. Nuetzel's books.

In retirement he has become involved in swing dancing, a long time lover of Big Band jazz. But more interestingly world travels have taken him (and his wife Brigitte) across the world, to Hawaii, Caribbean, Mexico, Kenya, Egypt, Peru, having a lifelong interest in ancient civilizations. His website is full of thousands of pictures taken during these trips.

"Discovering these wonderful places actually exist and getting a chance to even touch those ancient stones and structures, climbing some of the Mesa-American pyramids to their very top, has been a life-inspiring adventure! It is fantastic to realize that our modern world is built upon such fascinating places, like the 2,000-year-old Petra, which was simply amazing to see. Almost as stunning as the pyramids of Egypt! All of which, I keep telling myself, are the remains of colonies from Haldolen some 30,000 years ago (related in *Swordmen of Vistar*)."

A number of his books, released here by Borgo Press, also include mention of the Haldolen civilization, subtly tying their storyline into the Noomas universe.

HEIDI GARRETT lives in the Washington DC area where she has spent most of her adult life. Her two grown sons each now has a son of his own.

She writes: "I have been engaged in reenactment activities from pirate feasts to courtly concerts, making music and merriment at various local festivals."

Her interest in science fiction fantasy brought her to a catchy roll-playing website called *The Gathering*. Here, as Damsel, she met a number of strange and charming personages all interacting together, weaving their own fantasy tale in this make believe world of chivalry within the pre-cast chat rooms of *The Gathering*. Several of her favorite cohorts had actually been created by one man, Charles Nuetzel. His favorite hero was named Thoris and "we played scenarios with knights in less-than-shining armor, rambled among the parapets and socialized in the imaginary halls—imbibing ale at the hearth and sharing tall tales until—at last—the damsel discovered her prolific counter-sparring partner was, indeed, a pro writer."

To learn more about him, she searched out some of his out-of-print books, including an incomplete manuscript the *Epic Dialogs of Mhyo* which is now published by Borgo Press. Since then, over the years, they've become great friends, and even met on the west coast, when she spent a few days with Charles and Brigitte.

They had always talked about doing some writing together and when Borgo Press suggested that Charles do some original books for them, he said: "Only with Heidi!" She had been working with him via the internet—email—on helping proof the revisions of his books when being prepared for their new updated reprinted editions. During this interval, Charles completed his autobiography; making use of Heidi's editing skills for his nonfiction writing, as well. The results of all this has created a long term relationship of collaborated writing which produced the *Slavegirl of Noomas* and this present book

Recently they met again on the east coast when the couple spent a couple of weeks with her touring the DC area. This also gave the co-writers a chance to work face to face at last, on this final version of the Conquest, which now concludes the Noomas Trilogy.

www.ingramcontent.com/pod-product-compliance
Lightning Source LLC
Chambersburg PA
CBHW030237030726
47493CB00022B/86